ONE MORE RUN

THE ROADHOUSE CHRONICLES BOOK 1

MATTHEW S. COX

DIVISION ZERO PRESS

One More Run
The Roadhouse Chronicles Book 1
© 2015 by Matthew S. Cox

ISBN (ebook): 978-1-949174-46-5

ISBN (print): 978-1-949174-47-2

CONTENTS

NICE SHOT, MAN

Worry and relief made for strange bedfellows—stranger still when the bed is only big enough for one. Civilization, such as it was, ended fifty-one years ago. A war started on some forgotten day in August of 2021 ended forty-five minutes later amid the smoky haze of nuclear fallout and blind panic. Most people never even knew what hit them.

The driver curled and uncurled black-gloved fingers around the rubberized steering wheel. Clouds of dust whipped past the windows and billowed into a plume that made the rear view screen in the middle of the console useless. The silt invaded the air vents, tainting the fragrance of sweaty leather with earth. Pale blue bar graphs on the pieced-together dashboard reassured him the vehicle had enough juice left to finish the job. Loose spiral wires of red and yellow snaked among gauges, wobbling with every motion. The steady vibrating thrum of four electric motors stoked his adrenaline. He grinned at the large red LED numbers in the center of the console behind the wheel: 86 MPH. The six flicked to a seven or a five every few seconds. He'd go faster, but road crews hadn't existed for a hundred years, and the last thing he needed would be to smash an e-motor out in the middle of nowhere.

The lack of bullets flying at him so far had him on edge, not to mention how wide open the road seemed. He sped past the occasional tangle of metal on one side or the other, a former vehicle picked to the frame by scavs. This far out in no-man's land, he should've encountered at least one bandit party—especially with the valuable cargo in the passenger seat. He glanced at the unassuming metal can and patted it. A broad smile distorted skin covered with days' worth of beard and road dirt. Gloves creaked over the wheel.

People tended to hear things, even in Wayne's place. The scavs would know he was coming.

The iron sights of two hood-mounted machine guns wobbled from the occasional dip or pit, nothing that would threaten the solid tires. Flickering brass glinted as the ammo belts danced in the wind. He'd gone cheap, settling for 7.62 instead of going whole hog with .50 Cal. Anything heavy enough to need ordinance like that couldn't catch this car.

He glanced again at the innocent-looking can. The payoff from this run would be another big step toward his dream, but the closer he got to reaching it, the more it felt like he'd never get there. Sure, the smaller guns saved him about three hundred coins, and with any luck, they wouldn't kill him.

Glowing light pierced the dust cloud behind him. He squinted at the rearview screen, mounted where the radio had once been. No one needed those anymore. Two leather-clad figures on motorcycles fanned apart out of his wake. On the right, a little speed-machine with a couple of sub-guns in the handlebars; to the left, a larger cycle, a retrofit Harley with electro-motors and a rotary gun mounted to a side car.

Damn shame if I have to torch that Harley. Screw the Ninja.

His finger poked a small, square red button on the edge of the four-by-six-inch display screen. It flickered with static for a split second before a grainy feed from a trunk-mounted camera replaced the wide-angle rear view. A hair-thin green crosshair formed across an image flecked with mud. He flicked a toggle switch and one of many tiny pushbuttons on the side of the steering wheel lit up orange. He hovered his thumb over it and weaved to avoid a spray of fire from the smaller, more maneuverable Ninja. The biker's attack ended a second later when he swerved in a desperate attempt to stay upright.

The driver grinned. "Watch them potholes, son."

A quick shift of the wheel lined up the crosshair with the Harley as the giant rotary cannon on its sidecar spun up. *I hope you go to hell for makin' me do this.* The driver pushed the thumb-trigger. In the trunk, mounted assault rifles barked to life: an AK on one side and an M-16 on the other. Muzzle flare blew like dragon's breath from his taillights. As usual, the '16 let off about six rounds before it jammed. The AK continued chattering for a few more seconds until he released the button. Bike and sidecar burst into a fireball. The e-Harley veered off the road into an end-over-end tumble.

The Ninja's engine wailed as its rider pinned the accelerator. A lone square headlight surrounded by dingy green rushed in on the rear view camera, hoping to get close enough for a 'can't-miss' shot. The driver stomped on the brakes, chirping the tires and causing the small bike to smash into the rear bumper. All four tires threw off plumes of white smoke. A heavy *whump* landed on the roof a second before the bandit rider slid onto the hood in a flailing, gangly mass.

"Hmph. Ethanol." The driver shook his head at the rearview. "That's gonna burn hot. Damn waste of parts, even if it is a Ninja. Fuck it."

The bandit pulled a revolver from his jacket and pointed it at the windshield. The driver cut the wheel and reversed hard. A shot went high as the bandit sailed off the long hood and fell onto the road. The driver straightened out of the turn and continued in reverse another few seconds before slamming on the brakes. He flicked the Challenger into drive and stomped on the pedal. Sand flew in torrents from all four wheels before the car caught traction and took off like a streak, straight at the prostrate figure. Sunlight glinted off the barrel of the old revolver as the man wobbled up to one knee. For a nanosecond, two men stared into each other's souls.

A thudding clank rocked the undercarriage as all four-thousand some-odd pounds of car crushed flesh into pavement. The driver slowed and steered back around, stopping near the body. He waited a few minutes, staring at scraps of shredded leather fluttering in the wind while breathing the smell of molten tires. Once he felt confident no threat remained, he got out.

A pair of submachine gun mechanisms welded to the Ninja's handlebars excited him, until he realized he'd found some H&K thing chambered in .40 cal. Despite having no guns that could use it, he still took the twenty-six rounds. The revolver looked in working order, albeit banged up. On the way back to his car, he pulled a leather belt full of .357 shells out of the semiliquid mass he had run over. Gun and bullets went into a bin he kept in the back, joining a handful of grenades, knives, and tools.

He fell into the driver's seat, his weight barely noticed by the bulk of his rebuilt Challenger. Aside from the dirt, for a sixty-year-old frame, it looked mint. Granted, all the exposed wires and add-on tech inside was quite a far cry from what the designers originally planned on when the thing had a gasoline engine. Electric motors had been a novelty before the war, but now gasoline joined a long list of ghosts humanity may never see again. One more forgotten thing of the past, and only fools still used air-filled tires. Some die-hards clung to ethanol for the sound and fury, but the Roadhouse network made charging cheaper. He shut down the weapons to save battery life before returning to his delivery. The solar-powered trickle charger in the trunk could take twelve to fourteen hours to help him limp back to a waystation, and he'd rather not be exposed that long.

The driver brushed a smudge of dust from the rear-view targeting monitor, leaving finger trails of clean plastic. He offered a moment of silence for the death of a Harley, humming some song his dad used to put on in the truck all the time. He leaned back in his seat, arm draped over the wheel at the wrist, tapping one foot to ancient music that played only in his mind.

"Nice shot, man."

IN THIRTY YEARS

The road stretched out to the horizon, so straight it seemed like a crease upon which the world could fold. Vigilance returned as the relief of surviving another ambush faded. He flicked the rear view back to the wide-angle. A faint chirp came from the camera in the plastic bubble on the back window. It seemed silly to have a third tail light in the window; the housing proved much more useful as a camera, not that anyone paid much attention to signals or lights these days. Within an hour, a bullet-riddled sign caught his eye. Artesia settlement, a mile away.

Within a few minutes, he slowed and turned onto a cracked and battered side street past a handful of crumbling RVs, trailers, and a half-dozen huts. He drove through the dead town, following a little-used back road that took him to a desolate outcropping of rocks a quarter-mile farther down with a single armored door. Ten paces away, the matte-black car whirred to a halt amid a rolling cloud of beige. Listening to the barely audible electric hum of the wheel motors, he waited. A narrow slit in the door pulled to the side, revealing eyes. They regarded him for a few seconds and the metal plate slid closed with a *clank*. The driver took hold of the innocuous silver can and got out. Clanks and squeaks emanated from the armored door, which opened a few seconds after he reached it. Warm air carrying the fragrance of stale humanity and wood washed over him.

"Took ya long 'nuff," said the old man in the doorway. Brown-white hair and beard fluttered in the wind for a moment of silence. "That it?"

"Yep." The driver patted the plastic lid like a drum. "Got the coins?"

Wrinkled hands clasped the metal can, failing to pull it out of the driver's grip. Yellow eyes widened. "You'll be understandin' if I wan' ta check it first."

"Fine, old man." The driver kept his grip on the can until both of them were inside.

Tattered coats, boots, and pipes hung along the length of the narrow entryway. Coils of rope and hose hung on one side opposite spindles of wire and twine. With some reluctance, Kevin surrendered the can to the shaking arms reaching for it and put one hand on his .45. The old man ducked deep into his burrow, scurrying off like a squirrel with the world's last acorn. After nudging the door closed, the driver followed.

A single naked light bulb hung from a wire above a wooden table in the center of a room bedecked with maps. Pre-war radio equipment sat on a longer table against the wall in back, next to a massive shell—the kind of thing once fired from tanks. The driver stiffened, staring at it, relaxing a touch at the lack of wires connecting it to a button.

"Heee!" The old man squealed and spun in a circle with his prize. A plain steel cylinder with a plastic lid—an old coffee can. He set it on a workbench, opened it, and inhaled the sickly sweet scent of pipe tobacco. "Tis the stuff."

"I watched Gil load it. Could'a told ya it was real. Don't much like gettin' shot at for bullshit."

The old man more or less ignored him, grabbing one of a dozen pipes from his wall and wiping it out with a grimy finger. He moved to the canister and set about packing the bowl.

"Care ta join me?"

The driver looked down at his boots, letting the air out of his lungs. "Nah, thanks. That shit'll kill ya."

Yellow eyes gazed at the driver's scuffed body armor, a red leather jacket with Kevlar panels sewn in here and there. He glanced at three pistols, two knives, and the face of a man who just got shot at to deliver tobacco across the Wildlands. "Heh. Kill ya. Yeah, I s'pose it would at that."

He set the pipe down and shuffled around a corner, deeper into his subterranean nest. The driver's hand tensed around the .45. At the scrape of coins sliding over a metal desk, he loosened the grip, but only a little.

"Thousand?" asked the old man.

"That's right."

The elder emerged from the hallway, carrying a burdened cloth sack, which he tossed to the driver. "Yanno, boy. They used ta use bits o' paper for curn-cee when I was teeny. Lot easier ta carry than these."

He caught the sack, moved to the table, and opened the pouch before poking a finger at the contents. "Yeah, but coins don't rot."

"Also, usta-be 'at the different size ones were worth different 'mounts. Now, coin's a coin."

You told me that last month... and the month before that. "Ya don't say."

The old man shrugged and went back to his beloved pipe. "Sure'n you don't wanna 'ave some?"

Minutes passed as the elder smoked and the younger counted. Satisfied at the amount, the driver cinched the bag closed and tucked it into a satchel. "Yeah. I'm sure. Need ta be gettin' back."

"Much obliged." After a handshake, the elder followed him to the exit and sealed the door behind him

The driver stood in silence, staring at the old hermit's place, pondering the bizarre kinship that occurred between two people who didn't trust anyone. *That's gonna be me in thirty years.* He flopped in behind the wheel and secured the coins in the glove box. A thumb swipe across six blue rocker-switches on the shroud over the instrument panel brought the car to life.

He laughed. *As if I'm gonna live that long.*

WAYNE'S

An hour and change later, the Challenger rolled to a halt in front of Wayne's Roadhouse in Hagerman, tucking in between a battered pickup truck and a flotilla of e-bikes. The bikes all bore the same mottled crimson sheriff-star logo. The word "New" filled the middle of the star by virtue of it not being crimson. A number of the gang congregated on the porch, lounging about on the disintegrating remains of a few old sofas.

Cautious stares lingered on the driver as he got out and locked the car. He ignored them; they were far more interested in fighting with the "Olds" over borders than bothering freelancers. Inside, the room smelled of food, beer, and fart. A dozen or so people sat scattered at tables and booth seats along the right wall. Wayne's only waitress, a jittery black-haired android everyone called Bee, waved at him. One artificial breast hung out of her torn shirt, and her tight leather pants didn't leave many curves to the imagination. Not that anyone really imagined much about a machine anyway. Probably why Wayne didn't waste a new shirt on her.

A man'd have to be *real* lonely to get off on a plastic tittie.

She followed the driver to the bar, leaning on it in a pose reminiscent of an Old West prostitute. Her smile might have been reassuring if not for the patches of visible metal on her cheek and the sporadic twitches shaking her body. Every so often, a bad one would come hand-in-hand with a spark and trace of burnt silicon in the air.

"Need anything, hon?"

"Got any burgers?"

"Y-y-yeah." Bee, in the throes of a violent spasm, grabbed the bar in an effort not to fall. "Little bitta deer, and some other furry critters. Won't even taste the tire marks."

"Fine."

She headed off toward the kitchen in her herky-jerky stride, strands of dark hair wobbled back and forth over the "B-19-C" on the back of her neck. Wayne emerged from a camouflage curtain behind the counter a few seconds after the brim of his cowboy hat. He was a head taller than the driver, and a decade or so older. Something like fourteen years ago, he'd been a driver himself. His ice blue eyes narrowed, and he pulled his thick mustache as if trying to figure out what to make of the man slouched over his bar.

"What's with all the News out front?" asked the driver.

Wrinkles deepened at the corners of Wayne's eyes as he laughed. He turned and held a mason jar up to a spigot on the wall behind him. "Buncha Olds are holed up south of here a ways, down by Carlsbad." He set the improvised glass, full of thick, brown beer, in front of the driver.

"Why do they give a dust-hopper's ass where 'Mexico' starts anymore?"

"Damn fine question, Kevin," said Wayne. "Best I can figure is men need to have somethin' to fight over or they ain't happy. Squabblin' over the borders o' two countries what don't no more exist seems like as good an excuse as any."

"Heh. I'm fixin' to be happy when I stop fightin'." Kevin fished the pouch out of his armored jacket and dropped it on the counter.

The *clatter* of coins attracted every eye in the room, except for Bee's.

"Finished that hermit delivery. 'Nother hundred today."

Wayne pulled out a worn ledger and set about counting. He slid a hundred coins to a separate pile, pulled ten out of it, and then another three. The mass of nine hundred coins went back in the pouch.

"Ten percent?" Kevin sat up as Bee put a plate in front of him, a burger and fried sweet potato strips. "Thought you said five."

A creak came from the counter as Wayne leaned his weight onto an elbow. "Read the fine print, boy. I get five percent commission on posted jobs, minimum ten coins. Gil contracted you to collect a thousand for his 'bacco. Your share o' that contract's a hundred. Roadhouse gets ten percent facilitatin' fee, an' you jes' paid me three for the food. Nine hundred goes to the seller."

Kevin ate a fry, grumbling the whole time. "Where's that leave me?"

After adding a 'deposit' line to the ledger under Kevin's name, Wayne pointed at a number: 9918.

Kevin smiled. "One more run." He gathered the burger.

Bee was right; he couldn't taste the tires.

Feminine grunting, accompanied by several heavy sets of footsteps and a woman yelling grew louder out front. The scent of meat filled Kevin's nostrils; nothing else mattered.

"Get off me," shouted a young woman, before emitting a long, straining groan of exertion.

Thump. Something hit the wall and the porch rattled with the clomping feet of several people.

A few patrons glanced at the entrance.

"Help! Please, someone!" screamed the same girl. "Let me go!"

Men snarled and grumbled. The door opened with a *crash*, revealing the steel-toed boot that had kicked it. Kevin stared over the bun at the mirror behind the counter. Everyone had turned to look, except Wayne, who didn't seem to care much about the ruckus beyond frowning at the man who'd punted the door.

Three men dressed in a random assemblage of mismatched garments loped in. Tee shirts, army coats, jeans, camo pants, and road dust covered them. Two carried a squirming, bound woman in a clean black jumpsuit as if she were a bundled carpet. Long, pure white hair waved about as she fought to get free. She had a lithe, delicate build, and seemed young—between seventeen and twenty. Cloud-white hands, tied behind her back, peeked out every few seconds as she futilely tried to grab her abductors. Her outfit looked far too clean to have been outside long.

Kevin returned his attention to the food and took a bite. The room went back to what they were doing as well. Wayne pulled the journal away, flipping it around. "Looks like one of the moles poked her head out."

"I heard them moles is pale, but damn." Kevin finished chewing. "What you figure's goin' on there?"

Wayne flashed an appraising smirk. "Don't know. Don't care so long as they don't break any o' my shit."

"Surprised the News didn't try to poach the bounty." Kevin took another bite of the burger. "Got any jobs waitin'?"

"Three on four ain't the kinda odds the News like ta pick." Wayne leaned on the bar and offered an expression of sincerity. "You might wanna do more than one run, kid. You spend all your bits on a Roadhouse up north, you won't have anything left to buy stock. Gonna make for some *real* lean times if all you got ta sell is chargin'."

The woman groaned and grunted; scuffing wood added to the din.

"I got a damn trailer full of crap to sell."

"What about food? People come here more to eat than anything else." Wayne un-leaned from the counter and snapped the book shut. He started to say something to Kevin, but looked up as the girl's pleading and cursing ended with the slam of a sliding chair. "Hey, easy on the furniture."

"Decent burger. Scav the meat yourself?"

"Yep. Picked it out of my grille yesterday." Wayne winked. "I'll add this ta yer balance." He pocketed his part of Kevin's money and re-bagged the remaining eighty-seven coins. He tossed it up and caught it. "Nah, few young bloods sell what they find on the short runs. Lot of dust-hoppers a little ways west."

Kevin lifted the burger to his mouth again; the scent of barbecue sauce and six different forms of road kill ground together swirled in his nostrils. He glanced over the bun at the mirror behind the bar. Wayne and his mirrors. The newcomers had taken a table in the back, near a small corridor that led to the bathrooms. He shuddered. The bathrooms of Wayne's Roadhouse were truly a haven for the desperate. Even Bee refused to clean them, and she had no sense of smell. The android wobbled up to the edge of the newcomers' table, taking orders while the captive squirmed. One man on either side kept the woman trapped behind the table in a corner seat. Snowy hair hid her face, save for the point of a delicate nose.

"Someone help!" She wailed. "I'm being kidnapped!"

"Don't forget the solar array." Wayne clucked his tongue. "Pays for itself in a couple months. Amarillo's the only place ta even get a decent set."

"Notice I'm aiming for ten grand?" Kevin sighed. "Most of that is the freakin' panels."

"Please… anyone," cried the woman.

Wayne carried the money into the back past the curtain.

Her captors, and everyone else in the bar, ignored her. Kevin added a fry to his next bite, savoring the taste of meat mixed with potato. Wayne knew his way around the grill all right. Somewhere down in the basement, the old man had a safe—supposedly past a half-dozen autoturrets programmed to incinerate anyone but him. It'd be damn inconvenient if Wayne died. Since banks hadn't existed for fifty-some-odd years, it beat carrying thousands of coins around.

Kevin dipped his fingers in a bowl of pepper, dusting the fries before eating two more. Bee wobbled past him, trays clattering, and dropped off food at the table. The men attacked their meals with wild abandon.

"How can you all just ignore me?" yelled the bound girl. "Please, someone… they're going to kill me." She strained and writhed.

No one moved.

Kevin swabbed some of the meat juice off his plate with a fry, before tossing the soggy thing into his mouth. A few minutes later, Wayne emerged and resumed his place behind the counter. The girl attempted to stand, but the man to her left shoved her down none too gently.

"Hey! I said watch the furniture." Wayne's shout echoed over silence for a short while before the din returned.

The woman gave him a dire look; the pointing finger seemed to blame her for being rough with the chair. "Please, someone, help. Many people will die if I fail." She set about trying to wrench her hands free for a little while before giving up with a fatigued sigh. "Someone…" Her voice fell to a tiny whisper. "Please don't let them rape me!"

One man in the back yawned. Someone farted. Wayne went over to check the lock on the roll top door protecting his gun & armor booth from casual shoplifters.

"Damn fine burger, Wayne." Kevin popped the last hunk in his mouth, using the one remaining fry to absorb as much liquid as he could from the plate. "Lemme get another brew?"

"I'll give a thousand coins to whoever helps me." The white-haired girl sniffled.

"Bah, you ain't got that kinda cash," said a deep male voice to the right.

The room got quiet for about four seconds. Her three captors looked up, ready for a throw-down, but no one moved. Soon, the din resumed and they returned their attention to their meals. Kevin ate the last fry, and wiped two spots of burger juice from his armored jacket before licking his finger. The woman tried to get out of her chair again, and one of the men pushed her back down. Wayne came by with another mason jar filled with homemade beer as Bee collected the empty plate. Kevin glanced into the opaque amber liquid. His gaze flicked up at the mirror's view of the room behind him. The girl made eye contact with him in the reflection. He lifted an eyebrow at her.

"You put honey in this, Wayne?"

"Found a bit, yeah." The older man chuckled. "Some guy put it up for transport, but got himself dead. Spoils of war."

She pouted at the table. "At least let me have some foo—"

Kevin kicked off the counter, rotating on the spinning barstool while drawing his steel-grey 1911. His first shot hit the right-side man in the neck, spattering the wall red. The second caught the left-side man in the lower chest as he started to get out of his chair, turning a lunge into an ungainly face plant. Kevin slid off the cushion as soon as he faced the back corner. His feet hit the ground, and he raised his pistol higher; the third man's turned back afforded him the time to aim for the head. Bullet number three flung a corpse across the table and seasoned the food with brain bits.

"Damn waste of eats," said a voice off to Kevin's left.

"I'd still eat it," wheezed an old-sounding voice.

"Nasty mother of a dust hopper," muttered Wayne.

A half dozen others had weapons drawn, aiming randomly. When Kevin let his arm drop, the slow process of relaxing started.

"S'only brain and blood. Ya'veet worse afore," replied a gurgling female.

The pale white-haired woman drew her knees up, cowering away from the split-open skull in front of her. She looked at the floor to her right and trembled, turning wide, innocent eyes up at Kevin. He approached, holstering his 1911 before crouching to check her captors' possessions.

"Hey, what do you think you're doin' there?" shouted Wayne.

Kevin grumbled. "Come on, man, I'm getting low on .45."

"Anyone dies in here, their shit is mine. You know the rules. Someday, you'll be takin' advantage o' that part of the Code. Bee, clean that up."

"Yeah… yeah." Kevin sighed.

The android grabbed a rag. "Sure thing, boss."

The woman, cringing from the gore, scooted closer to Kevin. "So, that's what it takes to get a man to do the decent thing? Money?"

Kevin wandered back to the bar. "I wanted to finish my burger first."

"Hey." She squirmed as if to remind him she was bound hand and foot. "Little help?"

"I just gave you a little help." He lowered himself onto the same stool he'd vacated, and removed the magazine from his pistol. "Crap, Wayne, I only got three left. You got any .45 in stock?"

"Eighteen. Three coins apiece."

Kevin grumbled. "That's robbery, and you know it. I got some .40 cal I can't use. Trade?"

"I'll have to see the trade, make sure it ain't too old to work."

The girl wobbled to her feet and hopped over to the bar.

"It ain't as old as you are." Kevin winked and took a sip of the beer. "The rounds have scratchings. Ween's work. Less than four months ago."

"That crazy old fucker on the houseboat?" Wayne laughed. "I thought he bit it a year ago."

"Hey, whatever your name is..." The white-haired woman bounced closer; her hair danced at her beltline. "How 'bout untying me?"

Kevin glanced sideways at her. "No problem. How 'bout that thousand coins?"

She bit her lip. Her black jumpsuit rustled as she squirmed. "It's not actually *on* me, but I can get it once I get where I'm going."

Wayne chuckled. "At least she's original."

"Now ain't that convenient." Kevin slid the magazine back into his .45 with a *click*.

"I'm not lying. I have something very important that's gotta get to Harrisburg. There are people there who will pay you for getting me there safe."

The room went quiet at the name.

Kevin chuckled and took another sip. "Oh, so you want to hire a driver to take you all the way to Harrisburg? I usually charge a thousand coins to drive a third of that distance. The area 'round Pitts ain't no joke."

A few others in the room joined in his amusement. Bee swayed by with a basin full of guns, knives, and other random items, which she carried into the back room.

"Yeah, okay. I want to hire you to take me to Harrisburg."

Kevin looked her up and down before he searched all eight pockets of her jumpsuit. An odd scent clung to her, somewhere between clean and chemical. She tried to wriggle away, but didn't get far. "You ain't got a damn thing to pay me with 'cept the usual. You're pretty cute"—he patted her on the cheek—"but you ain't thousand-coins-a-fuck cute. Can probably sell you for twice that to some Wilders down in old Mex."

"Bet'cha get two grand for her in Glimmertown," said a gurgling middle-aged woman in an armored vest made of steel belted radials. She toasted him with a half-full mason jar and took a healthy swig.

"Naw, more like 1800," mumbled Wayne.

Kevin took a sip of his beer as she shivered. "Lucky for you, I don't believe in slavery."

She sagged, sighing with relief. "Look, I know you probably don't trust me, but there's a doctor expecting me in Harrisburg. He can give you a thousand coins, I swear. Maybe more."

"Harrisburg's a long way from here," said Wayne. "Most drivers'd charge least five or six grand to go all that way." He clapped Kevin on the shoulder. "That would take care of that little nest egg you'd be needin' to set up yer own Roadhouse. Course, Kevin' ain't gonna wanna go anywhere near a population center. He's got a thing 'bout Infected."

"Who the hell doesn't?" yelled a man.

"Heh." Half of Kevin's mouth smiled as he sipped his beer. "How do I know you're not takin' me into some kind of ambush? I'm too damn close to retiring to take stupid chances."

Gem-blue eyes widened as she made her most earnest 'trust me' face. She added a little whine and bounce. Bee tottered by with a bundle of clothes, setting them on the counter. With a towel from her apron, she dabbed blood from the girl's cheek. Unable to resist, the woman tolerated it, cringing away from three naked dead men on the floor. Once satisfied she'd gotten all the blood off the girl, Bee walked across the room to the dead, grabbed the first corpse by the leg, and dragged him out the back.

"Nice try. I fell for that look once. Woke up bare-ass in the desert wrapped around a cactus, minus one pickup truck and all my gear." Kevin drained the beer and slammed the mason jar down. "That ain't happening again."

Wayne chuckled. "Did you ever find that bitch?"

"Nope." Kevin got up and tromped toward the exit.

"Hey, you can't leave me tied up like this! Come on." She hopped to face him as he went by.

He didn't react, heading outside to the Challenger.

THINK FAST

T he white-haired woman slumped against the counter, eyeing the patrons and trembling. All efforts to catch Wayne's attention failed as he seemed to make it a point not to even look at her. An attempt to glare the rope off her ankles failed as the room returned to the usual din. The regulars didn't try to hide their conversations about if she'd become Wayne's property, Kevin's property, or ripe for the taking. Some seemed hesitant to risk tangling with whoever might still be chasing her. She stared at the door, pondering hopping outside, but decided against it. Wayne ambled by, once more ignoring her. She bent forward, wringing her wrists around, but the rope proved too tight, and her skin too sore. A glint of metal caught her eye from a knife on the floor under the bloody table.

Cord bit into her ankles each time her weight came down as she hopped back across the barroom. Once close enough, she squatted and let gravity take her sideways. After rolling onto her belly, she wriggled between two chairs and reached out for the utensil. Bee tottered up alongside and worked a rag around the tabletop overhead. Two fingers touched the knife and got it a few inches off the ground, but the greasy metal slipped loose and hit the floor with a *clatter*.

"Oh, dear." Bee stooped to pick it up. "This'll need to be washed."

"Hey!" yelled the girl. "Cut me loose?"

Bee shifted to stare at the bar, but Wayne wasn't there. "I must ask permission."

The woman growled. "Someone? Anyone? Please help!"

When no one acknowledged her, she scrunched around and tried to grab the rope between her ankles. The more she fought, the tighter the rope felt. Soft grunts escaped past clenched teeth. She bit her lip as one finger teased at a knot. Feeling trapped and helpless, she sagged limp and out of breath.

"Wayne?" she asked, voice raised. She shifted onto her knees and threw her weight back, managing to get on her feet without falling. "Hey... Wayne?"

After a minute of staring at the empty bar, her eyes lit up with hope when Kevin returned, carrying an improvised cloth pouch. Shoulder-length light brown hair lofted from his brisk stride. He returned to where he'd been sitting, slapped a hand on the bar twice, and Wayne re-emerged from a curtained doorway.

He's gotta help me. He's not like rest of these people.

She bounced across the room again, stopping a few feet away, tired and disheveled from her futile battle for freedom.

NEW PROBLEMS

Kevin set the bag of bullets down and pushed it like a stack of poker chips across the bar. "Twenty-six .40 cal. Trade you for the eighteen .45 rounds."

Wayne picked open the bundle, holding up each bullet in turn as if examining diamonds. He dropped the last one into the batch with a *click*. "Fine."

Kevin folded one arm across his chest, bracing his elbow in his palm and picking at his lip while staring at the woman. *I'm an idiot for even considering trusting this bitch, but a thousand coins would do the trick and then some.* After a pregnant pause, he sighed. "Alright, suppose I do get your ass to Harrisburg. You think your doctor buddy will pay two thousand?"

She looked up at him like a child given a pony for her birthday. "I'm sure he would. You don't know how many lives you're going to save."

Wayne handed him back the pouch, a change in shape indicating fewer, heavier bullets. Kevin peeked, earning a smirk.

"What? You're the guy that told me never to take anything on faith."

"True." Wayne grinned. "Thought you'd forgotten that when you lost the Marauder."

Kevin's eyes burned. "I miss that damn truck. Two inches of armor and a rotating turret."

"You gonna plate up your new one?" Wayne gathered the empty

mason jar mugs. "Guess not till it gets shot up a bit, awful pretty machine."

"I dunno. I'm kind of liking being fast and agile." Kevin went for the door. "Alright, come on."

The girl hopped twice, lost her balance, and fell to her knees. When Kevin didn't stop, she yelled, "Hey, come on. You can't leave me tied up."

"Sure I can. It's easy. All I have to do is"—he opened his mouth with a mild gasp, feigning shock—"not untie you."

She wobbled back to her feet as he reached the door and fell again after one more hop. "Ow." She whined, and sniffled as if about to burst into tears.

Goddammit. "I'm not going to carry you."

The woman attempted to get back on her feet and fell flat on her chest. She rolled side to side for a few seconds and thrashed before sniveling. He tromped back over and shook his head. She whimpered. Kevin lifted her by a hand under each arm and set her on the nearest barstool. When he pulled a knife from his belt, she smiled and spun so her back faced him.

"Thank you." She tensed her arms.

Kevin pulled her around to face him and sawed the cord binding her legs. Her black shoes were heavy like boots, but short enough to expose bare ankles rubbed raw. He blinked at her, wondering how skin could turn *that* white. He hadn't seen anything that color since he'd found a few packs of old copier paper in a sealed cabinet. That had been a nice little payday.

The woman swiveled around and held out her wrists, but he walked away.

"Hey." She ran up behind him. "What the hell's wrong with you?"

He stopped on the porch. "You're worth one, maybe two-thousand coins. That, and the last bitch I let in my car stole it. I'm not taking any chances. I only cut your feet loose because I'm too lazy to carry you."

A little color appeared in her face, turning it pink around her nose. She stared at him with an expression halfway between exasperated and angry when four members of the 'New' gang wandered over and gathered around him.

"Cute bounty. Where's the turn in?" asked a stocky man he knew as Juan.

"She ain't a bounty, she's a client," said Kevin.

"Horseshit, man. You're runnin' her up to Roswell," said a New with a long scar down his face. "You know we run the law around here. We'll be takin this one off yer hands. Give us the details o' what she's wanted fer, and get lost."

"If you're some kind of law, why'd you let those idiots kidnap me?" The woman narrowed her eyes at Scar.

Kevin shook his head. "The only 'law' these shitheads enforce is whatever that fatass Raphael tells them to do, and four on one is their kind of odds. Four on three, not so much."

"Look, man…" A tall, thin biker, Weed according to the name patch on his cut, pulled the leather aside to show a pistol. "This don't need to be ugly. We're gonna take her and get that bounty."

"I ain't gonna warn you humps again." Kevin glared at Scar. "She ain't no wanted bounty. She's a fare."

"You keep all your fares tied?" Weed pulled his gun. "Or you inta slavin' now?"

Kevin dove with a roar, tackling the thin man flat. The gun bounced into the street as small armor plates in his glove pounded into the ganger's cheek. A longhaired New grabbed Kevin by the shoulders and tried to haul him off. Scar and Juan went after the girl. She backed up down the long porch, twisting and pulling at the binding on her wrists.

"I'm not a bounty; he's just being an asshole. Thinks I want to steal his car."

"Yeah, right," said the scarred one, reaching.

She feigned a whimper that lured him off guard. A snap kick to the crotch stunned him long enough for her to jump into a flip-over kick that left a shoeprint on his cheek. He kissed the wall of the Roadhouse and fell unconscious. The woman landed wobbly without being able to use her arms for balance, but stayed upright. Juan hesitated, staring at her.

Kevin shoved himself up, driving his elbow into the gut of the longhaired man above him. Beer-flavored wheeze washed over his head as the New enforcer stumbled to all fours. Weed sat up and punched for Kevin's balls, but he caught the skinny man's arm. Holding him by the wrist, Kevin pulled him forward into a kick that struck the side of the head, knocking him flat, and out cold. The longhaired man pulled a knife and lunged at Kevin as he recovered from the kick. The blade stalled on an armor panel in his jacket. Kevin trapped the knife-wielding arm and fell on it, using his weight to drag the man to the floor. He pinned longhair's arm under one knee, trapped the man's free arm with his left hand, and punched him repeatedly in the skull until he looked unconscious.

Kevin sat back on his heels, panting. Longhair didn't seem likely to get back up any time soon, but he punched him again for good measure.

Juan screamed and rushed at the woman. She spun out of his grab, escaping with only a torn breast pocket, and whipped her leg into a roundhouse kick. Her heavy-soled shoe caught him in the left ear, sending him flying headfirst through the Roadhouse railing onto five of the New gang's e-bikes, which collapsed like a row of dominoes. Juan moaned, still conscious, but apparently in too much pain to get up. She backed away, shaking her head in an effort to get her hair over her shoulders and out of her eyes.

Kevin helped himself to some loose coins from the two men he'd knocked out, keeping her in sight the whole time. She trotted up to stand nearby; her body shook from adrenaline, though her eyes held fear. The woman stared pleas at him until he walked to his car. He opened the passenger door and gestured for her to get in.

"Gonna untie me?"

He glanced at the two men she put down. "You're dangerous enough without hands. Be glad I'm too lazy to carry you. Now, get in."

She gave him a pouty face for all of four seconds, but the clatter of gangers waking up nudged her into the vehicle. Kevin disconnected the charging cable from a bank of plugs and let it reel back into its compartment in the right-front fender. He pushed the hatch cover closed with a *click*, made his way around, and opened his door. Juan tried to get up off the pile of bikes, but wound up tripping and rolling face first onto the road. Kevin shook his head.

"You guys are gonna feel dumb when you figure out she ain't no bounty." He fell into the driver's seat. "She's right, I am just an asshole."

Slam.

The closed door muted their grumbling.

A LITTLE SYMPATHY

Silence filled the car for almost a half hour. The girl fidgeted, trying to squirm into a position to rub the soreness out of her ankles. Rope burns against such white skin looked like lipstick marks. Kevin kept his eyes on the road, heading north.

"Why won't you trust me?" She stared at her lap.

"'Cause you're a woman." He glanced at her for a few seconds. "And a pretty one at that. Think you can get anything you want out of a man with a cute stare and a little bit of whimpering. Acting more helpless than you are. I saw how you moved on that porch. That spill you took in Wayne's was a pity plea." He scowled. "I shouldn't have let it work."

Her face turned pink around the nose again. "I'm not like that. I'm not gonna steal your damn car. I could even help if you cut me loose. I know my way around a gun."

"That's exactly what I'm afraid of."

She kept quiet for another twenty minutes before she sniffled.

"Go ahead, cry if you want." He tossed a rag in her lap. "You can blow your nose on that."

"You gonna hold it for me?" She glared. "You're going to think I'm trying to manipulate you into feeling sorry for me."

"I already do, so get on with it and sob already."

Her eyes narrowed. "In case you didn't notice, I have no weapons, I'm not very strong, I'm alone, and I have no idea where I'm going or where I even am. Even if I *did* want to steal your car—which I *don't*—I have no damn idea how to drive or which way to go." She worked herself up into a huff, seeming much closer to angry than scared.

"Lying won't help."

She flashed a look of confusion.

"Not strong? You knocked Juan through a railing with one kick. I wasn't that out of it. Wayne's gonna be pissed at the damage."

The woman got quiet.

"Didn't figure a mole'd know their way around."

She glanced past her hair at him. "What the hell is a mole?"

He tapped his fingers on the wheel for a moment before squinting at her. When her innocence didn't flinch, he sighed. "You look like one. Pale as a ghost, white hair. Moles are them dumb bastards who think the war's still going on and hide underground in old government shelters, sewers, or subways. After a few generations, they decided to expand the bunkers into cities rather than risk the outside world. Bunch o' crazy idiots."

She looked out the window on her side. "I'm not a mole. Please, I promise I won't steal any of your things. I'm trying to save humanity."

Kevin laughed. "You're just full of big promises. A thousand coins, two thousand, saving all of humanity now?" He waved his hand about as he spoke. "Can't say I blame you much. I don't expect those three would've been very gentle with you."

"What's your name?"

"You're trying to get in my head now. Get me to trust you. First it's a name, then it's a hug, maybe a kiss, maybe a handie, or maybe if you're really desperate, full-on head. Then, I let my guard down and I wake up naked and tied hugging a cactus without a car. Look, the only difference between you and my usual cargo is that you talk. I ain't gonna touch you. I ain't gonna hurt you. I'm going to take you where you wanna go and hope to get paid. If I don't get paid, then we might have a problem. Until we get there and I get my money, I'm not gonna take the chance of you runnin' off. I should probably have carried you."

"I'm Tris. I swear you'll get paid. The doctor's been waiting for this information his whole life." She lifted a leg and wiped her nose on her knee.

"What information? You've got nothing anywhere on you. Not a tattoo down your back is it?" He chuckled, swerving around some potholes.

The motion knocked her against the door; she grunted. "It's in my head."

"Of course it is."

"No, really. Look behind my ear." She twisted, exposing the side of her neck.

After a momentary pause to make sure he had enough clear road to glance away, he reached across to brush her hair aside. Behind her left ear, a tiny metal socket glinted. Tris didn't flinch from his touch, but she did curl into a ball when he screamed and pounded the wheel.

"Shit!"

"W-what?" She raised her knee as if expecting the next punch to be for her.

"That's an interface jack. You've got cybernetic implants." Kevin's glower darkened. "You're from the goddamned Enclave." He seethed.

Tris pressed herself into the passenger side door, trembling.

"Oh, knock that simpering shit off already. I'm not going to hit you. You're probably boosted to hell and back and could kill me with your hands tied behind your back."

"Doesn't seem like there's much point to leaving me tied then, is there?" She eased herself out of her fearful pose.

"Nice try." He glanced at her feet. "I should."

She stared at her lap. "Please don't."

His gloves creaked on the wheel. Several silent minutes passed.

"It worked a little, didn't it?" Tris didn't look at him. "You do feel just a little sympathy for me?"

"Yeah, maybe a little. Don't confuse sympathy with desperation. I'm a hundred coins short of my dream, and you offered a thousand. It's shit pay for this kind of drive, but it's enough to let me retire. Don't get too excited yet, sweetie. At least now I know why those three didn't rip your clothes off."

"What?"

"They must've figured out you were Enclave. If you're out here alone, that means you've run away or escaped or something. Probably ten thousand coins on your head if you're brought back alive—but they won't take you if there's any 'genetic impurities' going on. They find one swimmer, no cash."

Tris blushed a little again. "They don't need me for that anymore." He shot her a look, but she kept going. "My implant has data with medical information stolen from the Enclave computer. I'm carrying a cure for The Virus." She stared urgency at him, eyes widening.

"Oh bul—" He glared at her. Unable to find any trace of deceit in her face, he grumbled at the windshield. "If that's bullshit, you must believe it."

"It's not."

"You're not a fuckin' android are you?"

"No. Just tweaked. If I was an android, I'd have snapped the cord already." As if on cue, her stomach growled. "Those bastards didn't give me much food."

"Great. I got some Enclave chick in my car that's either batshit crazy, or has something so valuable the entire damn world is going to come after me for it."

"Nobody knows. Not even the Council of Four. I escaped. They don't want the cure getting out here." She squirmed, twisting at her arms. "It'll be easier if I can help."

Kevin stared into the distance, tracking the orange sun as it slipped westward, into the teeth of the mountains. When he didn't answer, Tris slumped in her seat with a sigh. As time dragged on, she alternated between seeming angry and terrified. Another attempt to brute-force her way to freedom left her sweating and out of breath.

Gloves creaked.

"You've been lonely for a long time, haven't you? That other woman, the one who took your car, really hurt you." She tried to make eye contact. "I'm not trying to manipulate you. I'm honestly frightened. You say you don't trust me, but... How scary do you think it is for a girl to be helpless out here, stuck in a car with a man she doesn't know who treats her like a piece of cargo? What if something happened to you?"

He let off the pedal; the car lost speed.

"You said you wanted to finish your food." Her stomach growled again. "Was that the truth or did it really take me offering money for you to help?"

Ahead, he spotted the boxy shape of a white van that scavs hadn't peeled to the frame yet crashed into the side of a small shack. Kevin pulled over a short distance away. He ran his thumb over the row of glowing blue rocker switches, turning them off. Wheel motors whined down to silence.

"Wait here. Van ain't been stripped yet, might have something useful."

"Did you help me, or did I change captors?"

He finally looked at her, but turned away from her pleading face after only a few seconds. "Name's Kevin."

He stood and walked off. Tris pulled her feet up and shimmied over the console to the driver's side. She stumbled out of the car and caught her balance by leaning against the door.

"That was guilt, Kevin. You do have a soul. Please trust me, you're my last chance."

He stomped over to the van. All four wheel-motors had burned. What had once been solid rubber tires had become misshapen puddles of cooled material beneath char-blackened hubs. Bullet holes decorated the side, and the air around it smelled of singed meat. He climbed inside and searched a number of storage compartments for anything easy to scavenge. A shiny padlock secured one hatch—irresistible temptation.

Tris approached the open door, and bent forward to peer inside. "Kevin, come on. You're a nice guy. You helped me. Cut me loose already."

"You're asking that too much, what do you really want?"

She stared at him, gawking. "Uhh, not to be helpless out here in the Wildlands. What kind of woman *wants* to be tied?"

"I can think of a handful." He looked back long enough to wink.

Her face tinted rose. "Let me rephrase that. What kind of woman wants to be tied out in the middle of the Wildlands?"

Kevin stood up straight, pondering. "Okay, that narrows it to one." He shivered. "Zephyra's a bit of a freak."

Tris screamed.

"Oh, will you knock it off." He turned around to say more, but found her backpedaling into a full sprint. "What the?" He jumped out of the van, winding up within arm's reach of two walking corpses.

At least, they looked, smelled, and groaned like walking corpses.

Large swaths of bruise and rot stained bloated, misshapen bodies greenish-purple. The one on the right had deteriorated further, having lost something quite dear to all men. Kevin gaped at the patch of exposed insides as some of the strength left his legs. It raised an arm and lurched forward. Eager grunts fired bloody pus from the nostrils.

Shit! Infected.

Kevin leapt backward. One of the creatures lurched at him, throwing its weight into a punch that tore a hole in the side of the van.

The other Infected took off at a rapid shamble after Tris, who sprinted down the road alternatively sobbing and calling Kevin an asshole as she tugged at her wrists.

The Infected in front of Kevin pulled its arm free with a groan of bending metal. It whipped itself sideways, sending an overextended haymaker at his head. Kevin's hasty evasion took his legs out from under him. He fell flat and scrambled in a backward crab-walk for a few feet before flipping over and running to the road. Once he had the safety of about forty yards between him and a walking dead man, he sighted over the .45 at the one chasing Tris, but changed his mind and aimed at the closer one. It gaped at him, snarling, yellow ooze seeping over its teeth as it stiff-legged its way toward him.

He waited another half second until he felt confident shooting it would not spatter any infected blood on the van. He wanted what was in that compartment, but wouldn't go near it if even one droplet marred the paint. As soon as it reached the paving, he fired twice. Gore blew out from its back as a slug tore through its chest. The second shot caught it in the cheek, detonating the entire back portion of its head. The Infected took one more step, twitching arms grasping at the air, before dropping to its knees and falling to the road. The sight of its body rupturing mesmerized him in a fit of phobic tunnel vision. *One drop... all it takes is one drop.*

"Kevin!" Tris, somewhat distant, shouted.

He turned toward her and loosed a startled yelp as the other one jumped at him. The force of the hit knocked him to the ground. The creature pounced, grabbing his forearm and smashing his knuckles against the street until the gun bounced out of his grip. Kevin got a hand up, pushing at the squishy chest of the howling monstrosity. Rational thought evaporated in a desperate flailing fit to get away. It reared back, hauling him by the arms off the ground with enough force to swing him over its head. Kevin screamed as he hung suspended for a fraction of a second before the Infected slammed him down on his chest.

Stunned from the impact, he gasped for breath, catching a brief glimpse of Tris jogging closer between sparkling lights. *One drop... One drop...* He shrieked like a six-year-old boy waking from a nightmare and clawed at the dirt, trying to get away.

The creature pounded its fist into the back of his armor twice before it lifted him by the belt and threw him. Without the armored jacket, every rib in his chest would've been fragments. Kevin hit the ground in a flopping roll, unable to gain control of his momentum before he collided with the rear end of the van. A little distance muted panic. *Shit, these fuckers are strong.*

He stuffed a hand into his jacket, going for a 9mm Beretta in a holster under his left arm.

The Infected was on him before he could get up. He rolled to the side as it drove two fists down onto the rear bumper, knocking it off the frame with a loud *clang*. He scrambled on all fours but didn't get far before it grabbed his boot and pulled him back. Kevin flipped over, getting his arms up in time to catch the creature as it fell on him. Desperate to keep his mouth closed, he braced the monstrosity's weight on his left forearm and drove his fist into its face. His punch crushed the man's cheek, covering his glove with bloody ooze the consistency of raw egg.

Vicelike hands squeezed his wrists, pinning him into the dirt. He pounded a knee into its side twice, but the wild-eyed thing did not react. Eager grunts like a rutting hog issued forth as it forced itself close enough to bite. The Infected pushed Kevin's arms wider and leaned in as if to kiss him. Its jaw distended beyond human width, revealing a serpentine tongue-like appendage covered in tiny suckers and dark black tendrils.

The wavering horror searched out his lips; it wanted to burrow down his throat. He grunted, unused to feeling weak. His heart pounded in his head as he thrashed his face back and forth to evade the deadly kiss.

Blam.

The back of the creature's head splattered to the side, throwing gore clear of Kevin. In an instant, its superhuman strength faded. A length of tentacle bounced away from Kevin's chest and hit the dirt. He shoved the corpse off and sat up, still panting, and put two in its chest from the Beretta. Tris peered through her knees at him from fifteen feet away. A curtain of white hair spread out around her upside-down face, touching the ground. She had bent over forward, holding his .45 behind her back. A stripe of pale brown dirt ran up the side of her jumpsuit from the somersault she must have used to pick it up.

He blinked, unable to move as he pondered the impossibility of the shot she had made.

Tris stood up straight and brought her feet together, the gun pointed straight down. She made no effort to go anywhere and waited for him to walk over. Still covered in sweat with his pulse drubbing in his eardrums, he looked her up and down.

"How…"

She let her head sag forward. "Cyberware, remember? I have some dex boosters."

"Some?" He blinked. "You fired a gun from behind your back, upside down, at a target six inches away from my head."

"I hit it, didn't I?" She fidgeted. "And didn't get any on you."

He eased it out of her bound hands. "How…"

"The Underground gave me some training before I left. Did you get any of its blood in your mouth?"

"No."

She twisted her wrists. "Trust me yet?"

"No." He plodded back to the Challenger. "No, not really."

LOOKING FOR CRACKS

Tris stared up at the clouds, unable to decide if she wanted to scream in rage or just cry. Amid a stalemate, she trudged back to the car. "You're sure you didn't get any of the blood on you?"

"Little drips on my armor and pants, yeah."

"You should clean the armor and burn the pants right away. The Virus can persist in the environment for up to twenty-seven weeks." She squinted into the oncoming wind; her hair lofted like the train of a specter. "It's warm here, so probably double that."

Kevin grumbled.

She meandered back to the car and sat on the hood while he took off his belt, armor, and pants, admiring the sight of his pectorals, biceps, and thighs. *He's a lot healthier than I'd thought possible.* If not for the cord biting her wrists, she might've found his almost boyish face cute.

He used the pants to clean his armored jacket and tossed them to the road. A brief rummage of the trunk located a replacement pair, which he pulled on. A zippo and some lighter fluid from a box facilitated the disposal of the discarded, blood-soaked pair. He held his right hand glove upside down over the burn, trying to cook the viral blood off it.

With that done, and crowbar in hand, he returned to the van and disappeared inside. She sat on the hood, tapping her foot on nothing while the repeated *clang, clank, clang, thump* echoed from inside. It took him about ten minutes to batter the padlock into submission. Eventually, he emerged from the hulk with a belt of ammunition—.50 Cal BMG—over his shoulder. He paused at the fender, sensing the stare she gave him.

"These are worth about four to six coins a bullet. Good find."

"Do you want me to beg? Cry? Suck you off? When are you gonna untie me?"

"When I get paid." He looked at the road.

"Kevin…" She slid off the hood and leaned into him. "I hit that Infected. I could've hit you. Why won't you trust me that I'm not a threat? Whatever that other girl did to you, I'm not her."

"I'll think about it." He moved forward and tossed the ammo belt into the backseat crate.

Tris scowled and trudged to the car, backing up to it and managing to get the door open. She flopped into the seat and pulled her legs up. He reached across her to close it.

"I'll blow you right now if you cut me loose."

He ignored her and pulled back onto the road, driving around the dead body. "So you know all about this virus thing, huh?"

She scowled at the door, somewhere between rage and futility. "I'm not a doctor, but I guess I know more about it than someone that grew up out here. I went to school as a kid. It's nasty stuff."

"Zombies." Kevin shivered.

"Not completely." She leaned her head back. A small time display floated in blue letters at the lower left of her vision, fed into her optic nerve: 6:42 p.m. "They're not dead. They rot alive in a condition similar to leprosy. The virus causes degeneration in parts of the brain that govern reason and personality while stimulating regions linked to aggression. It causes random cellular necrosis, causing victims to look like they're decaying once it progresses to stage three. Infection winds up being fatal after about six months, less for weak people, longer for healthier ones. We don't know why some of them seem to spawn tendril symbiotes. The Virus isn't supposed to be able to do that. They think it's another organism."

Kevin shivered. "If your timeline is correct, there shouldn't be any infected left. The Enclave set that shit loose like twenty years ago. And that symbio-whatever sounds like a weapon."

Tris rolled her head toward him. "Yes. It was. That's why I have to do this. The Enclave doesn't want it stopped. We're all vaccinated, and it lets them dominate what's left of the world even though there's forty people out here to every one of them."

He glanced at her and sighed. "Stop looking at me like that."

She gazed out the passenger window to hide a smile. "You're still going north."

"Yeah. Gonna hop on Route 40 and go east to 44. There's a connection somewhere up there to 70 or 76"—he scratched his head—"ain't never been up that far north or east, but Harrisburg used to be a big ass city, right? There should be signs."

"I'm surprised you're not heading west. Figured since you're treating me like a prisoner, you were going to take me back to the Enclave."

"I don't trust them either. Reward's too high. They'd probably kill me for my trouble. Knowing my luck, they'd let me go, but confiscate my car."

"Yeah." She sighed. "You're right. So, are you gonna leave me like this the whole trip? I'm wearing a jumpsuit. I can't take it off to piss with my hands tied. I'm sure you don't want me wetting myself in your nice car."

He smiled. "Sympathy isn't working so you're trying logic now?"

Her stare got wider. "I don't think sympathy failed all the way. You still have a heart in there somewhere, even under all those scars." She shifted in a search to get comfortable. "I just hope you find it before I have to take a whiz. Course, you got time. I haven't had anything to eat or drink in two days."

THE ENCLAVE

Dammit. His gloves creaked. *I'm not gonna fall for the guilt trip. I am not going to fall for the guilt trip.*

"Kevin?"

He let out a long sigh. "What?"

"You might want to speed up. There's a few Hoplites coming up behind us."

"Shit." He glared at the rearview.

Three black Enclave hovercrafts gained on them, dark spots on the forefront of a massive curtain of dust. One followed the road while the other two spread out to either side and lagged a length behind. Each was about twice the size of the Challenger and brimming with mounted weapons.

"I should just stop."

"They don't want me back, Kevin." She lifted her face to stare right at him, looking wan, tired, and terrified. "They want me dead... and probably you too for being with me. In case I told you too much."

As if to underscore her point, a dull pop came from behind. A split second later, explosions on either side of the car showered them with rocks and shrapnel. He swerved, avoiding the second volley. The hard maneuver bounced her into him and back against the door. She wailed as her head hit the window.

"Ow." She sniffled.

Kevin kept his gaze on the mirror, drifting side to side without pattern. Tris lifted one foot, bracing it on the dashboard in an attempt to avoid another hard encounter with automotive glass. She grunted as Kevin hit the brakes unexpectedly, causing the left hovercraft to glide up alongside. A man in a black flight helmet looked down at him. Kevin waved and pulled a cord along the roof over his head.

From a few inches behind the driver side window, an incendiary gel sprayer roared to life. Burning slime spewed all over the armor-plated rubber skirt, raising an instant cloud of greasy smoke. The hovercraft pilot pulled away, but not before taking on enough flaming material to cause a catastrophic failure of the air cushion. With a great concussive *boom*, the seal burst. The hovercraft bottomed out and came to a shuddering halt somewhere in the dust, two enormous fan blades kicking up dirt.

Kevin nailed the accelerator, pinning them both against the seats. Red LED numbers shot up past sixty, seventy, eighty, ninety, over a hundred. The other two hovercraft kept pace; slow to accelerate, but they soon gained ground and opened fire again, this time with machine guns. Kevin growled as red-hot tracers streamed overhead.

A quick swerve put Tris face-first in his lap. She grunted, trapped there by inertia and having no use of her arms. Kevin squirmed at the awkwardness of where her face landed, but stayed focused on weaving between streams of tracers. After two more muted explosions outside, he cut the wheel hard left and she slapped into the passenger door again.

"Cut me loose! You're gonna break my damn neck."

Kevin flicked on the rear-targeting screen, lining up the lead hovercraft for a shot.

"You bastard. You really *are* going to leave me like this until Harrisburg." She stomped her foot into the dash, barely in time to catch herself before another sudden evasion.

"Sorry, hon. Little busy right now."

Thumb on the button, one rifle in the trunk opened up. *Shit, forgot to clear the damn '16.* Sparks danced across the curtain of rubber and metal; the bullets didn't dent the armored panels. "Shit. Shit. They're not gonna fall for the flamethrower again." He twisted in the seat, reaching for the crate behind him. His fingertips about touched it when he had to swing around to correct for a giant pothole. Another explosion showered them with dirt and threw up a dust cloud that blocked his vision for three agonizing seconds.

"What's in the box?" she yelled.

"Couple of 'nades."

The deep rumble of a high-caliber cannon made him swerve off the road. Now he had to dodge scrub brush and rocks in addition to heavy weapons. Giant jackrabbits, not so much. Tris turned her back to him.

"I'll get them." She shook her wrists. "Please... Trust me."

She slid into him on a hard turn as a chain of explosions rippled along the ground to the left.

"What the fuck was—"

"Automatic grenade launcher." She tried to tear her arms loose. "What are you more afraid of, a girl that wants to help or a pair of Enclave hovercraft lobbing 40mm high explosive at 325 rounds per minute?"

He seized a fistful of her hair, not tight enough to hurt, and pulled her head around to face him. Tears ran from the corners of her eyes.

"Please... Trust me."

Another explosion made him let go and grab the wheel. The Challenger skidded the other way, into a wide, sweeping left turn that shoved her feet-first into the door. Kevin drew the knife from his belt and sank it into the knot. She pulled the bindings into the edge as he pushed. The rope failed in a sudden rip, and her left arm smacked into the dashboard.

"Ow, shit." She cradled her hands to her chest, but grabbed the handle overhead as he drove back onto the road amid the squealing of tires.

"Don't just sit there. Get those grenades."

She rubbed her wrist for another few seconds before climbing past the gap in the front seats. He fixated on the rear-targeting screen, nudging the car a little to the right. She poked her head into the front a moment later, holding three black hand-grenades.

"Center console. Pull the pin on one but hold the little metal fl—"

"The spoon. I know how grenades work." She lifted the flap. At the bottom of the chamber between the front seats, a six-inch square metal hatch opened to a view of road racing by. She nodded, pulled the pin, and held the death sphere with both hands over the opening.

"Get ready..." He nudged the car to the left, not flinching as a stream of heavy cannon fire tore up the road to their right, a few feet away from a hit. "Now!"

She dropped it; somehow, the metallic *clang* of the spoon flying off reached his ears among the chaos of gunfire. Tris leaned forward, hovering next to him as they both stared at the rear-view monitor. The skirt of the lead hovercraft devoured the tiny, bouncing black dot. A split-second later, the rubbery walls disintegrated in a hail of metal debris. Fan blades, armor chunks, and bits of rubber belched out to both sides.

After a brief hop from the explosion, the behemoth crashed down and went into a spinning slide, spewing sparks. The trailing Hoplite smashed into the rapidly decelerating one and dragged to a halt. The lead craft flipped upside down, fan blades gleaming on the underbelly. Soon, both vehicles shrank to a smoking spot in the distance behind them.

Tris crawled back to the passenger seat, cradling her sore wrists. "Thank you."

Kevin stared forward, wearing the hard face of a soldier, and drove until dark.

9

CAMPFIRE JITTERS

He took the crowbar, and the skinned, roasted dust-hopper impaled on it, off the fire. Tris sat on a large rock nearby, staring at the meat as he cut the forty-pound jackrabbit in pieces and handed her one entire rear leg.

Kevin, the Wildlands savage, nibbled on his food and gazed at the stars while the 'civilized' Enclave-born woman attacked her portion with the finesse of a starving mongrel. The irony of the situation made him grin for the first time since he'd laid eyes on her. He watched her out of the corner of his vision, waiting for some trace of duplicity. Her entire world at that moment existed in the flesh of the dead animal in her lap. The sight of the red marks on her skin made him look away.

Some minutes after she could eat no more, he offered her a canteen, which she took without hesitation. She drank so fast she choked, and he had to hold it back and feed it to her. He opened his mouth as if to say something, but wound up only shaking his head. After drinking, she slid from the rock and wandered away from the car into the dark. He leaned back, staring at the stars. The sound of an opening zipper broke the silence. Soon, she returned and sat nearby, leaning against the same boulder.

"Get some sleep."

Tris looked at the ground. "You have to drive, you should too."

He folded his hands across his lap.

"You still think I'm going to steal your car, don't you?"

"The thought'd crossed my mind."

She scooted over and tucked up to his side. "I'll sleep close so you'll wake up if I move."

He let gravity pull his head to the left until he made eye contact, and sighed. "You're good. I almost believe you."

Tris kept quiet for around ten minutes. Neither of them got any closer to sleeping. "You have to sleep so we don't crash."

"Mmm."

"That Infected did a number on you. Let me have a look?"

He squinted. "You're trying to get me out of my armor."

"Fine then, don't." She folded her arms. "If I wanted to kill you, I would've done it when you had an Infected on top of you."

"You still needed someone to untie you then."

After another six minutes of silence, he sat up, grumbled, removed his armored jacket as well as the Beretta in its holster, and set them to his right. She helped him get his black tee shirt off, and guided him to the ground, on his chest. Tris straddled him and kneaded the muscles of his back.

"You've got a lot of scars."

With one hand on his .45, he let his chin rest on his crossed forearms. "I was stupid and young, thought only old men needed armor." He tried to stifle relieved moans as she massaged him.

"There's some bruising"—he cringed as she touched the spots—"but it's not as bad as I thought it would be."

Crickets got loud as she continued to rub his shoulders, back, and sides.

"Okay, my arms are tired. Hope that helped." She slid off him to the side and he rolled over. After another uncomfortable few minutes, she sat up. "If it will let you sleep, you can tie my hands again."

Kevin got up and went to the car, returning with a length of cord. She slumped and closed her eyes, not moving as he took hold of her arms. A soft whine escaped as he touched the red marks. He ran his thumb along the skin of her wrist, back and forth. His cheek brushed the side of her head, lips right by her ear.

"S'pose I don't have to." He tossed the rope toward the car and sat down, pulling his shirt on. "I wanted to see how you'd react."

She stared at him with a weak smile, but a trace of a glare in her eyes. Kevin settled back and tried to get comfortable. He tensed when she lay at his side and put an arm over his chest. Soon, a short contest of who would close their eyes first went in his favor.

KEVIN AWOKE WITH A START, EXPECTING EVERYTHING HE OWNED TO BE missing. Instead, he found a waterfall of white hair across his chest and an exhausted woman at his side. The sun had not yet completed its rise into the sky.

He took a great breath and stretched, the motion caused her to mutter in her sleep and cling. *She's probably awake and trying to make me feel sorry for her even more.* An awkward crane of the neck confirmed the car still sat where he had left it, glinting in the early morning light.

"Come on." He nudged her.

She made a series of soft noises, an attempt to speak that drowned in her dream, and snuggled against his chest. Kevin laid his head back with an impatient sigh, deciding to give it a little while longer before carrying her to the car. The attempt to wait a few minutes cost close to an hour as he nodded off again. Her motion woke him out of the unwanted nap, sending his hand toward his gun. Tris gasped and pounced, holding his arm down, her eyes wide. Nose to nose, her hair fell around him, creating a tunnel of white that blocked out the world aside from her piercing sapphire eyes.

"I'm not stealing your car," she whispered.

Kevin relaxed, letting the pistol slip back in its holster as he struggled to peer out from under the fog of a brief nap that left him more tired than he'd been when he first woke up. Her lips hovered so close, all it would take would be a tiny lift of the neck and he could kiss her. The same way he got in trouble last time.

"Morning," he croaked.

Relief sighed out of her, washing over his cheeks. Her nervous expression became an innocent smile. The more harmless she looked, the less he trusted her. Tris blushed and rolled off him, sitting nearby with her arms around her legs. She handed him a canteen as he sat up.

"You sound like you're thirsty." She stood. "Don't go crazy on me now; I have an important matter to discuss with some bushes."

Kevin tilted the canteen back, taking a few large gulps while watching her walk a short distance away. Not inclined to intrude on her privacy, he dragged himself to his feet and got back into his armor. Tris returned and stood by the passenger door while he collected the camp into the trunk. They got in at the same time. He glanced out of the corner of his eye at her rubbing her wrists, though no trace of red remained—not even a bruise.

Another guilt trip.

"What are you thinking?" She looked at him.

He flicked on the six switches one after the next: main power, rear left, rear right, front left, front right, and the last turned on the weapons, targeting, and camera systems. The console flickered to life. "What I'm gonna name my Roadhouse."

"Oh." She shifted in her seat, leaning against the door and closing her eyes. "I hope those are harder to steal than a car. Maybe then you can sleep."

He stepped on the accelerator, kicking up some dust as he peeled out.

"Yeah. Unwritten law. They call it 'The Code.' No one messes with the 'houses because they're neutral." He glanced at her for a few seconds, wondering if she was still even awake to listen. "Everyone from honest cargo runners to slavers respects the 'houses. Bandits that'll cut my throat right now would trip over each other not to piss me off if I had a 'house."

He looked at her.

Out cold.

Kevin drove in silence for the better part of two hours before she stirred.

"We're on forty now, heading east."

She stretched and looked around, accepting his offer of a nutrient bar. "You seem to enjoy it out here. Why are you going to retire?"

"I'm tired of getting shot. I need ten thousand coins to buy into the franchise."

Tris blinked. "Can't you just get a building and run it like a bar with a gun shop?"

"Nope. Amarillo has a standing bounty they offer to anyone who trashes a competitor. Five grand."

"That's il—" Tris stared into space.

Kevin laughed. "No law out here, hon."

She folded her arms. "Maybe I like that."

"Now *that* I wasn't expecting." Five minutes of silence passed, broken only by the whirr of solid tires on road. "Come on, you can't tease me with a line like that and leave me hanging. So, what's your story?"

"There's only like a few thousand people in the Enclave. The Council of Four decreed that people have to be gene-matched to minimize inbreeding."

Kevin flicked a fingernail at the top of the steering wheel. "Won the asshole lottery?"

Tris stifled a laugh into her hand. Her mirth lasted only a second before she took on her usual morose stare. "I got assigned to this guy from the First-Tier administration. They expected me to just have his kids without ever having laid eyes on him before that."

"First tier administration... that sounds kind of important." He raised an eyebrow. "Rich maybe."

"Yeah... and quite proud of that. Treated me like a baby-producing peasant since my mom was from the labor force and Dad was..."

Kevin drifted off in his mind. For a few seconds, his surroundings changed to the sun-drenched cab of a big rig. To his left, a barely recognizable silhouette of a man sat behind the wheel. "I was four when mine died."

"Nine." Tris sighed. "I think. He worked a lot. I might've been eight."

"Hard to believe they tell you who to marry. Ugh, what about love and shit?"

She pulled hair off her face, flashing a wistful smile. "Well, you can fall in love and then find out you're basically close enough to be siblings. Like I said, a few thousand people. The society is xenophobic. Anyone who can't handle higher education gets sent to the labor force and looked down on. They won't let any outsiders in to widen the choices. Gene purity and all that. My father tried to convince them we were dooming ourselves."

"You grew up there, right? How did something like arranged marriage sneak up on you?"

Tris looked down. "I dunno. I always thought I'd have the choice to ask for another match. There had to be more than *one* possible guy."

He glanced at her until a shallow pothole caught him off guard. "Something tells me that didn't work out like you planned."

"When I refused to marry Dovarin, they arrested me and charged me with treason and sedition, fomenting rebellion, and all sorts of other bullshit. They said they'd drop the charges and let me out of Detention as soon as I 'just behaved myself' and did as I was told. After two weeks, they got tired of waiting. 'Standard vaccinations' turned out to be egg harvesting." She clamped her hands over her belly. "They *took* them."

Kevin spent a moment trying to think of something to say to that. "You okay? I… can't even imagine…"

She gave him a helpless stare. "That almost sounded like concern." She sniffled and wiped tears.

"Did they take all of them?"

I don't know. I don't think so, but they didn't need me anymore and were going to let me rot in that cell as an example."

"You obviously escaped."

"I had help. Nathan, a hacker with the resistance, got into the system. He popped onto the 're-education' monitor and offered to get me out if I helped the resistance. One downside to all-digital security in there, a good operator can break people out from a distance. Since I can't go back to the Enclave ever again, they wanted me to take data about the Virus to Doctor Andrews in Harrisburg. I've got a memory implant with about nine gigabytes of data on the cure. Either I could help them or spend the rest of my life in a tiny white room. Once he said he wanted me to bring the cure to the world, I couldn't say no. He guided me through the city to the underground. I spent a couple months training for the mission, plugged in and got an upload, and left via an old sewer line. Nathan kept me off the security system while I ran."

"How'd you wind up with those three idiots?"

"I was wandering. Once I'd gone too far inland to see the ocean, I had to guess which way led east for a few days. My implant has a waypoint, but all the GPS sats are down, so it'll only give me a directional signal when I get close enough to where I need to go. I found my way onto a caravan, traded a couple of handjobs for a ride. An Enclave hovercraft found us. Spineless bastards were going to just give me over, but I ran. Got into a sewer where the hovercraft couldn't go. I got totally lost after that. I ran until I passed out from exhaustion. Those bastards found me asleep. Woke up tied. They were taking me back for the bounty."

"Idiots. They would've been killed. Not to mention they went the wrong way."

"You're right. No witnesses. They'd assume I told them what I was carrying. People think the Enclave made The Virus, but that's not true, no one really knows which side did it. I think it predates the war. It might've been some other country. We—they have a vaccine that has to be administered before infection. The data in my head is for a cure that can help someone even after they are exposed if it's given soon enough. The cure will let the dregs retake the world, and they don't want that to happen."

"I'm surprised we haven't seen more hovercraft." He glanced at the rearview mirror.

"I think we're too distant. They won't to go too far from home. Nothing scares them like the thought of being stuck out here with the primitives. You should see those hoplite drivers. They rig up in suits thick enough to go to the Moon. Like the air out here would kill them in two breaths."

The cute little laugh that came out of her made him smile, as much as he tried not to. A telltale shimmer in the distance announced a patch of solar panels atop a roadhouse. Kevin slowed, steering to the right and pulling down a gravel and dirt path to a small parking lot.

"Gotta stop for a charge, might as well grab some food while we're here and hope our luck holds."

He hopped out, waited for Tris to close her door, and typed the code on four rubber buttons under the door handle to lock it. "Plug in?"

Tris looked back and forth from him to the car for a second before her expression went from confused to knowing. She took the charging cable from its hatch and unwound it until it reached a socket on a post by the parking space. "Number four."

He jogged to a small porch and brushed through the door. An imposing older woman hovered behind the counter, the only person in the room. Almost as wide as she was tall, she embodied a nightmare of Germanic folklore. She, too, had white locks, though it seemed like a substance peeled from the walls of a haunted house more than hair. Her left eye, greyed over, didn't move at all when she pointed the other one at him. The dour frown seemed the perfect complement to her green camouflage dress.

"Evenin'."

Kevin approached the counter and offered a polite nod. "Evenin'. Charge on four, room, and some food please."

"Thirteen." The woman eyed him as if doubting he had any money. "Ain't got rooms. Bunks. Three coins each per night."

"Thirteen?" *Dammit.*

A flap of skin wobbled along the underside of the woman's arm as she pointed at the door. "Three ta charge. Two apiece fer food, three apiece fer a bunk."

"Fine. One bunk." Kevin set out ten coins.

Tris kept quiet.

After a meal of some atrocity covered in grey slime the woman called 'scrapple,' Kevin followed her directions to a common room full of military style bunk beds. Tris curled up on the floor near one.

He gazed at the dusty roof for a few seconds before stooping to pick her up and set her on the mattress. "I'm used to sleepin' on the ground."

She blinked, seeming genuine in her surprise. A second later, she sat up and removed her shoes. "It's okay if you want to share it."

Kevin slipped his armored jacket off and hung it on the frame, pondering. *Last thing I need to do is get all tangled up with a girl.*

"Come on." She lay back and scooted to the side. "The blanket is thin."

He muttered under his breath as he pulled off his boots, then crawled in next to her, keeping the .45 in his hand under the pillow. Tris let him settle in and draped herself half on top of him, cheek at his shoulder. The warmth and motion of her gentle breathing made it difficult to focus on the door, though the odds of anyone else showing up at a roadhouse this far east were pretty slim. Whatever 'scrapple' was, it didn't agree at all with his angry gut. At a particularly loud warble, Tris stirred and snuggled tighter.

This whole trip is one giant mistake. Kevin closed his eyes.

10

HARRISBURG

Road slid under the matte-black hood for hours. The German roadblock had gouged him a coin each for jerked venison packets. Harrisburg wasn't too far away, down roads that as far as he knew, no sane person had driven in at least ten years. Not since the Infected had overrun the major population centers. Being within forty miles of a big city had him on edge.

Tris put a hand on his arm, making him jump.

"Shit," he muttered.

She squeezed. "What are you thinking about?"

"Harrisburg." He wrung his hands around the wheel.

"I'm not thrilled about the idea of more Infected either."

Kevin smirked. "What are you worried about. You're vaccinated… or do you doubt it works?"

"Virus or not, they can still bash my head in… and being chewed on isn't fun."

He shivered.

"Your dad?" Tris glanced at him. "Sorry."

"No." He took an off-ramp from the interstate, following a huge circle around to a north-south rural highway. "Dad died before Infected happened. Nothing like saving the world. Just a pack of lousy fuckin' bandits. Would'a killed me too if I wasn't so little."

"I'm sorry." She fidgeted with her jumpsuit legging. "In the Enclave, I never knew what it was like out here. The stories they feed us... I used to have nightmares as a little girl about bandits coming over the walls and taking me away into the wastes. Guess you think it's this cushy carefree life, but it's like being in prison... even free. They control everything."

Untainted food, comfortable beds, no one shooting at you. What's a little fascism? "Yeah. I guess. Grass is greener and all that horseshit."

"Infected killed someone you love?" She let her hand fall from his arm.

"No." He accelerated off the circle, slamming the shifter up two gears. "I don't wanna go out like that. Bullet? Sure. Crash? Fine. A slow, painful change into something not alive and not dead, mindless... Every time I get near one I have these waking nightmares for days not knowing if it's gonna be me... fuck that."

"You must want this roadhouse pretty bad if you're willing to risk it."

Kevin stared at her for a long four seconds. "Yeah." He stared straight ahead. "... and you looked kinda desperate."

———————————

A FEW SILENT HOURS LATER, THE CHALLENGER CAME TO A HALT ON THE crest of a hill overlooking the city of Harrisburg. Tris rubbed her hands back and forth over her thighs while staring at the gloom. Skyscrapers, jutting spires of blackened ruin, rose out of a sea of roiling grey smog. As if clouds had fallen from the sky, vaporous trails slithered among the pylons of three bridges spanning a massive river. Gaps opened every so often, granting a clear view of streets littered with trash, the smashed and burned corpses of cars, and numerous skeletons. A layer of abandonment and death blanketed the city, thicker even than the fog.

Aside from a haze of green plant life growing from the sides of tall buildings, and a handful of barriers made of dead cars, the place looked like a snapshot into the past. By some miracle, the major city had avoided a proximal nuclear strike, and more or less survived—until the Virus came.

"This is Harrisburg?" Kevin cocked an eyebrow. "I guess your people are underground." He put it in reverse and backed through a U-turn. "I'm gonna stash the car in that barn we passed."

"Why not drive into town?"

"Call it a hunch." He accelerated along a crumbling highway, slaloming smashed concrete dividers. "I don't want to wind up having a pile of Infected between us and the car."

Tris smiled.

"What?" He squinted at her.

Her blue eyes glimmered. "You said *us*."

Kevin chuckled. "You still owe me a thousand coins, sweetie."

She folded her arms. An angry look lasted a few seconds, and dissipated. "Yep. So you better keep me alive. You sure it's wise to leave the car all the way out here?"

"The last thing I want is to wind up with a thousand infected surrounding it, and not be able to get back to it."

"So it's better to risk attack on foot for a two-mile walk?"

He wrung his hands around the wheel. A trickle of sweat ran down the side of his head. Losing the Marauder to a girl was bad enough, having to walk away from the Challenger because it had a pack of Infected around it... no way. "Easier to hide on foot."

She seemed to sense the fear in him and looked to the road. "Okay."

About a mile away, he pulled up to a weather-beaten barn at the end of a dirt road. From the looks of it, a private farm had once occupied the land. Tris hopped out and jogged around front to haul the door open. She waited outside while he pulled the car in. He swiped a finger over the switches to power down and headed around behind the car. Kevin gathered a couple spare magazines for his .45 and stuffed them in his jacket pocket. A flashlight came next, which he hung on the back of his belt before grabbing a pair of canteens, a padlock, and slamming the trunk. After locking down the Challenger, he slipped out the door and secured the padlock on the hasp. Tris took the canteen he offered. Kevin started toward the city, but took only three steps. He turned to face her. She gave him a confused look tinged with worry. He reached into his jacket and removed the Beretta—offering it to her grip-first.

She grasped it, but he didn't let go right away, exchanging a meaningful stare.

Moment of truth. If she's gonna do it, now's the moment. I guess I trust her... or maybe I'm more afraid of zombies.

Tris stared at him, seeming more innocent and vulnerable than ever before. He released the weapon and resumed heading toward the city. Tris walked alongside him, patting herself down in search of somewhere to put the pistol. She tried a few pockets, but didn't seem to like the way it wobbled about with her stride. The jumpsuit had no belt in which to tuck a handgun, so she wound up holding it. It took around a half hour for them to reach the outskirts of the city. They moved among old, burned cars and broken glass, peering into the vacant maws of dozens of abandoned buildings. Old newspaper machines littered the road as if a great housecat had swatted them around until it got bored. A few of the vehicles looked up-modded, electric motors and all, but the vast majority dated from before the war.

"Something doesn't feel right," she whispered.

"No shit. You're just realizing that now?" Kevin led her out of the open, into a narrow alley. "Where exactly are we going? Your *thingee* in range yet?"

"Yeah, I'm close enough now. I have no idea what the safe house looks like, but the implant is letting me see a yellow line." She pointed. "That way. It's feeding a signal to my optic nerve."

"So your eyes aren't electronic?"

She shook her head. "No. I don't have any major parts. A couple small implants and some wiring."

Kevin studied her face. "They look too blue to be natural. Like gems."

Tris blushed.

"Okay, lead on." He gestured forward. "Be careful."

She leaned around the corner, pistol first, and crept out along the sidewalk. Two blocks over, she crossed the street and entered another alley. Kevin followed, head on a swivel, certain Infected would come out of everywhere.

An echoing metallic clatter from the right made them both twitch. At the end of the alley, a fallen basketball hoop shifted. Four people in tattered clothing, three men in police uniforms and a young woman in a torn sundress, climbed out of a rubble pile, sniffing the air. All had manic bloodshot eyes and dark patches of necrosis scattered about their bodies. The woman's toes had reduced to black stubs. Kevin's throat closed up from fear. As fast as an eye blink, Tris shot the woman in the forehead and the nearest 'cop' in the heart one after the next. The female Infected stood in place for a few seconds, gazing into the sky as if confused. She collapsed over backward, leaving the shot cop staring at his chest as if he couldn't figure out what happened. A black tendril symbiote forced its way out of his lips, fleeing the now-useless body.

Tris shot it.

The wormlike creature exploded in a shower of black ichor.

Kevin cringed as the remaining pair zeroed in on the gunfire and charged. Tris fired again, striking a dark-skinned cop in the left cheek. A spritz of brain flew out of his head, spattering on the last one's face.

Kevin got his .45 out and pumped two rounds into the last shambler's chest.

The two former cops slumped to the street at the same time, moaning. Alleys and cross streets filled with the echoes of scraping and scratching.

***

"GREAT, NOW EVERYTHING IN TOWN'S HEARD US," SAID KEVIN

"Oops." Tris bit her lip. "Sorry."

He grabbed her by the left wrist and ran ahead, dragging her across the small courtyard and down another street.

He's panicking.

Moaning and breaking glass came from behind as dozens of Infected swarmed out of buildings and windows. She glanced back over her shoulder at the echoing *boom* of a body striking an empty dumpster. Some were so determined to pursue the untainted that they jumped out of windows at fatal heights. The wet splats of their deaths upon the pavement made her gag.

"Sorry," she said, choking back vomit while trying to keep her feet underneath her.

Tris raised the Beretta to the rear, but he hauled her around a corner, too fast for her to get a clear shot.

"Don't bother. Shooting will only tell them where we are. You'll run out of ammo before you kill half of that swarm."

Dammit. Her heart raced. The dancing yellow line streaking off into the distance in her vision snaked around a parking garage four blocks ahead. "There. That weird looking building full of cars. Turn left once we pass it."

He followed her direction, but skidded to a stop by a half-open manhole. "Down here."

"No, the line goes that way." Tris pointed at the glowing streamer fed to her optic nerve on wires thinner than a human hair. "It's dark down there. We have no idea what—"

"Yeah, and take a good goddamned look that way." He shoved the manhole cover aside.

Tris stared down the length of the gleaming ribbon. The entire area around where it went moved. Thousands of Infected swelled out from every alley, oozing from windows like a mudslide of flesh. Her stomach did a backflip.

"Oh… shit."

"Yeah. Oh shit is right. Damn erudite of you."

Tris yelped when he grabbed her under the armpits and half threw her into the hole in the street.

KEVIN DIDN'T BOTHER LOOKING AROUND. THE SHUFFLING DRAG OF MORE infected than he wanted to see closed in from everywhere. He waited for her snowy head to drop in a few feet and jumped down onto the ladder. Fear boosted his strength such that the manhole cover felt like aluminum as he pulled it back into place.

Darkness.

He climbed down, not needing to see to figure out how to operate a ladder. The city had been empty so long the sewer didn't stink like shit, only must and mold. Tris's hand pressed into his back when he reached the bottom.

"It's dark."

"Yeah." He pulled the flashlight off his belt and turned it on.

Kevin held a finger to his lips. She nodded. They stood in silence, save for the dripping of distant water. The wails and groans grew louder to a point. His heart skipped a beat whenever the manhole cover clanked from a heavy footstep. The small hand on his back became two arms threaded around his waist. Her breath blew warm over the back of his neck. After a moment, the noise overhead faded away.

Both of them exhaled. She let her weight hang on him. He found himself not minding the contact, holding her in silence until their second wind arrived.

"Still got the line?"

She pointed. "Yes. It's going that way, down the tunnel."

For the next hour or so, she led the way through the sewers, guided by some phantom line. Kevin didn't have a lot of trust or faith in technology, but she chose turns and jumped sewage channels without any hesitation, as if she'd been here before. Several times, she squeezed his hand numb as she stepped in shin-deep water, reducing the urge to scream at the cold to a muted whimper.

"Almost there," she whispered. "It's reading under fifty meters around that corner up ahead to the right."

He nodded and crept up to a rounded offshoot. After a brief hesitation at the corner, he whirled around, gun aimed. A pair of corpses draped over wooden crates on either side of the shaft about ten yards ahead. Their clothing, what remained of it, had a quasi-military aesthetic. Spent brass scattered around in the muck, 7.62 from the look of it. Normally, the urge to search them for valuables would be overwhelming. After the swarm, though, he wanted little to do with going near a dead body. These two were obviously rotting, but the Infected were also supposed to last only a few months... not years. He trained his .45 at the one on the left. Tris walked past them without care, as if she hadn't even noticed them. Kevin hesitated, but neither one so much as twitched as she got close. He closed his eyes for a second and took a few deep breaths. Eyes open, he sprinted ahead.

The rapid clomp of his boots made her spin around with the Beretta raised.

"Whoa..." He held a hand up.

Tris lowered her arm and sighed. "What's got you... Oh, the dead..." Her lip quivered. "They look like resistance."

"You knew them?" He shifted to face her, keeping the corpses in sight.

"Not personally." She backed up. "Their uniforms look like the info I received before I escaped. They won't get up. There's no such thing as undead... Infected are alive."

"And they're also supposed to drop dead in three months, right?" He guided her back another step before he stopped pointing a gun at the dead man.

"I..." She ran to a door fifteen yards past the corpses, a metal barrier that hung an inch away from closed. "They're still alive. The heart shot kills. Maybe the increased lifespan has something to do with that symbiote?"

Kevin kept half his attention on the dead guys as he backed up to where she'd stopped.

"In there," she whispered. "The line is going through this door."

11

FINAL STAND

He swapped magazines in the .45, loading a full one, and slipped past her. At the gap, he listened for a minute. Silence. He gritted his teeth and eased the old, rusted door to the side, attempting to be as quiet as possible. Tris took a step back, clutching the Beretta in both hands, but keeping it pointed down and away.

Inside, the space appeared to have once been some manner of safe house or command center. Cots lined one wall near lockers. The air hung damp with the stagnant scent of moss and earth. Desks and tables were set up with maps covered in mold, and a handful of portable computers clustered on the other side of the room, collecting cobwebs. Additional tunnels went off to areas that looked like more sleeping space and another metal door spray-painted with the word 'armory.'

"Where's the line going?"

Tris crept forward, looking around. She stopped by one of the tables, picking up a notebook full of drawings of things that seemed medical in nature. "I-it's gone. It… led me here." She shot him a look filled with dread. "This…" She closed the notebook, pointing out 'Dr. Martin Andrews' written in ballpoint ink on the cover. The bloody handprint over the name spoke volumes.

Kevin's eyes narrowed. "All those Infected outside. Something tells me the resistance didn't have much resistance."

She slouched, leaning on the desk to keep from falling over. "No… It can't be true. We were so close to a cure."

Close only matters with hand grenades. Kevin glanced at her shoulder, thinking about offering a comforting hand. *Crap. Guess I'm not getting paid.*

Tris grabbed for the piles of maps and notebooks. "There's gotta be some kinda notes here. There's no bodies. They can't all be dead."

"Maybe they got up and walked away." He folded his arms, draping the .45 over his left elbow.

"That's not funny." She moved on to search the drawers, finding nothing of interest before heading to the table full of laptops. Of eight, only one responded to the power button. It came out of sleep mode on a CAD screen that looked like a schematic pointing out the different components of a human cell. "There's got to be something here… a backup plan, an escape plan… something."

Kevin paced around while she fiddled with the computer. A bank of lockers on the left had two folded tee shirts and a pair of briefs, which he pocketed. *Guess it's not a total loss.*

"Wow," said Tris. "This thing has a satellite feed."

"Satellite?" Kevin hurried over. "I thought the nukes made them all fry?"

Tris nodded, making her hair dance. "They did… this must've been launched afterward or maybe got lucky, I dunno. I didn't think we could still put stuff in orbit. Maybe I can get a hold of Nathan. He'll know what to do."

He frowned at the little computer. "The only thing I distrust more than pretty women is technology."

She clicked on something, which opened a black window, in which she typed a series of numbers and letters. "Maybe… technology certainly helped kill the planet."

A man's face, blonde, early thirties, and paper-white like Tris, filled the screen. "Oh, I see you *did* make it." Static crackled the voice in time with pixilation and dropouts in the image.

"Nathan!" She smiled. "Good to see you. I'm here. But, everyone's gone. Did you hear anything from Dennis or Bill?"

The man on the screen sighed. "No, I'm afraid. All gone, you say? Pity. I'm so sorry to waste your time, my dear. It seems your services wound up not being required. Sometimes the caveman approach *does* work. The little package you've delivered for me won't be necessary after all." He smiled. "Not since they're already all dead."

"What are you talking about?" She leaned away from the terminal, shaking.

"That nonsense about a cure"—Nathan turned to the side to mock stifle a haughty laugh—"it was something to help us destroy the resistance out there for good. The Virus is doing its job nicely, but those Neanderthals had built up to a worrisome level. We felt it best to take an extra step."

"Y-you're not a hacker, are you?" Tris covered her mouth with both hands. "You're... Tier Two?"

"One actually." He examined his fingernails. "Don't feel so glum. You think a mere hacker can let people out of Detention so easily? Poor girl, so naïve. At least you had your freedom for a little while, such as it was out there in that ghastly place."

"L-little while?" She looked up at the moss-covered ceiling. "Are they coming?"

"Oh, heavens, Tris. You overestimate your importance. It's a shame to waste such a marvel of technology, don't you think? Just because the resistance is already dead doesn't mean I can't send you off with a bang. You know, loose end and all. Besides, you've got the cure in that pretty little head of yours, and we'd rather not let it get away from us. Ciao." He winked, and the terminal went out.

Tris gulped and jumped back with a shriek. She clawed at her jumpsuit, jerking the zipper down to expose her chest and stomach. A dull red light pulsed below the surface of her skin, left of her navel by two inches.

"No! No!" She screamed, bawling as she pressed and squeezed at the area.

A golf-ball sized object shifted below the skin.

She gawked at Kevin, mouthing, "I'm sorry" as the strength faded from her legs.

"Tris..." Kevin pulled a large combat knife from his belt and held it up. "Do you trust me?"

12

GUT FEELING

Cynicism, for some people, is elevated to an art form.
Suspicion had kept Kevin alive, kept him profitable, and kept his dream a fingertip away from reality. But in a second that felt like minutes, staring into the panic radiating from Tris's deep blue eyes, both left him high and dry.

The abandoned room around them, dented desks, loose wires, moldy concrete walls, froze in time. A weak flash of red light from beneath the milky white skin of her stomach failed to break his eye contact. Of all the women left in this beat up, shit-on world, it figures he'd wind up with one who was about to die—and take him along for the ride.

The tip of his combat knife came into focus as she blurred. His hair tickled the back of his neck.

"Yes," she yelled. "Yes, I trust you."

Kevin snapped back to real time. He grabbed her by her jumpsuit and flung her hundred-pound body over the nearest desk. Dead radio equipment and waterlogged laptops clattered to the ground. Tris seemed to know what was coming; she clamped her hands on the sides of the table and closed her eyes. Kevin pinched the skin by the red glow and dragged the knife over it as if slicing an avocado.

Tris screamed.

Blood welled around the blade as he pulled up on the skin, as careful as his haste allowed him to be. If he didn't cut too deep, she might live. If he nicked something inside, this might all be a waste of time. She squirmed and thrashed, keeping her mouth closed to mute herself.

He sliced and squeezed for two seconds, urging a milky transparent sphere about an inch in diameter from the wound. Amid electronics and a cube of light grey material, six red LEDs flashed with increasing speed. Kevin dropped the knife and plunged his fingers into the oozing cut, grasping the detonator and wrenched it loose, grateful after the fact no wiring connected it to anything else inside her. Tris screamed and passed out. He baseball-pitched the explosive into a passage leading away from the cistern-turned-command center and grabbed Tris, dragging her to the floor behind the desk.

The tiny plastic sphere clicked twice on distant concrete before an explosion slammed the air from his lungs and peppered the area around him with debris. Silence, save for a high-pitched tone dominated his consciousness. Each breath sucked in dust; he choked on the taste of decades-old sewer. A cloud of pale grey silt rolled over them, obscuring everything more than an arm's length away. He leapt on top of her and placed a hand over the laceration. Tris lay limp and unresponsive. A minute or so passed before the tinnitus tone faded with a sucking *whoosh*, and the raspy wheeze of his breathing flooded his ears.

Off to his right, a heavy metallic *thud* shook the floor when a metal door gave out. Random *clicks* and *clangs* announced falling rocks and fragments of pipe hitting the ground. Kevin sat back on his boot heels, straddling her, and peered over the desk. Beyond the shifting cloud of smoke and dust, the collapsed ceiling let in traces of sunlight. More bits of road and dirt fell in; the whole place looked ready to collapse. Along both walls, old sewage lines had twisted into modern art. Fortunately, it had been at least forty years since anything flowed in them.

Kevin blinked at a spherical absence of passage.

Damn that's a big ass hole vaporized. He looked down at her. *Holy shit. I should've slugged her in the head and gotten the fuck out of here.* His racing heart slowed as he studied the delicate lines of her face. He thought of her kicking the 'New' ganger over the railing at Wayne's. *She looks so innocent when she's out cold.* Blood seeped between his fingers from the three-inch slice a touch south of her navel, near the left hip.

"Crap." With one hand still on the wound, he leaned to the side until he got two fingers on the knife. "So much for getting paid."

The room, him, her, the laptops, everything looked as if a madman had run amok with a can of white spray paint. *She didn't change color.* Kevin chuckled. He squinted, coughed, and looked around for something to use as a bandage. The bomb had coated everything with dust, no doubt full of wonderful little microbes. Thinking about inhaling fifty-year-old shit particles made him gag. He pulled open her jumpsuit a few inches more, eyeing her plain, white panties. He smirked at his jeans and flannel shirt, covered in dust not to mention underneath an armored, long sleeved, red leather jacket.

Kevin smiled. "Looks like it's the only clean cloth within ten miles." He grasped the elastic waistband in preparation to cut it to make a bandage, but stopped when the wound didn't gush with blood as his hand came away. "What the hell?"

Traces of crimson foam bubbled from an angry red scab, as if he'd dribbled hydrogen peroxide on it. The edges stuck together. It no longer bled at an alarming rate, though the cut appeared liable to pop open if disturbed. He let go of the waistband, which snapped back against her stomach, wiped the blood from the knife on her jumpsuit leg, and slid it into its sheath on his belt.

Tris let off a soft moan.

He caught himself admiring her profile and fixating on her lips. Her voice replayed in his memory, offering to give him a blowjob in exchange for untying her. For a few seconds, he regretted passing on the offer. Even days later, it still seemed too much like 'taking advantage' of her.

"What the hell is wrong with me?" He wiped dust from his face.

Thud.

His head snapped up. The demolished hallway came alive with shambling figures.

Infected.

"Damn."

The weight of handguns pressed into his ribs under each arm and tugged at the right side of his belt. *Too many... I'll only attract more.* He quick-crawled to the Beretta Tris dropped and grabbed it. After tossing it on her bare stomach, he zipped her jumpsuit closed and scooped her up.

One of the Infected groaned and surged forward when her limp leg hit the desk with a hollow, metallic *thump.*

Shit! He contemplated leaving her for two seconds. Having to carry her might doom them both. *Aww hell.*

Kevin cradled her with one arm around her back and the other behind her knees. Her feet bobbed as he ran for the door they'd come in from. Throaty wheezes and moans intensified. Flakes of concrete skittered away from shuffling feet; desks and chairs bumped and banged as the swarm of barely-alive people zeroed in on them. He swiveled to slide her headfirst past the opening and kicked the door with a weak attempt to close it, not wanting to put her down to see if the latch even worked.

Tris opened her eyes while he sprinted around the improvised crates and boxes fortification her former allies made. *Bastards could've at least left a machine gun or something I could sell... Inconsiderate fucks.*

"Ngh. Ow." Tris grabbed her gut. Her eyes widened "What the?"

"You dropped the Beretta."

She leaned her head back, white hair trailing like a gossamer spirit. "Damn! There's—"

At an offshoot, he skidded over a metal grate bridging a deeper channel. "I noticed. Don't suppose you have that little map thing pointing the way out?"

"No... Only a waypoint." She cringed. "Shit this hurts."

"Bomb would've hurt more."

"I doubt that." She cringed. "Wouldn't have felt shit."

An infected's moan roared down the tunnel a second before a splintering crunch.

Tris glanced to the rear, then up at him. "They smashed the barricade."

"I think I'd have preferred not knowing." He jumped another deep channel, walls stained green from whatever awfulness it once carried. "Can you run?"

She pressed a hand over where he'd opened her up. "Not fast enough. It burns so bad."

Sweat flew from the sides of his head. He pumped his legs, arguing with himself about wearing twelve pounds of armor. It took him years, and nine bullets, before the burden seemed worth it. Much like the Challenger over his old Marauder, sometimes speed *did* prove better than toughness. Constant moans, scrapes, and wails behind him kept him moving. The wisp of a woman in his arms might've weighed a mere hundred pounds, but she seemed to get heavier with every step.

She glanced back for another second, unzipped her jumpsuit, and grasped the Beretta. Kevin cringed when she reached an arm around and fired three shots. His right ear felt like it flooded with water while his left rang from the discharge in a tight concrete tunnel. A hint of bodies smacking to the ground pierced his temporary deafness.

"Save your ammo," yelled Kevin. "They're strong, but I'm faster."

Tris looked forward and pointed at a torso-sized grey box mounted to the wall near an offshoot. Two arm-thick pipes connected to one side wrapped around the corner. "Go right by the junction box."

He risked a peek to the rear while rounding the corner. His heart thumped at the sight of an avalanche of once-people spilling over three dead bodies. She'd shot them within a step or two of the sewage trench. The first ones tripped over the dead and fell in, the next wave followed suit. More Infected kept piling on until the unfortunates struggling to climb up became a fleshy bridge, trapped under the weight of their mindless brethren.

"Shit!" he yelled.

The branch-off she'd indicated *did* look somewhat familiar. Maybe they had come this way, but everything down here looked the same. More boxes, cans, and cots—signs of early survivors seeking refuge underground from fallout. Up ahead, a square of sunlight illuminated the left wall. Inspired by the promise of escape, he pushed himself up to another hard sprint. Tris put a hand on her wound and gasped.

"It itches *so* bad." She whined. "It's gotta be loaded with bacteria."

"Next time you're about to detonate, I'll make sure to sterilize the room first."

She closed her eyes and hissed. "And wash your hands."

Kevin stopped at the base of a plain metal ladder. A narrow storm drain slit overhead glowed with daylight two feet away from a manhole cover. Tris reached for the ladder.

"You sure you can climb?"

"Yeah." She grunted and pulled herself upright. "The tunnel's full of motivation."

He pulled his .45 and aimed, hesitating at not wanting to waste ammo. It didn't matter much if he killed one, ten, or zero. Infected were supposed to die in a couple months anyway. *Why are there so damn many of them?*

A skinny middle-aged man in a doctor's white coat broke forward from the pack, windmilling his arms and moaning. Kevin raised the gun and squeezed the trigger. The Infected's face imploded, gore sucked out the back of his head, following the bullet. The body took two more steps, collapsed forward, and pulled itself another foot closer before going still.

Kevin gawked. *They're alive, right?* He jumped at a *clang* of metal overhead. Tris's mousy grunt echoed in the narrow shaft a second before the heavy scraping of the manhole cover she dislodged one-handed. A column of sunlight fell on him, illuminating flakes of dust. He stuffed the

.45 under his belt and hauled himself up. Tris slithered over the rim and rolled onto the street. Kevin scrambled out behind her and dragged the cover back in place before tamping it down with his boot.

Out of breath, he slumped forward, hands on his knees. "Shit. Glad they can't figure out ladders."

"We shouldn't stay out in the open." Tris cradled her gut in both hands.

Kevin swayed his head from side to side, trying to dislodge a ten-inch ribbon of snot from his left nostril without touching it. "Yeah, we shouldn't."

Minutes passed without words, as they both gulped down air.

Tris rolled her head to the side to look at him. "You're not moving."

"Neither are you."

"You cut a hole in my gut. I'm not feeling much like standing right now." She gazed up. "Gonna be dark soon. Maybe I'll lie here and bleed."

Kevin frowned at the manhole cover, and the continuous, confused moaning beneath it. "Sorry. If I knew it would hurt so much, I'd have let the bomb go off."

"Heh." Her body convulsed. Stands of her hair shifted in the breeze like cobweb on the macadam. "Ow."

"Don't try to laugh." He forced himself to stand straight and leaned backward to stretch.

Tris pushed up to sit and grimaced with a hissing inhale. "I'm sorry. I had no idea there was a bomb inside me. Damn. Fuck this itching. Argh!"

"I believe you." He offered a hand. "Can't fake a face like that."

She reached up; they grasped forearms. "A face like what?"

"Like you're about to shit yourself." He pulled her upright. "After what that little thing did to the tunnel, I can't say I blame you much."

"Thanks." She looked around and slumped into him.

"Come on." He picked her up again and headed down the street, trying to figure out where in Harrisburg they'd wound up. "Car's in the southwest, but we're losing light. No way am I gonna risk running that far in the dark." A heavy rolling security door, a quarter of the way open, caught his eye. "There."

She held on as he carried her up to an old service station garage. Safe bet if anything lurked in the underground tanks, it was far removed from usable fuel after fifty years. He set her back on her feet, and crouched to peer under the door. At the center of a garage big enough to house one car with a small 'office' in the back corner, a V8 dangled on a chain from a bright orange engine lift. Bare grey cinderblock walls peeked from between ancient centerfold images. Tits of every imaginable size, color, and shape adorned the two longer walls from magazine cutouts. Three windows on the right, covered by heavy steel gridding, sat above a row of hubcaps and a single door in the back left corner connected to the service station.

"This'll do." He braced a hand on the lower edge as he slipped under and crawled inside.

Tris followed, cradling her gut and grunting.

He locked eyes with a bikini-clad blonde gracing a Budweiser calendar showing August 2021.

Tris sidled up behind him. "No one's been here since the war happened… All forty-five or so minutes of it."

"You ever wonder what it was like before?" He looked around at the pre-electric car parts. If it wasn't surrounded by Infected, this would be a gold mine. "I haven't seen a gas engine since I was knee high."

Tris stumbled past him and stifled a scream as she lowered herself into a rolling chair at a desk in front of a shelf overflowing with rotting cardboard boxes containing air filters, spark plugs, and belts. "You're older than me."

"Yeah, but you had school, right?" To the right of the rolling garage door, a hanging loop of chain wound up and over a gear sprocket at the end of a housing. Kevin pulled on it until the door closed, muscles tensing from the amount of noise it made. He eyed the interior door, wanting to push the old engine block in front of it, but the lift wouldn't fit close due to the desk and shelves. "I don't like leaving a back way in."

"We didn't go too deep in pre-war history. Only bits and pieces. Before the war, most people went to offices and typed on computers for eight hours a day."

Kevin squinted. "What the hell for?"

Tris shrugged. "Jobs. I dunno. There was a lot of street violence in the months leading up to it. Riots, protests, and stuff."

"Trying to stop the war?" He dragged a metal shelf in front of the inside door, spilling a few dozen oil filters.

"No. They were angry about jobs going overseas. The government had to subsidize everyone too lazy to work, so it needed money. Probably why they started the war."

"Wait." Kevin pinched the bridge of his nose. "Didn't you say that they sent the work overseas? How are people lazy if there are no jobs to get?"

Tris shrugged. "It's what the teacher said."

"Enclave. Right." He shook his head. "They used to be some kinda military corporation, right?"

"I guess. They never said much about it, only how they're the only hope for humanity to continue." She put her feet up on the desk and closed her eyes. "Damn this stings. I've had cuts before, but not like this."

"Fifty years of germs in that dust." He ripped open an air filter and held it up. "No water in here, but you should try to clean it.

"That'll rip open the scab and hurt more."

She hadn't zipped her jumpsuit up since taking the gun out. Kevin removed his jacket and walked over. He started to put it over her like a blanket, but froze, watching her stomach rise and fall with her breathing. The cut had receded to a mark resembling an angry housecat's scratch. He lowered his arms and took a knee, mesmerized as the skin moved. Inflammation faded, leaving a thin red line as if drawn by a ballpoint pen. Moments later, the scratch disappeared. He stared at a spot of pristine skin, save for smears of dirt and blood.

Tris muttered when he traced his fingers over the spot.

"What the fuck..." Kevin whispered.

"Hmm?"

He pressed his fingers down, light pressure. "Does that hurt?"

"No, why." A moment later, his poking and prodding made her giggle. She sat up and grabbed his hand. "Stop! That tickles."

"Tris... what the hell." He pointed. "I don't think it's been an hour since I cut you open."

She took an air filter out of its box and used it to wipe at the almost-dried blood. "Nanites."

"English please."

Tris stuck her tongue out. "That *was* English. Tiny robots inside me. I told you I have some cybernetics, right?"

"You've got little robots inside you?" He blinked and leaned back.

"Microscopic. They help repair damaged tissue." She zipped up her jumpsuit and settled back in for a nap.

"How long do their batteries last?"

"No idea. Couple weeks maybe."

He draped his jacket over her and sat on the floor. "So it'll eventually stop working?"

"Maybe. As far as I know, the system keeps making more as the old ones are recycled. I don't really know how it works."

"Not sure I'd be so calm about havin' little machines running around inside me." He considered covering her with his armor, but changed his mind at the scuff of shoes outside. When signs of activity faded, he leaned close to her and whispered, "Stay quiet, they're outside."

Tris held up one thumb.

Kevin sat cross-legged, .45 out and ready. Red-orange squares on the wall faded as the sun disappeared into the distant horizon. He eyed the black windows with suspicion. All sorts of rumors about the Infected played through his head. They could hear a heartbeat from two hundred yards, they could smell people the way dogs do, or they could see body heat. He grinned to himself. The third one he had proven false. He'd stayed still, not making a sound, and one had tottered by less than forty feet away. *Either they can't smell us, or I stink as bad as they do.*

He watched Tris sleep for some time, until the weight of fatigue tugged on his eyelids. The next thing he knew, he'd slumped face-first into her. Kevin sat up straight and wiped his eyes. All three windows remained dark. He stood and stretched stiffness out of his body from his earlier sprint, and availed himself of an oil drain in the ground. Pissing made him feel like a new man.

A second after he'd zipped up, a hand at his side almost stained the back of his pants.

Tris's face took on a normal skin tone with a pronounced blush. He walked off to give her some privacy, and stretched out on the floor next to the chair, keeping his back to the front part of the garage. In the deafening silence, the creak of her zipper opening seemed loud enough to draw every Infected from here to New Mexico. He tried to get comfortable on the concrete garage floor, and kept his eyes closed.

A few minutes later, the chair next to him squeaked, followed by the hollow thump of shoes hitting desk.

"You need to get rid of that jumpsuit," muttered Kevin.

Tris sighed. "What, because this is the Wildlands, a girl's gotta run around naked?"

"Not where I was going, but"—Kevin grinned—"sounds like an awesome idea."

The chair springs screeched, and she kicked him in the side. "Ass."

"I got a metal bikini in the trunk."

"Ass," she muttered, and kicked him again.

"I'm kidding." Kevin laced his fingers behind his head and opened his eyes. "At least about the bikini."

A hint of color returned to her face. "I am not—"

"Shh. Don't get loud. I mean the jumpsuit, not clothes in general. That outfit will tell everyone you're Enclave."

"Former." She scowled. "They want to kill me, remember?"

"How can I forget? So who was that shithead on the screen?"

Tris kicked the desk. "Nathan. Argh! I can't believe I trusted him."

"Sounds like he's the one who sprang you from jail?"

"Detention. Yeah." She glanced down, lip quivering.

"There's gotta be something more to it than you not wanting to marry who they told you to. Enclave are a bunch of fascist shitheads, but that seems like a bit much even for them."

She shrugged. "If there is, I have no idea what I did. Probably all a setup to send me out here."

Thump.

Both of them jumped. Kevin shot upright, glaring at the rolling door. Tris cringed, her expression apologizing for making noise. He held his hand up and made a running motion with his fingers. Tris nodded and patted her gut before giving another thumbs-up.

Damn. I need me somma them nanite things.

Seconds of silence passed before another heavy *slam* rattled the entire rolling door. Kevin held a hand up to her as if to say 'relax.' The unmistakable moan of an Infected emanated from outside, so close he pictured it pressing its face against the metal.

"Will that hold them?" Tris whispered as she leaned forward in the chair and put her feet down.

Kevin nodded. "We should—"

Wham!

A human arm punched through the slats, flailing for something to grab inside. Bloodshot eyes locked on Kevin, pupils narrowing to points. Shattering glass echoed from the right, on the other side of cinderblocks. He pictured Infected pressing past the gas station's convenience store window like a lava flow of warm corpses.

"Run!" yelled Kevin.

13

STAY SHARP

The Infected raked and pulled at the garage door, peeling the slats apart with a screech of stressed metal. Kevin aimed his .45 as he backed up to the inner doorway. Tris leapt out of the chair, launching it into the shelf behind the desk. A few cardboard-boxed oil filters fell to the floor. Skin peeled away from the Infected's face as it forced its head into the widening breach in the flexible barrier. Steel slats buckled and broke apart. Kevin clapped his second hand on the pistol, sighted, and fired. Blood spattered up and down on the metal. With a final, heaving groan, the dead man hung in place, stuck by his neck and arm.

Tris braced her hands on the side of the shelf and shoved it away from the inner door with a mild grunt. Kevin blinked. She ignored the incredulous face he made and rushed out. He backed after her. A short hallway to the right contained a single bathroom opposite a white door with black letters spelling out 'private.' Straight ahead, a red-tiled corridor led to a modest convenience store, full of overturned grocery-style shelves and trash. Six sliced and bloody Infected staggered over the wreckage.

A chubby Asian woman with a foot-long piece of glass sticking out of her shoulder swiveled to face him. Milky eyes held no trace of higher brain function, and rolled up into her head as a black serpent-like tendril emerged from her mouth. It, more than the woman, seemed to be staring at him.

He shivered. "Oh, fuck no."

Kevin fired, missing on the first shot. The other five ambling figures behind her whirled toward the noise. His second shot caught her in the shoulder, staining more of her peach colored shirt red. She took a step closer, the thing in her throat straining forward. The third slug struck at the base of her nose, spraying gore over the rest. The serpentine tongue surged out to three feet in length, whipping side to side as the body careened over backward.

Tris raised the Beretta. "Five, we can do that."

Metal clanged in the street outside.

"Shit, the ones from the garage are comin' 'round."

She lowered her arms and ran for the door marked private. Kevin shot a second one in the chest, putting it down in one. *Dammit. I got one or two bullets left.* "I hate Infected... I fucking hate infected."

Rattling came from his right. "Does anyone like them? Shit, it's locked."

"You're vaccinated at least. One speck of blood in my face and I'm fucked."

Tris flipped 180 degrees and went for the bathroom. "Damn, the window's too small."

"Look out." Kevin aimed at the private door and pumped his last two .45 rounds into it. Splinters flew, but it held. "Shit."

"I got it." Tris jumped up, grabbed the top of the bathroom doorway, and drove a two-legged mule kick into the private door. It shook, but held.

Infected rushed the corridor, gripping and punching at the air. Kevin pulled a Sig 226 out from under his right arm and shot a charging Indian man as well as two dark-skinned women with cornrows and bloody eyes. They collapsed. Two burly men in flannel shirts stumbled over the crawling bodies. The fallen seemed so desperate to get to him they didn't bother trying to stand back up.

Tris kicked the door again, and it broke open. Kevin shot the crawling men once each in the head and ran after her up a flight of stairs to a tan-carpeted apartment. A Confederate flag adorned a wood-paneled wall over a battered sofa facing a massive flat-panel TV set. Aside from that, every scrap of decoration in the room appeared to bear a Steelers logo:

pennants, mugs, framed shirts, posters. Even the trash can in the kitchen had a team sticker on it.

"Oh, hello you beautiful thing..." Tris jogged around the coffee table to a bookshelf between the couch and the wall.

Kevin followed her gaze to the top where a Japanese sword set sat under a thick layer of dust. She climbed up and took the katana, pulling it out enough to check the edge.

Tris whirled about with a child-at-Christmas grin. "It's sharp!"

He rushed for the kitchen. "All yours. I ain't gettin' that close to them."

"What now?" Tris jogged up behind him. "Infected know how stairs work."

As if to underscore her point, commotion echoed up the hallway. Kevin crossed the kitchen in four steps, heading for a door out to a small patio. He squinted at the moonlit streets, shivering at silhouettes moving with the telltale mannerisms of Infected as far as three blocks away.

"What the hell! Do they have radios or something?" Panic bubbled in the back of his throat. "Shit."

Tris ran out onto the patio with him and slammed the sliding door closed. "Seven of 'em coming up the stairs. We don't have much choice."

He frowned at the tiny slab of safety with two folding chairs. Glass doors wouldn't hold them at all. "Roof."

Kevin grabbed her by the hips and hoisted her up. She got her arms over the rain gutter; the katana hit the tarpaper with a *clack*. A few seconds after she shimmied over, she reappeared and reached down.

"Grab my hand."

He jumped up, but missed the edge. Something crashed inside.

"Kevin!"

"You're half my weight."

She scowled. "Thanks, but I doubt that. Don't be an idiot."

After another miss, he grumbled and leapt at the same instant the door smashed outward in a rain of glass fragments. His grip closed around her frail wrist. He expected to drag her down into the grasping arms of a pair of Infected, but she closed her fingers around his forearm and hauled him up. Her mousy little grunt of exertion would've been cute if he hadn't been about to shit himself.

Scratching fingers pulled down his legs. He booted a jowl-faced business suit in the nose, knocking him over the patio railing. Tris scooted backward, dragging Kevin away from the edge. The portly man hit the ground with a noise similar to a trash bag full of pudding bursting on the pavement.

"Ugh." Kevin cringed. "I do *not* want to see that."

Moaning and rattling metal echoed from down below. A shallow lip about ten inches high ran around the flat-roofed building. Aside from a handful of pipes with spinning vent cowls, and a long-dead air handler, the area was wide open.

"You okay?" Tris picked at his shirt.

"Yeah." He stood and walked to the edge. Six Infected had crammed themselves onto the patio, reaching up at the roof as if trying to will themselves to fly. "Damn, what a mess. I think they're exceeding the weight limit on that patio."

"Get away from the edge. If they don't see us, maybe they'll lose interest."

"I ain't that lucky." He moved from the alley side to the front, where at least forty more half-alive wretches wobbled past the old gas pumps. The mere sight of them got his hands shaking. He paced. "This is why I don't go to cities."

"Sorry." She walked to the air handler and pulled open an access panel. "I feel like it's my fault we're stuck here."

"Probably because it is." He folded his arms, backing away from a tarmac full of groaning, mindless, virus-carrying nastiness.

A piece of sheet metal clattered to the ground.

"You're supposed to say no it isn't, or it'll be okay, or it's not my fault."

At the front-facing corner opposite the patio side, he squinted at the darkened street. "It's not your fault this went to shit, but you *are* the reason we're in Harrisburg."

She grunted an instant before something broke with a loud *snap*. "It wasn't supposed to be like this."

"I can't tell where the hell we are. Every street looks the damn same at night."

A deep moan rumbled up from inside.

"We should be safe up here until morning," said Tris.

He retreated farther from the edge. She knelt by the air handler, rigging some salvaged wires into a harness so she could wear the sword on her back. Tears caught the moonlight, making her cheek glint. Kevin trudged up to the narrow end of the old air conditioner and leaned against it. The box was a few inches too tall to make hopping up on it like a seat easy enough to bother.

"You had no way to know. It's not your fault those people are dead."

She stopped knotting wire and let her hands fall in her lap. "I know." After a pause, she sniffled and wiped her face. "The Resistance represented our last chance. I was supposed to have the cure. Save the world. Now everyone's going to die."

"Look…" He put a hand on her shoulder. "You did all you could. Blame the sick bastard who came up with the Virus in the first place."

"What if I wasn't so slow? It was my fault those idiots caught me. If I'd been a little more resourceful, I wouldn't have been abducted and—"

"You'd have showed up in time to die from whatever killed them." Kevin shook his head. "I can't say I'm terribly impressed with this 'resistance' if they're dumb enough to set up shop in the middle of a damn hive."

Tris pulled a knot tight to the scabbard. "They made the Virus to 'scrub' the world of those with genetic impurities. They're paranoid about DNA damage from nuclear fallout, inbreeding, toxic chemicals… Those poor people."

"What's the Resistance hope to accomplish anyway? The Enclave is one city. It's not like they're in control of anything but themselves."

She shrugged the sword over her shoulder onto her back, measuring a length of wire around front as she let off a somber chuckle. "They wanted to break down the wall. Open the Enclave up. It started inside with a small group of dissidents. I remember being a little girl and seeing the head talk about it."

"The head?" He lowered himself to sit and waited for his heart to slow back to normal. "I gotta hear this."

"Oh." She smiled. "It's not a real head. Everything's scary to a five-year-old. The Speaker. He's appointed by the Council of Four. Most citizens think he's in charge, like a president or something. His face is everywhere. There's TV screens all over the place."

"Maybe they tossed you in jail because you found out about this council thing."

"No. The Council is common knowledge." Tris fidgeted until the sword sat right, and shifted around to sit next to him with her back to the air handler. "I might've been six or seven when the Speaker announced there were people among us who were trying to destroy us from within. At the time, I was terrified. I had no idea what was really going on. They weren't trying to kill us." She tapped her shoes together. "They wanted to overthrow the council."

"And do what? Stop trying to kill everyone else?" He contemplated closing his eyes, until another moan floated up from below.

"Either that or escape. Civilians aren't allowed to leave." She pulled her feet close and rested her chin on her knee. "I think the Virus might have mutated in ways they never expected. Now they're afraid of their own weapon. The victims weren't supposed to live more than a couple months after contracting the disease."

Kevin shivered. "Infected have been around at least ten years. I don't think it's 'working as intended.' Sure, there were survivors in big pop centers, but not enough to keep it this bad, this long."

"I thought you said Harrisburg was one of the worst."

He chuckled. "It is."

For a while, they sat in silence, listening to scratches and moans while gazing at the stars. Tris leaned to her right and rested her head on his shoulder. He raised an eyebrow at her, noticing silent tears.

Tris hung her head. "Those people didn't deserve to die."

"They're not dead yet. If they were, shooting them in the heart wouldn't do much."

She squinted into a breeze that lifted her hair. "Not much different. The people they used to be… The world that used to be."

"Hey." He grabbed her hand. "The nukes came down long before those Enclave bastards set the Virus loose."

"Yeah." She sighed. "I don't know what to do."

"Why do you have to *do* anything? Try to stay alive, that's enough."

She glanced up at him with a sour expression. "Get a roadhouse, sell guns and booze, and hope no one breaks those 'rules' you keep talking about? You think that's a goal?"

Kevin closed his eyes. "Oh, it's definitely a goal." He opened one eye. "Might be a petty and selfish goal, but it *is* a goal." He shut his eye and tried to relax.

Tris sighed.

SUNLIGHT KNOCKED ON KEVIN'S EYELIDS UNTIL THE RED GLOW DRAGGED him kicking and screaming out of sleep. He grunted, raised a hand to shield his face, and squinted at a world tinted green. At a nearby cough, he pushed himself up and looked toward it.

Tris knelt near the roof edge, doubled over and holding her gut. She gagged and dry heaved. Kevin flailed in an uncoordinated attempt to stand.

"You okay?"

"No." She shrank in on herself, shaking. "I had a fucking bomb inside me for months. I could've died any time Nathan wanted to push a button." She gurgled. "So, no. I'm not okay."

"Hey…" He crouched by her side. "You—"

Tris whirled and wrapped her arms around him. "Thank you."

Kevin wheezed at the slender arms forcing most of the air out of his chest. "Urk."

She relaxed, but didn't let go, and bit her lower lip. "Sorry, still not used to the augments. They're still new… I got them right before the 'escape.'"

"Probably when they put the hot pepper in you."

Tris shivered. "Yeah. Wonder if there's any other nasty surprises."

"I might be a bit rusty, but if you need someone to do a cavity search…" He raised both eyebrows. "I've got a medical degree."

"You?"

He nodded. "Yep. Found it with some salvage awhile back."

She gazed at the sunrise for a quiet moment. "If we get out of this alive, maybe."

He nodded toward a pair of metal bars looping over the south edge of the roof. "Not that hard. Sun's up."

"Infected don't burst into flame in the day." She let her arms drop and wandered to the ladder. "We don't really know why they avoid light. People who contract rabies become hydrophobic, so maybe it's similar."

"I'd shit myself if I saw a hydra too." Kevin followed.

"Ass." She threw a leg over the wall and descended, pausing when her face hovered over the edge. "Hydra's are mythological."

He raised both eyebrows. "So were zombies."

She poked him in the side. "How the hell do you know what a hydra is anyway?"

"I spent most of my life hunting for crap to sell. I usually read any books before I turn them into coin. One had hydras in it, but usually its dragons."

Tris muttered the whole way to the street level. Kevin hustled after her.

"Dragon's aren't real either."

"Thanks for the clarification there." She sighed. "As far as I know, the

Enclave isn't working on any giant reptiles. Be right back." She jogged into the service station through the front door, glass crunching under her shoes.

"Yeah?" He moved to the center of the street, turning in a slow spin, searching for anything familiar in the shapes of buildings. At least with the sun up, he could head generally west and south. "Enclave ain't much known for 'restraint' when it comes to what they tinker with."

Kevin glanced at the smashed windows. *What the hell is she doing?* He trotted up to the wall, leaning past the twisted aluminum frame. Blood trailed in the grooves in the bricks below the window, pooling inside and out. Looters had long ago taken anything of value from the store, before anyone knew such a thing as an Infected could exist.

He backed away from the blood, not trusting breathing that close to it. Every direction he looked, the streets lay empty. The imagined ghosts of survivors walked about, continuing in some manner of life devoid of electricity and modern conveniences, but life nonetheless. Then the Virus happened.

"We had a chance…"

Glass crunched behind him. He looked back at Tris tiptoeing around the shelves, carrying his red leather jacket. Realizing why she'd gone inside, he cracked up laughing. After handing it to him, she swatted dust out of her jumpsuit, raising the muted smell of sewer for the span of a few breaths.

"You went back for this?" Kevin checked his jacket for blood. Finding none, he put it on. "Thanks."

"I didn't want you giving me crap for making you lose it. I know how much you like your jacket, and you'd say it was my fault because you let me borrow it for a blanket."

A somewhat combative reply died at the tip of his brain when she grinned. "Busting my balls, huh?"

"Yeah." She pawed at her sleeves.

"Ugh. Burn that damn thing. You smell like shit." He coughed. "And I don't mean that as a euphemism either. You smell like actual shit."

"I'm not streaking."

He walked to the west, following a road. "Do you want to get shot at or jumped by someone looking for an Enclave bounty?"

"I don't think the Infected care." She trotted to keep up with his long stride. "Unlike you, I'm not attached to a particular item of clothing, just clothing in general."

"Wayne'll have some stuff I bet. Ornery bastard'll squeeze you for it though."

She made a blasé face. "If you mean money, I don't have any."

Kevin sighed.

After several blocks walking past crashed cars, scorched buildings, and the destructive aftermath of mass riots, Tris fell behind, gazing at the road. Kevin paused until she caught up, and took her arm.

"No point getting in a funk about it. Feeling shitty isn't gonna undo any of it."

She looked up at him with red ringing her wide sapphire eyes. If he couldn't see the rest of her, the face she gave him would've made her look fourteen.

"What?"

Tris sniffled. "What do you mean 'what?'"

"Women only make *that* face when they want something." He stopped. "What do you want?"

"Nothing you can give me." She stomped past him. "Get rid of the Virus, undo nuclear war, you know… nothing big."

"Yeah. Do me a favor. Use that face on Wayne when I tell him I need ammo."

She scowled at him. A couple minutes of quiet walking later, she smirked. "I took a vow not to use my powers of cute for evil."

"Getting Wayne to knock a few coins off a sale isn't evil."

"Hey." She pointed at a mangled traffic light hanging from wires. "I remember that light. We went underground over there…"

He squeezed her arm. "That means there's Infected around here. Stay quiet."

Tris gestured at a side street. With no better ideas, he followed her suggestion. At the end of the next block, a compact car embedded in a bus stop struck him as familiar. He recognized the road they'd walked in on and followed it for about forty minutes to a grassy field outside the city. Between daylight, and the wide-open terrain, he felt confident no Infected were anywhere nearby, and allowed himself to relax. Adrenaline waned, letting exhaustion creep in. He stopped at the side of the road, hand pressed to his face, and found zen rubbing his eyes.

"It's in that barn, right?" asked Tris.

"Yeah."

The thought of his Challenger gave him a second wind, and a long stretch of mild downhill road made the walk easier. Stiff muscles continued to protest; a night sleeping sitting up after an extended sprint and a near-bomb experience gave him fond daydreams about Wayne's crappy beds.

Kevin cut his way past waist-high grass between the road and the old barn. His padlock gleamed in the sunlight, a welcome sign no one had bothered his ride. Without thinking, he reached into the jacket's inside pocket and grabbed the key. As soon as fingers touched metal, he shot a look at Tris.

She smiled.

"You almost had me with the sentimental shit. You remembered the key."

Tris folded her arms. "Happy accident."

"Bullshit." He chuckled.

She gave him a raspberry as he opened the padlock and pocketed it.

"Who carries a padlock around?" She leaned out of the way of the opening door.

The Challenger sat in a haze of light brown dust, exactly as he'd left it. Kevin flung the two large wooden doors to the side and drew his hands together like a meditating monk. "Someone with a car to protect. Never know when you'll need one."

He traced his fingers along the fender to the driver's side door.

Tris glanced at him over the roof. "The rifle in the back is still jammed."

"Too tired." Kevin fell into the leather seat and moaned. "Oh, yeah. I think I'm going to take a nap."

She pulled the other door open enough to peek in. "Are you sure you want to waste daylight?"

He opened one eye. "Are you sure you want me driving right now?"

Tris slid into the passenger seat and let her head lean back. Her jumpsuit flattened out as the cushioned seat absorbed her body, giving her the appearance of a deflated person-shaped balloon. From her expression and half-closed eyes, the padding had done the same thing to her as it did to him.

"Sucks the will to move right outta ya, don't it?"

"Yeah," she whispered. "Nap sounds okay. Are we safe here?"

"Probably not." He punched buttons on a keypad secured to the dashboard by plastic wire ties. "Settin' an alarm for two hours."

14

GLASS HALF EMPTY

K evin ignored the sharp buzzing for seven minutes before opening his eyes. A brief rush of panic subsided at feeling his car's seat still under him. He glanced to his right. Tris curled up facing him, fingers in her ears. When he hit the button to kill the alarm, her pained grimace faded to a pleasant smile and she let her arms slide down into her lap.

He remembered a roadhouse about three hours west along Route 76 and ran his thumb across the edge of the dashboard cowl over the console. The row of rocker switches lit up one after the next with a series of soft *clicks*. A subtle vibration in the frame provided the only indication other than the row of blue lights in front of him that the car was on.

He closed his eyes, and for a few seconds, tried to remember what a gasoline engine sounded like, smelled like, felt like. A fleeting image of 'Dad' came and went, little more than a huge figure in silhouette against the sun smiling down at four-year-old him from the driver's seat of a 2020 Camaro. Kevin inhaled the memory of burning gasoline. The last ride before the car got the electrofit conversion. The semi had been electric too. Kevin stopped trying to remember—he'd spent too long trying to forget the semi.

I can't remember what my damn father looked like, but I know it was a '20 Camaro.

He grumbled, opened his eyes, and pulled out of the barn. Fortunately, the roads hadn't suffered too much after fifty years and nuclear war. 'Too much' being a relative thing. He slalomed around potholes big enough to eat the Challenger whole and went off road for a quarter mile to avoid the aftereffects of a crashed airliner. No one had much idea what existed farther east than Harrisburg. Everyone he'd ever heard of going there to check it out never returned. Roadhouse gamblers laid odds forty-two to one it was disaster or utopia.

"Damn place is probably *still* glowing..." he muttered.

Tris shifted in her seat and yawned. "What place?"

"The east coast."

Kevin leaned back, clenching a fist at the top of the wheel, and accelerated up to eighty-two over a stretch where the worst problem in the road was grass growing up from cracks. The hypnotic *ka-whump ka-whump* of tires passing over seams made it difficult to stay awake, even after a two-hour nap. He headed south along Route 15, heading for 76, a roadhouse, and a real bed. His stomach growled, a reminder he hadn't had anything to eat or drink in over a day. The canteens that would usually be in the passenger seat wound up behind him, out of reach unless he pulled over. A war raged in his head as he tried to decide between stopping for a drink or arriving faster. He'd come too close to Infected, and the urge to keep putting distance between him and them won out.

"Where are we?" Tris sat up and faced forward, stretching as much as she could.

"Almost to 76. 'Bout two hours away from food and a bed."

She squinted at him under a veil of snowy, disheveled hair. "I need to find out what this data is."

"Probably ain't no data. Or if there is, it's bogus shit." He changed lanes to avoid a cluster of debris from a collapsed overpass. "That pinhead on the monitor is full of shit."

"It's gotta be real." She sulked. "The resistance had a guy on the inside go over the data. He said it looked legit."

"How sure are you this guy wasn't working for that needledick?"

Tris picked at the folds in her jumpsuit leg. "He had radio contact with Doctor Andrews. If he was playing us, he'd fooled everyone."

"I still don't see them letting the cure out of the Enclave so easy."

"So easy?" She yelled. "I had a fucking bomb inside me. What if Nathan spilled coffee on his computer? Or tripped and fell on his desk, or however the hell else he sent the kill signal." Tris collapsed against the door, hands over her face, shaking again.

"Sorry. Look, I'm just saying I don't think it's worth getting your hopes up. After a double-cross like that, I wouldn't trust a damn thing from them. Gonna head to Wayne's and find a run that'll actually pay."

"Think, Kevin…" She slapped her hands on her thighs. "There's got to be something to it. Why else would he have tried to kill me? To them, being stuck out here in the Wildlands is worse than death. If he wanted to be a shit to me, he would've let me live. He's trying to destroy the data."

He slowed to take the on-ramp to 76 and pulled over once they were on the highway. "You're more than welcome to walk anywhere you want, but I'm going back to Wayne's. I'm too close to ten K. I can't give up now." Kevin reached around behind his seat and grabbed a canteen.

Tris stared with lust in her eyes as he gulped the tepid plastic-flavored water down. Once the thought of taking another sip felt nauseating, he handed it to her. She held it in both hands like a baby with a bottle. When she choked, he pushed it down.

"Easy, don't breathe the water."

She slapped herself on the chest, gagging and crying, though she tried to smile. "I did that last time too."

"Yep." He stared out at the wavering grass. "Sure wouldn't mind a dust-hopper steak about now."

"Are they this far east?" She drank more, trying to peer out the window at the same time.

"No idea. Dust hoppers are a meal for the desperate. When you start *wanting* it, you know you're starving."

She laughed, shooting water out of her nose. Kevin caught the canteen as she lapsed into another choking fit.

"You're still here."

Her smile faded. "Yeah." She stared into her lap.

"Look, I know you don't wanna hear it… but all that shit about the cure was to get you revved up to run out here as a meat torpedo."

"What?" She blinked.

Kevin waved his hand around. "You know, a guided missile made outta person."

"Oh." Tris glanced down, grumbling. "I think Nathan's enough of an arrogant bastard to use real data. It would be more ironic for him."

"It's stupid." He wedged the canteen between seat and center console, checked the rearview monitor, and laid rubber.

Tris waited for the g-forces of rapid acceleration to wear off before she spoke. "Is it? First, he'd never expect the 'savages' to have the equipment needed to synthesize a viable preventative vaccine or post-infection antiviral drug. Second, they invented the Virus to begin with, so they know it back and forth. To them, it's no big mystery. It's not like teams of doctors have been searching for the cure for thirty years and it doesn't exist."

"Hmm."

She crossed her arms. "And, Nathan is apparently *that* kind of asshole."

Kevin leaned to the side to make eye contact in an exaggerated loll of his head. "Even if I believed the data was real, I don't think there's anyone out here with the tech to get it out of you. Can't you like access it inside or something? The way you saw that glowing line?"

"No." She scowled. "They said it's the kind of implant that low-level military intelligence operatives once used to transport classified information they weren't cleared to know. It's a memory fob embedded in my head. Only way to read it is by plugging a wire into the port behind my left ear."

"You probably don't even have the memory implant."

"I do. I was there when they uploaded it." She pointed at her neck. "Kinda had to be. I saw the storage interface."

"But not what's in it?" He shot her a distrustful glare.

"Have you ever used a computer? It was a file transfer bar, they didn't open the file."

"Yeah. I used a computer once."

"Really?" She smirked.

"Yup... for target practice. Damn thing exploded in a cloud of silver glitter."

"Cretin." She moaned into her hands.

Quiet took over the car for the better part of the next hour. Overgrown fields passed on both sides, as did the occasional wrecked vehicle. Most had been stripped all the way to the frame, leaving nothing worth taking. He grumbled. Even a little salvage would help. As it was, this excursion would set him back about forty coins in charging fees alone, never mind ammo. He glared at the striped yellow line pulsing into the bottom of the windshield, like a cheesy laser effect from some old movie he'd watched on a half-dead flat panel. Eventually, Kevin's head grew heavy, the road became blurry, and he caught himself nodding off. Tris noticed too, and slapped him on the arm a second after his head snapped up.

"Shit." He grumbled. "I'm fried."

"You let me sleep a bit, want me to drive?"

"Have you ever used a car?" He grinned.

Tris picked at her eye with her middle finger. "No, but how hard can it be. You turn the wheel to go left and right and the pedal controls speed."

"Oh, yeah, it's that easy." He chuckled. "Hey, we've only got a little while left. Keep talking and I'll be okay."

"What about?"

He forced air out his lips, making a noise halfway between fart and angry elephant. "I dunno. Anything. Make sound effects…"

"Do you think the resistance died in there? I didn't see any bodies." She squirmed in her seat. "Did you?"

"Only the ones chasing us." The red LED in the middle of the dash fluttered between eighty-eight and eighty-nine MPH. "Some of them were probably your resistance. All it takes is one drop of blood in a wound or a scratch from a tooth. One jackass that doesn't admit what happened and everyone's dead."

Tris stared into space. "The Virus is asymptomatic for up to twenty-four hours after initial exposure. After six hours, other Infected can somehow tell… and leave you alone. Between twenty-four and forty-eight hours, the subject appears to be suffering a common cold or flu. After forty-eight hours, second-order symptoms manifest. Initial signs are reduced intellect, disorientation, and fever, occasionally accompanied by muscle spasms. Ten to fourteen hours later, the subject appears to have an advanced case of dementia. By day three, higher brain function stops and they're not a person anymore."

"Jesus H. Christ," said Kevin. "Morbid much? And why do you sound like you were reading that?"

"Because I *am* reading it. Data implant. Got a little floating virtual screen in front of me now." Tris continued speaking in a monotone. "The Virus is non-aerosolized. Transmission vectors consist solely of the exchange of bodily fluid. Blood. Sweat. Other secretions."

"I asked you to keep me awake for the ride, not give me nightmares for the rest of my life." Kevin drummed his fingers on the steering wheel. "Subject change."

Tris seemed to snap out of the daze. "How'd you know cutting out the bomb would work?" She pressed her hand over the spot. "You could've run."

"You still owe me a grand." He grinned. "So, what was detention like?"

"You're a lousy liar." She almost smiled at him, but turned a sad expression out over the passing countryside. "They stuck me in a tiny little room. Everything was white or black except for the bed." Her eyes twitched. "Grey sheets."

"What's up with the tic?" Kevin helped himself to another swig from the canteen.

She glanced toward him, the fingers of her right hand still at her temple. "Strange memory that doesn't make sense."

"Dare I ask?" He offered her the canteen.

Her right arm fell in her lap as she grabbed the water with her left. "I'd been in Detention for about eight months. All they let me do was access educational media from a wall terminal. Not once did I leave that little room. The day Nathan offered to help me escape, my hair was damp when I woke up."

"Why is that strange?" Kevin opened his window, hoping a blast of fresh air would ward off the sleep stalking up behind him.

"It was me, a bed, and a wall terminal. No source of water. I can't figure out how it got wet."

He squinted at her. "No toilet?"

She shook her head while drinking.

"You got some kinda cyberware that dries it all up to farts or something?"

Tris glared, then looked confused. "I... don't remember. The food was bland. Oatmeal or something. Porridge." She stuck her tongue out. "It was probably high-utilization."

"You should've still had to piss."

"I have parents," Tris yelled, hesitated, and slouched. "Had... I think."

He chuckled. "You think you had parents?"

"No. I think it's *had* instead of have." She frowned. "I don't remember my mother at all, and my Dad died when I was nine. The couple I got assigned to acted like my Dad never existed. I haven't seen them since I got arrested for refusing the pairing."

"Mmm." He slowed, pulling as far left as the lane allowed.

The Challenger rocked as he turned left onto a gravel-covered connector between east and westbound lanes. One small, white sign still read 'For Official Use Only.' He went right at the other end, bouncing onto what would have once been lanes full of oncoming traffic. Tris sighed.

"Dad had it in his head that the Enclave's mission should be to reclaim Earth. Spread out from the Enclave and take back our planet."

"Yeah. That's what they want alright." He shook his head. "After they kill us all."

"No." She pouted. "Dad wasn't like that. The Enclave is too small. They need a damn computer to tell everyone who they can have babies with already. It'll never work. They *need* the survivors. Some of them know that… the Resistance."

Beautiful red-orange light bathed the wavering grass ahead on the left. Above a sprawling one-story building with four garage doors on the right, an attempt at a giant neon sign in the shape of an R glowed in all its glory. Kevin drooled, already imagining the taste of food.

"Okay, maybe they're not all assholes." He pulled to a stop near the building's small porch. The smell of meat blew on his face from the air vents. "Oh, that's beautiful."

"Yeah." She gazed down.

"Sorry." He flicked the switches off. "What makes you think he's dead?"

"Dad vanished. No one would talk about it. I got reassigned to a new family. Whenever I asked about him, they treated me as if I was making up people who never existed. I pretended to forget him, so they stopped acting like I was crazy."

"Damn." Kevin traced his finger around the master switch for a second or two before pushing it. The console went dark. "That's harsh."

"Hungry?"

She didn't look up. "No coins, remember."

Kevin mouthed 'what did I do?' at the roof. "Come on… And you can lay off with the guilt. I ain't gonna let you starve."

Tris let off a cute grunt as she shoved the door open and got out. He followed and keyed 4-1-9-4 into the buttons under the door handle. The Challenger chirped.

"I thought you said it's under the roadhouse protection if it's parked here." Tris stuffed her hands in her pockets and trudged around the front end of the car to the porch. "Don't you trust the code?"

"The Code I trust." He crossed the porch and put a hand on the door. A quiet murmur of voices emanated from inside. "It's the people I worry about."

"I don't understand." Tris leaned back as he opened the door. "There's no guards. Not like there's any kind of communication grid out here. How's it work?"

Dusty air laced with stale beer and wood washed over him. Kevin's attention went first to the two men at a round table in the back end of the room sandwiched between a decades-dead jukebox and a small cabinet that held the remains of a touchscreen monitor and a cash drawer. The older man's pewter-colored hair hung in long, straight strands over a black armored shirt with Kevlar panels sewn into the material. *Might stop a pistol.* His traveling companion looked less than half his age, not-yet-twenty as far as he could guess. The younger man gave the customary quick glance at the squeak of an opening door, started to look away, but left his stare on Tris.

"They still got radio. Don't take long for word to get around, then Amarillo puts a few thousand coins on your head… you're done." Kevin glared at the younger man. "Somethin' I can do for you, friend?"

"Nah." He kept staring, chewing something, for another few seconds before shifting to face the table.

Kevin grasped her arm above the left elbow and pulled her toward the bar. "Come on."

"Was that 'I wanna fuck it' or 'I wanna kill it?'" Tris yanked her arm away. "I can walk, you know. I'm not six."

"Could'a been either one." He tugged on her jumpsuit. "Until you lose this, won't know. People do a lotta stupid shit for ten thousand coins."

"You know they're fake right?" Tris leaned on the bar.

"Those tits look real enough to me, honey," said a wiry woman a day or four away from sixty. "If you're lookin' for work, we could come to an arrangement."

"I meant the coins." Tris glared up at Kevin. "They stamp steel or aluminum."

"So?" Kevin chuckled. "Not like it matters anymore. No government to counterfeit against. If it looks like a coin, some people will take it. Amarillo's a bit picky, though."

The proprietor leaned back, making her breasts prominent against her patched red tee shirt. Straight brown hair, as long as her belt, slipped off her shoulders as she tilted her head and winked at Kevin. "I'm Beth. This is my place. What'cha need?"

"Meat. Preferably cooked. Whatever you got's hot."

"Sweetie…" Beth leaned forward. "Everything I've got's hot."

The younger man behind them choked on something.

"Go fuck yourself, Roy," said Beth in a saccharin sweet tone with a bat of her eyelashes before standing straight and looking at Kevin. "Fries?"

"Yeah." He nodded at Tris. "Same for her 'less she wants somethin' different."

"Nah, I'm okay with that." She sighed. "He's paying, I don't have an opinion."

"George," yelled Beth, "need two hood ornaments with collateral damage."

"On it," said a baritone from behind the wall.

Kevin suppressed a wince. *That's going to hurt on the way out.*

"Five coins." The woman leaned both hands on the counter, arms wide. When he counted out five and went to hand it to her, she chuckled. "Each."

Kevin squinted at her for a few seconds. "Little high."

"You remember where you are?" The woman gestured at the door. "Eastern fringe."

"So you jack the prices?"

Beth sighed. "Not like there's many people runnin' supplies out to me this far. I'd charge less if I didn't have to pay cowboys like you to scav supplies."

"Don't 'spect you get much traffic this far up." He set down ten coins, a mixture of pennies and dimes. "Got anything to drink that won't give me the shits for a week?"

"Filtered water or engine cleaner, and enough. There's couple settlements up 522 what trade in ammo and shine. Gets a routine flow through here."

He grinned. "Shit, I haven't had engine cleaner in years. That'll do. She—"

"Water." Tris raised her hands. "Just water."

The woman showed three fingers.

Kevin dropped another few coins on the counter while Beth filled a huge plastic cup from a spigot on the wall behind her. After setting it in front of Tris, she reached below the counter to retrieve a sealed mason jar of clear liquid, which she handed him. Kevin headed to his left, toward a booth in the front corner, where he could watch Beth, the two men, and the front door without craning his neck. He settled into high-backed bench built into the wall, with a fat strip of red cushion. Grime pressed into the red and white checkered tablecloth highlighted tiny squares in the material. Beth had even managed to find salt and pepper shakers, though he didn't trust what was in them.

Tris slid into the adjacent spot on the bench and looked from him to the room and back. "What? I'm not trying to be cute. Keeping my eyes on possible threats."

"Mm-hmm." He opened the jar. In seconds, fumes watered his eyes.

"That's not actual engine cleaner is it?" She cringed.

"Nah. Moonshine. Course... you *could* clean an engine with it... if anyone still had one."

Tris leaned into him, eyeing the two men. "Maybe you're right about this jumpsuit."

"I'll hold your sword if you wanna take it off." He grabbed the scabbard.

"No!" She clamped her hands over the wire harness between her breasts. "I'm not running around in my skivvies. See if Beth has any clothes to sell."

Kevin scoffed. "After what we paid for the food, clothes can wait for Wayne's. Besides, those two've already seen you."

Beth walked over with two metal plates, each with an irregular lump of meat between thick cut slabs of bread next to a pile of fried potato discs. She winked at Kevin again and went back behind the counter.

"So... ten thousand some odd coins you're trying to save up." Tris plucked one of the potatoes from her plate and held it up in two fingers. "So you can ask people if they want fries with it."

Kevin held up a hand. "Shh. This is a special moment." He clasped the sandwich with reverence due a holy relic and raised it to his nose. Growling emanated from his stomach; he salivated. After taking a long, deep breath and savoring the fragrance of... *Probably deer. Eh, fuck it.* He chomped, and spent a good three minutes chewing the first mouthful.

Tris's face turned pink.

"What?" He glanced sideways at her. "Why are you givin' me that look?"

"Stop moaning like that. They'll think I've got my hand down your pants. It's only food."

Kevin smiled. "No such thing as *only* food." He enjoyed another bite. "And yeah... I'd rather sell potatoes than get shot."

"Will those two be a problem?" Tris examined her burger as if looking for the proper angle from which to grasp it.

"Shouldn't be. We're so damn far away from the Enclave I doubt they believe it. 'Sides... locked door."

Chomp. *Oh, yeah...*

15

DEBTS

Two days later, Kevin guided the Challenger down the familiar streets of Hagerman, New Mexico... or at least what used to be Hagerman, New Mexico before politicians made maps and borders irrelevant. People still tended to call it Hagerman, but almost no one bothered with the other part. The few that did liked to make a big deal about it, the kind of big deal that often involved blood and bullets. He squinted at a pair of motorcycles parked by Wayne's porch, and the two men with brown leather biker cuts emblazoned with the crimson star 'sheriff badge' logo of the News. They shifted at the crunch of his tires on the dirt as he pulled into his usual spot.

"Looks like Wayne fixed the railing," said Tris. "Think he'll be mad if I break it again?"

Kevin swept his thumb over the rocker switches, shutting down the car. "No idea what you're talking about. Some New idiot fell on it." He pushed his door open and stood, locking eyes with the self-appointed 'law' in the area. "They won't do shit."

The taller, thinner man swatted the other in the arm twice as his eyes widened with apparent recognition. His stockier friend still had a bruise on the side of his face from where he'd had a close encounter with Tris's shoe. He leaned forward as if about to rush at her.

Tris raised her arms in a combat stance. "Come on. I got my hands this time. See what happens."

"She's *not* a damn bounty." Kevin forced his way between them. "You got balls lookin' to start shit so close to Wayne's."

Tris ducked around him. "I can take this idiot."

"Hey." The taller New held up a hand. "No trouble. Juan. Let it go."

Juan squinted.

"She put your ass down with one kick last time. You should listen to your friend." Kevin winked. "Unless you want another dance."

Juan spat to the side and walked off, shaking his head and muttering.

"You know they're going to get friends." Tris folded her arms.

Kevin put an arm around her back and guided her through the saloon doors. "We tried. Next time it's on them."

"This is your fault." She followed.

He looked back, but kept walking. "How is this my fault?"

"If you had untied me when I asked, they wouldn't have bothered with us on the way out."

"Oh, sure." Kevin shook his head. "If you hadn't gotten yourself kidnapped in the first—"

Her fist in his back made him yelp. He rubbed the spot over his left kidney, one eye closed from the pain, and grimaced.

"Hello, Kevin," said Bee. The android woman in a torn shirt and knee-length denim skirt shuffled across the room with a gait like an Infected in the middle of being electrocuted. A spark sizzled by a patch of exposed metal under her left collarbone. "Hello again, girl."

"Nice of them to leave her tit hanging out." Tris let her arms fall.

"It. It's a robot. Not a real tit. Trust me; no one is looking at Bee and thinking about anything but how long it takes to bring food to the table."

"Kev," shouted Wayne from behind the bar. "I was not expecting to see *you* again. How's it feel to own a roadhouse?"

For a long minute, Kevin scowled at the fifty-something cowboy, trying to come up with a reason to hate every grey whisker on his face. "Go to Hell, Wayne."

The older man threw his head back and laughed. Bee caught his cowboy hat when it fell and put it back on for him. His bushy goatee and mustache twisted with a smirk. He sent a playful wink at Tris. "Had a feeling. The innocent looking ones ain't never what they seem."

Kevin climbed onto a barstool. "Usual... and one for her."

"Oh, dammit... there it goes." Wayne shook his head, causing his hair to dance over his shoulders. "She's got you already."

"It's a tab." Kevin stared at the ceiling and grumbled. "I got some .50 Browning in the trunk, bout sixty some odd rounds."

"Ween make it?" Wayne raised an eyebrow.

"Nah, salvage."

Wayne's interest seemed to melt out of his face. "So you don't know how old it is… or if it still works?"

"Looks in decent shape. Signs of hand loading on the brass. It's not prewar." Kevin stretched. "Need something else for her to wear. Got anything?"

"Possible." Wayne turned to shout into the alcove behind him. "Bee."

The robot woman tottered into view. "Yes, boss?"

"Two burgers." Wayne indicated Tris with his thumb. "We got anything in her size in the back ta wear?"

Bee shuddered with a spasmodic twitch, made a noise much like a sneeze, and walked like a normal human around the bar. Her fluid motion lasted about three more steps before her left leg seized at the knee.

"Christ, Wayne. You ever gonna fix that? Almost seems cruel." Kevin cringed.

Bee's right eye glowed red, projecting a grid of laser light on Tris.

"Ain't got the parts or the knowhow." Wayne shook his head.

"Bee r-r-r-ight b-b-b-ack," said Bee, as she convulsed in place and bent forward at an angle. Her black hair slid off her neck, exposing the B-19-C. "Pain detected. Ouch."

Tris moved up behind Bee and pushed the destroyed shirt up. After a moment of prodding at the imitation skin on the android's back, a square panel rose out and opened. Inside, flickering light illuminated a cloud of smoke around something whirring.

"You know what you're doing in there? Kill Bee, and your ass belongs to Wayne." Kevin cringed around as Tris stuck her fingers inside the machine.

"I only had the intro courses on robotics… Everyone gets it in high school. Been awhile." Tris made a series of contemplative noises. "When was the last time you had her serviced?"

"Serviced?" Wayne raised an eyebrow. "Case you hadn't noticed, little lady, this ain't the sorta place what's got android shops."

Tris grumbled. "Got a star driver at least? Maybe a toothbrush?"

"A what?" asked Wayne.

"Really?" Tris sounded annoyed. Kevin chuckled. "It's a screwdriver with a tiny tip that looks like an asterisk."

Wayne looked past Kevin at the source of her voice. "What the fuck's an asterisk?"

"Isn't that a bird?" asked an old woman in the back.

"That's apteryx," said Tris. "Dammit."

Wayne, mouth half open, stared at her for another few seconds before shifting his gaze to Kevin, who returned a 'yeah, I know' glance.

"Guess that's some 'o that *fancy book learnin'* eh?" Wayne slapped the counter. "Be right back with them burgers."

"Need a charge too." Kevin's back muscles tensed at a loud, sizzling spark from behind him.

"That did not feel pleasant," said Bee.

"Port Three," yelled Wayne from a room separated from the bar by a camouflage curtain.

Tris mumbled. "All the connectors are loose. It's a wonder you can move at all."

Kevin stood, wanting to be as far away from Bee as possible when she exploded. He jogged to the door, keeping an eye out for any members of the New gang, but the porch was empty. He walked around to the Challenger's driver side door and punched 4-1-9-4 into the buttons under the handle. The door *clicked.* He ducked in long enough to hit the release for the trunk as well as the charging port on the front right fender. After closing and locking the door, he retrieved the belt of .50 Cal ammo from the pile of salvage in the back. Kevin draped it over his shoulder, glancing around for any sign of trouble. Seeing none, he slammed the trunk and walked along the passenger side to where the small panel about the size of an old gas hatch tilted outward a few inches behind the wheel well. A light push on the near side levered it open the rest of the way, and he drew out a few feet of wire in clear plastic insulation, which he plugged into a bank of sockets by the porch stairs.

The scent of ozone floated out from under the hood within seconds. He squinted up at the roof of solar panels, which accounted for most of the cost of starting a roadhouse. The people in Amarillo charged through the nose for them, since as far as anyone knew, they were the only source. Not that the world had many cars left, but the ones that remained needed charging.

They control the power. They control us all.

He shook his head and tromped up the stairs followed by the clattering of ammunition. Wayne, three unfamiliar men about his age, a dark-skinned woman with an explosion of dreadlocks, and one ancient man all looked up as the tin can door chimes rang. Tris remained forearm deep in Bee. From that angle, it looked like she worked an old ventriloquist dummy, her arm was in so far. The android emitted a series of disturbing phrases like: "Oh, that feels wonderful," "Please do that again," and "Yes… yes… that's the spot."

Kevin resumed his place on the same stool he always tried to sit in. Third in from the left. Whenever someone else sat on it, he'd give them the squiggy eye until they moved. Once, he'd gotten into a fistfight over it. Brass hit the counter with a *clatter* that got everyone looking again as if the treasure of a dragon's hoard had landed on the wood. On top of the stink of stale beer and fart, a weak trace of cooking meat drifted by.

"Hmm." Wayne picked up one end of the belt, appraising the bullets like a jeweler. "Don't look in too bad o' shape." He shook it, listening to the powder move. "Four per bullet."

"Fuck you too, Wayne." Kevin chuckled. "You're gonna sell it for twelve each. There's a reason I never got a .50 mounted on the Challenger."

"Seven and I'll throw in clothes for the little woman." Wayne winked.

"I'll pay fer her duds if'n she changes out here," said the old man.

"Seven and the clothes," said Tris, sounding unamused.

"Seven." Kevin reached out to shake. "Plus whatever you pick off the old horndog's corpse."

The elder squealed. "Easy, I ain't want trouble."

Tris snuck a smile over her shoulder at Kevin.

"Done." Wayne shook.

"The meat is ready," said Bee, still bent forward at a ninety-degree angle.

"Sec." Tris tried to reconnect an uncooperative copper-colored ribbon cable and snarled after a few seconds of it not fitting in place. Eventually, a loud *snap* came from inside Bee, and she shot upright. "There."

The android woman convulsed in place and her head thrashed side to side.

"Oh, shit. What did you do?" Kevin leaned back.

"She's rebooting." Tris raised a hand. "Calm down."

"I'm about to re-boot someone's ass if you broke her." Wayne rested his elbows on the counter, sniffing the air. "I smell smoke."

"You sure that's not my dinner?" Kevin grinned. "I'm not paying for charcoal."

Bee stood up straight, turned to face the bar, and smiled. "Operational."

Tris lunged after the android to close the panel as it walked off with only a faint limp in its stride. Bee rounded the bar and hurried into the kitchen past the camo curtain. Tris slid onto the stool at Kevin's left.

"Can't do much for that hip actuator. All the parts are worn out and dirty. Someone needs to take her apart and clean everything, replace that actuator, and put her back together. I think the frequent shocks are also giving her memory read errors, and her gyroscopic stabilizer is on its last legs."

Wayne leaned back, his upper lip twitching. "What in the hell language was that?"

"Got me," said Kevin.

Tris leaned forward, speaking a hair over a whisper. "Wayne? Do you know anyone with any kind of high-tech gear? Someone who might be able to umm… There's a data port on Bee. Standard interface connector."

Wayne drifted back two steps to fill a pair of mason jars with his homemade beer. "You mean like the one you got?"

Tris sat up, lowered her hands to her lap, and stared at the bar. "Yeah."

Kevin moaned and rubbed his face.

"Aw, relax." Wayne set the drinks down in front of them. "Ain't got no reason to stir up trouble for you two."

Bee reappeared with a plate in each hand, setting a burger and fries down next to each beer before speed-walking back through the curtain.

"Great." Kevin forgot all about everything when the smell of the deer-rat-something meat reached his nostrils. He battled his growling stomach's urge to eat the whole thing in four bites.

"So…" Tris lifted her head to look at Wayne. "Know anyone with the gear necessary to take data out of a cranial implant?"

A light came on in the armory room past the bar, revealing a handful of rifles and shotguns on pegs behind a security cage.

"One… if they're still even there." Wayne scratched at his goatee. "Pack 'o Enclave dissidents supposedly set up shop under the south end of the Golden Gate."

At hearing 'Golden Gate,' Kevin drew a sharp breath, which launched a small piece of bread down his throat. He choked for a second before squinting at Wayne with one eye wider than the other and wheezing, "Fuck that."

"But—" said Tris.

"He's got a point. Area's near Enclave H.Q." Wayne glanced to his left as the light went off in the armory. "Even ignorin' that, it's a bad, bad area. The Boatmen more or less own it."

"If the area's so bad, why would these people go there?" Tris ate a fry.

"Keeps the Enclave away," muttered Kevin past a mouthful of burger.

Bee emerged from the curtain and set a pair of women's jeans and a medium-sleeved shirt seemingly made of brown leather on the bar in front of Tris. Kevin chuckled.

Tris put her hand on it. "It's softer than it looks. What is this?"

"Dust hopper," said Wayne. "'Less you want long-sleeved flannel in a man's size."

Kevin surrendered to the wonderful flavor. His gut won, and he devoured the last half of his meal in two huge mouthfuls. This batch of Wayne's beer had odd fruity notes. *I don't want to know.*

"Can you get there?" Tris picked up her burger as if she'd never seen anything like it. After a tentative sniff, she nibbled.

"No point in goin' there. There's no way they put anything useful in that implant of yours. I'm gonna grab a run, earn some coins, and get the hell off the road while I'm still alive."

She lowered the food from her face, her expression mournful. "But you don't—"

"Wanna save the world? Pff." He shook his head. "Better people 'an me have tried, and we're still fucked. Not my stone to haul."

Tris's expression made her seem disinterested in food, but she kept nibbling on it.

"Two for the charge. Six for the food." Wayne twitched an eyebrow at Tris. "So, what'll you be doin'? Might find a use for you 'round here if you ain't got plans."

"She still owes me a grand." Kevin tilted his head back and chugged the beer. "She's with me till she pays it off."

Tris rubbed her hand over her abdomen where the bomb had been. She peered past a drape of hair at him, her eyes sad sad, but a hint of a smile on her lips. "Yeah."

"Rooms." Kevin started to reach for his pocket.

Wayne held up his hand. "I'll take it off the books." He reached under the bar and held up two keys.

Kevin took his, while Wayne set the other on the bar by Tris's plate, as her hands were full of food. She glanced from the key to Kevin and shrugged.

He slid off the stool to his feet. "I'm so damn tired, sleeping feels like work."

"That, my dear"—Wayne grinned—"is why he's so set on gettin' hisself a 'house of his own. The hours be regular like."

"Hmf," said Tris.

"See ya in the morning," Kevin muttered.

He trudged across the room full of tables, went past the bathrooms, and dragged himself up a flight of stairs at the end of the little hallway. Ten rooms occupied the upstairs, five on either side, behind doors painted dark green. One small window at the far end let a feeble breeze in. A handwritten sign hung next to it on the wall reading: "No pissin' out the window." He went door to door until the key worked in the third on the left. Inside, a plain eight-by-ten-foot room waited with a single bed consisting of a naked metal frame, a mattress, and box spring with a tattered excuse for a sheet.

Paradise.

Door locked, deadbolt flipped, he shrugged off his armor and boots. Content, he let gravity take him face down on the bed.

He didn't even smell the mold.

16

LITTLE BLACK BOX

Gentle pressure on his left shoulder, accompanied by a series of light shakes, pulled Kevin from the depths of an exhaustive sleep. Tiny needles of pain stabbed his eyelids as they fought a seal of dried crumbles that glued his eyelashes together. Through the meager gap they afforded without the intervention of a hand to wipe crud away, he stared at a blurry bare breast hovering inches from his face. Interest died faster than the Infected from his dream. A black scuff mark to the right of the nipple gave away the owner.

Bee.

"Wayne told me to wake you before you gotta pay for another night."

As fried as he felt, the voice sounded almost human. Kevin moaned and worked his right arm out from under his weight to scrape the sand from his eyes. "Ngh. What time is it?"

The android breast rose out of his field of view amid the whirr of electric motors. "Wednesday June 15th, 2072. 10:54 a.m."

He pushed himself over on his back, muscles leaden and stiff. "'Nother hour."

Bee's arms whirred as she crossed them. "Suit yourself, but past eleven, he'll bill you for the room again."

Mercenary cocksucker. Kevin grumbled and reached an arm out. "Alright, alright."

"Good morning, Kevin." Bee grasped his hand and pulled him upright, catching him by the shoulders when his balance failed. "Oversleeping is as bad as not getting enough."

"Yeah. So what's for breakfast?" He rubbed his fingers around his eyes before snapping them open and taking a deep breath. "Smells like grease."

Bee tottered to the door. "Eggs, bacon, coffee. Two coins."

"Wayne can call it bacon, but cutting dust hopper meat thin doesn't make it bacon."

Kevin snagged his armor and shrugged into it before taking the key from a small nightstand made out of an old footlocker on end. The stairs *clonked* and *banged* as he tromped down to the first floor and walked into a cloud of misery seeping out of the men's. He clamped a hand over his mouth as his eyes watered and forced his way into the stench to relieve himself. Furry black *something* grew up and down the walls around the toilet. Kevin decided to work on long distance marksmanship. After, he hurried down the short hall to the main room.

Tris's white hair grabbed his attention first. She sat at the bar, with her back to Wayne. Her new 'rabbit-leather' shirt fit quite well, though if her bust was as big as Bee's, it would've been a second skin. The katana remained on her back. In addition to the jeans, she'd added a belt with a holster that held the Beretta. Only the black shoes remained from her Enclave uniform. Their all-terrain soles would likely be helpful, but Infected loved to grab ankles when a person went down.

Nervousness melted out of her when she looked his way. The two men that had been there when they arrived seemed more interested in the last few crumbs of their breakfast than Tris, and the old man who suggested a striptease for a discount was nowhere to be seen. Kevin approached the bar, stared at the red LED clock behind it showing 11:01, and set the key down.

"Don't even think about it."

Wayne chuckled as he slid the key toward him. "Wasn't gun'ta."

"Hey," said Tris.

Kevin glanced at her belt. "What'd that cost?"

"Two." Wayne hung the room key on its nail in the cabinet behind the bar. "She bought it herself."

"What?" Kevin glared at her. "You have money?"

She raised an eyebrow. "I used to."

"Paid her twenty coins for fixin' up ol' Bee. She's been zippin' 'round here like almost new. Only seized up once all mornin' so far."

Kevin climbed onto a stool, set his elbows on the bar, and held his head in both hands. Tris rubbed his shoulder. The scent of eggs and thin strips of unidentifiable meat came in from between them as Bee set two plates down.

"I told him to put the other eighteen in your account since I owe you." Tris eyed her plate.

Wayne grinned at Kevin. "Took the lib'tee of assumin' you'd be coverin' her food again. She did wait fer ya ta be down."

Kevin teased a fork at the eggs for a few seconds. "No sense takin' her last coin. She earned 'em. We'll work some kinda payment plan out."

They ate in silence for a few minutes.

Wayne set a stack of coins, nickels and pennies, in front of Tris. "Sixteen. Two fer the belt, two fer breakfast."

"Thanks." Tris collected them, shot a smile at Kevin, and kept eating.

"Since H-Burg turned to crap on ya, figger you might be interested in an iffy little run that walked in the door an hour ago." Wayne set his hands on the bar and locked his elbows. "Your cut's two hundred and fifty."

Shock sent a few crumbs of egg down the wrong pipe. Kevin choked and pounded a fist into his sternum. "W-what is it?"

"If your reaction to pay like that is any indication, probably too dangerous." Tris picked up a piece of 'bacon' and sniffed it.

"Eat it," said Wayne. "S'good for ya."

"It's only dangerous if you drag-ass. Do it quick and it's easy money." Wayne looked around before ducking and whispering, "Takin' a box of void salt to Glimmertown."

Fuck me. "I told you I don't touch that shit."

Tris smiled.

Kevin slammed a fist into his chest and coughed. "Too much risk."

She smirked.

Wayne stood and held up his hands. "Not forcin' the issue. Two fifty on the hook. No one knows it's here yet."

"That's too much money for something so 'easy,' isn't it?" Tris narrowed her eyes at Kevin.

"Yep." He folded an entire strip of 'bacon' into his mouth at once, chewing it slow like tobacco. Once it reduced to mush he could speak around, he shook his head. "Have anything with wheels comin' after us constantly. They're payin' me two-fifty to haul it, so that means the shit's worth at least two grand."

"Too risky," said Tris.

"In order for there to be risk, people would gotta know what yer doin'.

I haven't even posted the run on the board yet. Wanted ta keep it quiet an' offer ya first dibs."

"How charitable of you, Wayne." Kevin chuckled.

"Well, you got a bad deal on that whole Harrisburg thing." Wayne winked. "Least she's easy on the eyes."

"Yeah, she's a real blast." Kevin stabbed his eggs.

Tris hung her head.

"There's a story there." Wayne rubbed his chin. "Not sure I wanna know."

"I'll do it." Kevin pushed the empty plate back to Wayne. "Leavin' right away."

"I don't like this." Tris looked up at him. "Feels wrong."

He patted her on the shoulder. "Consider this your first paid job then. We should come to an agreement. Twenty percent of all payouts is yours."

"Twenty?" She poked him in the side. "I'm worth more than that. How many people out here you think could've made that upside down behind-the-back shot?"

For an instant, the image of an Infected's serpentine tongue inches from his face played back in his head. He shivered and scraped the rest of his breakfast into his mouth. "Okay, fine. Thirty."

"I'll accept on the condition you agree to consider forty the next time I save your life."

"My car. You're making runs easier, not possible."

Tris twirled some hair around her finger. "So all a girl needs is a car?"

Kevin eyed her. "Hey Wayne, you got any rope?"

She slugged him in the arm.

Wayne laughed as he wandered into the back room. Bee hustled out to take a position behind the bar. The android winked at Tris. A second later, she stood rigid with a startled face that made Kevin think someone stuck a finger in an opening the android lacked. One spark flickered out of the exposed metal under Bee's right eye, and she settled back to a normal human posture.

"It is not perfect," said Bee. "But I feel much better."

The *clonk* of boots on rickety wooden steps echoed from the back room. Wayne emerged from the curtain and set an eight-inch black cube on the bar in front of him. Four raised channels about as wide as his pinky nail glowed with cobalt-blue light in the middle of each face.

"Jesus, Wayne. That looks like it came outta the Enclave." Kevin leaned back.

Wayne covered the box with a rag. "I wouldn't try openin' it. Look, just get it to Glimmertown and give it to Neon at a place called Cloud 9."

"Oh, this keeps getting better and better." Kevin pulled his hand down over his face. Risk and reward battled in his head. *The more time I waste hesitating, the harder this is gonna get.* "Okay."

Tris made a face at him as if he were about to give away her pet dog. "That's drugs, isn't it?"

"Relax." Kevin wrapped the box up in the rag and stood. "What could go wrong?"

Wayne groaned. "Never ask that. God's an asshole."

"Heh, no shit." Kevin headed for the door. At the window, he spotted a pudgy man in New regalia sitting on the Challenger's hood by the charging cable. The man had a mustache as big as a dead sparrow, which twisted with the start of a smile. "Fuck." He jogged back to the bar and handed Wayne the box. "Hold this for a sec. Gotta scrape some bird shit offa my car."

"Careful," said Wayne.

"Railing wasn't me." He jogged out, shoving the saloon doors hard. "Fatass. Off the car."

The porch bounced under him. Four more News, waiting on either side of the door, rushed at him. In his haste to get to the steps, he hadn't noticed them. Kevin roared and threw himself at the closer man on the right, a thirty-something white dude with a scar down his left cheek. The man didn't seem to expect the charge, and Kevin caught him with a fist to the jaw, knocking him into a stagger. The other man on the right, a muscular Native American with long hair, grabbed Kevin by his armored jacket and slammed his back into the wall.

Tris flew in like a white wraith out of the corner of his eye. Her jumping kick connected with the tall, thin New they'd seen the other day, who'd been rushing at Kevin from the left of the door. He went over backward like a dropped plank. Tris ducked two punches from the stocky one before she caught his arm and flipped him over by it, dropping him on his chin.

Long Hair cocked his arm back. Kevin let the shot hit him in the gut, trading it for an elbow to the man's cheek. Scar snarled and wiped blood from his lip. He let out a roar and ran in. Kevin ducked and twisted to his left causing Scar to punch the wall. As the man doubled over cradling his wrist, Kevin moved to kick him in the face, but Long Hair again grabbed him by the armored jacket.

The world blurred as his feet left the ground: ceiling, floor, ceiling, floor, and he smashed into the porch on his chest, seeing stars and unable to breathe. Tris screamed a war cry somewhere nearby. Kevin cringed, expecting the kick to the gut, but none came. Long Hair staggered backward. Tris grunted and snarled. Kevin pushed himself up.

The huge Native American had Tris in a bear hug from behind, pinning her arms. Scar, Stocky, and Wiry converged on her with murder in their eyes. Stocky held up a pair of black military-style handcuffs. Tris let her weight hang in Long Hair's arms. Her legs vanished in smears of blue. They appeared solid for an instant with simultaneous meaty *smacks,* her feet stopped in the crotches of Scar and Wiry. The hit lifted Scar on tiptoe and Wiry a few inches off the ground. Before either man's heels returned to the porch, she'd twisted and kicked Stocky across the face with her left leg, again knocking him into the railing, which broke under the force of impact and dumped him onto the street.

Kevin sucked air into his lungs and jumped on Long Hair. Tris kicked and squirmed. Wiry curled fetal with his hands over his balls, whimpering. Scar seemed to experience a paradoxical effect from a kick in the nuts, going red-faced and enraged instead of stunned. He unwound a length of chain from his waist and spun it up to bash Tris in the head. Kevin let go of Long Hair to intercept, tackling the man flat.

"Damn, this bitch is strong," said Long Hair.

"Get the fuck off me." Tris snarled. "I'm not a fucking bounty."

"Don't matter now," said the man sitting on the hood. "You resisted arrest last time. Now you belong to the News."

Stocky moaned from the road.

Wayne appeared in the doorway, holding a shotgun. He gestured at the railing and flashed a pained expression. "Goddammit. Again?"

"Stay outta this, Wayne," said the hood-sitter. "We followin' the Code."

"Messin' with another man's car while it's parked at a roadhouse is skirtin' the line, Raphael." Wayne leaned back as Kevin grappled with Scar, trying to stay in too close for the chain to work. "Even your dumb ass should know that."

"Dumb?" Raphael yelled. "Where you get off?"

Kevin forced Scar into the wall, squeezing his forearm into the man's neck and getting a close view of the man's name patch. "Road Rash eh? Guess you should learn to ride before you join a pack of morons."

Rash gurgled, unable to get Kevin's arm off his throat. His eyes rolled up.

"He knocks motherfuckers off their bikes," whined the skinny man, still on the ground holding his crotch.

"Yeah, dumb," said Wayne. "Who the hell gives a flying fuck where the Mexican border is now?"

Stocky grabbed the porch and pulled himself upright.

"Cuff this bitch already," said Long Hair, still struggling to contain her.

Kevin let go of Rash, letting him slide to sit on the floor, and ran at the man holding Tris. He grabbed Long Hair's leather at the same instant Tris faked a kick to Stocky's face with her left, and drove her right foot into his groin.

Smack.

The hit echoed loud enough to cause every man on the porch to cringe. Stocky fell to his knees, emitting a high-pitched keening wail. The handcuffs slipped from his fingers and clattered to the porch.

She slipped away from Long Hair as Kevin wrestled him backward. An unexpected fist found Kevin in the forehead and knocked him scrambling for balance as the big man stomped after him. He rolled to the side and got upright a second before Long Hair punched again. His already-tender ribs didn't need another dose, so he threw himself to the right and adopted a boxer's defensive stance.

He traded jabs and blocks with the big man for a few seconds. Rash recovered and got to his feet, heading for Tris with a swinging chain. Wiry limped upright and pulled a knife. Wayne coughed. Tris shrugged the katana off her back, still in its sheath. Kevin looked away to duck an overextended haymaker and capitalized with a right hook to Long Hair's jaw that sent him reeling. A rapid three-smack echoed, like a burst from a low-caliber assault rifle.

Wiry, head turned and spit flying from his lips, tilted back on his heels as if he'd taken a baseball bat to the cheek. Stocky fell to his left, blood spraying from his nose. Rash stumbled away, favoring his broken right arm as the chain fell from his grip. Tris blurred again, smashing the katana once on each of Rash's knees before crowning him with a glancing stroke across the top of his head, all in the span of a second and a half. Kevin winced at the thought of what the attack would've done were the blade exposed.

Rash, unconscious, hit the ground, forearm and knees broken.

"Don't," yelled Wayne, aiming at Raphael.

Kevin managed a two-second look at the revolver in the fat man's hand before Long Hair staggered at him again. The leader of the News stared at Tris with an expression as though he faced off against some manner of demon he needed to send back to hell. Kevin leaned away from the first punch, but the second caught him in the chest and bounced him into the wall next to the door. This time, Long Hair didn't come right in. Kevin coughed and wheezed, searching for a second wind.

Raphael stared at Wayne, though his gun aimed in Tris's direction. "You got a li'l Enclave exile. Ten grand you know. Split it with ya."

"You know as well as I do that's bullshit." Wayne narrowed his eyes. "They'd sooner kill either one of us than pay."

"That's a rumor." Long Hair took a step back, relaxing his posture a little. "They can make all the coins they want. Shit's worthless to them. Won't bother 'em none ta pay."

"Alamo's right, Wayne."

"No, he isn't." Tris faced Raphael. She didn't even seem to be breathing hard. "They don't think of anyone out here as a person. They made the goddamned Virus to wipe everything out so they had nice open land to take over. Do you honestly think a group capable of doing that is going to pay you? Killing you brings them closer to their goal."

"Listen to her," wheezed Kevin. "We're dogs to them."

The Challenger's shocks creaked when Raphael stood. "We can handle it."

"Can you?" Kevin filled his lungs and stepped forward. "Look what one little woman from the Enclave did to your crew. She's not even trained for combat."

Tris glared at him. "I got combat training… two weeks' worth before they sent me out here."

"Two whole weeks." Kevin gazed up at the cobwebs in the porch roof. "Now think about full-time soldiers?"

Raphael's right eye twitched.

"Look," said Kevin. "Why don't you go prick and dick about with the Olds about where Mexico starts and leave us the hell alone. The only reward you're gonna get for her is a painful death."

Tris blurred forward, drawn katana gleaming in the sun. The point stopped at Raphael's neck. "If I even *think* that you and your boys intend to cause me problems, the Wildlands are going to be minus one pack of shitheads."

Silence reigned for a moment. A steady breeze lofted Tris's waist-long hair to the side. Alamo tensed, eyeing Kevin. The other three remained unconscious. Wayne lowered the shotgun. Raphael held his hands up.

"It's only out of respect for Wayne I haven't killed anyone yet." Tris took a step back. "You were about to shoot me in the back. I really should kill you."

Wayne spat over the railing. "I'm a neutral party. I got no 'pinion 'bout it s'long as it ain't my blood hittin' the floor. Then Amarillo gets involved. If you do it on the porch, their shit is mine."

"I'm half tempted to shoot the fat bastard for sitting on my car." Kevin pressed a hand on his side where Alamo hit him. "Damn, you got an arm."

Alamo grunted.

Raphael holstered his revolver. "Come on, let's go."

Kevin glanced at the three still on the ground. "Your boys look tired, Raph. Guess she wore them out."

Wayne handed him the cube. "Clock's tickin'."

"Yeah." Kevin swiped the box. "I'll get right on it."

Bang.

Clatter.

Kevin twitched. His hand slapped on the handle of his .45 as he spun toward the sound. Tris had the Beretta out, inches from the holster. The katana she'd dropped to free her hand had hit the porch after she fired from the hip. Raphael lingered upright for three more seconds, a trickle of blood from the small red hole in the middle of his left eyebrow ran over his nose and dripped from his chin. His revolver fell from his grip, far enough out of the holster to topple over and hit the road.

Kevin glanced at Alamo. "Well, looks like you got promoted."

"Bee," yelled Wayne. "Need ya ta gather some stuff."

"Horseshit." Kevin rounded on Wayne. "He's in the middle of the damn street."

"Her boots were on my porch when she fired." Wayne winked. "Shit belongs to the house."

"Not all of it." Alamo loomed at Wayne. "His cut stays with the News."

Wayne made a 'be my guest' gesture at the big man.

Tris put her gun away and picked up the sword. "It's okay. Let him have it."

"Good eyes," said Wayne. "Was wonderin' if you were gonna see that coming."

Kevin stared at him. "You were—"

"Neutral party." Wayne leaned the shotgun up, balancing it on his shoulder.

Bee slipped through the door behind Wayne, who pointed at Raphael.

Kevin shook his head. He jogged to the plug board and disconnected the Challenger's line before walking it back as the spring-loaded spool pulled it into the fender. Tris passed behind him and stood by the passenger side door. Bee ambled by in front of the car.

Kevin slapped the charging port closed. "How many rounds you got left?"

Tris pulled the Beretta and checked it. "Eleven."

He whirled toward Wayne. "Got any nine?"

Wayne scratched his goatee. "Think so." He raised his voice to a yell. "Bee. Nine mil para?"

"Seventy-four ball and thirteen hollow point." The android seized Raphael by the belt and dragged him toward the side of the roadhouse building.

"Lemme get thirty ball." Kevin keyed in the code to open the car. "She's gonna need it for this one, and I'll take twenty .45 too."

"That's a lot of ordinance. What're ya runnin'?" asked Alamo.

"Tampons," mumbled Kevin. "Whole trunk full. She's a bit of a bleeder."

Tris glared.

"You're a funny man." Alamo grunted and slapped the skinny man until he woke up.

Kevin dropped into the driver's seat, but left the door open while watching Alamo and Stocky drag the still-unconscious Rash off down the street. A few minutes later, Bee emerged with a small cloth sack, which she carried to his window.

"Thanks, Bee."

"Welcome." The android smiled, ducked to wave at Tris, and limped back inside.

Kevin swiped his hand over the switches, causing the dashboard to light up like a Christmas tree. He tossed the ammo in her lap. "Here goes."

Tris glanced down at it and frowned at the 'package' stuffed in the center console. "Did that count for forty percent?"

This girl is scary. He squeezed the wheel, wringing his hands on it. *Heck with it. The longer I'm with this one, the shorter my life will be.*

"Sure."

Silence lasted for a hair shy of an hour before Tris broke it by snapping bullets into the Beretta's magazine. Dry, dusty nothingness streaked by on all sides, the road a line of dark over the endless beige. Kevin's jaw twitched as each bullet clicked in. Half of his brain screamed with worry that the innocent looking, small, wide-eyed girl he sat next to could probably leave him wrapped around a cactus, stranded and car-less for the second time in his recent life.

He watched her with a sideways stare, measuring his odds at taking her out if he had to. From what he'd seen, she didn't seem any stronger than a human could be. *She's definitely stronger than a girl her size should be. Speed's the problem.*

"What are you thinking?" Tris looked up with a hint of a smile.

The red LED ticked up to ninety MPH. At least Route 285 north of Roswell had remained relatively intact. Old abandoned cars and trailers flew by every so often, long ago picked clean of anything worth taking. One disgorged a family of dust-hoppers, startled by an approaching car.

"Wondering if those jackasses are going to cause more trouble."

Tris sighed. "What's wrong with them anyway? They try to grab me and they're acting like we started it."

"They think they're peacekeepers or some shit."

"Yeah right. Keeping the peace by abducting me?" She holstered the Beretta. "Thanks for the ammo. I'll try not to waste it."

"You really only had two weeks of training?" He risked a three-second look away from the road at her.

"Well, yes and no."

"If you don't wanna talk about it…"

Tris flashed an impish smile. "I wasn't sure if your tech-limited mind could handle it. Two weeks of real time plugged into virtual reality. It felt like eight months."

"What, like a dream or something?"

"Close enough." She leaned left to peer at the rearview monitor. "So you've been paid almost ten thousand coins for driving stuff around?"

He flared his fingers up for a second, keeping the wheel steady with his thumbs. "It ain't that simple."

"Driving stuff back and forth?"

"There ain't that many cars left. An' the ones that are ain't in the best shape. They need constant work."

"You're a mechanic?" Tris raised an eyebrow. "The wheel motors on this thing aren't so different from Bee."

"Different enough, and yeah. I've been around cars since I was three."

He steered around a scattering of wreckage, a truck judging by the amount of scrap. "There's parts here an' there, but none of that fancy prewar shit. You wanna drive, you better know how to fix the damn thing."

"If working cars are so rare, why do people shoot at each other on the road?"

Kevin tilted his head side to side. "Couple reasons I can think of. Stupidity, greed, because they can. Someone gets wind of that box of void salt, they're gonna come after us hard. They ain't gonna care about somethin' like one less working car in the world when they're thinking of an easy couple thousand coins."

"That's why it's important for me to get this data out of my head." Tris raked her fingers through her hair, trying to gather it in some attempt at order. "Without the Enclave's manufacturing and tech resources, we're headed straight back to the Dark Ages."

He shook his head. "Maybe humanity will be better off living in small isolated pockets that never talk to each other. The Enclave tried to kill the world. Even if you did have the cure, it's not gonna make them want to play nice."

Tris sighed, and turned away with a hand over her mouth.

Great. Here come the waterworks. He squeezed the wheel.

"Shit." Tris whipped her head around and stared at the center console targeting screen. "Bikes."

Kevin glanced at the door mirror. Sure enough, a pair of motorcycles gained on them. "No sidecar guns." He leaned to his right, almost touching heads with her. A tweak of a button on the steering wheel zoomed in the view. "Doesn't look like any mounted guns. Amateurs."

"Maybe they're not planning to attack us?" Tris glanced at him.

"They are." Kevin couldn't tell from looking if they were electric or ethanol, not that it mattered. Either way, the bikes wouldn't have any problem catching up. "If this thing still had a gas engine, I'd smoke them…"

"How can you know they're hostile?"

"Same guys from Wayne's. No reason they'd come after us unless they overheard what we're carrying."

The man on the left pulled a compact submachine gun out from under his jacket.

"Did you clear the '16 yet?" Tris asked.

"Fuck!" Kevin punched the center of the steering wheel.

"I got it." Tris twisted through the gap in the front seats and crawled into the back. "Can I get to the trunk from inside?"

"Yeah, little pull strap." Kevin swerved left two lanes when the man aimed.

Tris screamed and bumped into his seat.

He cut the wheel the other way. "Sorry."

"No… no… keep doing that. There's a tank of incinerator fuel behind you. Don't get shot."

The idea of catching a biker with the side-mounted flamethrower made him smile. He glanced up and left at the thin steel cable along the roof at the top edge of the window. Effective as it was, if a lucky bullet hit the tank… it would be him going crispy instead of a biker. *I should really move that fucker elsewhere.*

Bullets whizzed overhead and left, ricocheting off the paving. Kevin steered hard toward the barrage, expecting the biker to overcompensate. The next shots hit the road on the other side. Kevin eyed the rear viewscreen. Bike two rode the centerline, trying to line up a shot with a massive revolver.

Crap. He's either an idiot or he's got explosive bullets.

Kevin flicked the arm switch for the rear-facing guns. The AK-47 mechanism still worked, even if the '16 on the other side remained jammed.

"You turned them on?" Tris yelled. "They're moving."

"Can't help it." Kevin feathered the steering wheel, wagging the tail of the car and easing the crosshair over the bike.

A short burst of fire came from the subgun, pinging off the road. At least one slug hit the car—somewhere—with a *clank*. Kevin swerved right, sliding across three lanes.

"Son of a bitch!" He looked over his shoulder at Tris's ass sticking out from a folded-down rear seatback. "You okay?"

"Yeah. Didn't see the hit."

"Hang on to something." Kevin hit the toggle to switch the firing system to the twin M60 machine guns on the hood.

"What are you do—"

Kevin swung the wheel left while simultaneously yanking the parking brake and stomping on an improvised clutch pedal to throw the in-wheel motors to neutral. Tris's question became a scream as the Challenger screeched into a flat spin, tires emitting a banshee's wail.

He jammed down on a glowing red thumb button at the top right part of the steering wheel. Both machine guns went off, throwing three feet of muzzle flare. Bullets raked over the bikes as the car spun past. He let off the brake and clutch as the Challenger completed the three-sixty, powering out of the spin.

The submachine gun biker fell backward off his ride a second before it burst into flames. His body tumbled on the road behind a skidding fireball. Handgun biker broke off his pursuit, guiding his bike to a stop a few seconds later before collapsing. Sweat ran down the sides of Kevin's head; he focused on not rolling or losing control of the car. Once sure he'd recovered, he slowed down, stopped, and backed into a K-turn.

Tris crawled into the passenger seat and held up a single 5.56mm bullet. She twisted it to show off the bottom. "There's your problem."

"No primer." He grumbled. "That's gotta be one of Wayne's."

"Where else do you buy ammo?" Tris blinked at the windshield. "You're going back?"

"Yep." Kevin stopped the car about ten paces from the unexploded bike. "These two idiots made me use about twenty rounds of 7.62. They owe me eighty coins."

Kevin shoved his door open and stood, pulling his .45 at the same time. Handgun biker stopped dragging himself away from his bike. For an instant, he expected the man to beg for help. As soon as a glint of steel flashed by the biker's hand, Kevin fired.

One round to the head.

He took a few steps closer, frowning at the battery fluid pouring in four piss-streams onto the pavement. The M60 had shredded the rear drive wheel and the power cell. He'd need a truck or van to salvage the bike, and he had neither that nor the time.

"You're pretty good at that." Tris walked up behind him. "Hitting the head."

"I hate Infected."

She set off in the direction of the other man. "You know that's a myth, right? Infected are still alive. Shooting them in the heart works fine."

"Yeah… yeah." He stooped to collect a Ruger Super Redhawk in .44 magnum. Much to his disappointment, the bullets looked plain. *An idiot then.* "Well, that'll pay for the ammo I burned on your dumb ass."

He searched the man, collecting nineteen rounds of .44 ammo, a decent sized handful of coins, two knives, and a hip flask. He stood, tucked the Ruger in his belt, and opened the bottle to sniff. Whiskey. He took a small sip, enough to taste but not feel. Fire swam down his throat.

"I got lucky," said Tris. "Other guy had an Uzi. More nine-mil ammo." She wagged a long box magazine at him. "And a spare. Thirty rounds plus whatever's still in the gun."

He glanced at her, noting a leather jacket bundled around a pair of boots under her left arm.

"Not gonna take the clothes?" Tris raised an eyebrow. "Other one's shirt and pants were a bloody mess. Looks like you got three rounds on him. One went through the gas tank and caught him in the dick."

Kevin winced. "Nah. I ain't desperate enough to take a man's clothes."

"Can sell them to Wayne."

"Snort?" He offered her a drink.

Tris stuck the Uzi magazine into the bundle and took the flask. She tilted it back, swallowed, and returned it. "Not bad."

One... two...

Her eyes widened and she coughed. "Okay. Little kick."

"Heh. You want his pants, you take 'em." He hustled to the car and set the Ruger and other loot in the back seat. "Fuckin' primer."

Kevin found random things to look at while Tris relieved the other biker of his boots, and jacket. Impatient, he drummed his fingers on the wheel until she threw the clothes in the back seat on her side and jumped in.

"What's with the look?" Tris pulled her door shut with a heavy *thud*. "Those jackets alone will pay for a meal... unless you wanna wear one."

"Nah. Got a thing 'bout wearing a dead man's stuff. Besides. I like *mine*." He tugged at the nonexistent lapels of his armored jacket. "It's one of a kind."

Tris settled down in her seat. She slid one hand under her hair and rubbed the side of her head, below her left ear. He lost a few seconds staring into space, listening to a barely audible hum from the electronics in the dash.

Kevin spun the wheel all the way right and backed around in a half circle. When the car faced north again, he stopped. "S'pose you are too."

THE COMMON GOOD

A bout two hours after sundown, Kevin headed down an off-ramp toward a cluster of lights that hinted at the shape of a small community. He dropped below thirty as the road went from smashed paving to even rougher dirt. Dim spots on the ground ahead from the feeble headlights warned him of potholes, but only with enough time to brace for impact.

"Skimped on the lights too?" Tris yawned, but didn't bother sitting up from the ball she'd compacted herself into. "I thought Glimmertown would be... brighter."

"This ain't Glimmertown. Place is called Cortez. Bunch of settlers. Beats spending a night out in the open."

She flashed a whimsical grin. "Are you still worried I'm going to steal your car?"

"No." He smiled at her. "But you're not the only one out here."

Buildings, by looks made from box trucks or old semi trailers, stood on either side of a central 'street,' a strip of dirt that seemed to exist as a road more as a product of circumstance than a deliberate attempt to make a place to drive. A handful of steel camper trailers filled in some spaces behind the trucks, among a couple of hand-built shacks. Eight children, ranging in age from five or six to early teens, came out of nowhere and ran alongside the car. All wore handmade clothes, and several were shirtless. Between their youth and long, wild hair, he couldn't tell boy from girl in the dark.

Three adults in long-sleeved flannel shirts and jeans approached after he came to a halt at what appeared to be a central crossroads, where an east-west stretch of path led away from the 'main drag.' An older-looking man with a white beard and two women who may have been his daughters clutched hunting rifles, aimed low and to the side. The man lifted the brim of a camo baseball cap and studied the car.

A muffled mechanical whine emanated from the door as Kevin rolled down his window. A small pair of dark-skinned hands grabbed the edge and a little boy stuck his head in, gawking at the lit-up console. More curious faces appeared in Tris's window, ogling the car. She seemed nervous, and stared at them.

"Evenin' all," said Kevin.

"Howdy," said the man. He stooped to peer in at Tris and nodded in greeting. "Miss." His gaze shifted back to Kevin. "What ya lookin' for, son?"

"Hoping you had a bed for rent, maybe a charge and some food."

Tris yelped. Kevin looked over. A child's face occupied the entirety of the targeting screen, warped by the girl's proximity to the lens. She seemed to have mistaken the camera lens for a peephole. He couldn't help himself at Tris's reaction, and laughed.

"Kids terrify me too." He winked.

She scowled. The four children at her window smiled.

"Think we can help ya out. You got any tradin'?" asked the old man.

The women behind him relaxed their stance. Tris rolled down her window and let the little ones lean in. One boy reached up and touched her hair. The others seemed mesmerized by the lights on the console. The maybe five-year-old behind the car gave up on checking out the camera and climbed onto the trunk. She bounced a few times before walking up the rear window to the roof.

"Gabby, get down from there." The woman to the old man's left slung her rifle over her shoulder and walked up to the car, reaching for the roof. "Sorry, she's a handful."

Childish giggling rang out overhead. The woman collected the girl, who waved at Kevin before being carried a few steps away and set on her feet.

"I think we can 'comma-date yas." The man pointed west. "You read?"

Kevin nodded.

"Stop at the place wit' the sign what reads 'Billy's.' I'll be along in a tick." The old man backed away. "'Mon, kids. Git 'way from the car."

Once the children gave him some space, Kevin tapped the accelerator and turned left. The eighth building on the right looked like it had been an automotive service place before the war. With a forest of solar panels on the roof, it now probably served as the town's source of power. He stopped half in the driveway, eyeing three garage doors. Tris stared into the dark.

"What's got you so nervous?"

"I'm waiting for someone to try and grab me." She seemed unable to let go of the door handle.

"These people are friendly. They ain't gonna grab you."

Tris stared at him. "Try spending a couple days out here with a pair of tits and see how you feel. Everyone looks at me like... Well. Like you know."

Kevin raised an eyebrow. "So you do have emotion."

She sighed. "Go to hell."

"We're already there." He winked.

"Yeah... That's what I'm afraid of."

At the scuff of the old man's boots on dirt, she startled and whipped her head to the right to watch him pass. He drifted out of the 'road,' and walked in front of the car, gesturing at the leftmost garage door. Kevin pulled up to the indicated lane and waited while the elder went inside. Soon, the door rattled its way upward. Once it got high enough to clear, he pulled into the service bay, straddling an open pit in the floor.

Clattering resonated in the air. The old man worked a chain hand-over-hand to close the door. Both spaces to the right were empty of cars, but cluttered with an assortment of ancient automotive diagnostic machines, air compressors, and tools. Kevin shut the Challenger down and got out.

"Appreciate the parking spot." He looked around for a socket. "Where do I plug it in?"

"Name's Brian," said the old man, approaching with an extended hand.

"Kevin." He accepted the shake.

"Underneath in the pit, front wall."

Kevin walked around the nose end of the car and opened the charging port before crouching to peer under the bumper. An old oil cart sat in the pit beneath the Challenger, littered with cylindrical filters and tools. Cracking rubber pads lined the floor, curled and skewed, and a narrow passage near the door side connected to the other two pits. The charging port sat on the wall two feet below his left boot. He lay flat on his chest and stretched to plug in. After a bit of grunting and wriggling, the prongs snapped in, and a *chirp* from overhead indicated a good connection. Cobalt blue light bathed him from above as the enormous battery went into charging mode.

Brian offered him a hand up. "Once you're settled in, I'll send food. Not rightly sure what Jean made though."

"Doesn't matter. Food's food." Kevin stuffed his hand in his jacket pocket, where he'd stashed the dead biker's coins. "What do I owe ya?"

Brian raised both eyebrows at Tris as she trudged over, arms folded tight across her front. He seemed to be staring at the katana. "You folks in trouble or somethin'?"

"Nah. Runnin' a shipment north ta some collector type offa route six. An old book."

Tris narrowed her eyes.

"Ahh. Hell of a thing to risk travel for." The elder smiled. "How's six coins sound? Prefer if ya got somethin' to trade. Ain't got much use for metal chips out here."

"Six is fair." Kevin sifted six quarters out of the handful. He liked getting rid of the big, heavy ones. "Not much else I got you'd be wanting."

"Leather jackets?" asked Tris. "Only two bullet holes."

Brian chuckled. "Let's 'ave a look."

She fetched the jackets from the car and held them up. Brian looked them over.

"Take both of 'em instead?"

Kevin pursed his lips. "Could get five coins for one."

"Aye, ya might." Brian smiled. "Throw in a hot bath and breakfast?"

Tris stared at Kevin.

"Okay." He let the quarters roll down his finger into the pocket.

"Pleasure." Brian took the coats. "'Mon inside. I'll show ya to the guest room."

Kevin followed the old man through a door in the back of the service area, which led to what had once been an office. From there, a flight of stairs led to a second-floor apartment full of clutter. A timid-looking black-haired girl of about eleven sat cross-legged on a ratty couch with a book in her lap, wearing a dress made from an adult's tee shirt. She twisted around as they passed, peering over the back of the sofa at them. Two women, one Brian's age and one in her later twenties, sat facing each other at a small table in the kitchen. Both offered pleasant looks. Brian crossed the living room and entered a narrow hallway. He walked all the way to the end, where three doors surrounded him.

"Straight ahead door is the bathroom. I'll see about some hot water. Trade's good for one batch, so's ya can share it or take turns. Up ta you." Brian pushed open the door to the right. "Kin sleep in here."

Kevin shook Brian's hand again. "Thanks."

The older man nodded and went to the kitchen. Kevin stepped past the doorway, holding it for Tris to follow. The size of the old bed and military aircraft posters on the wall implied the former owner had been a boy.

Tris paused by a dresser full of little league trophies, examining them with a somber expression. "I wonder if he survived." She slipped around him and took a seat on the end of the bed. "Poor kid, he must've been terrified."

Kevin approached the dresser. All of the trophies had the name 'Brian Werner' engraved on them, and seemed to be from third or fourth grade. He held one up for Tris to see. "I think he made it."

She chuckled. "What are the odds it's the same Brian?"

"I dunno." He dropped the plaque back where he found it. "If he was nine or ten when the war happened, he'd be in his early sixties now. Could be."

"Umm, hello?" asked a child's voice. The girl from the sofa leaned in, using one bare foot to push the door open wider. She carried a green bowl in each hand, filled with some manner of stew and a protruding spoon handle. "Gran'pa asked me to bring you food."

Kevin waved her in and sat on the edge of the bed. "Thanks, kid."

"Hannah." The girl walked up to the bed and handed the bowls over, staring at Tris.

A scent reminiscent of gumbo with sausage absorbed his attention. Six spoonfuls later, he looked up at the child, who remained in the same spot, toes clenching and releasing the rug. Her tee shirt dress looked at least three times her age, patched, sewn, and re-patched. Though she had the disheveled appearance common to settlers, she seemed healthy enough.

"What's on your mind, girl?" asked Kevin.

Hanna tilted her head to the right. "Why is her hair white and she's not old?"

Tris smiled. "It's always been this color. I don't know why."

"Same reason yours is black." Kevin winked.

"I've seen lots of people with black hair, but no one ever has white hair." Hanna took a step back. "Did you grow up near radiation?"

Tris shook her head. "Nope."

"Hannah," yelled a woman. "Stop bothering our guests."

"I gotta go." Hannah backed up to the door, where she lingered for a few more seconds before darting out of sight.

An older woman leaned in and smiled. "Sorry about that. She's curious, like her mama was at that age."

Kevin waved her off. "No problem. I don't know what this is, but I'd drive for a week to have another bowl."

"Oh, you." The woman winked. "You're too kind. Ain't nothin' but an old recipe of mine. Brian's sick to tears of it."

"Impossible." Kevin scraped at the bowl.

"Well, you let me know if you need anything. I'm Jean. My daughter's Caitlin."

"Thank you, ma'am." Kevin bowed his head.

A minute or so after Jean walked off, Tris looked at him. "You're not at all worried?"

"Nope. Most people are pretty friendly. Wayne says it's like it was hundreds of years before the war, when horses were still how most got around. People were a lot nicer t'each other back then."

"I've seen historical documentaries about the Wildlands when I was in school. I know what happens to women out here." She shivered. "They're probably acting nice until we're asleep. That girl is creepy. I bet she tries to cut my throat in the middle of the night." Her eyes shot open wide. "Oh, no! What if this is people we're eating?"

Kevin smirked. "What 'historical documentaries' did you see?"

Tris glanced up in thought for a second. "Umm, *Mad Max*, *Damnation Alley*, *Cyborg*, and *Escape from New York*."

He burst out laughing.

Tris scowled. "What?"

Tears flowed out of his eyes. He cradled the precious bowl so he didn't drop it until he got control of himself. "Historical documentaries? Really?"

She growled. "What!"

"Those are old-ass movies. Fiction. Pre-war stuff making up what it would be like after a nuclear war."

"Doctor Gaurav said the Enclave had surveillance drones out in the Wildlands, and they recorded those images."

"Holy shit." Kevin leaned forward, still chuckling. "Tris, it's bullshit. Have you ever heard of Hollywood?"

She stirred her food. "Yeah. It was one of the first major population centers struck by nuclear weapons. The enemies of the old United States attacked it as a symbolic gesture against capitalism and Western ideals."

"Right. Do you know why they felt that way?"

Tris squinted.

"They made movies there. All those 'documentaries' they showed you are fictional. None of it is real. Humans don't all degenerate into mindless savages the instant there's no longer organized law. Where do you think organized law came from in the first place?"

She stared at the rug. "Umm…"

"There's something about disasters and living with the constant threat of imminent death. It awakens some instinctual need for people to come together and help each other. Most settlers you run into out here are good people."

"I'm not sure I believe you." She sniffed a spoonful of stew. "Why would the Enclave lie about that?"

"If you have to ask that, you're a lot more clueless than I gave you credit for."

A knock at the door preceded Brian peeking in. "Bath's hot."

Kevin glanced at her. "You go first."

She smiled for a few seconds before nervousness overwhelmed her.

"Course, if you don't want to be alone."

Tris made her sad-eyes at him and looked back and forth from him to the door. "If you want."

"Do you?" He smiled. "It's been a little while for me. I might touch something I'm not supposed to."

Her cheeks and nose went from porcelain to pink. "I trust you."

Well, shit… she's offering. Who am I to say no? "Lead on."

He stood, shrugged out of his armored jacket, and removed his boots. Tris kicked her shoes off and padded out the door. The bathroom, two steps from the bedroom, had already filled with steam. He followed her in and nudged the door closed before locking it. Tris pulled the leather shirt off over her head, causing a cascade of cottony white hair to spill down over her back. Kevin set his .45 atop the toilet tank in easy reach of the bathtub and pulled his shirt off as Tris worked her way out of her jeans, pushing them and her panties down at the same time.

Kevin momentarily forgot how to work a belt buckle.

Tris looked over her shoulder at him. He couldn't reconcile the thought of a woman with such a slender figure kicking a man hard enough to smash a railing. Gazing at the little heart-shaped gap between her perfect thighs brought a grunt of discomfort as his interest struggled to break out of his jeans.

What is she up to?

She tested the water with a toe before smiling and lowering herself in to sit. "It's perfect."

He discarded the rest of his clothes and hopped in facing her. Two seconds later, every muscle in his back locked.

"Shit! It's hot!" His teeth chattered.

Tris took a bar of soap from a recessed cubby in the wall. "I wasn't expecting this place to feel so... normal."

It took a minute for him to settle in, millimeter by millimeter as his skin adapted to the temperature. He stared at her breasts, large A-cups or small Bs, hovering a few inches over the steam-shrouded water. Her blasé demeanor raised his guard, a too-sudden shift from modesty to not caring.

"I'm telling you." He eased himself against the tub wall, trying to acclimate to the water. "Most people are normal."

She worked the soap up and down her arms and over her chest. He couldn't pull his gaze off wherever her hands moved.

"We shouldn't stay here long." She aimed a nervous glance at the door. "Turn around. You are filthy."

He did and rested his elbows on his knees. She rubbed the soap over his shoulders and into his hair. As Tris leaned in close enough for her nipples to graze across his back, his 'little warrior' sprang to attention again, forgetting how hot the water was. Kevin groaned.

Tris whispered at his ear. "If these people are nice, I'd prefer we get out of here before the Enclave comes for me. I don't want them to get hurt."

Kevin reached up and grasped her hand, which rested on his shoulder. Eye contact. Her face hovered close enough to kiss. "They think you're dead."

"I'm not." She bit her lower lip. "Because of you."

Kevin twisted sideways and ran a finger over the spot he'd cut. *Not even a scar...*

She shivered and squirmed, evidently ticklish.

"Yeah, don't get used to it. I'm usually an asshole." He smiled. "Rare attack of conscience."

Tris covered her mouth to mute a giggle. She brushed a soapy hand over his forehead and worked her fingers through his shoulder-length hair. Droplets hit the water in front of him, exploding into small clouds of grime. "When you said it's been awhile, did you mean a bath or being with a woman?"

"Yes."

"I can tell." She smirked at his crotch, and at how grey the water had become.

"You don't have to do this as some kind of thank you." *You're an asshole, not an idiot. She's offering. Take it.* "Really."

"What if I want to?" She leaned closer, pushing him backward until he lay almost flat, with only his head above the water. "Do you want to?"

"I could be talked into it. But it might take a bit of do—" He closed his eyes as she lowered herself to kiss him.

Water lapped at the sides of the tub as they writhed, joined at the lip for several minutes. She pushed up, gasping for breath and smiling. The soap bumped his shin, bobbing in the water, forgotten at the other end. He ran a hand up her thigh and over her hip.

"I've only done this a couple of times before." She put on a demure expression he wasn't inclined to trust. "But I've seen a lot of historical documentaries about it."

Kevin muffled a laugh into the crook of her neck. She giggled.

A PATCH OF MOONLIGHT GLOWED ON THE WALL PAST THE FOOT END OF THE bed, a skewed rectangle taller on the right side. The silhouette of an old combat aircraft, a 'Raptor' according to the poster, lurked in shadow near the corner. Kevin let his gaze wander to the ceiling. Tris lay flat on her back next to him, using his right bicep as a pillow, her head turned toward him. More relaxed than he could ever remember being, he closed his eyes and waited for sleep.

Scattered gunfire went off in the distance.

Tris shot upright, staring at the window.

"It's not the Enclave." He put a hand on her shoulder and tugged. "Relax."

"I thought you said people are friendly."

Kevin yawned. "There's always the exception. Besides, they might be shooting at a dust hopper or coyotes."

Soft, rapid *thumps* vibrated the floor with the cadence of a child running. A door out in the hallway opened and slammed.

Two more shots split the silence with sharp *cracks*. A woman's voice yelled something like "Over there."

"Aren't you going to help?" She leaned over him, trying to peer out the window. After a few seconds, she lay back down.

"Whoever it is ain't shooting at us." He closed his eyes again. "Ammo's expensive."

18

GLIMMERTOWN

T he Challenger devoured miles of road in relative silence. A pervasive rattle seemed minor enough to dismiss for the time being, but constant enough he couldn't stop wondering about it. If the nozzle for the incendiary chem sprayer had been knocked loose, using the weapon could send a stream of flames onto the back of his head. If the noise came from one of the rear-mounted rifle mechanisms, it presented less of an issue. Inaccuracy didn't kill… at least not right away. *Can't be drive train, sounds too light.*

He glanced sideways at Tris. Since the sun had gone down after a full day of driving, she'd settled in the passenger seat and closed her eyes. Fleeting memories of last night in the bathtub played a slideshow in his head, punctuated by scenes of what she'd done to the News. Crossing *that* line with her left the aftertaste of a guilt cocktail boosted with dread in his mouth. Guilt as though he'd taken advantage of an innocent girl in need mixed with fear he'd slipped further into a bog he'd not be able to get out of. Not that he had much of an attention span to spare in the midst of it, but she *had* seemed to be enjoying herself… not merely waiting for it to be over.

With the exception of Zephyra's working girls, only one other woman had offered sex so soon after meeting him—and she stole the Marauder. Kevin missed everything about that truck, from the chromed skull gearshift knob to the two-inch armor plating. *That old war-wagon got me through 8320 coins.* It wasn't fast, but it didn't need to be. He tried to figure out what her motivation was. Maybe it'd been some kind of desperation play to make him want to protect her. Perhaps nothing more than a 'thanks for saving my life.' He shrugged. *Maybe she just wanted to get laid.*

Pitch black horizon held no answers to his wandering gaze.

Kevin sighed, making Tris stir. She looked at him with half-open eyes, stretched, and sat up with a yawn. A swath of artificial light simmered along the horizon, filtering among innumerable tangled iron girders and struts. The unmistakable radiance of Glimmertown set him on edge. This was as 'civilized' as the Wildlands got, which meant it wasn't civil at all. His own voice replayed in his mind, telling Tris most people were friendly.

Okay, bit of a white lie there. Most people... except the ones in Glimmertown.

"Salt Lake?" Tris looked away from a green blur passing outside her window.

Kevin chuckled. "Not anymore."

"Are you sure?" All traces of sleep faded from her eyes. "Wasn't it a major population center. Infected?"

Kevin shook his head. "Doesn't matter. Glimmertown'll chew up and spit out anyone that doesn't have money... Even Infected."

"What are we walking into?"

He shrugged. "Gambling, drugs, prostitution... When I was little, they weren't much different from a pack of bandits. They shot up settlements, took slaves, chased down drivers like me. Eventually, there were so many of them, people moved in on their own. They didn't need to raid anymore 'cause they got all they needed comin' to them."

Tris scowled. "I already don't like the place."

Gravity lessened for an instant as the Challenger crested the top of a small hill in the road. Up head, a blinding light source hung in the air above a walled-in settlement a few miles square. The glare came from a forty-four-foot scaffold tower bedecked with hundreds of headlights, light bulbs, stadium gas lamps, and anything else they could find. An expanse of buildings, many made from old vehicle parts, surrounded the spire. Outside the walls of Glimmertown, the ruins of old Salt Lake City sprawled over the earth. The war had pulverized many of the prewar structures into a bed of rubble reminiscent of a Japanese Zen garden. A handful of tents and small trailers stood around the outskirts, casting long shadows in the glow from the central spire.

Kevin slowed to thirty along a cracked-but-navigable stretch of highway. A half-mile from the edge of the rebuilt city, dividers sat horizontally across the road, alternating left and right. Reflective flakes embedded in the concrete flickered in his sweeping headlights. The back and forth route around the barriers forced the Challenger down to a slow creep.

"We could walk faster than this," said Tris. "I feel like a target."

Kevin kept his gaze on the men with rifles watching them from the safety of nooks nearest the ends of each switchback, clad in tattered leather and old military body armor.

"That's the point. Welcome to Glimmertown."

"They don't look happy to see us," said Tris.

Kevin locked eyes with one and offered a nod of greeting. The man didn't react. "I don't think they're happy to see anyone."

The gauntlet ended at a courtyard framed on all sides by fifteen-foot fences capped with razor wire, which connected to the city's outer wall. Traces of curb hinted that the open space used to be an intersection between two huge streets. To the left sat a long yellow and red building with six garage doors and a window full of old hubcaps sandwiched between yellowing blinds and glass. A brothel took up most of the right wall, judging by the suggestive nature of the spray-painted figures adorning it and a cluster of half-dressed women by the door. Straight ahead, in the center of the reinforced fence, a person-sized opening led into Glimmertown proper.

"Guess we walk from here?" asked Tris.

Kevin pulled up to the garage. "Yeah. In a town where everyone's trying to screw each other over, the last thing they want is wheels. Makes it too easy to get away I guess." He opened his door. "Do me a favor? Watch the car."

Tris pulled the Beretta out and smiled at him. "Okay."

Kevin trotted to a garish pink door between the window and the garage bays and walked in. Behind a desk covered in wood paneling, an Asian man, shirtless save for a black leather pistol harness, looked up from a functioning flat panel monitor. He flashed a broad grin, making his jawline almost a perfect square. Tons of color printouts of naked women adorned the wall to the man's left, their poses varying degrees of 'artistic.' On his right, a similar collage of nude men papered the other wall.

"Hello, friend. Welcome to the garage. I am Takeshi. Are you in need of a parking space, a charge, repairs, or modifications? I have an extensive selection of customization options available. Everything from paint to onboard weaponry. I'm particularly fond of large missiles."

Kevin let out a *hmph* noise. "Not like I can drive in. Charge too."

"Excellent. Storage fees are ten coins per day and—"

"Ten? Are you nuts?"

Takeshi paused with the same placid smile on his face. "And that includes the charge. You could park out there in the quad, however, ten coins is much cheaper than buying a new car."

Kevin glared.

"You misunderstand me, friend." Takeshi held his hands up in a gesture of innocence. "I would have nothing to do with any misfortune that befalls your vehicle. This place is full of thieves you see."

"Yeah, I see." Kevin leaned on the counter. "And I'm looking at one of them."

The man's saccharin smile showed no signs of denting. "If my services exceed your budget, you could always have your associate remain on guard duty." Takeshi lowered his voice. "But, in this city, they'll steal her too."

"Five, and even that's about double a fair rate."

Takeshi brought his hands together in front of him. "Ah, friend. This is Glimmertown. Nothing about this place is fair."

Kevin pinched the bridge of his nose.

"I will accept six per day, plus a trade of you or your associate posing." Takeshi indicated his wall of 'art.'

"Ten is fine." Kevin counted ten coins out of what he'd taken from the biker. A quick feel said he had at least a hundred or so left.

Takeshi poked a finger at his monitor. "Door four."

A distant motor whirred to life, amid the clattering of a chain. Kevin pushed the coins over a scuffed laminated calendar for 2018.

Takeshi bowed at him. "How long do you expect to stay?"

"One night, if I can help it."

"Glimmertown has a way of getting under your skin." Takeshi winked.

Kevin shook his head and walked out. "That's what I'm worried about."

By the time he got to the car, the fourth garage door had opened all the way, revealing an empty bay with a hydraulic lift. He grumbled again at the price and got in.

"What's wrong?" Tris put the Beretta away. "Your face is red."

He backed up, spinning the wheel under his palm as fast as he could wind it. "Son of a bitch is charging ten coins a night to park."

She trotted alongside. "That's crazy. Maybe I could show a little skin and get a discount."

"Nah. I don't think it'd matter." He parked on the jack and killed the switches.

The door motored down as soon as he stopped. Kevin grabbed 'the box' and got out, heading for a walkway separated from the garage bays by a painted red line. Bay three held an orange van with too-small tires and numerous gun ports for people inside to use handheld weapons. A silver sedan with white leather interior parked in the next space, not a scratch on it. Bay one had a pair of motorbikes refit with electric wheel motors.

"I'm surprised he didn't make them rent two spaces," muttered Kevin.

"I did," said Takeshi from behind the wall. "They are each paying."

Kevin pushed the flapping red door open and headed for the way out. Tris hesitated. He glanced back and found her eyeing the 'wall o' nudes.' She turned away from it, gaze down, a trace of a smile on her lips.

He headed left out of the garage, following the ghost of a sidewalk around the perimeter. At the middle of the north edge, a person-sized gate offered entry to Glimmertown proper. Despite it being well after sundown, the city was bathed in light. Most came from the tower, though hundreds of neon signs hung in windows along the main drag, buzzing, flickering, and flashing.

Glass tubes in the form of pink and orange breasts wagged in some, glowing green silhouettes of playing cards flashed in others. Many of the rest advertised prewar beers or sports teams, hung for the sake of having more neon. Kevin headed in a straight line, ignoring small clusters of prostitutes or hawkers trying to lure them into gambling houses. He stuck his hand in his left jacket pocket and cradled the lump of coins.

Every so often amid the smell of rust and dirt, a lick of something edible drifted by. Tris lagged behind a few paces when they passed a weapon store, checking out the guns hanging on a pegboard behind a short, older man who appeared to have steel wool attached to his face.

"Trust nothing here," said Kevin. "As soon as you bring anything out of the store, the bastard who sold it to you 'never saw you before.'"

"Is *everyone* here out to cheat?" She took a few quick steps to catch up.

"More or less."

He headed in the direction of the artificial sun overhead, arriving in

Glimmertown's central square about fifteen minutes after passing the gate. Atop what may once have been a fountain stood a drunken idiot's rendition of the Eiffel tower, if it had been built with scrap metal, old cars, and no understanding of straight lines. Three of the storefronts around the square belonged to what might be called restaurants, if one felt generous. One had the look of a hotel, a couple looked like general stores, and a handful were casinos. The largest of those, a silver-and-white structure with more than its fair share of chrome trim, bore the name 'Cloud 9' in silver spray paint over a set of powder blue double doors with round, black windows.

Four men wearing what passed for fancy suits in Glimmertown flanked the entrance, each with submachine guns.

"That thing is gonna fall." Tris shielded her eyes and peered up at the tower.

Kevin shrugged. "Been there at least six years or so."

"Where's that cable go?"

He followed her stare to a wire as thick as his wrist, draped between the tower and the hotel. It paralleled the street heading north, in a series of swinging arcs mounted to rooftops and poles.

"Solar farm, north of here." Kevin crossed the courtyard, marching straight for Cloud 9. "This place has more power than it knows what to do with. Why else do they waste it on light?"

"Some species of fish hunt by making light in the dark ocean." Tris hovered close behind him. "They're trying to lure people in."

A tan, stocky meathead to the left of the door raised a hand. "Hold up. You ain't dressed nice enough."

Kevin suppressed the urge to roll his eyes. "I'm not here for fun. Got a delivery for Neon."

"That's a dangerous load of bullshit to sling." The man's eyebrows furrowed.

"Ain't BS," said Kevin. "Go ahead and ask him if he's expecting a little box."

All four thugs looked at Tris.

Kevin scowled. "Not her."

"Alright man. You wanna roll them dice, go on in." A thin six-footer on the right with a massive cluster of butt-length dreadlocks smiled.

Music, some manner of guitar-heavy rock from before the war, leaked from tinny speakers somewhere overhead. Most of the interior contained red-cushioned bench seats with more chrome trim around booth tables.

A bar sat on the left, beyond which a small stage held a trio of women dancing in cages, wearing black lacy bras and almost-nonexistent thongs.

Kevin shot a quick glance around the room, noting numerous couples seated at various tables. All were dressed in some sad attempt to recreate expensive high-society clothes from scavenged prewar garments. The women had low-cut necklines and shimmery gowns; a few had high heels. Mismatched logo tee shirts, flannel scraps, denim, and colored cloth stitched together into monstrosities as if someone had tried to recreate Old West Saloon dresses.

Three men sat at the bar, in more austere attire, riding leathers, armor panels, and heavy boots. Tris squeezed his arm and directed his attention with a pointed glance at a young blonde woman struggling to clean a table. Her wrists were locked in cuffs linked to leg irons by a chain, preventing her from raising her hands higher than her waist. She had to climb into the bench seat to wipe a rag at a smear of sauce on the formica. A length of dingy white cloth tied around her waist and between her legs attempted to be clothing, helped along by another strip over her breasts.

Another 'waitress' across the room sported leg irons in addition to a cheerleader miniskirt and white lace bra. Her dark hair hung wild, almost hiding a bruise on her light brown cheek. Kevin closed his eyes.

Not my problem.

"Are they slaves?" Tris snarled. "We have to—"

"We should keep our heads down," whispered Kevin. "Unless you want to wind up waiting tables here yourself. Don't start any shit."

She shot him a wounded look. He put an arm around her and pulled her close enough to whisper in her ear. "Look, it's not like I don't *want* to. No one deserves that… but this is Glimmertown, and shit doesn't work that way here. I can't take out fifty guys."

Tris's eyebrows moved together. "I only see five."

"Out in the open…" He got quiet as heavy footsteps thudded up behind them.

"Yo," said a deep voice. Meathead One pointed to the nearest table. "Have a seat while we check wit' Neon."

The other patrons glanced at him as he walked over to the indicated table, staring down their noses at him. He basked in their derision. *They have no damn idea how much coin I got.* Kevin smiled at them, which seemed to further piss them off. These idiots probably thought *two* thousand coins was a fortune.

A moment after they settled in, the blonde who had been wiping the other table shuffled over. Around her neck, a thin leather choker sported a round brass disc stamped with a number twelve. It didn't seem sturdy enough to be a restraint, but in this town, the symbolism was enough.

She raised her hands up to her navel, making the chain *clink,* and waved. "Hi. Welcome to Cloud 9. I'm Barbie. What can I get you?"

"Barbie?" asked Tris. "Really?"

The girl looked downcast. "My name is whatever Neon says it is. I'm his."

This one must be on someone's shit list. She can barely move. Kevin made it a point not to look at her—or Tris. *Two hundred fifty coins. In and out. No complications. Not my circus; not my monkeys.*

"How are you supposed to carry our food like that?" asked Tris.

"I manage." 'Barbie' puffed at a strand of hair in her face, twisting at her handcuffs as she spoke. "The dust hopper soup is fresh. We've also got yam fries, meatloaf, and chicken."

"Soup," said Kevin. "Water too."

"Same." Tris tried to stare holes in Kevin's face.

"Okay." Barbie shuffled across the aisle to retrieve a bin of dirty dishes from the other table, and drifted off amid the clatter of leg irons that didn't even allow her a normal walking stride.

Tris tapped her fingernails on the worn faux-wood Formica table. "Bet those dancers are locked inside."

"We are not going to piss in Neon's Wheaties. We're here to deliver a package, get paid, and get out."

"What possible reason can you have for leaving them here?" Tris leaned close as she whispered.

"Not wanting bullets in my ass and a chain around *your* neck too." Kevin grabbed her hand. "I'm no crusader. All I want is a nice quiet life selling food and booze to other idiots young enough to get shot at for a living. I did my time. I'm done with it."

"All that's necessary for evil to win…" Tris folded her arms. "You're not old."

Kevin chuckled. "I'm twenty seven. For a driver, that's a damn old man. If you live to see nineteen, you'll understand."

She frowned. "Too late. I'm twenty."

A dark skinned woman with shoulder length black hair and a delicate frame carried a tray full of drinks to another table. Her gauzy shirt, ankle-long skirt, and lack of restraints made Kevin gesture.

"See? They're not all slaves. That one's even got shoes."

Tris frowned. "More likely she's never tried to run away. She's still got a price tag on her neck."

"Huh?"

"You didn't notice?" Tris tapped her throat. "They've all got a tag on with numbers. Probably how much it costs to fuck them. Barbie's said twelve, and she's not that young. It's gotta be a price."

"Or maybe their auction ID." Kevin clenched his hands into fists. "You're trying to talk me into doing something stupid."

"You know it's wrong. Transporting drugs is bad enough, but you can't look away from what's happening to these people."

"Let's get paid first, then we'll talk."

I'm an asshole... it's what I do. Ain't no money in it. Only thing I'll get paid in is lead.

She didn't try tears, though a little red ringed her eyes. Sapphire irises darkened as she stared at him without another word until Barbie returned with a death grip on the edge of a round serving tray.

The woman shoved it onto the table before gingerly grabbing one of the bowls of soup in both hands and climbing half in to the bench seat with Kevin in order to put it in front of him. Tris reached over and took her bowl.

Barbie offered a weak smile.

"It's stupid to make you work like that." Tris scowled. "You'd be more efficient if you could use your hands."

"It forces me to get close to customers so they can touch me and pay for..."

"She got a hold of a weapon once." Kevin didn't look up. The barely-dressed figure in the periphery of his vision froze. A strip of thin cloth dangling at her knee level fluttered back and forth. He ate one spoonful of soup. "You did, didn't you?"

"Knife," whispered Barbie. She grasped Tris's drink and climbed onto her seat so she could reach to set it close. "Luisa tried to run away two months ago. You're Enclave aren't you?"

"Not anymore," muttered Tris. She watched the unchained woman cross the room with a tray of beer mugs. "Is that one going to be a problem?"

Kevin kept his attention in his food.

"Shailaja? No. She is not happy either." Barbie chafed at her restraints. "Please get me out of here. I can't take this anymore. They never let me out of these fucking things."

"Any coins in it?" asked Kevin.

Barbie glared. Tris kicked him in the shin.

"Hey, I had to ask." He looked up at Barbie, catching a glint from the brass tag at the front of her thin leather collar. "Need to think on it."

Barbie hung her head, backed out of the seat, and started to shuffle away.

"Hey," said Kevin.

"Yes?" The waitress glanced back over her shoulder.

Kevin smiled. "Still got that rag?"

19

A SPECIAL KIND OF STUPID

Kevin scraped the last of the dust hopper soup out of the black bowl. It wasn't bad, but it couldn't hold a candle to Jean's stew. Tris ate while continuing to stare at him. The three dancers gyrated in their cages, entertaining a group of men seated at round tables in front of the stage. Two men leaned on the wall to the right, submachine guns at their side. A knuckle-dragging mouthbreather with long, brown hair lurked in the shadows near the cages, though his weaponry appeared limited to a sledgehammer. Behind the bar, an older man, missing a left arm and wearing an eyepatch, seemed low on the threat scale. *He's probably got the biggest damn gun in the place.*

"Two on the right with MAC-10s," said Kevin. "Paul Bunyan over by the cages has a sledgehammer. Might have a handgun concealed. Bartender's gonna be a problem."

"How do you know his name?" Tris finally broke her stare to look around.

"Books." Kevin hung his head. "Ugh."

Tris raised an eyebrow. "Bartender's old and he's missing an arm. Don't forget the four goons outside."

"Goons?" Kevin chuckled. "Normal people don't use that word. Bartender's dangerous because he looks harmless. He's probably got a roomsweeper under the bar."

"What the hell is that?"

Kevin finished off his water. "Automatic shotgun."

The clatter of light chain dragging on the floor announced Barbie walking up behind him. She stopped at the edge of the table, resting her hands on it. "Was everything okay? Do you want anything else?"

I'm an idiot. He managed to keep the annoyance off his face while gazing into Tris's pleading eyes. *So close to ten grand... I'm going to die within sight of my roadhouse.*

Kevin pulled the damp rag she'd been using to wipe tables out from under her fingers. He snuck the P226 off his belt and wrapped the gun in the cloth. Barbie nodded. He set it on the seat to his left, out of sight between him and the wall. "Nah, we're good."

"Seven coins please," said Barbie.

He dropped the money into her upturned palm. The cuffs looked like standard pre-war police hardware, easy enough to pick when it wouldn't get anyone shot to do so. "Thanks."

Barbie eyed the rag, and shuffled to the bar to hand over the payment.

"Yo," said a deep voice. Tall and Dreadlocked waved. "Neon's ready for you."

The room got quiet.

"This guy sounds like a happy ball of fun." Kevin slid out of the seat and stood.

Tris followed.

The other three meatheads from the front shadowed them as they crossed the restaurant portion of Cloud 9. Dreadlock pushed past a pair of swinging double doors covered in red padded leather with little buttons in three rows. Dim light emanated from clamshell sconces made of frosted glass every few feet along both walls of the corridor beyond. They passed two smaller doors on the right, labelled 'men' and 'women.' Another set of double doors fifteen yards from the first offered the only other path.

A huge wooden desk stood on the far side of a square burgundy colored throw rug, at the center of a large office. Kevin stared at the fluorescent blue hair on the man seated behind it, glowing from the effect of ceiling-mounted blacklights that made his blazer appear luminous indigo. Eerie green luminescence emanated from in-wall fish tanks along the left, though it was likely many years since anything lived in them.

"Ah, that was fast." The man who had to be Neon smiled. "I wasn't expecting the shipment for at least another few days."

The four thugs formed a wall of meat behind Kevin and Tris, blocking them off from the door. Kevin approached the desk with the usual 'I'm not up to anything' slowness he'd become accustomed to in such situations. He held the cloth bundle high and unwrapped the black cube with cobalt blue light strips down the sides.

"Cargo like this, it pays not to waste time." He set the cube on the desk and took a step back.

"Quite true." Neon's iridescent blue eyes twinkled. He leaned forward and pressed his thumb on a small spot of gloss amid the otherwise flat black surface.

The top split down the middle, opening like the hatch of an old missile silo. Four trays rose one after the next, pivoting to the sides like an aluminum flower. A fifth tray clicked into place in the center. Each pad held a twelve-by-twelve grid of one-inch glass ampules, containing about six drops worth of violet liquid apiece—720 doses of a drug called void salt.

Neon plucked one out, upending it to appraise the quarter-inch needle protruding from a plastic cap. He held it under his nose, sniffed once, and replaced it in the pod before a light touch on the glossy square caused the cube to motor closed.

"It's all there," said Kevin. "I'm supposed to collect 2700 coins. No offense, but this is an official contract from the roadhouse network. Everything by the book."

"Oh, ye of little faith." Neon clucked his tongue. "I have no intention of reneging on the arrangement. Bad deals create supply problems in the future. I do, however, want to make you an additional offer."

Dammit. You're done. 250 coins and it's roadhouse time. Get out. "I'm not sure I'm for hire right now."

"Oh, I don't wish to hire you." Neon smiled, touching all his fingertips together in front of his face. "You've got quite an exotic little beauty with you. I'd like to take her off your hands. Say, 1800 coins?"

Fuck. Kevin bit his lip. There it was. All set. Done. Finished. No more runs. Roadhouse. Beer, food, and guns to idiots. He glanced at her and puckered his lips so hard they had to resemble an asshole. A wounded look formed on her face. *Yeah, I'm an asshole...* "She ain't up for sale. Ain't mine to sell."

Neon's smile fell flat. "Let me rephrase then. I'll pay you a thousand coins then to do nothing. Glimmertown belongs to me, and I always get the things I want." He stood. "And I want this fuck toy."

Kevin cringed inside as two of the meatheads seized Tris by the arms from behind, right below her armpits.

"She'll bring in a lot of coins," said Neon. "What's she eighteen maybe? Exotic hair…"

Meathead Three grabbed her Beretta.

"I can't wait to break this tiny little ass in," said Dreadlock.

Tris's hands moved in a blur, appearing solid for an instant as she swiped pistols from the belts of the men holding her. Before Kevin could open his mouth to shout, she crossed her arms and fired both guns, nailing each man in the side of the head. A patch of scalp with a long trailing wad of dreadlocks stuck to the wall. She stepped forward, raising her arms and firing backward over her shoulders, squeezing off three shots from each pistol at a speed fast enough to pass for automatic fire. Meaty slaps preceded the *thud* of two bodies hitting the ground behind them.

Kevin got his .45 out and aimed at Neon. "Methinks the lady doth protest."

"This 'tiny little ass' isn't on the market." Tris scowled.

"Hold on." Neon raised a hand. "You don't understand this situation very well. I own this town. You'd have to be some special kind of stupid to piss me off." He smiled, though a trickle of sweat ran down the side of his head, glinting in the wavering emerald light from the fish tank. "I've never seen someone with moves like that. Perhaps we could come to an arrangement?"

"What kind of arrangement?" asked Kevin.

Tris adjusted her grip on her guns, a Glock and a Sig. "I don't trust him. He'd only come after me for revenge, plus he's a slaver pig."

"There's a certain problem of mine that needs eliminating." Neon smiled.

"Assassination isn't my scene," said Kevin.

"I wasn't trying to hire *you*." Neon tilted his head. "This girl is a lot more than she appears to be. Besides…" He gestured at the dead men. "You'd better make it your scene. I can't let something like this go without some kind of response. Bad for business, you see."

"You're not in the best negotiating position right now." Kevin focused on the .45 in his hand, rendering Neon in blur.

"Neither are you." Neon eased his weight back into his chair. "Official roadhouse business and all. Isn't killing the client against your 'code?' You could say no, but one way or another, this girl is going to work for me. Either on her feet or on her ba—"

Bang.

Neon's iridescent blue eyes became gaping voids; the back of his head exploded in a spray of gore. He rocked back in the seat, still with a cocky grin on his face, and slumped down.

Trails of smoke wisped from both of Tris's guns.

"Fuck." Kevin let his arm fall limp at his side. "You're not much for planning stuff out are you?"

"Nah." She lowered her weapons. "Guess I'm that special kind of stupid."

DREAM KILLER

Kevin kicked the front of the desk. "Goddammit!"

Neon slid farther down in his chair, mouth gaping. Blood ran from empty eye sockets, down his cheeks like tears. The music from the main room was at least loud enough to mask the gunfire. That, plus no one expected two on five would have had any chance. If anyone had heard gunshots, Kevin and Tris were the ones they'd assume got the bad end of it.

Kevin headed for a curtain a few feet behind the fish tank where a hint of a safe poked out.

Locked.

He ransacked the desk drawers. Tris threw Neon to the floor and went through his pockets. The drawers held little of any use: old ledgers, a few music CDs, spent brass, post-it note pads, pens that probably hadn't worked in decades, and a couple of bottle caps. Kevin pocketed some jewelry, hoping it wasn't costume crap.

"Found the keys." Tris, near a folding table on the right side of the room, held up a jingling bundle.

"Great. No money." He grabbed the cube. "You do realize that it's on me to get the payment for the shipment right? How the fuck am I gonna retire if I get a rep for killing the damn clients."

"*You* didn't kill him." She smirked. "You didn't even get a single shot off."

Kevin looked at the two men by the door. One took all three slugs, two to the chest and one right in the nose. The other man only got hit once, but it caught him in the forehead. "You're starting to scare me, Tris."

"Starting?" She winked. "Glock 17 and another 226." She tossed the Sig to him.

He caught it and stuffed it in his belt on his way to search the two by the door. Both had MAC-10s. After slinging the weapons over his shoulder on their straps, he plucked three spare magazines and a knife.

"Don't take their clothes this time. One, no one with any self-respect will wear this shit. Two, we don't have time."

Kevin wrapped the cube in the cloth, and hurried out.

Tris jogged behind him.

He slowed from storming to trudging at the second set of double doors and slipped into the restaurant area as though nothing went wrong. *Hope no one notices the new guns.* Barbie hovered by the table they'd been using. She looked over her shoulder at him. At the sight of him heading for the exit, she seemed ready to burst into tears.

The waitress with the miniskirt and leg irons, Luisa according to Barbie, eyed him from across the room, as if aware of some manner of plot. After a quick look at the cages, and all three girls staring at him, he stopped, gazing at his boots. Tris bumped into him.

Shit. Why did I have to go and make eye contact? That one in the middle cage is too young.

"Well, I suppose if we're going to stir some shit, we might as well bring it to a boil."

She grinned.

Kevin directed a meaningful look at Barbie and flicked his gaze to the oaf in the back with the sledgehammer. Her eyes shone with eagerness. She nodded and fidgeted with her chains as if hating them more all of a sudden. "Tris, you get the two on the right. I'll get the bartender."

"Go," whispered Tris.

"Need one for the road." Kevin spoke loud, hurrying to the bar.

Luisa slipped under a flap on the narrow side of the bar. At Kevin's purposeful stride, the bartender looked at him and smiled. *He does look harmless. I don't trust it.* Shailaja approached the dancing cages with a bucket and ladle. She scooted past the giant with the hammer, after which, she locked her glare on Kevin.

Last time I trust a blonde to keep a secret.

He smiled his best false smile as he approached the older man. Luisa let out a shriek, produced a kitchen knife from under her cheerleader's skirt, and lunged at the bartender. Her leg irons tripped her into a dive, and the man caught her by the forearms, shouting.

Shit! Kevin yanked the .45 from its holster, not trusting his odds at firing into a melee without hitting the girl. Other patrons screamed and ducked. One or two pulled weapons. Kevin whirled to the right and fired at a man aiming a long-barreled revolver at Luisa. The heavy round caught the guy in the upper chest, killing him in an instant. The woman seated with him screamed and slid to the floor.

Behind Kevin, a ripple of gunfire scared him into thinking the two idiots opened up with their submachine guns. He glanced over his shoulder for a second. Tris had shot both men before they even got a hand on their weapons. Barbie, now less than fifteen feet in front of him and two tables right, threw herself on the towel and grabbed the concealed pistol. She slid off the bench seat to her knees, the chain leaving her unable to raise the weapon up high enough to sight over it while standing.

The bartender hurled Luisa into shelves of bottles behind him. She flailed for a handhold, but fell out of sight. Kevin pivoted to aim at him, but he dove down going for something under the bar. Luisa, screaming in Spanish, jumped on his back, and stabbed him. Kevin hesitated for half a second, and fired. A gouge of wood splinters sprayed the bartender in the face when he popped up, but the bullet didn't find meat. A man in a hideous green 'suit' at the bar went for a gun, his attention locked on Luisa.

Kevin fired one round into his back. He slumped forward and fell off the stool.

The hammer-wielding behemoth hurled a round table from the dancer's area at Tris like a Frisbee. She yelped and ducked. Shailaja screamed and cowered to the ground, looking meek and uninvolved. Barbie raised her hands as high as the chain allowed and fired shot after shot at the charging giant. He roared and went down, howling and screaming in pain rather than anger. The dancing girls shrieked and ducked as a few bullets ricocheted off their cages. The men watching them hit the deck. Kevin sprinted at the bar, gun up. Luisa yanked the knife out from the man's back and lunged again. The bartender flung a glass of something in her face, which made her retreat and shriek. Kevin aimed at the old one-armed man, but he dropped out of sight behind the bar again before he could squeeze off a shot.

Gunfire came from behind, followed by a gurgle and a yelp from a table to his left. A metallic *thud* struck the floor.

"I see a weapon, someone fucking dies," yelled Tris.

Shailaja pulled her hand out of the water bucket, with keys, and set to opening the cages. The bartender popped up with a shotgun, though it looked like a pump rather than an automatic. He seemed torn for an instant between firing on the blinded Luisa or Kevin. A shot from the .45 winged the bartender on the shoulder, forcing him down out of sight. Luisa's shrieks went from hurt to pissed off. She wiped a hand over her eyes and spat before diving to the floor behind the bar. The shotgun discharged, blowing a head-sized chunk out of the wood paneling and pulping the left calf of a man seated at a table near the bar. Luisa's hand rose into view, clutching the knife, and went down. Again it came up, and went down.

A potbellied man in a black tee under a blue button-down ran in the front door while pulling a pistol from his belt. Kevin pivoted and fired, drilling him in the chest twice. The handgun, half out of the holster, went off. A ricochet caused a puff of dust from the ceiling and floor at almost the same time.

Kevin kept his gun trained on the door, half his attention on the nervous whimpers of patrons who hadn't been stupid enough to get involved. For a few seconds, eerie silence settled over everything. Dust hung in the air, and the loudest noise came from Barbie's rattling chains.

The blonde shivered, not having moved from where she knelt. She kept the pistol pointed at the last place she'd seen the big man. Tris hopped up onto tables, leaping from one to the next until she reached the spot.

She aimed a pair of MAC-10s at the floor behind the barrier. "Neon's dead. You wanna join him?"

"Fuck Neon," said a labored deep voice.

"No thanks," said Tris. "Get outta here… and leave the hammer."

The big man staggered upright, a hand clamped over his bleeding thigh. Barbie aimed at him, but held her fire. Cage doors grated open, and the three underwear-clad women jumped down to the floor.

Ka-chuck.

Everyone looked toward the sound.

Luisa, leg irons clicking, padded out from behind the bar and leveled the shotgun at a table with two couples and an extra man. "Clothes. Now."

A mixture of head shaking and murmurs of protest came from the people.

"Bloody clothes are better than no clothes." Luisa aimed at the head of a woman in a red dress. "It won't show on red."

The dancers gathered around Luisa, trying to cover their miniscule thongs and see-through bras with their hands. One by one, they snapped the leather 'price collars' off their necks and hurled them away. The smallest, who didn't look much older than sixteen, reached up and removed Luisa's choker. Tris tossed the keys to Barbie who seemed all too ready to drop the pistol and search the mass of metal bits for freedom.

Tris collected the MAC-10s from Kevin and offered one to Shailaja, the other to the tallest of the dancers. Luisa kept the shotgun trained on the people at the table while they peeled off their outer clothes and handed them to the former dancers.

The youngest wriggled into the red dress. "I can't believe he didn't see you take the keys." She gawked at Shalaja. "I thought we were all gonna get beat."

"Wait," asked Kevin. "How'd you wind up with keys in the bucket?"

Shailaja blinked at him. "Barbie said you were here to help us escape. I slipped them off Pedro's belt while he was squeezing my tits."

The grateful look on the smallest dancer's face made her look more like fifteen.

Thoughts of the women all revved up for freedom, then watching him stride right out the front door brought on a cringe. *I'm gonna go out just like Dad.* Kevin holstered his .45 and walked over to Barbie, who still hadn't found a single key that worked. She fumbled, trying to get one to go into the cuff on her left ankle. He took a knee, grasped her shaking hands, and made eye contact. "Calm down, Barbie."

She stared at him. "Tina. My name's really Tina. Get this shit offa me."

Except for three keys likely meant for the cages, the other nine were identical. He unlocked her and snapped the leather strip off her neck. Tina rubbed the angry marks on her wrists and cried.

"Don't thank me yet. I'm sure Neon has friends." He waved her at the shotgun-toting woman and pressed the keys into her hand. "Here, go unlock her and get some real clothes."

Tris walked over and stood beside him, grinning. "Tell me that didn't feel good."

"It feels like I spent two thousand coins on fucking up a delivery." He scowled at the cube. "Why are you giving away guns?"

She put her hands on her hips and shifted her weight onto her right leg. "Because I didn't think you'd want to babysit six women or try and stuff them into your back seat."

Kevin scowled. "If we leave them in this city, they're gonna wind up someone else's toy. They'd have a better shot in Cortez."

Tris grabbed him by the shoulders and kissed him. "You're right. Let's get out of here."

"Not yet." He patted the cube. "I've still gotta deal with this. Look. Tell them to hole up somewhere. This place has to have a hotel. When we leave, we'll play clown car."

"What the hell does that mean?"

Kevin chuckled. "Cramming six women in a Challenger's back seat."

"What about that silver shark? I bet that's Neon's."

"You know his codes? Oh, that's right... you splattered the codes all over the wall. Not to mention, killing a man is one thing... but stealing his car?" Kevin cringed.

"He's dead." Tris smirked. "He's not gonna miss it."

Kevin sighed and stomped for the door. A ripple of automatic fire made him spin, .45 raised.

The middle dancer, a slender brunette now in a frilly Frankenstein version of a saloon girl dress, held a smoking MAC-10. A man who'd been sitting by the cages collapsed in a leaky heap of meat.

Kevin glanced at Tris. "Guess he was a lousy tipper."

She glared.

He holstered the .45 and went outside, heading right, wanting to get as far away from Cloud 9 as he could, as fast as he could. Thugs, punks, and prostitutes observed him from the shadowed patches between buildings, one of which consisted of an upside down metro bus. None did more than look. *If they only knew what I was carrying. Enough void salt to go to Pluto... and not come back.*

He wandered with no particular direction in mind, searching and thinking of what he could possibly do with the drugs. Minutes later, scuffing footsteps approached at a light run. He whirled, hand on his sidearm, but relaxed when he saw white hair.

Tris stopped beside him. "The girls are at Mom's Hotel in the northwest. They looted the bar, so they should be okay for a few days."

"We're not gonna be here that long. As soon as I sell this shit, we're out."

"Drugs?" She glared. "Forget the job. We should destroy them."

Kevin grumbled in his head. When he caught sight of a red neon 'diner' sign, he grabbed her by the right wrist and pulled her across the street. "Not outside."

She followed without protest. He stiff-armed the door out of his way and walked in to a place lit by the flickering light of a handful of recessed fluorescent corkscrew bulbs. Red stools lined a short counter, behind which a middle-aged woman with ginger hair and a permanent frown gave him a distrustful squint. He went to the right and stopped at a plain maroon table. Tris slid into the booth on the same side.

"Sorry. Don't want the wrong people hearing the wrong thing."

She didn't let go of his hand. "I understand. I'm sorry, too... I know you didn't want to start anything in there, but... I couldn't just—"

"What'cha need?" asked a boy about thirteen or so with freckles and red hair, in an apron and a non-snobbish tee shirt and black jeans. His shoes appeared made from old tires. "We got the best fries in the area."

Kevin pulled his jacket over the cube. "Coffee is fine. Just ate."

"Same," said Tris.

The boy nodded and walked off.

Tris kept her voice low. "How can you profit from destroying people's lives?"

Kevin raised his eyebrows in a blasé smirk. "By selling this box."

She sighed.

"Look around you." Kevin gestured at a few bedraggled patrons, most little more than skin-wrapped skeletons propped up against the wall in booth seats. "The world is fucked. Who gives a shit if people get high? They get a few minutes of not suffering. So what if it shaves years off their life? We're all dead anyway."

She let go of his hand. "It's wrong. I can't help you hurt innocent people."

He leaned back as the boy set two cups of coffee down. When the kid made eye contact, he handed him three coins.

The waiter flashed an excited smile. "Thanks!"

Kevin sipped. *Not bad. Can barely taste the motor oil.* "You spent most of your life in that Enclave bubble. Okay, so maybe the world isn't quite as bad as those movies said it would be, but it's still pretty shitty. You're a naïve idealist. Without some kind of organized society, two things motivate people: survival and pleasure."

"So now you're going Freud on me?"

Kevin blinked. "What?"

Tris stared into her cup, a somber expression on her face. "I thought you were different. Thought that whole asshole thing was an act. You know, don't let anyone in. I guess you really *are* obsessed with money."

"It's not money." He scowled, shaking his head for a few seconds to let his anger ebb. "I'm sick and tired of getting shot at. Every goddamned time I leave Wayne's with someone else's bullshit in my back seat, I'm risking my ass. Half of these spackheads get off on the thrill of the run… I used to be one of them." He took a sip. "I didn't wear armor till I was twenty-four. Thought I was too good. Too fast."

"What happened?" She slurped.

"You saw the scars." He glanced sideways at her. "Not everyone puts themselves back together as fast as you. I don't want money. I want my dream. I was one run away, and now it seems everything I touch turns to shit."

"I'm sorry. Doctor Andrews really did have money. He would've paid you what I promised if he wasn't dead."

He looked at her. Something in her eyes got under his skin. Anger at borking the deal with Neon faded to sympathy. "Look, we don't know for sure he's dead. Maybe he ran from the Infected or something. Your boy Nathan certainly didn't expect them to be gone."

"He's not *my boy*." Tris pounded her fist into the seat with a cushioned *thump*. "I'm still not gonna help you sell poison."

"Then I'll sell it without ya. You can wait with the women." He picked at the cube. "I didn't sell you to Neon 'cause I figured you'd have shot me too when you pulled the ol' blurry arm thing. Real tempting. That would'a been that. Retired. Roadhouse. Set for life."

Tris leaned toward him. "Kevin, you're a shitty liar."

He stared at the cube. "Yeah… I suppose I am."

21

TYRANT

Kevin resisted the urge to stuff his hands in the pockets of his armored jacket. He shifted his gaze from left to right, watching every dark spot between walls. His hand hovered by the .45, fully loaded after a brief stop at the garage to visit his trunk. The weight of eyes settled on him, both seen and unseen. It took a certain kind of individual to live full-time in Glimmertown, though to be fair, not everyone was cut out for constant roaming.

If anyone ever made a top ten list of stupid shit to do in the Wildlands, walking around this place at night would be four or five. He twitched at the scrape of a shoe to his left, and stared into impenetrable shadow. *Doing it alone is probably number three... right under drinking glowing water.*

Something about the way it looked when people shifted in the alleys came too close to reminding him of the mindless shambling of Infected. He jumped every time motion caught his eye. Tris hadn't been kidding when she refused to help him sell the void salt. Two thousand coins or nothing. Even offering her half hadn't budged her. *Stupid righteous woman... Bad enough I may have just started a friggin' Wildland war with Glimmertown because she has a giant bleeding heart for slaves.* Kevin stopped and leaned on a lamppost made from a steel I-beam stuck end-first into the ground. Four clip lights dangled from the top, their extension cords braided in a lazy arc to a nearby trailer.

Tina's grateful face when he unlocked her cuffs haunted his thoughts. *Yeah, okay fine.* He looked up at the blackness overhead. Anywhere else in the world, he'd have been able to see stars. Too much artificial light rained down from the central tower to see a damn thing. *I keep doing sympathetic shit like this, I'll be seein' you soon, Dad.*

A boot scuffed on the dirt behind him, close and to the left.

Kevin whirled around the I-beam and yanked the .45 off his belt. The tip of the barrel came to a halt under the nose of an emaciated man with shaggy black hair and a heavy five o'clock shadow. A hasty disarming smile bared yellow teeth between quivering lips.

"'Sup. Just out for a walk."

Kevin smirked. "Uh huh. Sure. Out for a walk right up behind me. With a knife."

The man twitched as he laughed, seeming taken by an involuntary spasm. He looked down at the spring blade concealed in the long sleeve of a green army coat, and folded it closed. "Hey, you got any shit man?"

"I oughta aerate—"

The man whimpered, cringed, and shut his eyes.

Kevin squinted. "Maybe we *can* help each other."

"W-what?" The junkie risked a peek out of his left eye.

"Say I'm looking to get rid of some junk quick like, and I don't wanna deal with Cloud 9." Kevin relaxed his gun arm, aiming at the man's chest instead of his face. "You know anyone might be in a buying mood?"

"I d-d-don't d-d-do d-d-drugs, man." The vagrant shivered.

"Yeah, sure you don't. And I got wings growing outta my ass." Kevin pulled the hammer back with his thumb. "If you ain't a junkie, you're just a thief I got no use for."

"K-k-kay." The man held up two shaking hands. "You w-wanna talk to Tyrant in the train graveyard."

"Tyrant huh?"

"Yeah." The junkie reached across his chest and clutched his left arm above the elbow. He lost a few seconds ticking and blinking. "He sells all the cheap stuff the Cloud won't touch."

"How do I know this isn't bullshit?"

"Swear, man. Swear." The vagrant thrashed his head side to side with such force it seemed his eyeballs might go flying.

"Lead the way." Kevin gestured with the .45.

"Y-you gonna shoot me in the back?" He stumbled ahead facing sideways, staring at the gun.

Kevin eased the hammer forward with his thumb so it didn't go off. "You got a point. Might not look too good me walkin' you in there at gunpoint. Let's make a deal. You don't stab me, and I don't shoot you. I'll even give ya five percent of whatever I sell it for."

"Uhh okay." The bedraggled skeleton-in-skin took two steps before looking back over his shoulder again. "That a lot?"

"For you? Yeah. A shitload." Kevin put the .45 back in its holster, but kept a hand on it.

"Mmm." The man sniffled and wiped at his nose. "Nice. I'm Mike." He held a grimy hand out for a few seconds, but dropped it when Kevin didn't react. "Nice dealin' with ya." He beckoned with a wave. "C'mon."

Mike scurried off like a two-legged rat into the bowels of Glimmertown. He avoided the central square and its blinding glow, favoring a series of narrow channels between the rear walls of dwellings or other buildings. *Guess people in Glimmertown don't believe in back doors.*

After a walk that felt as if he'd gone around the entire city twice, congested buildings ended where an open channel held four parallel train tracks. The rails continued for about a hundred yards to the right, a mixture of rust and glint, before making a left turn through a gate in a decaying chain link fence. Broken glass littered the ground, sparkling as if he stood inside a snow globe of ruin. Even this far from the center of town, the tower lights cast long shadows over everything. Dozens of bullet holes in the surroundings suggested copious violence, but not a single trace of brass remained. *These people'd steal each others underwear to sell for a hit. If they could sell dirt, they'd do it.*

Rectangular forms flickered in the orange of distant fires beyond the fence. A hodgepodge of old boxcars and dead eighteen-wheelers stood on the near side of an open tarmac, like metal dinosaurs come to die at the boneyard. The air carried the stink of wood smoke brushed with industrial chemicals. *They're burning creosote.*

While Mike shambled off along the tracks, Kevin spent a few seconds staring up at the gleaming mass floating like a tiny electric star. *I bet she's right. This whole place is one big trap.*

"You comin'?" Mike's voice echoed in the open space.

Kevin pulled his gaze away from the truck graveyard and jogged to catch up. "Yeah, yeah…"

"N-not the kinda place a guy like you w-wants ta hang out."

"No shit." Kevin glanced at the tower again before gesturing at Mike. "After you."

Mike trotted along the tracks, following the curve left past the tattered strips of aluminum where something huge had smashed the fence years earlier. About twenty yards beyond the breach, a section of road ran alongside the tracks past two doublewide 'office' trailers built into permanent structures. A handful of people, most in their teens, lounged around in various states of consciousness.

The only one lucid enough to move, a strung-out looking girl somewhere between fourteen and sixteen with caramel-hued skin, pulled black hair off her face and smiled at him. Almond-shaped eyes widened, and she tried to strike a seductive pose. A brief gust of wind fluttered scraps of torn cloth on her thin tank top, and she barely managed to hide shivers and chattering teeth.

"Don't trust Fix, man," whispered Mike. "She'll knock ya out 'fore ya get anywhere and you'll wake up wit nothin'. Fell for that skank once. Ain't doin' again."

Kevin stared at her. "Yeah. I know the drill." *That redhead looked innocent too.*

Fix seemed to realize sexy wasn't working and turned up the pathetic. She shivered and changed her posture. *Shit, is that girl even thirteen yet?* Kevin looked away. The kid reminded him of some of the girls the Olds used near the 'Mexican border' as bait. A twinge low and outside of his left nipple reminded him why he wore armor. *Little bitch shot me as soon as I untied her.*

One by one, other faces emerged from the dark. Boys still. Not one of them looked eighteen yet. Tris's words whispered at the back of his mind. These are the lives he was about to destroy. He thumbed the cube, his pace slowing. He caught Fix staring at him again, huddled in a ball and peering at him over her knees. If not for having witnessed her 'sexy' act before, he'd have mistaken her now for twelve.

She's playing me. Shit, they'd all slit my throat in an instant if they knew what I was carrying.

He stomped after Mike, who'd gained a six or seven pace lead. The junkie led him past three huge semi-trailers with open sides. The first had been merged with another, forming an open-faced barroom. The second trailer, a single, had a boxcar-like door cut out of the facing wall blocked off by a U-shaped counter full of shitty looking handguns and knives. A woman in a black lace corset, old enough to be his mother and definitely too large to wear the fishnets cutting into her legs, winked at him from the gun shop.

"Holy shit." Kevin rubbed his eyes. "I think I'm catching a contact high from being here."

The third car held only mattresses strewn with bodies that may or may not have been alive. A reek of feces and urine wafted by, causing him to choke back the urge to gag. Mike cut between it and the next one, walking four rows deep before turning right down a 'corridor' formed by boxcars. After passing four of them, they emerged in a semicircular clearing with a handful of burn barrels throwing off firelight. A dozen or more people lounged in improvised chairs and drank murky green liquid from fat glass bottles. Except for a few young women evidently here to trade themselves for drugs, the gang seemed to have made an effort to dress as close to the same as possible: black leather jackets, black pants, and blue shirts.

Mike indicated a couch near the blue boxcar that formed the rear wall of the 'courtyard.' A large dark-skinned man sat between a pair of women who draped themselves on him from either side. He shifted to give Kevin a look-over, causing his leather jacket to creak as it strained to contain his muscles. Thick cornrows wrapped over his head and an enormous silver handgun sat on a table near his right hand.

"The hell is this?" asked the man, eyeing Kevin.

"You Tyrant?" Kevin stopped by a battered coffee table made from a slab of metal balanced on a plastic crate, covered with pills, needles, coins, and ammo.

Clicking weapons played a cricket song in the dark all around him.

"Yeah. An' who the fuck are you? Imma give you 'bout ten goddamned seconds 'fore I school you on the meanin' of sovereign territory."

"I'm a driver. 'Less ya fancy Amarillo comin' down on ya, relax."

Tyrant scoffed. "Shit, man. Them uptight bitches ain't got no sway here. Not ta mention, if you here talkin' ta me, I think they'd be more after yo' ass than anything."

"You'd be right, except for the original client's not around to complain." Kevin held up the cloth sack. "I need to sell this quick, and *Mike* here says you're the man to talk to."

"What'cha got?" Tyrant picked his gun off the table and held it in his lap. "Let's see it. Easy and shit."

Kevin unwrapped the bundle. At the sight of the black box with glowing blue strips, a concentrated quiet settled over the gang. Tyrant's hostility melted away. He gestured Kevin closer.

"It's legit." Kevin cleared a space on the table with his boot and set the cube down. After a dramatic pause, he pushed the small shiny spot, causing it to open as it had in Neon's office.

"Motherfucker…" Tyrant's eyes bulged. "Ain' never seen sah much damn Salt."

"Yeah." Kevin folded his arms.

Mike grabbed him from behind to keep from falling over. The wiry man's entire body shook with need. He tried to speak, but all that came out of him sounded like 'mama' over and over. Kevin pushed him off to arm's length.

"Give ya two hundred coins, cold." Tyrant lifted one ampule, holding it to the light. "This shit from the Enclave, ain't it?"

"Two hundred?" Kevin shook his head. "It's worth more than ten times that."

Tyrant grinned. "Yeah, it is. But you ain't sellin' to no Cloud 9 here. And if what you say is true… if Neon is no more… than your ass best be getting the fuck out on the sooner side of later."

"Contract was for twenty-four hundred. I can't go back with less than two grand."

Mike emitted a sound like a chicken being run over by a truck as he slumped to his knees.

"Two hundred's my best offer." Tyrant's smile hardened.

Kevin leaned forward and snagged the ampule from Tyrant's fingers. "I can't do two hundred." He dropped it in the tray and poked the button to close the cube.

"Pity." Tyrant turned his head to the left. "Yo, Al. Time to negotiate."

Shit. Kevin went for the .45, but the woman to Tyrant's right leapt at him, shrieking and waving knives. He backpedaled, cringing from the bombastic assault, trying not to trip over Mike.

Bang.

A slug slammed into his back, stalled on his armored jacket, but it knocked the breath from his lungs. The dervish woman feinted high and kicked his legs out from under him. Kevin hit the gravel on his back, raised the .45, and squeezed off one shot before a flurry of chains, clubs, and fists fell on him. Pain exploded in his wrist. His gun hit the stones somewhere to his right.

He stomped the nearest shin, driving the knee backward with a splintering crunch. An aluminum bat smashed into his stomach, making him sit up into a massive leather-clad fist. Rocks hit the back of his head. For a few seconds, the haze of over-illumination faded.

I can see the stars...

22

LITTLE RED

An inch of water sloshed in the bottom of a highball glass as Tris slid it back and forth between her hands. Every few minutes, she looked up at the window and searched the dark street. The rhythmic sound of glass sliding over whatever synthetic material covered the table seemed to drown out the rest of the world.

"Refill, hon?" asked a kindly middle-aged woman holding a bubble-shaped coffee pot full of water.

"I guess." Tris let her glass stop.

"What'd you two fight about?" The woman poured. "Shame ya let a cutie like him get away."

"Oh…" Tris stared at the water until the bubbles stopped swirling, and glanced out the window again. "We didn't fight that bad. He's coming back."

"Hope you're right, sweetie. You g'won and lemme know if you need ta talk." The woman shuffled back to the counter.

Tris's focus traded blur between her reflection and the street. The dirt road outside twinkled wherever bits of silica or broken glass caught the incessant glow from the main spire. Pale blue numbers floating at the lower left of her vision read 23:18. The two dots blinked in a slow cadence, marking the passage of seconds. She closed her eyes, but the clock remained superimposed over the black. Somewhere inside her head, little wires fed it directly into her optic nerve... or at least that's what Nathan told her.

I don't remember going to the bathroom once while in Detention. I had to have, but why can't I picture where the toilet was in my cell? Lines drawn in memory appeared in her thoughts. Octagonal grey room with floor-to-ceiling chrome strips at every corner. Tiny table on the south wall. Gel-filled mattress on the north wall. Door on the left. Education terminal on the right. Gloss-black floor icy underfoot.

Tris sighed and rubbed her fingers into the sides of her nose. She thought back to the look on Kevin's face when she'd taken out Neon's bodyguards. To her, everything had seemed to stop when her boosters kicked in. She'd pulled guns from a pair of mannequins and shot them in the head before they even knew she'd gotten their weapons. The predictive targeting system embedded in her brain stem painted thin lines out of the front of any gun she held, estimating the bullet path. Reflections in the fish tank let her hit the two other thugs behind them without needing to turn around.

He looked at me like I was a... machine. She shivered. *They can implant memories. Months of combat training in two real weeks. What else did they feed me?* A handful of fleeting glimpses of her father, an oldish man with snowy white beard and hair. *He's so old. How can that be my father?*

She picked up the glass. "I'm drinking this. I can't be an android."

"You need something, hon?" yelled the diner owner.

"Fine, thanks. Just talking to myself." She chugged the entire glass in one breath.

If I'm a machine, I'm about to short out.

Again she looked at the street. *Dammit, where is he? I should've thrown that stupid box over the wall. I never should've let him go alone.*

She stood, slung the katana across her back, and rushed out. Four steps into the street, she stopped, unsure which way to go.

"Hey," yelled the woman. "You forgettin' something?"

"Oh." Tris turned. "Sorry. I gotta find him. What do I owe you for the water?"

"Just one, sweetie." The older woman smiled, and let go of something in the back of her belt.

"Sorry." Tris handed over a dime. "I was too pissed. Did you notice which way he went?"

The woman pointed left. "Toward the bad part of town."

"There's a *bad* part?" *Other than everywhere?*

"Oh, ho…" The woman shook her head. "You're still new here. You'll find out. Little thing like you might wanna come on back inside and wait for him."

"I've already waited too long." She squinted into a breeze blowing in from the west. "I got a bad feeling."

"Pity if anything happened to a pretty face like yours. Be careful." The woman ambled back into her diner.

Tris thought about marking a waypoint. A faint *beep* sounded in her ears and a directional arrow, in the same shade of pale blue as the clock, appeared next to the numbers. She followed the road for a few minutes before it dead-ended in a cul-de-sac with three brothels. The last possible right turn led past a row of private residences that used to be passenger vans, small cargo trucks, and a few made from welded-together dumpsters. All manner of sounds emanated from within. Snoring, sex, and everything in between.

She fought the urge to start shouting his name. Urgency hastened her stride and she proceeded to jog in a regular back and forth sweep pattern. One side of Glimmertown to the other, up one block, then reverse. The second time she reached the farthest east point before the walled-off end, a flash of red caught her eye to the left. A wisp of a teenaged girl had Kevin's armored jacket. *How many long-sleeved, red, ridged jackets are there in the Wildlands?* She pivoted on her heel and ran up behind the girl.

"Hey, kid."

"I'm not your kid, *blanca*." The girl kept walking in a wobbly gait that made it seem like she'd fall over at any second.

"Nice jacket."

The girl narrowed dark green eyes at her. "Fuck you, it's mine."

"Where'd you get it?" Tris grabbed the sleeve.

"Offa me!" The girl whipped her body around to jerk her arm loose and fell on her ass. She grabbed Tris's wrist and pulled, unable to move her. Fear widened her eyes. "Fuck do you care?"

"I really want to know." Tris squatted, draping her elbows over her knees. "Where'd you get it?"

"Offa some dead guy." The girl made a sour face.

A wave of lightheadedness came on and passed. By the time Tris returned to the here and now, the girl was upright and half a block away. *No… Kevin.*

Tris stood and yelled, "Show me where."

The girl shrieked something incomprehensible and took off at an ungainly sprint. Tris bolted after her, gaining ground with ease. She got close enough to shove the teen with two hands, knocking her forward into a tumbling roll. After a somersault, the girl curled on her side, clutching her right knee.

"Ugh, bitch."

Tris pulled the Beretta off her belt and pounced on the girl, holding the gun against her cheek. "You're going to show me where you found that jacket. If you move faster than a calm walk, I'm going to blow out both your knees. Got it?"

The girl stared at her, lip quivering as if about to burst into tears.

"Don't give me that bullshit." Tris leaned back and stood. "Get up."

"I'm Stacy, but everyone calls me Fix."

"Don't care." Tris wagged the Beretta at her. "Get up."

"Please don't shoot me, I'm only twelve."

"You're at least fifteen. Get the hell up."

Stacy rolled onto her hands and knees and crawled to a stack of tires someone likely intended as a 'crash absorber' at a street corner. She pulled herself upright and leaned on it. Tris closed to within two steps.

"Alright, alright." Stacy pushed off the tires and flailed her arms to keep balance. "You torched my fucking knee, gimme a little slack."

"Sorry. It was that or shoot you."

Stacy fixed her with a dark look, half pout and half venom. "He's over by Tyrant's, on the tracks."

"I'm still waiting."

The girl limped on. "Stay quiet. Tyrant's crew'll fuck you up if they hear ya."

"They leave you alone?" Tris raised an eyebrow.

"Yeah." Stacy raised and lowered her arms as if pantomiming a bird. "They don't mess with payin' customers. If you're not there to buy, you're there to steal."

Tris followed her as she hooked a right turn between a pair of rotting buses. "Seems like a bad way to get new customers. You sure they won't try talking first?"

"Not to you. You're like stupid hot. Crazy white bitch, beyond white. They'll try to sell you to Neon, like that other chick." The girl stopped at the front end of the bus, holding on to the metal to support herself as she peered past it. "Shh. He's right over there."

Tris wagged the Beretta.

Stacy grumbled, still scowling, as she trudged across a field of loose gravel. Four parallel sets of train tracks filled a wide channel between two sections of rebuilt city. Metal creaked and whined in all directions, keeping time with the rise and fall of a breeze. About a hundred yards ahead on the far side of the rails, Kevin lay in a pile of weeds and trash against a slatted chain link fence.

Shit! Tris grabbed Stacy's right wrist and pulled her up to a sprint. The girl stumbled on the rails, but didn't fall. Once they reached open gravel, she set her heels, though Tris dragged her along anyway. A few steps from Kevin, she shoved the girl to the ground. Stacy scooted away and cowered with her back to the fence.

"Don't move." Tris aimed at her for a second, before guilt and worry overwhelmed her caution. She hurried to his side and took a knee. Blood oozed from his nostrils, mouth, and a cut on his forehead. "Kevin?"

After transferring the gun to her left hand, she felt for a pulse. The instant she sensed one, he groaned. Tris let her head sag with relief.

Scratch.

The gravel shifted to her left. A blur of motion got her attention and her hand flew up to intercept something coming for her face. With a *slap,* she caught Stacy by the wrist. Tris stared past trembling fingers holding a one-inch square derm patch at a terrified teenaged girl. Her fear didn't seem quite as fake now.

Stacy's button-shaped nose, a little wide for her face, and her large green eyes made her look young. She offered a weak, apologetic smile, though any color her skin might have had drained away.

"H-holy shit... W-what the fuck was that? How did you move that fast?"

Tris glanced at the derm for a second and back to the girl. "What's that?"

"Nothing bad. Just some sleepy time." Stacy looked down, lowering her voice. "I thought you were gonna kill me."

"Bullshit. You were gonna pick me clean."

When Stacy didn't offer an immediate protest, Tris shoved. The quick thrust overpowered the girl with ease, smacking the derm patch onto her cheek.

"No! Please don't!" Stacy fell over backward. She tried to claw the derm off her face, but already had lost too much coordination to grab it, and flapped her arms like a wounded bird. "Don't leave me here unc... un..."

Tris pushed the girl's fingers down on the chem square, deforming the teen's cheek. "You were gonna leave *me* here unconscious... and probably naked."

Stacy moaned. She attempted to squirm, but seemed barely able to move. Her eyes rolled up and her head lolled to the side.

After holding the girl down for ten more seconds, Tris holstered the Beretta. She crept back to Kevin's side and jostled him. He moaned. She patted him on the cheek until his eyes fluttered open.

"Tris..." Blood seeped out of his smile.

She poked and pressed around his neck and sides, making him wince. "I don't feel anything broken."

"Ugh." He breathed hard for a moment before raising his hands to stare at them. "Shit." He patted his empty holster and sat up. "Fuck." His eyes crossed, and he flopped onto his back again, moaning. "My .45?"

"I don't know."

"Drugs?"

"Not here."

Kevin snarled and struggled to his feet. "Where's my fucking jacket?"

Tris grabbed his arm and pulled him upright. "There."

"Little rat." He staggered over to Stacy, squinted at her, and glanced at Tris. "You offed a kid?"

Tris frowned. "No. Look at her cheek. She tried to sneak me with a derm."

Kevin growled past clenched teeth as he bent down to grab his armored jacket. "I suppose you're gonna tell me I should let her keep it." He peeled her out of it, exposing a ratty tank top as thin as toilet paper and nothing underneath.

"Nah." Tris helped him into it before pulling his arm across her shoulders, steadying him on his feet. "She's not as innocent as she looks. Come on."

Kevin grabbed his side and winced as she supported most of his weight.

She eyed the chain link fence, peering at faint hints of fires burning a couple hundred yards in. He'd probably be okay for a few minutes... but what if something went wrong. Revenge never came with guarantees.

Tris hefted his arm and tucked into his side. *Not worth it.* "Let's get you to bed."

23

HAD IT COMING

Pain flared in Kevin's chest each time his boot struck the ground. Tris had a vice grip on his wrist, causing her bony little shoulder to jab him in the armpit as she helped him walk. His free left arm wound up swinging limp at his side, covered in throbbing bruises. Whenever he tried to put weight on his left knee, it tweaked out, but didn't feel broken. Flashes and glimpses of mocking grins and blurring fists came and went. Somehow, they'd focused most of their attention on his chest.

He reached up and grasped the jacket. *I love this thing.*

Droplets of fluid moved deep within his nose. The maddening tickle overwhelmed rational thought and filled him with the irresistible, uncontainable urge to make it stop. He clamped his palm over his face and rubbed side to side, before sticking his finger up to the second knuckle and setting off an atomic bomb of a migraine.

"Shit, you're bleeding again." Tris pushed something soft under his nose. "Hold that there. I think it's broken."

"Ng." All he wanted at that moment was for the pain to go away.

Tris gathered his arm over her shoulder again and pulled him. "Come on… Don't make me carry you like a baby."

He chuckled. "Ow."

Gravel crunched.

Kevin waved his arms around, gritting his teeth from the agony as Tris whirled away from him and let go without warning. He managed not to fall to his knees and looked up at her. An angry scream stalled in his throat at the sight of the huge guy from Cloud 9. Even without the sledgehammer, he struck a menacing silhouette. Tris already had her Beretta leveled at the giant's face. White cloth around his thigh soaked red where Tina had shot him.

"Wait." He raised his hands. "Not lookin' for any trouble. I wanted to warn you."

Tris didn't lower the gun. "Warn us?"

"You could'a killed me and didn't, so I felt like I owed you at least something." He stepped closer.

"Easy." Kevin wheezed. "She's got a little issue with slavers."

"Hmf." Tris smirked.

The man gestured toward the tower. "It got back to the boss you offed Neon. He ain't too happy 'bout it."

"I thought Neon *was* the boss," said Tris.

"Naw." Kevin coughed. "He's the face. A smart boss doesn't show himself to any idiot that walks in from the road."

"Somethin' like that. Cloud 9 was Neon's thing, but Glimmertown belongs to Mr. Petersen." The big man lowered his arms. "Look, I ain't here to start shit. Mr. P wants someone's ass bent in ways asses ain't made to bend on account of havin' his town shot up. He took it as an act of disrespect."

"I'll give him an act of disrespect." Tris lowered the Beretta… a little.

"He's got a pretty good idea what you look like. Most of the people in the place, 'specially the ones you forced to strip got good memories."

"That wasn't even us. The girl with the shotgun did that." Kevin shook his head. "We should've finished what we started."

"What, killed them all?" Tris sighed. "Then we'd be worse than Neon. Stupid damn people. How's it okay what Neon did to those women, but taking clothes—"

"Easy." Kevin coughed. "Aw, shit this hurts."

"So where do you fit into all this?" Tris pulled Kevin's right arm across her shoulders and braced her left around his back.

"Not much choice for me. Back to work. If we meet again, I'll be expected to do something mean to you. Course, with the pain from my shot leg, my vision ain't too good. I'd probably wind up wasting bullets over your heads." The big man took two steps back and wandered away into the dark.

Tris waited a minute more before securing her grip on him and resuming their walk. Being upright let him feel his ribs sliding around. She guided him ahead at a slow pace for several minutes. Details slipped in and out of his consciousness; one street blurred to the next. She stopped to let him catch his breath, and he dozed on his feet. A loud *whump* startled him into looking around at a small room with a plain bed, dented metal desk, one chair, and a tiny door that likely led to a bathroom.

"Where—" Words became a grunt of pain as she carried him across the room and set him down on the bed. "Are we?"

"A cheap hotel." She tugged his boots off and set them on the floor nearby. "Sorry."

Kevin reached a leaden arm up and rested his hand over his face. "Ugh. What for?"

"I shouldn't have let you go alone." She sat on the side of the bed, head forward, face hidden behind a cascade of arctic white hair.

He peered at her between his fingers. "If you were there, it would've been worse."

"Worse?" She glanced at him.

He tried to laugh, but grabbed his side and cringed. "More guns would've been involved."

"They might not have been so quick to steal from you after a show of force."

Kevin moaned. "Where are those women? We should get our asses out of here."

Tris helped him out of his armored jacket. "Different hotel. Didn't want to lead any of Neon's thugs there in case we were being followed."

"Petersen's boys." He gritted his teeth and went limp, letting her do all the work of undressing him.

"Easy enough to fix that problem." Her voice sounded cold. She opened his belt and pulled his jeans off.

"Not worth it. Petersen's been the king of Glimmertown as long as anyone remembers. Some people think he had power even before the war."

Tris threw a blanket over him and blinked. "That shouldn't be possible. The war happened fifty-one years ago... He'd have to have be ancient."

He coughed, cringed, and moaned. "Not so hard to believe. You got them nanites. Ugh. Spare a few?"

"Doesn't work like that." She brushed at his hair. "You need the control module implanted too. Maybe I can find some painkillers."

"I need a pill the size of a hamburger."

She fussed over him for another few minutes before making eye contact. "What now?"

"We leave… as soon as I can breathe without wanting to die."

Tris looked at the floor. "If you go back to Wayne's, he's going to expect the cash out for that box. He'll take it out of your bank."

"Shit." He grabbed at where his belt holster would've been had he been wearing pants. "Bastards got my .45 too. Fuck."

"Sorry for shooting Neon." She folded her hands in her lap, gaze downcast like a kid that ate too many cookies.

"Meh. He had it coming."

She smiled and leaned toward him, running a hand up and down his thigh while planting the gentlest of kisses on his lips. Somehow, she managed to find the one place on his body that didn't ache. "You need to rest. I'll deal with it."

"Don't." He tried to sit up, but she pushed him down. "No. I went off alone and look at me."

"Fair point." She smirked. "But you're in no shape to do anything right now other than bleed and moan."

"Great, I'm on the rag." He chuckled, and regretted it.

Tris made a fist, but decided against punching him. She scooted closer to the headboard and stroked his hair. "Stay here. I promise I won't do anything stupid."

"Mmm." Kevin tried to fight, but the cottony pillow sucked the wakefulness straight out of his skull.

PAYBACK'S A BITCH

Men's laughter echoed in swells from the train graveyard up ahead, punctuated by periods of total silence. Tris crept from shadow to shadow, hiding at the slightest hint of someone approaching. Two locals stumbled by, a scrawny bald man in black pants and boots, and a fat, long-haired man in a heavy coat. Drunk or high, they seemed to require leaning into each other to remain upright. She pressed herself into the wall of a half-crushed metro bus turned home. The acrid stink of someone cooking drugs inside made her hold her breath.

Once the wanderers disappeared around a rusty Peterbilt laying on its side, she emerged and hurried to the end of the row. The tracks appeared deserted, populated only by a handful of rats and other, smaller things scratching about. She darted across the open area, jumped the four sets of rails, and tucked into the shadow of the slatted chain link fence surrounding the lot where trucks had gone to die.

Trash, bottles, and old needles collected underfoot and in the crook between barrier and ground. A cluster of old fifty-gallon barrels a few yards to her right offered some cover from the light. She hurried to it, startled to find Fix already nestled in a hollow among them. The girl had her arms wrapped around herself, shivering. The girl's ripped up tank top fluttered in the wind, the fabric so thin it barely offered modesty much less warmth. She hadn't even peeled the drug patch from her cheek. Her green eyes drooped, unfocused.

Fix leaned back, raising an arm to defend her face. With Tris standing there, the mound of barrels had gone from shelter to cage. She offered an apologetic look, though it seemed well-rehearsed. *As soon as I lower my guard, this kid'll knife me in the back.*

Tris shook her head and climbed up onto the barrels, attempting to be as quiet as one could while disturbing hollow, rusted metal. She grasped the top of the fence and pulled herself up, crouching like an alley cat. From there, she surveyed the yard. A mixture of old trailers, cabs, and train cars packed the area. On the right side, the boxy vehicles formed neat rows. Organization deteriorated the farther west her gaze panned, as though whoever operated this place before the war had become lazy and taken to packing them in wherever they felt like it.

Firelight in the distance gave away the location of Tyrant's camp. Tris closed her eyes, suppressing the urge to pull a Kevin and charge right in. Anger welled up and faded. *They could've killed him. They didn't have to let him live.* She exhaled. *Sneaky time.*

She missed her black jumpsuit, though her brown leather shirt and jeans weren't her biggest problem as far as stealth was concerned. She scowled over her shoulder at the massive tower of lights, which made her pure white hair all but glow. It hadn't felt unusual before. Perhaps four in ten people in the Enclave had white hair... out here, she hadn't seen even one other. She dropped down, landing on all fours, and sprinted to the nearest hulk.

Yeah, the jumpsuit was the problem. She climbed onto the roof of a warped box trailer and crept up to the cab end. *I suppose it did make it more obvious. White hair and modern clothes...*

She leapt from the top of the truck, landing on the edge of another trailer bedecked with refrigeration pods. At the *skiff* of approaching boots, she got down flat. A man and woman passed on the right, whispering about how much money they were going to make selling 'the good shit.' Tris grumbled in her head. She despised the idea of recreational drugs, knowing what it did to the people who used. The historical documentaries they'd shown her in school made it clear what kind of harm they caused. She tried to rationalize the users had a choice to buy or not against Kevin dangling on a hook for almost three thousand coins. Her loathing for such poison seemed petty compared to his lifelong dream, though her attempt to placate guilt by thinking these people were responsible for their own misery brought a sick feeling to her gut.

Tris crawled to the front end of the trailer, hiding on her belly behind a shot-to-pieces refrigeration unit. *I could sell myself to Petersen and worry about escaping later... Neon was going to pay him almost two thousand for me.* She touched the tiny metal socket behind her ear. *What if I can't escape? What'll they force me to do?* Her eyebrows drew together. *Hell with that. I'd rather kill Petersen. These poor bastards are already chemmed-up past the point of no return. Maybe he's right. Maybe it* is *a kindness.*

She sighed.

Seven trucks later, she climbed onto a boxcar and jogged over four more before slithering onto a catwalk running along the top of a tanker car. A hint of train tracks peeked here and there out from windblown dirt and about ten million cigarette butts. After waiting for a pair of punks to walk by, she crawled to the forward end. Cold steel grating chilled her thighs despite her jeans, but the perch offered her a good view of Tyrant's camp. A half-circle shaped clearing contained seventeen gang members. Four people had paired off, having sex in the not-too-private cover of old sofas or beds set up under canvas tarp roofs while everyone else drank.

Purple and pink light emanated from within a shiny blue boxcar at the center point of the rounded wall. Silver spray paint formed blocky letters to the right of the door. It took a moment of staring to figure out the over-stylized word spelled 'Tyrant.' The two men seated on a sofa right outside the door gave off the vibe of enforcers or bodyguards.

Tris moved to the farther edge of the tank car and slid to the ground. With four barrels of flame burning bright, the shadows outside the courtyard deepened. *How did they manage to move all the trailers out of here to make a camp?* She crawled amid the wheels to get a closer look. *Probably before they banned vehicles inside the city.*

The overall layout resembled one of those toilet seats with a gap lined up with where she hid. Deciding against parading right in the front, she decided to try the other side of Tyrant's boxcar and backed away. A quick crawl over rotten railroad ties covered in bugs let her out into a narrow passage between train cars. Junk packed the closest walkable path that seemed likely to lead her where she wanted to go. Stacks of pipes, more barrels, old appliances, dumpsters, propane tanks, and a couple of bare mattresses littered the ground. Every breath tasted like corroded metal and desperation.

She followed the rightward curve for a few minutes until a wall of refrigerators and filing cabinets blocked her path, beyond which lay a small clearing. Two rectangular sections of chain link fence with metal wheels along the bottom had been propped up against the junk and secured with a padlocked chain. A large boxcar formed the right-side wall of a secure yard. Tyrant hadn't bothered to paint the back blue, but based on how far she'd walked, she felt confident this was it. She examined the barricade for a few seconds, debating between squeezing through a narrow gap where the 'doors' met, or attempting to climb it.

Haste, and not wanting to crawl in dirt, won out. *Up I go.* When her fingers came within inches of the chain link, a faint tug at her shin preceded a cacophony of falling tin cans. Her heart skipped a beat and she froze. Before her brain could calm itself from thinking the tripwire could as easily have been an explosive as a crude alarm, the tromp of running boots came up behind her.

"Hey, what the hell?" yelled a man.

Tris turned, holding her hands up in a non-threatening way. The two men from the sofa in front of Tyrant's dwelling emerged from a gap between cars some distance back. A muscular thug with dark brown skin pointed at her. Behind him, a somewhat shorter man clung to a submachine gun. She tried to make herself seem wide-eyed and harmless. *Works for the kid...*

"Bitch is goin' for the vault," whispered the second.

She bit her lip. "Sorry. I'm not sure how to get out of here. I don't know anything about a vault. I'm lost."

"Yeah, right." The darker man stomped up to her and folded his arms. "Little scav tryin' for a freebie."

His associate looked her up and down. "Dunno, man. Not sure this one's a scav. She don' look wrecked."

"Nothin' to her though. Maybe you're lookin' for somethin' you can sell fer food?"

Tris edged backward a step. "I thought someone was following me and I got scared. I ducked in here to hide, but now I can't get out. This place is like a maze."

"Hey." The other man raised his submachine gun. "Skinny white-haired bitch. Ain't Petersen throwin' coin at that?"

"Think yer right." The dark-skinned man reached for her. "Hello, payday. Be a good little girl and we won't hurt ya."

"No, please!" She whimpered like a frightened teen, darting forward and left.

The man with the submachine gun mistook her rush for a

miscalculated attempt to run away, straight into his arms. He dropped his weapon on a strap, letting it fall against his side as he reached up to catch her. Time seemed to slow as she triggered her reflex boosters. Tris leaned to her right, spinning out of the wires that held the katana to her back. She ducked the grasping hands and rounded the still-sheathed sword into the side of his head.

Speed beyond human ability mixed with boosted strength knocked the oaf into a semiconscious forward stagger. Lunging became falling. He took two steps and landed on his face. She sprang at the dark-skinned man. He weathered the blunted sword stroke across the crown of his head, and grabbed her forearms, growling.

Tris grunted and struggled, shoving him toward the train car wall. The man's eyes shot open wide as she forced him back. The last thing he seemed to expect was to lose a battle of strength with a woman her size. But after a second, the initial shock faded from his glare, and he capitalized on his advantage—height. With a slight lean back, he lifted her feet from the ground and made her helpless. He spun around and slammed her against a stainless steel fridge, holding her in place.

"You be one funky little surprise." He shook his head, seeming to feel the effects of her first strike a moment after the fact.

Hanging like a caught fish, she couldn't overpower the hold he had on her arms. The second his gaze darted to the Beretta on her belt, she slammed her knee into his gut. He barked an "oof," and wheezed. She drove her knee into his side, in three rapid strikes the man likely saw only as a blur. Something cracked. He lost his hold and stumbled back, cradling his gut. Expecting the thug to hesitate from pain, she raised the sword to deliver a knockout strike.

He surged upward and punched her in the face. The hit bounced her skull off the metal fridge. The man gurgled, clutched his ribs, and fell over to the side. The truck yard spun, and the ground came up to kiss her. Cool dirt caressed her cheek. A high-pitched squeal vibrated in her head. Tiny crunching noises came from her jaw, which shifted ever so slightly as nanites repaired a break. A sense of pins and needles swam over her brain as the microscopic robots fought off the effects of a concussion. An explosion of dancing white lights and spots cascaded before her eyes. Her jaw popped back into place, mended before shock let her feel anything.

Tris grabbed her mouth and mumbled into her hand. The man coughed up blood and dragged himself across the dirt toward his unconscious associate, and an Uzi. She forced herself upright and ran three steps before kicking a field goal into the side of his head. He flipped onto his back and went still. She limped to the Uzi, favoring the now-throbbing foot she'd driven into a man's skull. She helped herself to a spare magazine tucked into his inner jacket pocket and slung the little gun over her other shoulder on its strap.

Coldness spread over her instep as the nanites tended to a bruise that would never form. By the time she reached the top of the 'vault' gate, her foot no longer hurt, but her stomach growled. *Great. The little bastards will start digesting* me *if I don't eat something soon.* She leapt to the ground inside and hurried over to a cluster of still-intact filing cabinets. Predictably, they were locked. Though her cybernetics amplified her strength far beyond what a woman her size should possess, the amount of force she could generate was no greater than the upper six percent of human potential.

The voice of Doctor Andrews, former Enclave scientist, replayed in her head from a grainy educational video she'd had to watch as a child. Something about cybernetic enhancements and future humans. "Someday, we hope to provide full augmentation and enhance the capabilities of the human body in more than simple speed. The density of human bone limits the effectiveness of certain components as the body cannot withstand the stresses involved."

"Yeah... so much for augmentation." She squinted up at the moon, racing for cover behind gloomy clouds. "People would kill each other for reliable food and electricity now."

Tris let the padlock fall out of her hand and squinted at the back of Tyrant's boxcar. Sure, she could shoot it out, but that would get every one of his thugs swarming back here with guns out. *I bet Tyrant has the key.*

At least being inside 'the vault' gave her clear access to the rear wall of his home. She jogged over the dirt lot, eyes scanning the ground for any more trip lines, finding none. A modest push failed to move the large sliding door, so she set her feet in the dirt and heaved. It still didn't move.

Barred. She scowled.

A ladder on the right end brought her to the roof. She kept low to avoid notice from any of the people inside the courtyard. *They're lazier than I thought... no one even reacted to jackass screaming.* On the far corner, an open hatch offered a way inside. Someone had rigged a small green plastic tarp over it to block rain, but not air. She slipped under, lowered her legs in, and slid down to hang on her fingertips.

A small table and chairs made of milk crates waited below her, near a crude shelf (also made of milk crates) on which sat a few cardboard boxes, their labels long ago faded. The center of the car held a pair of plush recliners facing a metal box used as a fireplace. Beyond that, at the opposite end of the boxcar, Tyrant lay upon a bed covered in a furry jaguar-patterned comforter with a woman on each side. On a nightstand (also made of milk crates), the cube of void salt sat within arm's reach of him, apparently untouched.

Tris breathed in slow and dropped into the stifling fragrance of sweating bodies, wet dog, and marijuana. All three had their eyes closed. *In and out. They'll never even know I was here.*

"Woof." A shaggy, filthy dog not much larger than a cat emitted a half-hearted bark from one of the recliners. It yawned, putting in the minimum possible effort a guard-dog possibly could. "Mrrff."

She'd mistaken it for a cushion.

"The hell?" Tyrant sat up, propping his weight on his elbows and staring at her.

The woman on his right leapt out of bed, her midnight dark skin covered only by a tiny pair of white lace panties. His other companion, a much smaller woman with traces of Asian and Hispanic in her features, hid behind him. The first woman's sudden exodus from the bed left Tyrant rather distractingly exposed.

Tris cringed, unable to pull her gaze away. *The man's not human.*

He took note of her expression and grinned.

"What the yell you doin' bitch?" The standing woman ran at her.

"I"—Tris leaned to the side to avoid a grab, and punched the woman in the side of the cheek, knocking her senseless with one hit—"need to talk to Tyrant."

The dark-skinned woman tottered backward and fell, draped against the foot of the bed. A second later, she slumped to the side. Tyrant's smaller girlfriend whimpered and eyed something beneath the pillows.

"Don't." Tris pulled the Beretta and aimed it at her. "You're cute, but that shit only works on men."

"You got some serious balls, bitch," said Tyrant.

Tris smiled. "Back at'cha."

Tyrant chuckled.

"What do you want?" The girl narrowed her eyes, seeming jealous.

"Oh, relax. That thing's all yours." Tris suppressed a shiver. "The box. You stole it from a friend of mine."

"Don't know a thing about that." Tyrant sat up, but made no effort to cover himself. "Some skinny bastard named Mike sold it to me."

"I respect that you didn't kill my friend. It's why I didn't come in the front door shooting everything that moved."

"I can recognize that." Tyrant pursed his lips and glanced at the open door leading to the courtyard. At the sight of the empty couch, he frowned. "You don't think you're gonna steal from me and walk on outta here do ya? You got 'nuff heat on your fine ass already from Petersen."

Tris kept the Beretta trained on the conscious woman, not trusting she wouldn't go for whatever sat under the pillow given the chance. "Someone told me you had a kind of honor code. Your boys beat my friend senseless. I returned the favor." She tilted her head toward the couch. "Let's call it a failed negotiation and go back to the start."

Tyrant sucked something out of his teeth. "What's your proposition?"

"I don't really want what's in the box. It's about money. That box was transported by a roadhouse courier. I heard they don't react well to bandits."

Tyrant held his hands up. "Your asses killed the client. Roadhouse be every bit as twisted up at you."

Tris smiled. "Neon wasn't the client. Petersen was. Neon's just an employee."

"Hmm." Tyrant's jaw shifted left and right.

The girl slid her hand along the mattress.

"Stupid bitch." Tris raised the Beretta. "Tyrant, you might wanna put those fuzzy cuffs to good use before your minus one pet vagina."

"*Mata a esta puta,*" said the woman.

"If you insist." Tris pulled the hammer back.

"Hold on." Tyrant pushed the small woman away from the pillow with one arm and held the other up to Tris.

"Two thousand coins or the cube." Tris narrowed her eyes.

He grinned. "Ain't got that much coin, an' you ain't got no way outta here."

"How 'bout a duel then?" Tris smiled. "You and me, hand to hand. First one out cold loses."

Tyrant chuckled and mimed grappling motions. "Why don't you get those clothes off and we can do it all Greco-Roman style."

"That's not happening." Tris shook her head.

"Neither is us fightin'. I saw you take Libby out with one hit, an' that bitch be hard. Yo' bony li'l ass got some shit."

"Guess we're at a stalemate. Look, I really don't want to have to kill anyone. I don't have a lot of time, so this is what's gonna happen." She wagged the Beretta. "You. Out of bed, grab that cube and bring it over here."

The woman blushed and stared.

"You still think you're walkin' outta here?" Tyrant raised an eyebrow.

"I took out Neon and four of his thugs in six seconds. What do you think I could do to your shitheads if I felt like it?"

"Aww, bullshit." Tyrant shook his head.

Libby moaned.

"S'pose you need a little encouragement." Tris glanced down at the semi-conscious Amazonian woman. "Had enough?"

Libby shook off the daze and snarled. She jumped to her feet, ignoring the rather obvious handgun pointed at the smaller woman. Time dragged to a near-standstill; Tris cracked Libby across the crown with the handle of the pistol, drove a hammer fist into the woman's gut, and smashed her over the back of the head with the gun as she doubled over. Time resumed.

The woman collapsed on her chest, unconscious.

"That enough motivation?" Tris had her weapon pointed at the smaller woman again before she could yank the object out from under the pillow. "Go ahead, pull it out. Unload it."

Tyrant stared daggers at Tris while his still-conscious playmate tugged a big chrome handgun out from under the pillow. She removed the magazine and dropped it, but held on to the pistol.

"Clear the slide too, sweetie. I'm snowy, not blonde."

The woman narrowed her eyes, but did so, ejecting a round.

Tris shot a nanosecond-long gaze at the drugs. "Move your ass. Bring me that cube."

Again, the woman turned red. At a nod from Tyrant, she slipped out of bed. Tris raised an eyebrow, not due to the woman's nudity or plethora of knife scars, but at the puffy foxtail hanging down to her knees. The short woman turned to grasp the cube, revealing the faux appendage dangled from between her ass cheeks.

Tris squirmed. *I don't even want to know why.*

Tyrant appeared to find humor in her discomfort and reached down between the mattress and the wall. He held up another butt plug tail, this one black like a panther's and twice as long as the fox. "Got extras if you're curious what it feels like."

When Tris glanced at it, the woman threw the void salt at her, grabbed a knife from the nightstand, and charged. Tris ignored the cube, which sailed over her head and hit the far wall with a loud *thud.* The dog emitted another unmotivated bark. The shrieking woman lunged. Tris dodged to the right, cringing at the sight of the 'tail' flaring out as she spun to pursue. She leapt back to avoid a slice at gut level. Tyrant's excitement at watching a naked, knife-wielding woman chase her around the boxcar grew… visibly.

Tris ducked and weaved, keeping one eye on Tyrant in case he remembered the Desert Eagle on the mattress behind him. Blind with rage, the woman didn't seem to notice their proximity to the courtyard-facing door until Tris caught her forearm out of a wild overhead stab and jiu jitsu-tossed her outside. Tail fluttering, the short woman flew onto the empty sofa, bounced up into a flip, and landed on her ass on the dirt in front of it.

Tris cringed, paralyzed for a split second by imagining how it felt to have all her weight come down on such an object stuffed in such a place. She slammed the door and flipped the locking bar while the stunned woman struggled to get up.

Tyrant shook his head, looking disappointed. She kept the Beretta leveled at him while backing up to where the cube sat on the floor near the 'fireplace,' and squatted over it. A poke of the button caused it to open and extend its four trays.

"Aww, don't you trust me?" Tyrant's baritone laugh vibrated the walls. "We only had the damn thing a couple hours. None 'o my people are crazy enough to dose that shit." A sense of genuine regret tinted his features. "'Sa one-way trip."

"Sounds like it's heat you don't need then." She closed it. "So here's what's next. You forget me, I forget you, and we both go on like tonight never happened."

"Not a whole lot of upside for me in that arrangement."

"You know what this stuff is, don't' you?" She sighed.

"A lot of cash." He chuckled, deep baritone vibrating the walls.

She shook her head. "This is the Enclave trying to kill whoever survived the Virus."

He held his hands up in a gesture of surrender. "I don' *make* anyone buy that shit, but it's good money."

Pounding fists struck the door accompanied by rapid Spanish yelling in a pleading tone.

"Oh, she sounds upset." Tris glanced at the wall.

Tyrant chuckled. "Natasha's a bit shy."

Tris walked to the rear-facing door, opened the lock, and pulled the slab of wood and steel far enough to slip out. "No one's got a bullet in them. I'm only taking back what you stole. Don't press the issue, or you'll be leading a gang of one."

He glanced down, shaking his head.

A dark purple sweatshirt caught her eye, draped over the back of the chair by the dog. She snatched it and jumped out. Metal clattering announced Tyrant jamming the mag into his handgun and racking it. Thuds moved across the boxcar as he stomped. Tris jogged backward, aiming at the door. Scraping preceded the flickering glow of firelight invading the interior. *He's letting Natasha back in.* She sprinted for the gate, climbing it in three leaping strides. At the top, Tris glanced back over her shoulder. Tyrant leaned out of the doorway, Desert Eagle in hand. He aimed for a second, but let his arm drop. After another disappointed head shake, he shoved the door closed.

Tris jumped down and ran past the two moaning thugs. She headed to the right, going around behind the gang's courtyard and emerging with a few rows of dead trucks between her and Tyrant. At that distance, stealth became a triviality. The more organized section of wrecks left her navigating a tighter channel between decaying trailers, and several times forced her to climb collapsed piles of debris.

She found a pull out loading ramp on the underside of a box truck near the fence and propped it in place against the razor wire to use as an easy way up and over. The Uzi and katana rattled against each other when she leapt to the street, seeming loud and painfully obvious in the stillness of the railway path. Fortunately, no one but a few cats came to check out the noise.

Sixty meters or so later, she passed the cluster of barrels where Fix still huddled. The teen's teeth ceased chattering as she peered up, wearing an expression of surprise. Much of the drowsiness of the drug had faded from her expression. She looked awake, but forlorn.

"Don't be so shocked. I'm hard to kill." Tris threw the hoodie at her. "Might wanna peel that thing off your face."

Fix blinked, staring mute.

"You should get out of here. That used to be Tyrant's."

The girl squirmed into the massive sweatshirt, using the oversized sleeves as mittens.

Tris trudged off in the direction of the hotel, tracing her thumb back and forth over the cube.

This has got bad idea written all over it.

25

PLAN B

Sunlight seared a shimmering glare across the horizon, making Kevin squint and raise a peach-fuzz covered arm to shield his face. The hand hovering in front of his face belonged to a four-year-old. The rumble of a semi diesel vibrated his ass from a poorly padded seat. He smiled up at the indistinct silhouette of a bearded man behind the wheel. A plastic hula girl swayed on the dash, next to a taller, thinner cartoon cowboy holding a guitar. Kevin looked down at his gaunt little shirtless body. His jeans were pink, but he didn't care. Dad had found them, and they fit.

He looked back up at the man, a question at the tip of his child brain that could not find a way off his tongue.

"Kevin?" asked a whispery, distant woman.

He peered around the seatback into the sleeper cabin, toward where the voice seemed to have come. Sinuous blackness whorled within, scaring a gasp out of him.

"Kevin?" The voice sounded closer, inches from his ear.

His eyes snapped open. Bland grey ceiling blurred overhead for two seconds before gaining focus. The placidity of sleep gave way to a dull ache throbbing in his arms and legs. Sweat melted out of every pore, a sweltering blanket up to his chest.

"Good morning," said a familiar woman.

Tris. He shifted his head to the left. She lay at his side, naked save for the Beretta dangling from a hand attached to an arm draped over her hip. Porcelain skin glistened with a light coating of perspiration. He stared at a spot halfway between her navel and sex, three inches toward her left hip. Not even a scar remained where the bomb had been.

"Do you feel any better?" She traced a finger over his pectoral. "You're one big bruise."

Kevin closed his eyes again, distracted from lustful thoughts by feeling his pulse in his face and chest. He flung off the blanket in a search for cool. "I'll live."

Something cold landed on his chest, taking a bit of the pain away from a tender spot. He leaned his head up, opened his eyes, and stared at the cube. A second later, he sat up clutching it in both hands and poked the button to open it. At the sight of all the ampules still in their trays, he sagged with relief.

"How the hell did you…"

Tris rolled off the bed, leaving the Beretta. "I can be sneaky. By the way, there's no hot water, but there is a shower."

"I'll be right there."

She kept going. "Better not. Keep a gun on the door in case we have visitors."

He reached for the pistol, freezing when he spotted the Uzi hung over the back of the desk chair. "You went shopping?"

A metallic *squeak* preceded the pattering of water. "Shit! This is cold. Not exactly. Pinch of opportunity."

The floor creaked as if someone approached the door outside.

"You didn't see my .45 did you?" He forced himself out of bed and took the Uzi. It seemed in dire need of cleaning, but mechanically intact. "Did you fire this or see it fire?"

"N-n-no." Her teeth chattered.

He dropped it back on the seat, sat on the edge of the bed, and put a hand on the Beretta, watching the door. Whoever it was outside either kept going or had fallen asleep on their feet. A few minutes later, Tris emerged, covered from armpit to mid-thigh with a towel. Kevin handed her the pistol and trotted into the bathroom. A little toilet sat so close to the shower one could barely take a dump without getting their feet wet. He flung off his briefs and stood under a stream of chilly water. The stagnant heat of the motel room baking in the sun of a desert morning made the frigid downpour feel amazing.

Kevin tried not to think about closed-circuit plumbing systems, poor filters, and how many other people's piss he might have in his hair at that moment. Once the shower went from 'ahh' to 'damn, this is cold,' he hopped out and stumbled into the room. Much to his disappointment, Tris had her clothes on—though he had to admit to himself his body wasn't quite up for that yet. Being on his feet and walking was already asking a bit much.

After struggling into his jeans, shirt, and boots, he forced himself to put the jacket on, but left it open. During a hunt for something to conceal the cube with, he found another surprise in the bathroom: TP. Kevin pondered stealing it. He knew places he could sell a three-quarter-full roll for six coins, but decided against any more jinxes. Takin' someone's shitter paper was about as low as it got... well, next to stealin' his car.

"Ready?"

Tris glanced at the Uzi. "Not interested?"

"Untested."

"I took it off a guy who was about to shoot me with it. He trusted it."

Kevin smirked, but accepted the Uzi when she handed it to him. "What the hell did you do?"

"I'll tell you about it over food." She rubbed her stomach with both hands. "I'm about to eat myself."

OVER THE COURSE OF A MEAL INCLUDING UNIDENTIFIABLE MEAT PATTIES and home fries, Tris explained the gory details. Kevin kept eying the diner windows, not too comfortable being out in the open with the cube while the 'King of Glimmertown' had his people looking for them. At any second, the quiet murmurs of a handful of what passed for 'citizens' here having a late breakfast could become screaming and shooting.

"What's bothering you?" Tris sipped her coffee.

He looked down at his untouched burger and toast and sighed. "I've had that 1911 since I was nine. Really, I guess I ought to be glad I managed not to lose it this long... but—" He flicked a fingernail on the edge of the table.

"Your dad's?"

Kevin moved only his eyes to stare at her, still sitting slouched. "What makes you say that?"

She gave him a sympathetic look. "Well, men only get like that about firearms if they're damaged in the head or if their dad gave it to them."

She picked up her coffee, but hesitated before drinking. "And you were muttering in your sleep, apologizing to him for losing it."

"Oh." He shifted in the seat, unable to look at her. "Well, he didn't exactly give it to me. He died when I was like four. One of his friends found me later and passed it on."

Tris smiled. "Nothing to be ashamed of. I miss my dad too."

"What happened to him?"

"I don't know." She gazed into her mug. "He vanished one day and I got reassigned to new parents. Mom2 and Dad2 treated me like I'd always been theirs. Kinda creepy. They thought I was having 'mental problems' when I asked about my real father. The entire city seemed to think he'd never even existed. No one talked about him, and whenever I asked, they were all condescending and stuff like I was having imaginary friends."

"That's twisted." He felt a little awkward at being sentimental over a gun by comparison. "Bet he was involved with the resistance."

"What?" Tris looked up. "Where did that come from?"

"Well, think about it." He scooted back in the bench seat and leaned forward. "A small society like the Enclave that's heavy on propaganda and mind control needs to wipe out any trace of dissent, right? Everyone's supposed to eat the same bullshit for breakfast, lunch, and dinner. If someone steps out of line... questions that council of four or whatever they are... it makes sense for them to stop existing. Preserves the illusion for the rest of the sheep."

Red appeared around Tris's eyes.

"Hey, sorry... just a theory. I'm guessing."

"I can go back for it." She sniffled. "Tyrant's girls might pose a bit of a problem, but maybe he'll sell your gun back to us."

He wrapped a half-patty in a piece of toast and jammed it into his mouth, chewing the salty mush slow enough to dare tasting it. A tinny clatter of improvised bells announced the door opening. He left the 'sandwich' dangling from his teeth and grabbed the Uzi. Tris spun to face behind her at the door as a short figure in a dark violet hoodie walked in with her hands stuffed in the front pockets. Black hair hung to the belt down the front. Fix pulled her hood back, and looked off at the left end of the diner, evidently searching. When she swung her gaze to the right, she locked stares with Tris and trudged over. Her expression held the begrudging politeness of a teen forced to go apologize against their will.

"I don't believe this kid." Tris turned her head as the girl approached, sliding back into a normal seated position by the time Fix stood at the end of their table, eyes downcast.

"Hey," said the girl.

A small red mark on her cheek remained where the 'sleepy time' derm had been.

"Get outta here, ya little rat," yelled a bearded guy behind the counter. "I already told you, I catch you stealin' in here again I'm—"

Kevin raised a placating hand at him.

"You got some balls, kid." Tris squinted. "What the hell are you doing?"

She sniffled.

"You can skip the pathetic act." Kevin folded his arms. "I've been around long enough not to fall for the old crying beggar kid with a hidden knife."

"Not acting." Fix bit her lip. "Sorry for tryin' to steal your stuff."

"Yeah, well. Be happy you're a kid." Kevin made a shooing gesture. "G'won afore the cook has a stroke."

Fix glanced at Tris's chest, avoiding eye contact. "Thanks for the jacket."

"Lucky it happened to be there when I was leaving." Tris shot Kevin an unreadable stare, somewhere between apologizing for being nice to the girl and guilt.

"Yeah. Still, you didn't have to give it to me."

"Apology accepted." Kevin glanced at the windows again, relieved that no one hustled up in ambush while the kid distracted them.

Fix didn't budge.

"Oh for fuck's sake." Tris scooted toward the window. "Sit down." She waved at the cook. "'Nother burger please."

"You're payin for it. Ain't my charity," yelled the man behind the counter.

"Such friendly neighbors in this place." Kevin winked.

Fix eased herself into the bench seat, perching on the edge and sitting rigid.

"Knock it off with the pathetic bit." Kevin sighed. "We're not going to hurt you." He swabbed meat juice up with his toast. "Unless you try something shifty."

"You got a car, right?" She kept her gaze on her lap.

Kevin squeezed the Uzi. She looked like an older version of the 'hand grenade orphans' from closer to the Mexican border. Round face, wide, innocent eyes, and a backpack full of badness to throw at you when you stopped watching them. They weren't orphans though. If the grenade didn't ·finish you off, Mom or Dad would… or one of their siblings too old to be 'cute' anymore. Fortunately, the Marauder had thick armor.

Damn, I miss that truck.

"The only way you're going near my car is hogtied and in the trunk." Kevin pointed over the table. "I'm not losing another one."

Tris chuckled. "Don't feel bad, I had to be tied up to ride the first time too."

Fix looked up, fear plain on her face. "R-really?"

Kevin frowned. "I found her like that."

"And he didn't trust me enough to cut me loose. Thought I was gonna steal his car."

"The last woman I let near my car stole it." He scowled.

"Oh, so everyone with tits is a car thief?" Tris rolled her eyes.

"No…" He tapped a finger on the table. "Everyone who's alone and not as harmless as they look is a car thief."

Tris stuck her tongue out. "I never wanted to steal your car."

"I don't." Fix looked down. "I just wanna get out of this place."

The cook arrived with a plate. She cringed away, raising a hand to shield her face. The portly man set the meal in front of her and gave Kevin a look of mutual annoyance at her 'overacted' pitifulness. Kevin nodded. Tris handed him two coins.

Fix stared at the food without taking her hands out of the sweatshirt pocket. "I gotta get outta Glimmertown. I don't care if you tie me up. I'll ride in the trunk if you want. Just get me outta here."

"What's the rush?" Tris glanced at the window. "Who'd you piss off that'll shoot us for helping you?"

"Wow. I thought I was the cynic." Kevin chuckled.

Tris winked. "Must be rubbing off."

"Not yet. Too much pain." Kevin managed not to grimace while stretching.

A little pink appeared in Tris's cheeks.

"No one." Fix risked making eye contact with Tris. "I'm fifteen. Won't be long before those assholes at Cloud 9 come after me. I don't wanna be a whore… you know, like you didn't wanna be. They'da grabbed me already, but I'm good at lookin' like a little kid."

Tris glared at the girl with such a look of rage Kevin started to reach over the table to grasp her hand.

"I mean... you killed Neon right 'cause he wanted to buy you." Fix leaned away, shivering. "That's all I meant."

"Oh. Yeah... and four of his guys." She sighed. "It's his car, but I don't see the harm in giving you a ride to the first roadhouse we hit."

"I'll have to buy some rope." Kevin drummed his fingers on the table.

"Okay." After a moment, Fix summoned her most pitiful expression and looked up at him. "What if I did you a favor?"

"I'm not sure I want to know where you're going to take that." Kevin pursed his lips. "You seem to be part of the scene here... Think you can set up a buy with Petersen for some stuff?"

"The Salt?" Fix shivered. "Uhh, no. If I go in there, I ain't comin' out. You stole all their women. They wouldn't even care how old I am."

"Dunno, man." The cook walked over and topped off their coffees. "Rumor goin' round Petersen and Neon weren't rightly eye to eye."

"How's that?" Kevin looked up at a sweaty face covered by a wild brown beard streaked with grey.

"Petersen's about power and business. Neon had his... vices. Slaving gets some people all sorts of sentimental. Tempers flare. No one comes blazing into town ready to die to rescue their drugs." The cook gave Fix a pointed stare before walking off.

"I mean another kind of favor." Fix let a little hope creep into her green eyes. "I'm sneaky too."

"We know," said Kevin and Tris at the same time.

Fix pulled her hands out of the pocket, revealing a 1911 pistol. She cradled it flat across her palms, careful not to seem as if she intended to use it, and set it on the Formica table. Kevin gawked at the American Eagle grips and familiar scratches on the left side. "My real name's Stacy."

Kevin grabbed it. Tris tried to hide a smile behind her hand.

"Is gettin' that back for you enough for a ride outta here?"

"This is it." He ran his fingers over the weapon before putting it back in its holster. "I think I can about forgive you for trying to steal my jacket."

Tris smirked at him. Her expression said 'really?'

Stacy seemed to relax. "I know someone lookin' for a driver to move some stuff. Last I heard, they're payin' 1800 coins."

Kevin pointed at Tris. "This one offered me a thousand for a ride and I still haven't seen a tenth of it."

The amused tone in his voice kept her from appearing too upset, but Tris still looked down.

"Isn't me payin'." Stacy at last attacked her food, devouring it as if she hadn't eaten in days. "I'll set up a meeting, 'an you can decide from there. It ain't Cloud 9."

Tris drained her coffee. "If that other job pans out, you could offload that crap to Petersen for say one thousand… tell him you'll take the loss as a 'make-it-right' gesture or something."

Stacy almost smiled at him. "Yeah, he might forgive you for killing Neon."

Kevin's eyebrows formed a flat ridge. "*I* didn't kill Neon."

26

A MATTER OF PERSPECTIVE

By some strange paradox, Glimmertown seemed far quieter at ten in the morning than at two hours after midnight. Sun-beaten streets, some paved, most dirt, saw only a few scattered pieces of trash moving about. Old tin cans and battered plastic cartons scraped along in a fitful breeze. The distant shadow of the reinforced barrier around the settlement made it feel more like a prison than an oasis.

Tris followed Stacy for five or so minutes, staring at the girl's hands for any sign of deceit. *Is this how Kevin felt when he first met me?* She wanted to trust the innocent-looking face, but the attempted ambush with a drug patch validated Kevin's worry. The girl paused to look back before taking a left turn, stepping over a collapsed stack of aluminum shipping boxes. She'd gone into a narrow alley that ran in a rightward curve between the backs of two rows of ramshackle dwellings, thick with shadows despite the daylight. Somewhere, an electric fan motor whirred and rattled. Tris slid her katana out of its sheath.

A quick two-step rush caught up to the teen. Tris grabbed her by the shoulder and flung her into the wall, leveling the sword point at her throat. "Okay, kid. What's your game?"

Stacy stared for a half second before the tears started. "G-game?"

"You got us to split up, and now you're leading me into a dark alley. Who's waiting for us?"

"N-no one." Stacy held her hands up. "I promise… no bullshit. Please don't kill me."

Tris stared down the gleaming length of steel and narrowed her eyes.

"Please…" Stacy whined and rose up on tiptoe to get away from the point at her throat. "You're the only one in this place who's ever been nice to me. I wasn't always like this. I swear I ain't gamin' you."

Tris lowered the sword one inch. "You've seen how fast I can move."

"Yeah." Stacy nodded.

"I've got some Enclave tech. One of my toys is a kind of lie detector." Tris touched the point of the katana to the base of the girl's throat. "It measures facial gestures and stress responses. Look me right in the eye and tell me you're not leading me into some kind of ambush. If it tells me you're lying, I'm going to cut your head off right here."

Stacy shivered, sniveled, and cried. She stared at Tris without blinking. "I'm not lying. Her name's Jasmin. She runs the general store. Has a job. I wanna get out of this town."

If this kid's acting, she's pretty damn good at it. Tris sighed and lowered the sword. "Okay. Sorry. It's been shitty for us lately. Gotta be careful."

Stacy covered her face with her hands, shivering and breathing hard. She wiped her eyes and moved away from the wall. "S'okay. I did, like, try to sleepy you and everything. I understand why you don't trust me."

The teen's sorrowful look bloomed into one of startlement. Instinctively, Tris's cybernetic boost kicked on. A scuff of dirt came from behind. She whirled. A skinny man with wild hair and a thin goatee down to his belly leapt out of a gap between two huts, a syringe held high like an assassin's dagger.

Tris whipped her blade around, severing his arm midway between wrist and elbow. The pain from the strike only began to register on his face when her follow through took his head off. He hit the ground with a weak *thump.* Stacy whimpered.

Tris glanced back to find the girl trembling. "Pee yourself?"

Stacy shook her head. "Almost. Ain't never seen anyone die before… not that close."

"Sorry. I've got a problem with slavers." Tris squatted and gathered a bit of the man's coat in her hand, using it to clean the blade. "If you're with us for any length of time, you'll probably see death a lot more."

"Hey… I ain't like lookin' to be adopted or some shit. Too old for that now. I just wanna get outta here 'fore… you know."

Tris stood. "Kevin said most people out here are friendly and helpful."

"He ain't from Glimmertown. This place ain't 'most people.'"

"Lead on." Tris slid the katana back in the scabbard and crushed the syringe under her shoe.

"Sec." Stacy cringed as she crouched over the body and rummaged his pockets. She collected a couple coins, a knife, and three needle-tipped ampules of white liquid. "'Kay."

Tris glowered at her until she dropped the drugs. *Poor kid.* "How'd you wind up here?"

Stacy's pleading look back and forth from Tris to the injectors failed to sway her. "Don't really remember much. I was pretty small. When you're real little, everyone's nice. 'Ventually, I stopped being a 'little kid' and it changed. People didn't wanna give me food and stuff unless I did *things.* So I started stealing. The drugs... I don't really remember how; they kinda happened."

"Just say no." Tris smiled.

Stacy blinked. "What?"

Tris tugged her along by the sweatshirt. "I've seen historical documentaries about what drugs do to people. You're supposed to 'just say no' and everything will be okay."

"Uhh, whatever." Stacy trudged on. "I haven't had any in a while. Startin' to feel like ass."

"What were you taking?"

"I dunno. Whatever I could get my hands on. Not VS. Fuck that with a capital f. Most people who take that crap don't come back. They get high and stay there."

Tris cringed. *The Enclave... I never should've let him take that stuff to sell.* "It's as much my fault as his now. I didn't have to get it back."

"Huh?" Stacy looked back.

"That box. It's uhh... full of void salt."

Stacy's light brown skin faded to almost Caucasian for a second. "No way. Uhh, maybe I shouldn't go with you two."

"Oh, it's not happening again." She glared at the wall, where someone had painted a giant jalapeño pepper with a sombrero and eyes. "Guilt makes a person do strange things."

"Yeah." Stacy gathered the purple sweatshirt tight. "I guess. Sorry."

Eighteen minutes later according to the time floating in the lower left corner of her vision, Tris followed Stacy along a passage between two large buildings. The alley forced them to turn sideways and shimmy in spots, except for a protruding ventilation fan that required a little crawling to get by.

"Where the hell are you going?" Tris dragged herself past the gap and stood.

Stacy replied in a whisper. "You got Petersen's crew looking for you, and probably Tyrant's as well. Jasmin's place is right in the main quad. Sneaking in the back way."

The girl crept to the end of the building and poked her head out into the sun. A few seconds later, she slipped around to the right. Tris followed into a wide-open quad surrounded by various shops, casinos, and brothels. The garage where the Challenger waited sat less than sixty yards away, on the far side of the reinforced gate. Stacy kept close to the wall and ducked into the first doorway she reached.

Tris walked in behind her, eyeing a room set up like an old-timey store with shelves of seemingly random stuff: canteens, coils of wire, a pile of mass-produced machetes, tackle boxes, a handful of mismatched boots, one sleeping bag, matches, candles, a number of shirts, and even some canned goods. Over the shelves on the right, a selection of cowboy hats hung on pegs. Tris debated getting one for Kevin, but expected he'd only complain about wasting money.

At the back end of the store, a woman who could've been Stacy's cousin by looks stood behind a glass counter. She had a pair of handguns in a nylon harness over a grey tank top that struggled to contain her rather generous bosom. The clerk had a second pair of handguns on her belt, camo fatigues, and flip-flops. A pair of well-worn black combat boots sat near a doorway that led deeper into the back.

Tris approached, still mulling the hat. She pictured him wearing *only* the hat and grinned to herself. Red velvet material on the enclosed shelves bore dark spots in the shapes of handguns, though the only items inside consisted of a handful of chintzy rings and a box of bandages.

"What's this?" asked the woman, speaking to Stacy but giving Tris a look. "Somethin' not natural here."

Stacy leaned back, elbows on the counter, and smiled. "Jaz, I found some people who might be interested in that job."

The woman regarded Tris with a critical eye. "Well, you definitely not from Glimmertown."

"No... no I'm not." Tris nodded at Jasmin's belt. "That's a lot of hardware to protect a couple pairs of boots and some camping gear."

Little trace of warmth lurked in the eyes locked on her. "What's the Enclave doin' out here?"

"Beats me." Tris put her hands on her hips. "They want me dead. What's a shop owner willing to pay 1800 coins for someone to drive somewhere? I'm guessing you've got some *special* merchandise. We're not interested if it's drugs."

"Oh, a crusader." Jasmin's hard glare relaxed. "Next thing, you'll be tellin' me you're the one that offed Neon."

Stacy coughed.

Tris shrugged. "Not sure I know anything about that. Though, I've heard some guns tend to go off on their own if they're brought too close to stupid people."

Jasmin smiled. "Took his pets too, huh?"

"They're safe." Tris kept half an eye on the window, watching shapes she assumed to be armed men move around outside. "Not havin' a whole ton of time here. What's the run?"

"Well." Jasmin chuckled. "It is drugs, but not the kind you're thinkin' of. Medical supplies. Antibiotics, some pain killers, couple antivirals, basic stuff."

"And you're going to trust someone you've never met to take it where you want it to go?" Tris blinked. "Seems like an awful lot of faith to have in a town like this."

"I've got a lot of faith in GPS and tamper-proof cases." Jasmin folded her arms. "The kind of tamper proofing that puts a permanent end to thieves."

Tris tilted her head to one side. "GPS hasn't worked in years. All the satellites got toasted during the war."

"Damn. Fuckin' Enclave would know that." Jasmin glared at the floor.

Stacy covered her mouth to hide her grin.

"Why would we steal it? Bandits aren't all that interested in medical supplies. Besides, Kevin's a driver for the roadhouse. If something goes wrong, you can take it up with them."

Jasmin tapped a foot, seeming to debate the issue.

"Not to mention," said Tris, "1800 coins is a lot to pay for a bunch of painkillers and antibiotics. Where's it going? That's the catch, isn't it? It's going somewhere shitty."

"Not that bad." Jasmin pursed her lips. "Dallas."

That sounds familiar... must be a big city. Kevin's gonna love that. "I think we can do it. How large a shipment are you talking? We've got car, not a cargo truck."

"One box." Jasmin outlined a shape about the size of a footlocker in midair. "Should fit in a trunk. Sergeant Ralston is the contact in Dallas. He's got the code for the box and the money for you. I've already got my cut of it, so you don't have to come back."

Oh, sure. The guy we're going to has the money. She froze, staring at the wall. *Wow. Hypocrite much?* "Okay. Meet at the garage tomorrow morning?"

"Sounds like a deal." Jasmin reached over the counter to shake hands.

Tris accepted. "See you then. Oh, hey you got any spare ibuprofen around? Friend of mine went face first down the stairs."

Jasmin disappeared into the back room, returning half a minute later with a brown plastic bottle.

Tris stuffed a hand in her pocket. "How much?"

"Only six pills… Call it a good faith gesture." Jasmin set the meds down and slid them across the counter.

"Thanks." Tris tossed the bottle up, caught it, and headed for the door.

Stacy led the way back across the courtyard, skimming along in the shadows. Once they cleared the far end of the too-narrow passageway, she spun and looked Tris in the eye.

"That whole lie detector thing was bullshit, wasn't it?"

Tris smiled. "Yeah, a little."

Stacy looked annoyed, but laughed it off. She tapped her sneaker on the dirt. "What's GPS?"

"Old tech for navigation. It used satellites to tell people where they were."

"What's a satellite?" Stacy fell in step at her side.

Tris whistled. "Electronics people used to launch into outer space. They'd float around the planet and do all sorts of different things. Some even had lasers on them that could assassinate people."

"Wow…" Stacy shivered. "That's scary as shit. How do you know all this stuff?"

Tris shrugged. "I watched a lot of historical documentaries."

KEVIN LEANED ON A WALL AT THE CORNER OF AN ALLEY, GLANCING AT THE front of Cloud 9 out of the corner of his eye. He tapped his foot and shifted his weight from leg to leg. At this hour, the place looked abandoned. After what had happened there, it wouldn't be a stretch to imagine it *was* abandoned. Tris did have a point... he couldn't summon much respect for the sort of people to be more upset at having their clothing stolen than they were at enslaved women. *With Tris going apeshit and titties bouncing everywhere, maybe no one noticed me. Not my circus. Not my monkeys.* He sighed. *This is the king of shitty ideas on a mountain of shit.*

"I should write that on a coffee mug." He shoved off the wall and strode across the clearing.

He fidgeted with the empty holster on his belt as he walked. Leaving the .45 in the hotel room was a calculated risk. Assuming this idiotic plan worked out even close to a way that didn't leave him twisted into a human pretzel knot, odds were high they'd disarm him before he got within shouting distance of Petersen. The chance they'd 'lose' it was a chance he didn't want to take. The Uzi would suffice.

The front doors of Cloud 9 were open, which surprised him. He stepped inside, and found the place in much the same condition as he'd left it in, except for the lack of bodies. The dancing cages remained empty and open, someone had cleaned up the blood on the floor, and the absence of unbearable stench had to mean Neon's office got cleaned out as well.

"W'aint open yet." An imposing bald man behind the bar, patch over his left eye, looked up from a porno magazine that looked three times older than him.

Kevin tapped into something halfway between courage and idiocy. "Man, those pages were stuck together before you were a dirty thought in someone's head."

"Yeah." Tall and Bald flipped it closed to examine the cover. "2018, and it ain't for sale."

"Not buyin'." Kevin put one hand on the bar. "Or drinkin'. I got a package for Mr. Petersen. Roadhouse job."

"Leave it. I'll get it to him." The man fluttered pages back to his place. A few did seem fused together.

"Can't, pal. You know the drill. Gotta bring it to him."

The security guy grumbled and got that look in his eye like he was about to do whatever it took to regain his previous solitude. He shifted his weight forward as if to stand.

"700 ampules of void salt." Kevin scratched his head. "You look like a no-bullshit kinda guy, so I figure before you throw me out the door and get the big man's panties in a knot, you should know."

The man froze with one ass cheek still on his chair. "Have a seat."

Kevin took the nearest stool and leaned on the bar while the security man fiddled with what appeared to be a CB radio under the bar.

"Pedro, it's Al. Got some dude here says he's got a box of Salt for Mr. P."

Static crackled as he let off the talk button.

"Sec, Al." About a minute later, the radio crackled. "Sendin' an escort."

"Copy." Tall and Bald set the mic down and reclined with his back to the wall. "You're in luck, buddy. He'll see you."

Yeah. Luck. I guess that's one way to put it.

Kevin stared around at the place for a while, trying to guess which bullet holes came from Tris's attack of conscience, and which had been there for years. A chewed on table leg lined up with a recent patch in the front of the bar. *Wow, they fixed that pretty damn fast.*

"Hey," yelled an average looking man in the doorway. His voice sounded far too deep for his build. "You the driver?"

"Yep." Kevin threw a half-hearted salute at the bald man and headed to the door. Two other, much larger, men waited on the road. Both had shotguns, and more lame attempts at fancy suits. "Wow, red carpet time."

"Comedian," said the closer man. "I'll need the Uzi till you're done with the boss. Plus any others you got on ya. We find one later on, it's going up your ass."

Kevin shrugged the strap off his shoulder and heaved the weapon to the guy. "Figured. I'm just finishin' a job. Don't want any trouble. Only brought that one." He pulled his jacket open to show off his lack of other weapons.

"Yeah, yeah. That's what they always say."

The dark-haired guy waved him to follow and headed off down a side street. The two leg breakers with shotguns took up the rear. They meandered in no great hurry down streets wide enough for two cars to pass abreast. Most of the facing buildings had the look of bars, casinos, or abandoned houses. An old, twisted street sign identified an intersection as S. Temple going one way and S 400 E branching off at a T, but the way it had bent left it anyone's guess which was which.

Hmmf. Temple my ass. If there is a god, he's left this place way behind.

His guide hooked a right past the sign, which put the mountains to their left. About five minutes of walking later, he turned toward the mountains and passed a collapsed multi-tier parking deck and a plain beige brick building beyond it before cutting across a dirt lot full of car parts that may once have been a well-tended lawn. A short concrete porch led up to the face of a three-story building that bore a mild resemblance to an ancient castle. On the third floor, metal gratings protected windows long-since devoid of glass, where men stood behind belt-fed machine guns mounted on posts. The entire first floor had layer upon layer of metal armor plates arranged around it, several with car-shaped dents.

That explains the thing with cars.

The man stopped at the door. "Before we go inside. You got any hidden weapons you don't have room in your ass for?"

"Just my mouth." Kevin winked. "Feel free to check. I haven't been felt up by a dude in about six months. Kinda miss it."

"I'll take yer word for it." The deep-voiced man opened the door and went in.

After a brief trip down a hallway and up two flights of stairs, they followed a moldy carpet beneath a skylight installed via high explosives to a dull red door that looked as if it could stop missiles. The man opened it for him and waited.

Kevin forced a smile and stepped past him into a dark wood-paneled office that seemed to have escaped the very existence of a nuclear war. A subtle hint of unsmoked cigar lingered in the air. Overstuffed bookshelves surrounded a desk at which an older man stared imperiously down at him from a wingback chair.

Mr. Petersen could've been fifty as easily as ninety. The appearance of his face, pale, stout, and veiny, had the texture of a nonagenarian, but the structure and shape of a much younger man. Despite a plain white button-down shirt that seemed far too clean for anyone in Glimmertown to be wearing, the man's eyes pinned him in place. Kevin had the distinct urge to turn around and haul ass.

"This is the driver?" asked Mr. Petersen, raising a steel-wool eyebrow. "Ahh, yes. The red jacket."—he gestured at a facing chair covered in gold velveteen—"Please."

Against his better judgement, Kevin approached the desk and sat. A weak mechanical noise emanated from somewhere behind the desk. Rhythmic, it whirred, hissed and popped in an endless cycle. He managed a pleasant smile. The two shotgun meatheads entered, but remained by the wall on either side of the door.

"You've caused quite a stir in my city, mister..."

"Kevin."

Mr. Petersen's eyebrows edged closer.

"No idea what my last name is. Dad got himself dead before I was five."

"Well... *Kevin*... I would be most interested in hearing your side of what happened."

Something in Petersen's unflinching glare unsettled him. He had the tone of one who spoke to a soon-to-be dead man. Kevin's heart raced as he tried to channel the attitude that had thus far kept him alive. In the back of his head, he pictured Wayne pointing at a patch of empty dirt behind the roadhouse. *Behold, the garden in which I grow my fucks. You might notice it's barren.*

"I wound up running into this crazy bitch. Promised me all kinds of money for a ride, and... well. That didn't work out. So since she's handy with a gun I figured I'd keep her ass around till she covered what she owed."

Petersen steepled his fingers in front of his face, nodding once.

"Get the job to bring your package here. Instructions said to bring it to Neon at Cloud 9. So, we go in there. He's got these women..."

"I am aware." A hint of disdain warped Petersen's mouth, giving Kevin a spark of hope.

"So, Neon's in the middle of finalizing the drop off when he offers me money for the woman. She had a small objection to being taken as a slave."

"So you killed Neon, six of my employees, four customers, and robbed half a dozen others?"

Kevin let out a nervous chuckle. "Well, if you don't mind me splitting hairs... I sort of stood there watching. She's had some work done. The whole Neon thing was pretty much over before I even pulled a gun out."

Mr. Petersen tapped his fingertips together in a rotating pattern from pinky to thumb. "You must understand how this looks. My people are dead and seven of the club's assets are missing."

"Six." Kevin held up a finger. "Tris isn't a slave. A person ain't a slave till they get captured, and Neon wasn't tall enough to ride that ride."

"I assume you decided to bring more than glib witticisms with you today?" Petersen pulled his hands apart and let them rest on the desk.

"Correct. The original delivery stipulated I was to exchange the package and collect 2700 coins. Considering the... problems, I'd like to suggest we do the exchange for one thousand."

Petersen at last shifted his drilling gaze away from Kevin's eyes. He seemed to mull the idea, and the dour, imposing presence faded to a more cordial smile. "We have an agreement. You have the package with you?"

"Uhh." Kevin scratched his head. "It's in my room at the hotel. I… well… I half expected you to just kill me and figured I'd make you work for it if that was how it went down."

Mr. Petersen laughed. "So you aren't as dumb as you look."

Kevin cringed inside, but smiled. "I keep hearing that."

"Don't worry, Kevin… Neon was getting to be a bit of a problem. Outgrowing his position. I assumed the man would attempt some manner of power play soon. You did me a favor. I'll consider your eating the 1700 coins and the bounty I was contemplating putting on Neon as a break even on the damage your out of control woman caused."

"Sounds good." Kevin pointed over his shoulder with a thumb. "I'll go grab the stuff and be right back?"

Mr. Petersen's stare seemed to slice into his soul. The unsettling quality returned after a few seconds, made worse by a sourceless, repetitive mechanical noise that occupied the silence. Kevin shifted in his seat.

"That is fine." Mr. Petersen flashed a broad smile. "See that you do return. It would be most unfortunate if you did not."

Kevin stood. "I won't be long." He started for the door, but stopped. "Can I ask something?"

"Questions can always be asked, Kevin. The answers are often the problem."

He hesitated. "Is it… true you were around before the war? You, uhh, don't look that old."

Mr. Petersen smiled and gestured at the door. "Why don't you go and retrieve my package, and we can talk about history when you return. I'll put on some tea in the meantime."

"Uhh, sure."

One of the shotgun meatheads opened the door.

Kevin leaned back with a smile. "Tea sounds lovely. See you in a few minutes."

IT AIN'T ME

An hour after leaving Mr. Petersen's office for the second time, Kevin's heart continued racing. He decided against coffee and sipped metal-flavored water. Anxiety got his foot tapping. Another minute later, he set the glass down and drummed his fingers on the table. Tris appeared from an alley across the street about forty seconds before he got up to go look for her. Stacy trailed behind as they hurried across to the diner and slipped into the opposite seat.

The girl seemed wearier than before, but also at ease. Dark rings around her eyes had appeared since the last time he'd seen her, only three hours ago. A twinge of concern needled at him, but he swallowed it. All he needed was for her to sniff out a strand of vulnerability and she'd exploit it.

"How'd it go?" He smiled at Tris.

She wobbled her head side to side. "Not bad. Got the job set up. Seems legit. 1800 coins to drop off some painkillers. Oh... here."

Kevin glanced at a pill bottle rolling across the table toward him. "What's that?"

"Ibuprofen."

Kevin blinked. "Gesundheit."

"Are you still sore?" She grabbed the bottle before it fell off the edge and stood it on end. "Take one. It's a non-narcotic pain pill."

As soon as she mentioned pain, his bones ached. "Thanks for reminding me I got my ass kicked."

Tris kept quiet for a moment, fixing him with an earnest stare. "How'd it go with the... uhh..."

"I'm here aren't I?" He opened the bottle and poured one capsule into his palm. "Petersen's quite a talker. Either he really is over a hundred, or he's living in his own fantasy world." Kevin tossed the pill in his mouth and slugged down the rest of his water. "Told me all about how he used to live around this area before the war... worked for a robotics manufacturer trying to get people to buy actuators."

"Sounds like fun." Tris leaned back as the cook brought her a coffee. She handed him a penny. "Thanks. So the 'king of Glimmertown' is settled with us?"

"Yeah, I got a talking to about how I can't 'control my woman,' but it's over and done with." Tris scoffed. "I hope that kid's job works out, or I'm gonna take a beating at Wayne's."

"Control your woman?" Tris fumed. "I'll show him controlling—"

"Hey, easy... or I'll have to break out the rope again."

She kicked him in the shin.

"Ow. Aww." He rubbed it. "Easy... I'm wounded."

Stacy shivered, seeming feverish. She looked up as if to add something to the conversation, but her head dipped down.

"Well, the upside is, Petersen's not a big fan of Neon and his slave trade. Too many complications. Though the drug thing is here to stay. So, about that job."

Tris sipped her coffee in silence for a few minutes. "1800 coins to run medical supplies to a settlement. It's not on any roadhouse channels, so it should be a mystery run."

"That's good." He stared at her. "You haven't once mentioned the destination, so I'm going to assume I won't like it."

"Dalmmnfths." She mumbled into her hand.

His eyebrows flattened. "Out with it."

"Dallas."

Kevin stared at the ceiling. "Oh for fuckety fuck's fucking fucked sake."

An uninspired giggle hiccupped from Stacy, sounding half-alive. She raised a hand in a lame attempt to point at him. "He said a bad word."

"Do I want to know?" Tris raised an eyebrow.

"Dallas took a direct hit. The place practically glows at night. Plus, it's a major pop center, so there's gonna be Infected coming out of the goddamned walls." He glared at Stacy, not that she noticed. *If she hadn't suggested it...* "I'd rather eat the 1700."

Tris grabbed his hand. "Hey, don't be like that. There's a settlement there, so obviously the stories are a little exaggerated. Jasmin did say we *had* to take route 75 in from the north, so maybe it's not inside the city itself, but near enough to be called Dallas?"

He grumbled.

"Hey, can I tell you something?"

The sincerity in her voice caught him off guard. "Yeah."

"When I heard the payment's waiting for us in Dallas, my first thought was 'bullshit.' I... I get why you didn't trust me. I understand now."

He let all the air out of his lungs in a slow sigh. A feeble sense of vindication withered away at the look in her eyes. He felt like the guy who told a little girl Santa Claus was made up. "Yeah...."

<hr />

KEVIN STOMPED OUT THE SMALL DOOR FROM THE GARAGE OFFICE TO THE parking area, twenty coins light. *Greedy, mercenary prick.* He ignored the shiny silver car and hooked a right past the cinderblock wall separating it from the Challenger. Tris, Stacy, Tina, Shailaja, and the four other women from Cloud 9 all crowded at the passenger side door.

"Oh, hell." He grumbled. "I'm gonna need that rope."

Stacy whined, but held her hands up, wrists together.

"Must you?" asked Tris.

He gestured. "Not for her. I'm gonna have to tie two of them to the roof." Kevin rubbed his chin and pointed at the smallest dancer. "Might be room in the trunk for her and the junkie."

"You can't put a person in the trunk." Tris stomped. "For one thing, it's cruel. For another, you have a pile of random shit in there already, and last, that's where the cargo's going."

Kevin muttered, running over maps in his head. If he pushed the car, they could probably make it to Cortez in one day. Nice little town. Good place to drop off all the baggage. "Okay, but this is going to be a damn rolling orgy. Get ready to get intimate."

Over the next half hour, Kevin grumbled and cursed under his breath as he transferred all his "quick access" supplies from the back seat to the trunk. Jasmin arrived when he'd all but filled it, dragging a metal case. He tried not to see it as a massive pain in the ass, instead as 1800 coins.

Another twenty minutes of unloading random bits of salvage he'd taken from roadside husks made room for the box. He slammed the trunk lid, shook Jasmin's hand, and backed toward the Garage office once again, pointing at Tris.

"No one touch the car. I'll be right back."

He opened the door with his ass and whipped around to confront the clerk.

Takeshi smiled at him. "Back so soon?"

"I needed to make room. Interested in salvage?"

"Ahh, I sense a deep discount since you'd be abandoning it anyway. What sort of parts do you have?"

Motherf... "Tie rods, a pair of traction bands for a Class E wheel, four swivel mounts for light machine guns, bunch of serviceable brackets and bolts, two power filters, fourteen feet of fuel line, and a fluid pump from a"—*don't call it a flamer*—"heavy incendiary unit."

"Sounds lovely." Takeshi tapped his chin. "I'll need to see."

Kevin gestured at the door. "It's all unloaded."

⸻ ⸻

THE CHALLENGER GLIDED OVER THE ROAD, WHEEL MOTORS EMITTING A worrisome whine. Not yet twenty minutes out of Glimmertown, and already he figured he couldn't push it past about fifty miles an hour with all the weight. Stacy sat on the floor in a ball between Tris's legs, facing him and shivering. The black bags under her eyes kept him glancing at her every few minutes, fearing she'd contracted the Virus and would bite someone any second. Bits of white stuff dribbling off her lip didn't do much for his nerves. As much as he still didn't trust her, he couldn't bring himself to carry through with his threat to tie her. The state she was in, she looked helpless already.

He'd crammed his seat as far forward as it would go. The six women from Cloud 9 filled the back, three in the laps of three others. Hair and legs seemed to be everywhere; every five or six minutes, someone's knee poked him in the spine. Fortunately, the car didn't use an inside mirror for rear-view, or all he'd see was tits. With each passing mile, his frown deepened.

Tris put a hand on his arm. "What's wrong? You look like you want to rip someone's testicles off."

"Colorful." He sighed. "The car can't take this much estrogen."

Tris raised an eyebrow. "You're smarter than I gave you credit for."

"So I hear."

The women in the back muttered. One asked what estrogen was, which set Tris off on a twenty-minute explanation that nearly put Kevin out cold at the wheel.

Stacy made a series of huffing noises, sounding like a giant cat about to spit up a hairball.

"Really." Tris squeezed his forearm. "What's bothering you? Are we going to run out of charge in the middle of nowhere?"

The women got quiet.

"No, but I have to keep it slower than I'd like to be going. *This* is the kind of weepy horseshit what got Dad killed." He twisted his grip at the wheel. "He was like you. Soft heart. Saw slaves and *had* to get involved. He had a friggin' truckload of girls, and I don't mean that as a turn of phrase. An actual truck trailer ass-to-tit with women. I can't even remember where the hell we were. Somewhere in Arizona. Word got out and bandits came out of freakin' everywhere. We never had a goddamned chance."

Tris gasped. "Sorry."

"They didn't have any use for a boy, but I guess they didn't wanna kill a four-year-old. Only thing I remember is they dropped me off in Clifton. They took Dad's rig, and all the women with 'em." He looked at the back seat. "Right now, I feel like a big fat fucking target… and what the hell is wrong with the thief? She's gonna go zombie on us?"

"She's in withdrawal. She never told me what she was on, so I have no idea how bad she'll be."

Stacy tried to say something, but couldn't seem to get her jaw open, so it came out as a long, stressed "nnnnn."

Kevin sighed out his nose and tried to get comfortable despite the steering wheel rubbing his nuts. Tris tended to Stacy as best she could. The girl faded in and out of coherence, sweat buckets, and trembled. The women muttered amongst themselves about their odds of winding up stranded on the side of the road. Within an hour, they resumed their animated conversation about everything and nothing—mostly about how happy they were to be out of Glimmertown. They quieted to listen after asking Tris to tell them about Neon's final minutes.

Stacy had passed out, her head back in Tris's lap.

He tried not to feel good for helping them. Another couple of hours, and he'd drop the lot of them in Cortez… maybe enjoy a night in a bed. As stories of what had been done to them at Cloud 9 circulated, he tuned their voices out to indistinct feminine warbling, attention focused on the endless pulse of a yellow line down the center of the street. Each cruel fact twisted the guilt deeper at being ready to walk out and ignore them. The speedometer wavered between forty-five and forty-eight; the sports suspension made him feel as though his ass scraped the road.

Another couple hours... He eyed the rearview screen as the remembered scent of his father's truck cabin came to mind. *What the hell is wrong with me?*

KEVIN SQUINTED AT PALE DESERT, AFLAME IN THE SHIMMERING GLOW OF THE relentless sun. The Challenger's wheel motors purred like their old selves, without the added weight of so many passengers. Rattling from behind reassured him, his box of miscellaneous handy crap once again in easy reach. Cortez settlement seemed more than happy to welcome six women and a girl. A middle-aged couple had agreed to take Stacy in. The best part about stopping there had been another helping of Jean's gumbo. Tris had been quiet since they left, and kept her head turned to the right.

"That didn't take long." Kevin tapped his fingers on the wheel.

"What?" she muttered, not looking.

"That kid got under your skin already. You fell for it."

Tris smirked at him. "She said I was the only one who'd ever done anything nice for her."

"What was that? Not kill her?"

"The purple sweatshirt. Used to be Tyrant's." Tris sighed. "She's had a crummy life. She's only fifteen."

"And you're only twenty and I'm only twenty... something. Seven?" He accelerated to ninety. "Fuck it. Everyone's got a shitty life. Keep your eyes open for dust trails."

"What's that you keep looking at?" Tris pointed to a dark two-inch screen below and left of the rear view, hooked into the dash by four exposed spiral wires.

"Rad meter."

She kept quiet for a little while, but continued to fidget in her seat as if she couldn't get comfortable.

"Piss break?"

"Not a bad idea, but... What happened to that whole people are friendly thing? Couple days ago, you were trying to tell me the documentaries are wrong, now you're all 'the world is shit.'"

"I'm pissed off."

"So close but so far?"

He twitched when the rad meter lit up with 0018. "Crap. Hope you brought sunblock. If that fucker hits 100, I'm turning around and there won't be any negotiation."

"100? Please tell me that's not Gray."

"No, it's red. You colorblind?"

Tris stared at him. "Remember the other day when I said you're smarter than you look? Yeah, forget it. Gray is a measurement. 100 Gray would melt someone. You wouldn't have time to turn around."

"It's rads."

She blinked. "Who uses rads anymore?"

"Sorry, I don't have Enclave tech."

She shoved him on the shoulder. "It's not Enclave. It's been around a long time."

Parts of the paving had broken apart in jagged junks. Here and there, the bumps forced him off onto the dirt for a smoother ride. Blasted out shells of steel trailers dotted the road, the metal blued near jagged tears along the south-facing parts. Large hunks of debris, pieces of former buildings, cars, and a set of train wheels, sat at the ends of angled furrows going in the same direction, a frightening indication of proximity to ground zero in Dallas. Kevin grumbled. Taking a ride to Harrisburg on Tris's flimsy promise for a thousand coins was one thing... but driving this close to an impact crater stressed the limits of reason.

He slowed to a halt. Twisted iron and steel claws rose from the scorch mark that had once been Dallas, Texas, a dark stain across the horizon. The rad meter displayed 042, causing a bead of sweat to slide down the left side of his head. Striations in color over the open nothingness before him radiated outward from the distant city, crossed by the occasional tumbleweed or dust-hopper oblivious to the radiation.

"So, another couple months of small runs will make up for it." He sighed.

Tris glanced at him. "We're already here."

Kevin tapped the corner of the rad meter. It hopped up to forty-four. "Can barely see the city from here and the dose is almost halfway to 'screw this.'"

She leaned forward and shielded her eyes with her hand. "There's gotta be something here."

"You almost sound upset." He chuckled, flicking his fingers at the gearshift in contemplation of backing off.

"We're here because I believed Jasmin about the run." Tris leaned from left to right, surveying the distance.

He dropped the Challenger into reverse. "Ain't no point o' me retirin' to run a roadhouse if I grow a third testicle."

"Wait." Tris lunged through the gap between the front seats and grabbed a pair of dusty green binoculars from the box. After flinging herself upright again, she pointed them off to the right and held them to her eyes. "Yes… Tire marks over there. Seems like they're converging on one place."

"How far?" Kevin squinted, but couldn't make anything out of the blinding glare.

"Four hundred yards maybe?" She pointed almost right at the spar between windshield and door window. "That way."

He pursed his lips, eyeing the rad meter. "No sense wasting time debating. Couple hundred more yards won't change much."

The gearshift moved forward with a *clunk,* and he steered where she indicated. A few minutes later, distinct vehicle trails emerged from the smooth beige landscape. Someone (in fact many someones) had driven onto a strip of paving more or less covered by dirt, all heading toward the southwest. The sight of it made him cringe. In all likelihood, the resettled sand had been fallout, and probably still 'glowed.' A quick glance at the rad readout tightened his grip on the wheel: 52.

Kevin held out another few seconds until the Challenger reached the old road, and he went in the direction of the tracks. "You know, this could be a damn bandit nest. If it is, this is going to get real damn ugly."

"What happened to 'people want to help each other?'"

"There'll always be a bad element. Human nature. What I meant was *most* people are helpful. The two you gotta watch out for are the ones who don't give a shit about shit, and the ones who've given the fuck up."

"You're wasting yourself behind the wheel." Tris leaned her elbow on the door and smiled over the fingers supporting her chin. "You should've been a poet."

"Hey…" He accelerated. "Looks like there's some kind of old tunnel up ahead."

A pair of figures in long, brown coats wearing full bug-eyed gas masks stood from behind white concrete lane dividers repurposed as barricades on either side of the sunken roadway. Both had AK47s. A hundred or so yards closer to where the road diverted down into a culvert, two more figures crouched behind similar barriers with huge rifles.

"Oh, shit. They have Barrets." Kevin stopped the car and held his hands up in a non-threatening manner.

"That's bad?" She mimicked his hands-up pose.

"Yep. Barret will shoot through the battery, me, the trunk, Cortez, and lodge in Wayne's ass all the way back in Hagerman."

"Right, so don't get shot by it." She rolled her eyes.

The figure on the left approached in a cautious stride, AK47 held not-quite-aimed at the car while the other moved up on Tris's side. Dark lenses in the gas masks concealed any clue about their disposition.

"Hey," said Kevin. "Not lookin' for any trouble. You know where we can find a Sergeant Ralston?"

"Why?" asked a female voice.

Sunlight flashed on distant scopes. Kevin's sphincter clenched at the thought of a .50 Cal Browning round pointed at him. The figure on the passenger side seemed more on edge than the woman and kept the AK trained on Tris.

"Got a box from…" He glanced at Tris.

"Jasmin." Tris offered a smile at the figure pointing a rifle at her.

"Let's see it." The woman backed up a step and let the rifle down a few inches. "Damn, did a perfume factory explode in there?"

"It's a long damn story." He pushed the door open and got out, heading for the trunk. The other sentry kept the AK pointed at Tris. He glanced at his escort and flicked his gaze to the other one.

"My sister doesn't trust her," said the woman.

Kevin chuckled. "She has that effect. Neither did I at first." He opened the trunk lid. "She grows on ya though."

Hissing breath from the woman's gas mask paused as she leaned forward to examine the box from Glimmertown's general store. She reached in and moved a few car parts to the side to clear away the front face, and pointed at a tiny black doodle that resembled a poor attempt at a biohazard symbol, or an even sadder flower. Kevin tensed when she patted him on the shoulder.

"Sorry for the rough greeting. Welcome to New Dallas. I'm Samantha. My sister's Marcie." The woman backed up three steps and made a series of exaggerated hand motions at the two distant snipers before yelling, "It's good" to her sister.

Tris waved at Marcie after she lowered the rifle.

Kevin shut the trunk. "Now what?"

Samantha pointed down the road. "Drive on down to the gate."

"New Dallas is underground?" He felt as nervous as a hamster in a microwave and hurried back to the door.

"Yeah." Samantha followed. "We don't get a lot of drivers out this way. Sorry again for almost shooting you."

He hopped in and closed the door. Tris turned her head to continue staring at Marcie as the car pulled forward. The woman's posture conveyed disappointment at not getting to kill someone, but the opaque lenses over her eyes hid any sense of emotion. Concrete lane dividers rippled by on both sides, flashing in the sun. Finally, he reached the point where the road angled downward. The snipers had set up behind the first set of dividers after the downgrade, where the terrain gave them protection from the sides and rear. Both men wore full gas masks, military armor vests, and camo-covered helmets. Despite the intimidating hardware draped over their barricade, they both offered enthusiastic waves.

Tris smiled at the man on her side. "Okay, these two seem friendly."

"Friendly enough for two guys who would've shot us a minute ago without losing sleep." Kevin grumbled as he guided the Challenger down a sunken roadway lined on both sides with stacks and stacks of sandbags. Thirty meters after the road leveled out at the bottom, they entered a rounded tunnel. Three weak incandescent bulbs overhead gave off enough light to see a huge darkened metal door covered in lines of rivets streaked with green smears of corrosion. He pulled up to within three feet.

"You're the one that told *me* people are friendly." She sounded sad. "Except for the Enclave, I was almost ready to believe you."

He sighed. "Recent events haven't done much for my optimism."

A resounding *clank* filled the tunnel a second before a seam appeared down the middle of the door. Two halves peeled away to the sides, revealing the barrier to be eight inches thick. Behind it, two more doors of similar dimension opened at a somewhat slower pace. Each great slab slid into the wall, riding rollers in recessed tracks. Though the tunnel was wide enough for three cars to drive abreast, the doors halted with only inches to spare on either side of the Challenger. Beyond, the tunnel continued, lit every fifteen yards or so with a somewhat less feeble light than the ones nearer the entrance. Another man, also in a camouflage uniform, waited inside with a black M4 held to his chest. He waved in a manner indicating Kevin should follow.

"Wow." Tris leaned up. "That door would stop a damn nuke."

He drove in, following the jogging figure along a subterranean road. The rad meter ticked down to 008 about a minute later when the tunnel opened into a large chamber supported by thick columns. The space had the appearance of an old subway platform converted into a garage. The rails had been ripped up and replaced with a crude asphalt surface. Carts of tools and clustered around most of the columns. Five military-style Humvees occupied parking spots defined by yellow spray paint, as well as an M35 truck with a canvas-covered back.

A handful of men and women in loose camo pants and tank tops peered up from various places around the vehicles, pausing in their work. Tris looked from them to Kevin with wide eyes. Their escort stopped, turned on his heel, and waved him at an open parking space near a long wall of pale white tiles. Old US flags hung wherever the lack of stuff piled against the wall allowed it, some covering glass cases with prewar advertising posters. Kevin pulled into the spot and killed the switches. The soldier who led them in, a little winded from the jog, met him with a warm handshake as he got out.

"Can't say how good it is to see ya. I'm Corporal Kendall." The man looked to be in his younger twenties and had a sharp jaw. "Been waitin' on these meds for months."

Tris's door closed with a *clunk*. Her shoes skiffed over the black paving as she came up behind him. Another man and a woman with short brown hair emerged from the far side of the deuce-and-a-half. Unlike the others, their clothes looked civilian: flannel shirts and jeans.

"Yeah… I've been runnin' shit for the 'house for years and I ain't never seen a job posted for Dallas. Can't say I know anyone crazy enough to get this close."

"Well…" Kendall chuckled. "Hope you're not *too* crazy. This here's Doc, and her trainee, Josh."

The woman nodded. "Candace. Not really a MD, but I do what I can."

Josh also shook hands.

Kevin opened the trunk and stepped back as Candace and Josh unloaded it and struggled to two-person carry it back the way they came.

"We're supposed to give that to Sergeant Ralston," said Tris.

"That's a name drop." Kendall smiled. "Code so we know you're on the level."

"So there's no Ralston?"

Kendall waved. "C'mon." He headed off down the line of vehicles. "Yeah, there is... but there's no need to bug him. Sarge is already pulling out what little hair he's got left with motor pool logistics."

Kevin paused to wonder at the urgent look on Tris's face before he followed Kendall past three Humvees and up a small stairwell to what had once been the platform where people waited for trains. A middle-aged man in a camo jacket hunched over a desk shifting papers around and grumbling about someone not keeping track of parts properly. He glanced up as they passed. Kevin got a friendly nod, though he squinted at Tris.

She grabbed Kevin's hand.

Kendall gestured at a passage through a pair of smashed turnstiles, which opened out at the rear left corner of the raised area. "New Dallas isn't the biggest of places, but we get by. You're welcome to spend a day or two if you need. Any longer, you'll go from visitor to resident and be expected to help out in some way."

Past the opening, they entered a rectangular concourse marked with the scars of absent bolted-down seats. A chain-link fence/cage surrounded rows of metal shelves filled with weapons from pistols to rifles to larger machine guns. Men and women in a mixture of camo uniforms, Wildlands leathers, and patched-up civilian clothes occupied stations here and there. Several, carrying rifles, appeared to be internal security. Almost everyone afforded them at least a passing smile.

Jury-rigged wiring dangled in shallow arcs, stranded from hooks and brackets driven into the ceiling. Fluorescent lights bathed the area in brightness, proving New Dallas had a decent solar farm somewhere.

The far wall had the look of a mall of sorts, containing a series of open alcoves packed with the trappings of ancient commerce. One had empty garment racks, another, row upon row of bookshelves. Candace and Josh stood in the third storefront going through the contents of the box. White flags with red crosses hung on poles on either side of a space that looked like it had once been a deli.

Kendall walked straight across and went down another connecting passage labeled 'Platform 3.' The air carried the mixed fragrance of garlicy vegetables and body odor, tinged with a wisp of industrial grease. Traces of light glinted off ink-black walls from up ahead. The dimness compared to the open mall left Kevin blind for the thirty or so feet before he emerged in a rounded train tunnel. Cabinets and storage shelves occupied a dead end by where they entered. On the right, a passage wide enough for two subway trains stretched into a gentle leftward turn. Double-deck bunk beds packed the inward face of the curve, each pair occupying cubbies walled off by tall steel cabinets.

They kept going to the right, Kendall waving at people as he passed. Men, women, and children sat among the beds or on the floor in front of them. The smaller children wore handmade ponchos or other well-worn garments while the adults seemed evenly split between camouflage and tattered prewar garments. Many stared at Tris with curiosity or worry. A few seconds after they passed a small blonde girl, a tiny voice demanded white hair too.

Tris grinned.

Kevin raised an eyebrow at the sixth cubby they passed. Sandwiched between a pair of bulkheads, a slightly larger than usual area had flags over every visible square inch of wall, including the metal cabinets positioned at the end of the bulkheads. Most were the Stars and Stripes, though a huge black POW-MIA banner occupied the center of this 'shrine,' and a number of smaller flags bore logos from an old military unit. A grey-bearded man with a blue bandanna over his head crouched over a small workbench, engrossed in the task of hand-loading 5.56 ammunition.

"Here." Kendall gestured at an empty cubby two spaces past the old man. Two sets of bunk beds sat between olive-drab cabinets, both of which hung open to reveal nothing inside. "I'll have someone send over some blankets. Feel free to spend the night or two if ya need." He pointed further down the tunnel. "'Bout a hundred yards further down's the mess. Tell Paula you're a guest and she'll set you up with some chow."

"Thanks," said Kevin. "I'm supposed to pick up a payment for the supplies."

Kendall glanced back the way they'd come with an uncertain expression. "Uhh, that'd be something you take up with Sarge. More than likely, once Doc approves what ya brought, it'll get cleared through Sarge. Might take a couple hours or so."

Kevin sat on the left bunk, draped his arms over his knees, and nodded. "Thanks."

"Welcome." Kendall started to walk off, but stopped. "Anyone ya see inside carryin' an M4 is part of the security patrol. If y'all need anything, just let 'em know."

Tris sat next to Kevin as their escort wandered off. Echoes of conversations and snippets of voices bounced off the dingy white tiles on the facing wall. The weak breeze imparted by distant fans teased at a scorched US flag hung on thin copper wire. Giggling children occasionally broke the monotony. Within a few minutes of them sitting idle, several tiny faces peered around the wardrobe cabinet.

Kevin reclined and laced his fingers behind his head, leaving his boots on the ground. Some of the kids approached, asking Tris about her hair. She entertained them with stories for a little while as he drifted in and out of consciousness, grumbling at the jostling of small bodies climbing over the bed. At the feeling of weight settling into the mattress to the left of his head, he opened his eyes. A scrawny boy, perhaps five, with light brown skin and black hair, knelt half a foot away with a wide-eyed expression. A plain white tee shirt fit him like a shift dress. Six handwritten names descended in a column over the left breast. Five had cross-outs, leaving 'Tommy' at the end.

"What?" asked Kevin.

Tommy waved. "Hi."

"Hi." Kevin returned the wave and closed his eyes again.

Tris rambled on through a story about a bunch of kids who went into a hole in the wall of a train station to study magic so they could survive a trip to bring a cursed ring to a plasma forge in the middle of a giant space station and defeat the evil Lord Vader. Kevin faded in and out, the story jumping from some haunted forest to the kids flying in a space dogfight.

Tommy waved. "Hi."

Kevin furrowed his eyebrows. His audience of one hadn't moved. "What?"

"Can I see your car?" Tommy smiled.

"Maybe tomorrow." Kevin glanced at the boy. He thought about relocating the kid so he could lie fully on the mattress, but resigned himself to not moving.

"Okay," said Tommy.

Tris, well into the story of a climactic battle in which the bad guy's laser sword kept swatting the heroes' magic spells aside, had the rest of the kids' attention in her hands. Tommy seemed more fascinated by staring at Kevin. He tried to ignore the boy and shut his eyes again. The next thing he knew, Tris nudged him awake. The other children had gone, though Tommy remained.

"Hungry?" asked Tris.

Now that you said that, I am. Kevin scratched at his stomach and sat up. "Yeah."

Tris seemed to take notice of the names on the boy's shirt and gave him a sad look. "Why are those names crossed out?"

Tommy smiled at her. "It's mine now. They're too big."

Tris relaxed.

"Are you and her gonna make kids now?" Tommy looked at him.

Laughing, Kevin grasped the boy about the chest and set him on his feet. "Not right now."

"You can make kids with my mom if you wanna. I need a li'l brother or sister."

Kevin covered his face to keep from laughing too loud. Tris coughed and gave him a strange, unreadable look. He patted Tommy on the head, ruffling his hair. "Not right now."

The boy took two steps away before looking back. "Can I still see your car?"

"Ask your mom. And, in the morning." Kevin stood and took a deep breath laden with the fragrance of cooking beans. "Food?"

Tris, with a trace of blush in her cheeks, kept her gaze down as she got up and followed him deeper into the train tunnel. The smell of cooking food grew stronger the farther they walked. Power fluctuations manifested as regular flickers in the lights that affected the entire settlement. He glanced at one corkscrew bulb as they passed under it, wondering what these people would do when they ran out of them. *Guess they're gonna live like moles when the lights go out.* While debating how long it would take for humanity to regain the ability to manufacture light bulbs, he sidestepped boxes, toys, running children, and a handful of fifteen-to-thirty-year-old women who tried to catch his eye.

"Reminds me of home," muttered Tris.

"How's that?"

She glanced over her shoulder. "All those girls are checking you out. There can't be that many people here. They probably want some outside DNA."

"Hmm." He chuckled. "And here I thought it was my good looks."

"You planning to donate?" Tris swung her arms as she walked, not looking at him.

Kevin halted by a metal counter, where a kitchen had been set up in place of bunks. "Nah. Still too sore from Tyrant's lack of ethical business practices."

Tris nibbled on her lower lip.

A pale thirtyish woman with mouse-brown hair looked up from tending a stove full of pots. She had a 'kiss the chef' apron on over an olive drab tee and camo pants. A trio of preteens, a boy and two girls, sat on the floor nearby, making what appeared to be salsa in a metal bowl big enough for them to bathe in.

"Hello. You must be the driver who brought the medical supplies." The woman smiled.

The kids looked up with curious expressions.

"Yeah." Kevin took a handful of coins from his pocket. "Kendall said we should see you for food? Guessin' you're Paula?"

"Yep." She waved at him. "Put those away. We all help out here. Be just a moment." Paula tapped the boy on the shoulder.

"Yes, Mama." He jumped up and ran to a flat cooking surface, grabbing four little dough balls and making them into fresh tortillas.

Kevin leaned on the counter. "I got the explanation on the way in. Not sure I could tolerate staying underground so much."

"Oh, there's more than this." Paula pointed at the wall. "Tunnel D hits an open atrium about two miles in. That's where we grow all our vegetables. Used to be a platform, but the whole roof fell in. Plenty of dirt to grow things with."

"No rads? No Infected?" Kevin blinked.

Paula shook her head. "Haven't seen any Infected around here."

"Maybe everyone died in the blast," said Tris. "No one to get sick."

Kevin scrunched his face in thought. "We saw building frames on the way in. Had to be a high-altitude airburst. City as big as Dallas was, there had to be enough survivors for a major nest. The Virus landed in all the major population centers. I don't see why they'd have skipped this one."

The boy scraped the tortillas up and flipped each one before grinning back at them. "'Nother minute."

Paula stirred a thick brown paste in one of the pots. "All I know is we're safe down here."

Until the lights go out. Kevin glanced up.

The man who had been with the doctor emerged from the tunnel and waved at everyone.

"Hi, Josh," said Paula. She looked at the boy, but before she could say a word, he'd already grabbed two more dough balls for tortillas. "Maybe he could explain?"

"Explain?" Josh leaned on the counter.

"Infected," said Tris. "Paula said there aren't many around here."

"Any, actually..." Josh nodded. "We're not sure of the exact mechanism, but it seems like the radiation in the area kills the Virus... or kills any cells which uptake the virus. It would be great if we had the kind of diagnostic equipment that would let us study this in detail, but..."

"Yeah," said Kevin. "Any place big enough to have that kind of tech is either blasted to hell or too small to still have any sort of power." He sighed. "Seems like we're still sliding down."

Paula took the first four tortillas from her son and set to the task of turning them into bean burritos. "What do you mean?"

"We're still hanging on to scraps from how the world was. Using up whatever tech survived... but you don't really see anyone making more of it. Eventually, I figure we'll go back to the dark ages... and then we start the whole damn cycle over again... assuming we don't die off."

"Heh." Josh shook his head. "Let's hope we don't reinvent nuclear weapons."

"Oh, they will." Kevin accepted a hubcap with two fat burritos from Paula. "Thank you." He leaned back as Tris took hers, and glanced at Josh. "By the time they get there—if they get there—no one will remember this."

"Sad, but true." Josh sighed.

"So radiation"—Kevin held out his 'plate' as one of the girls doled out a ladle of salsa for him—"kills the Virus. Any idea if it could function as a cure? Or is the dose necessary to clear the virus gonna kill someone too?"

Josh laughed. "If you figure that out, we'd love to know."

"Your hair is so pretty," said the girl, after giving Tris a scoop of the salsa.

"Thanks." Tris returned the smile.

Kevin glanced at his food. "Take it easy, Josh. Gonna go eat."

"Keep yourself safe." Josh waved.

They wandered back down the tunnel to the bunk Kendall let them use. A few hesitant notes from an acoustic guitar twanged from the old man who had been reloading ammo before. The sound bent and warped as he tuned it. Kevin sat on the side of the bunk, stuffing one end of a still-hot bean burrito into his mouth. He scooped salsa with the hole he'd made.

"Maybe that's why the Virus hasn't wiped everyone out?" Tris bit the corner off her burrito and poured a little salsa in it. "Enough radiation zones to keep it in check?"

Kevin held up a finger while he finished chewing. "I don't know of any other settlements like this... so close to a strike point. Maybe it works as designed and kills people too fast to migrate over long patches of uninhabited ground?"

She shrugged, and continued eating.

"What about that vaccine?" Kevin drank the salsa between bites.

Tris shook her head. "The Enclave is one city... maybe a thousand people at most. They built up an area around what used to be a corporate industrial complex. The war happened in the middle of the day when people were at work. I..." She looked down as tears collected along her lower eyelid. "Sometimes I think about it. What it was like when everything happened. People not knowing if their families were still alive. Millions of lives vaporized in minutes. All the achievements of our civilization gone. I guess some of them tried to go home to find their families, but the Enclave formed from those who stayed behind. There's a big underground lab... I think it used to be some kind of physics thing with particles in a giant ring. No one cares about that anymore though."

He finished burrito one in three more bites and squeezed her shoulder. "You weren't even alive then. Hell, neither was I. You shouldn't feel guilty about something you had no control over."

"It's not that." She took a breath and wiped her face. "They still have some tech. The Enclave can make medicine and solar panels, cars, light bulbs... there's no reason we have to go back to the Stone Age again."

"Except they're zee-no whatever."

"Xenophobic." Tris attempted a smile, but it lasted only a second. "The Council of Four is convinced only they deserve the world. It wasn't bad enough nuclear war happened... they tried to kill everyone else. *That's* what I feel guilty about. Being associated with that kind of insanity."

A handful of kids ran by, re-enacting the climactic final battle from Tris's story. One boy yelled "I'm your father" seconds before a girl stomped her foot and screamed, "You shall not pass!"

The man two cubbies down began to play an ancient song. Kevin stared at a torn US flag on the wall outside their cubby as the elder sang *Fortunate Son.*

"There's not enough vaccine for the whole world." Tris stared at the remaining burrito on her hubcap. "Even if the Council changed their opinion."

He picked up the second half of his dinner. "It's a waste of time even considering people like that will change."

Tris looked up at him with innocence in her eyes. "Someone has to try."

"Yeah, maybe." He glanced sideways at the tattered flag. "But it ain't me."

CIRCLING THE DRAIN

K evin awoke to the sensation of warm breath at the crook of his neck. At some point while he slept, Tris had moved from the upper bunk to under his blanket. She lay on top of him with her head at his chin. He gazed down at the field of snowy white inches from his chin. The way she clung in her sleep made her seem frightened. *Not surprised. Out of her perfect little Eden.* He smirked. Awake, she'd seemed far from afraid. *She's either good at hiding it or this is my Dad coming out.* Having her body so close to his made the effect of morning even harder.

He slid a hand up onto her back, over a thin strip of cloth at her hip and smooth skin the rest of the way.

Tris smiled. "Is that a gun in your belt or are you happy to see me?"

"Gun's under the pillow." A strange feeling made him turn his head to the left. Tommy, crouched at the side of the bed, peered at him over the edge, eyes and half a nose visible.

"Hi," said the boy.

"Morning." Kevin yawned. Consciousness spread from one region of his brain to the next. His hand flew under the pillow, and he calmed at feeling the .45 right where he'd left it.

"Did you make a baby?" Tommy stood. "You said I can see your car."

"Need a minute, kid." Kevin rubbed his face. The more he tried to think about calming his erection, the more determined it seemed to be to remain.

Tris stirred. She seemed to lose the desperate clinginess her posture had given away in sleep and slid off him toward the wall side. "I promise you can see the car. Can you give us a little privacy?"

"Okay," said Tommy, not moving.

Kevin tried to ignore the images his brain gave him of Tris in only her panties and focused on how much he wanted to beat the hell out of Tyrant. Having a five-year-old stare at him helped kill the mood the rest of the way. He scooted to his left, sliding out from under the blanket while ensuring it continued to cover Tris. Seated on the edge of the bed, he stared at the boy. "Go on, we'll be a few minutes."

"Okay," said Tommy.

After it became clear the kid wasn't going to leave, Kevin grasped him under the arms and carried him across their cubby to the other side. He set the boy down inside the tall steel cabinet and closed the doors. Tris flung the blanket off, hopped out of bed, and grabbed her shirt and jeans from the top bunk.

"You've got a way with kids."

"Yeah." Kevin scratched himself. "Usually it involves not being around any."

She offered a playful smirk while she dressed. He shook his head and reached for his pants. Tris seemed to think he wasn't serious. *That's what got Dad killed. Feeling sorry for women and kids.* With a grumble, he put all thoughts of his father out of his mind and got the rest of the way dressed. He patted himself down once he'd put his armored jacket on, making sure everything was where he'd left it.

"You look surprised," said Tris. She pulled the last Velcro fastener closed over her right shoe. "Expecting something to be missing? The kid's only wearing a tee shirt… he's got nowhere to hide anything."

"I'm not a stealer." A little voice echoed inside the empty metal cabinet.

Kevin opened the door. Tommy stood exactly as he'd been placed. "Yeah, well… A guy drives all over the place, you get a little used to bein' taken advantage of."

The boy trailed them through the tunnel to the food counter, where Paula offered the three of them toast slathered with raspberry preserves. After thanking her for the food, Kevin made his way back to the mall area. Conversations filled the open concourse, everything from patrol schedules to one woman complaining about being put on a 'rest list' due to having taken in too many rads, to a crowd of older teens discussing ways to optimize the garden's dispersion of sunlight.

Kevin finished off his toast halfway across on the way to the garage. Fortunately 'straight across the big tunnel' was easy to remember. New Dallas appeared much larger than he ever could have imagined. Despite the radiation overhead, and being stuck underground, the thought that no Infected could exist here got an idea bouncing around his head of possibly returning at some point. He dismissed it as soon as the Challenger came into sight past a row of Humvees. There weren't many Infected out in no mans' land either, and he couldn't see spending the rest of his days hiding from the sun.

The older man behind the desk looked up. "Howdy there. You must be the driver."

"Yep." Kevin walked up to a desk littered with handwritten ledgers.

Tris stood at his side.

Tommy squeezed between them and grabbed the edge of the desk, pulling himself up on tiptoe. "They made a baby."

Kevin chuckled while Tris gasped.

Sergeant Ralston frowned at her and shook his head at the boy. "Doubt it, son."

Tommy looked up at her.

Tris frowned. "What?"

"Can't knock up a toaster." Ralston gestured at her. "White hair's a dead giveaway. Right before it all went to crap, the Air Force was experimenting with artificial intelligence and androids. They tried ta make 'em look as real as possible... but the first-gen batch was all given white hair so they could be easily identified."

Tris shivered.

Kevin put a hand on her arm. "She's not an android. I've seen an android before, and they don't bleed."

"Civvie models, sure." Ralston opened a drawer and took out a dented lockbox. "Military intelligence had ones that could bleed. Wouldn't be any good to fool people if it was obvious."

"Are you a robot?" asked Tommy.

"No." Tris scowled at Sergeant Ralston. "If I was, would I have memories of being a kid and growing up?"

The sergeant offered the lockbox to Kevin. "Maybe... maybe not. Depends on what the mission params were. Can't see why they'd bother to trick their own machine though."

She clenched her hands into fists.

"Of course, you won't mind if I count it?" Kevin smiled.

"Go right ahead." Ralston fell into his chair and tucked up to the desk. "I know you driver types aren't the most trusting sort. No sweat off my balls."

Tommy ran off toward the Challenger.

Tris tapped her foot for a few seconds before shifting her weight. "I'll go watch him, make sure he doesn't touch anything." She jogged off.

Kevin opened the lid and got to counting.

"So where'd you find that unit?" asked Ralston.

"She ain't an android. I've been under the hood." Kevin squinted, thinking back to the shot she'd made with her hands tied. The woman was strong enough to kick a man through Wayne's railing… twice. *Nah. If she was an android, she'd have broken the rope. She eats. She pisses. She fucks.* "Body heat. Bleeds." *She can't be…* He looked up from the coins. Tris had Tommy in one arm, balanced on her hip, and seemed to be pointing at various parts of the car. *No… no way.*

"Looks like I hit a nerve." Ralston grinned. "Ah well. Whatever floats your boat."

Kevin finished counting under a little black cloud. His count wound up being 1804, but he didn't feel like repeating it since the error went his way. More than likely it was 1800 and he overcounted due to feeling distracted. He closed the lid, shook hands with the quartermaster, and jogged over to his car with the burdensome payment under one arm.

A muscular, twentyish woman with an M4, full camo, and Hispanic features jogged in, hurrying after him. "Hey…"

"Yo." Kevin stopped. "What's up?"

"What's with the boy?" She gestured at Tommy.

"Oh." Kevin laughed. "He demanded to see the car. We ain't trying to take him. Hell no. Kid's pushy enough for one night, can't imagine having to live with him. Little bugger even wanted me to go nail his mom."

"Oh?" The security officer cocked her eyebrow.

He resumed walking. "Yeah. When he asked if I was going to be making a kid, I figured the next thing he'd say would be some kind of 'got a kid?' 'No.' 'Want one?' routine. Threw me off when he suggested I go 'make a kid' with his mother… Guess she works on her back and found a new way to advertise."

The soldier coughed.

Tommy, still attached to Tris's side, looked up from the car and waved. "Hi, Mom! Can I see inside?"

Kevin halted five feet from the trunk. "Shit." He glanced to his right with an overacted, sheepish smile.

After a momentary hard stare, the woman's gaze softened. "Well, I suppose being called a whore is better than you two trying to abduct him. He's a little forward and a lot fearless."

"Hey… I…" He raised his free hand. "Sight unseen… assuming."

"No harm done." She slung her rifle over her shoulder and walked around to where Tris stood, and collected the boy.

Kevin packed the lockbox of coins in the trunk. Tris unplugged the charging line and let it spool back into the fender before closing the hatch. Kevin tolerated a few minutes of a five-year-old crawling around and asking "what's that do?" about three dozen times. Both Kevin and the boy's mother denied his request to go for a ride.

"Aww, but why?" whined Tommy.

"You're not old enough to go outside yet." The woman dragged him out of the car by a fistful of tee shirt at the back of his neck. "There's bad stuff up there, and you're too little."

"I hate radiation." Tommy pouted at his bare feet.

"Me too, kid… me too." Kevin shot an apologetic glance at the mother before pulling his door closed. "Me too."

Tris hopped in. "Money good?"

"Yeah." He ran his thumb across the row of switches, each one lit azure with a *click*. "You're not an android."

She folded her hands in her lap and looked down.

"If you were an android, you wouldn't be ready to cry about the thought you might be an android." He looked around to make sure no one was behind them and backed into a K-turn between two columns. "Besides… you're from the Enclave, not the Air Force."

"A lot of people there have white hair." She looked up at him. "Almost half."

He drove up to the massive door. "Well, there you go."

Two rifle-toting men in camo approached the window. The closer one, name patch 'Clarke,' waved. "Quick in and out, just the way my wife likes it."

"Bullshit," said Kevin. "No girl likes it quick."

The sentries both laughed.

"Any lady who's gotta smell Clarke's breath does," said the other man, earning a middle finger.

Clarke pulled a metal tube from his left hip pocket, the kind of thing a cigar might've been shipped in. He twisted off the end cap and poured two pills into his hand before offering them. "Here, you two might wanna take this. Iodide. Helps protect from the rads topside."

"Thanks." Kevin accepted the pills, handed one to Tris, and reached for the canteen behind his seat. "Since I know you're here now, I might be inclined to do another run back this way if there's a need."

"Be safe." Clarke waved at his partner, who clapped his hand over a button that set the huge doors in motion.

"That's my dream..." Kevin hit the button that rolled up the window.

Once the doors opened wide enough, he eased the Challenger past them and up the quarter-mile ramp back to the surface. Early morning sun, after hours spent underground, left him unable to look out the window for a few minutes. Fortunately, the flat, barren area allowed him to drive with one eye closed and one barely open. He had the car up to ninety-four miles per hour within seconds of his eyes adjusting.

The Rad meter had leapt from zip to 051 as soon as they reached the end of the ramp, and proceeded to decline tick by tick with each passing minute they traveled north. Tris kept quiet for the better part of an hour, alternatively gazing out the passenger window or sending a morose stare into her lap.

Kevin found himself humming *Fortunate Son*, the song the old man had been strumming, tapping his fingers on the wheel as the Challenger devoured mile after mile of wide-open desert. A shadow of paving ahead lined up with his approximate memory of where Route 70 ran west. If not for legends of millions of Infected in Oklahoma City, he'd have gone straight for Route 40 and a smoother ride...

"Fuck Infected." He slowed to take a gradual left onto Route 40.

Tris looked over at him. "I wouldn't suggest that. The Virus is likely transmissible in all bodily fluids, not only blood."

He opened his mouth to retort, but closed it. *Not worth it.*

"That was supposed to be a joke." She gave his arm a light shove. "I'm trying to cheer myself up."

"You're not an android."

She stared at him.

"They raided your ovaries. You eat. You piss. You're awesome in bed."

Tris hid her face behind one hand. "You had a damn bomb inside you. Lot of blood there, and I saw... squishy bits too."

A laugh blurted out of her. "The egg thing could be a false memory... same with my childhood. Nanites can process food into other materials. They extract iron and metals from food, as well as scavenge 'dead' nanites to keep making new ones."

"I don't know how those nanite things work, but that doesn't prove you're a"—two large shadows from the right caught his eye—"shit."

Tris gawked. "I'm a shit?"

"Incoming!" he yelled.

A quick cut of the wheel launched them off the paving of Route 40 seconds before a ripple of sand geysers traced the path of a machine gun. He jammed up on the parking brake to cause the ass end to fishtail around and lined up the nearer shadow with the front-mounted M60s. A pair of near-identical black SUVs, probably rebuilt Excursions, roared over the desert at him, belching blue flames from exhaust ports along the underside between the wheels.

"Ethanol. Fuck." He flicked the master arm switch and a green laser projected a targeting crosshair on the windshield. "Hold on."

Kevin risked three seconds of driving straight at one while firing both guns. Sparks danced across black armor paneling on the front. Even the windshield had steel plates over it, with only a narrow slit for the driver to see.

"That's not good." Tris pulled on her seat belt. "Grenade trick?"

The second truck broke away, drifting off to the left while the one he'd fired on continued on a ramming trajectory. A turret on the top of the distancing vehicle swiveled to aim at them. Kevin stared out of the corner of his eye at what had to be a single-barreled 20mm machine gun. Sweat ran down his head.

"Goddammit. This is what I get for going cheap and not getting the .50 Cals." He slammed on the accelerator and turned to the right.

The Challenger slid around in a circle, kicking up a wall of sand. He straightened out in the general direction of west and stomped on the accelerator. A tremendous repeating *boom boom boom* went off somewhere to the rear and right, answered by a series of sharp *snaps* much closer.

Explosive rounds.

"Who are they? Why are they shooting at us?" yelled Tris.

He flicked the toggle to activate the rear-facing guns and lined up the second vehicle on the little targeting monitor. "You see any insignia or markings on them?"

Tris twisted around to look. Kevin's thumb touched the fire button, but he didn't press it hard enough to activate the guns. *What the hell am I doing? The '60s bounced off... these won't do shit.*

"No markings." She righted herself. "I think... inch-thick plate on the front and sides. Grenade trick won't work; looks like they got plows or something with spikes."

"Crap. Night Riders. They're looking for target practice. Bunch of complete psychos."

"Wasn't that a little tiny car?" She looked confused for a second until bullets clanked all around. She screamed.

"Goddammit!" Kevin swerved to the right, pushing the accelerator as hard as he could as a triplet of small explosions hit the ground next to them. "Where the hell did tiny car come from?"

Sand washed over the hood, spraying up onto the windshield.

Tris pressed herself into her seat, staring wide-eyed at him. "Historical documentaries. The car had an AI inside it that helped the driver."

"Never heard of it." He scanned the dash looking for any warning lights or signs of major damage. As soon as he dared to feel relief, both rear wheel status indicators went yellow. "Fuck."

"What?"

"Anything you wanna say before we die?"

Tris grabbed his arm. "What!"

"We lost two motors. We're not going to be able to outrun those ethanol-chugging monsters. These little pop guns aren't gonna do a fuckin' thing to an inch of armor. If I ever see that bitch again... So much for speed being an advantage."

She unhooked her belt and rolled her window down. "Hold me so I don't fall out."

"What the hell are you going to do? Flash your tits and hope they take up slaving?"

Tris punched him in the thigh, hard enough to numb the leg. "No. Asshole." She pulled the Beretta off her hip. "Gonna try for the viewport."

"Ow, son of a..." He reached to rub the leg, but seeing the gun coming back around, wound up with both hands on the wheel, throwing the car into a right turn that sucked Tris back inside.

Another row of dirt geysers passed on the left.

"Use the .357; it's got a longer reach. More accurate too."

She dove between the seats, reaching for the back.

Kevin swerved in as erratic a serpentine as he could manage. The Excursions came around and pulled in close with each other before their engines roared. The Challenger's speed bled from eighty to seventy and kept going down. Front wheel status went orange, indicating the motors were getting too hot. He glared at the speedometer as enormous black forms tipped with rows of welded spikes engulfed the rearview screen, engines roaring.

Tris slid back into her seat with the silver revolver in her hand. She grabbed Kevin's right hand and slapped it onto her belt. "Don't let me fall."

"Wait." He eyed the turret on the left Excursion moving. After a fake right swerve, he committed to the left as the 20mm gun opened up again. One *clank* came from overhead. "Shit!"

"Going!" Tris lunged half out her window.

Kevin held on to her belt with one hand, trying to watch the rear view for the next attack while slaloming among larger clods of sagebrush that might cause the car to flip. *Come on... Come on... what are you waiting for?*

Blam.

He frowned at the rear screen. At nothing happening.

The .357 went off again, two shots so fast it sounded like a burst.

The SUV with the turret veered into its companion, bounced away, and careened off in an aimless drift. Tris shifted and grunted. The other Excursion swerved left; black steel filled his door-mounted rearview mirror. Blue flames belched from four exhaust pipes behind the driver side door as the growl of a massive ethanol-swilling engine drowned out the world. Kevin palmed the wheel and cranked it clockwise while pulling back on his right arm in an effort to get Tris inside the car. He lurched forward in the seat as the huge vehicle rammed the Challenger from behind, knocking the car into a flat slide before thundering past. Tris screamed. The weight on his arm vanished. Kevin's heart skipped a beat at the sight of a bundle of denim in his fist around two black shoes.

Blood on the door only frightened him a little more.

She screamed again and slapped the roof. He twisted his head to look. She'd wrapped herself around the side of the car and somehow managed to hold on. Kevin kept pulling on her jeans while straightening out and slowing. At twelve MPH, Tris pushed off the car and slipped free of the denim. Kevin stomped on the brakes. She bounced to her feet, .357 aimed at the black mark in the distance leading a trail of dust back toward them. Dirt caked in the shape of bloody rivulets down her right leg.

He shoved the door open, pulled his .45, and aimed at the front of the Excursion barreling at them. *What am I doing?* Tris fired.

Plink.

She fired the last two rounds. Kevin stared at the muzzle flare.

Plink. Plink.

Tris grabbed at her hip for the Beretta, but got only a handful of thin elastic. "Shit."

"Here!" Kevin threw the .45 over the roof to her.

Rumbling engine noise vibrated the ground.

She caught it, aimed, and fired four times, once every half second.

Plink. Plink. Plink.

The Excursion's horn blared a second before it swerved hard to the right and flipped. The massive vehicle went from driving to rolling like a log at them.

"Fuck!"

Kevin hopped in, not bothering to close the door. Tris took off running. He slapped it into reverse; the tires spat dirt as he slid backward into a half turn. Dust, metal fragments, and a huge blur of darkness crashed and bounced past the front bumper. No shock wracked the frame. It might've been under an inch, but he'd take any miss fate would give him. Kevin let his head sag forward until it touched the wheel.

Holy shit. He sat there breathing for a few minutes.

Shoes scuffed up outside his door. He glanced to his left at Tris's panties.

"Hey cowboy, goin' my way?"

"That was incredible."

She bent forward, resting her elbows on the door, .45 draped from her hand. "So… Ya trust me yet?"

He reached a hand behind her head and pulled her into a long kiss. "Yeah."

"Oh, crap." She pushed herself up to look over the roof. "Got people coming out of the other truck."

"Get in."

Tris limped around the nose and dove headfirst in the window amid the *pops* and *snaps* of pistol and rifle fire. Kevin stomped on the accelerator, feeling a little dead inside at the lackluster response. On the car-shaped outline displayed on the little screen in the console, two red triangles where the back tires should be flashed with exclamation marks.

"Dammit. Dammit. Dammit." He banged his head against the seat with each word. "Now what the hell am I gonna do?"

Tris twirled a strand of hair around her finger. "I've already got my pants off."

"You know what I mean." He stared at the rearview monitor for a few seconds, until he felt safely out of range. "You're shot."

"It went all the way through my leg and out the floor. Didn't catch bone." She twisted to show off her perfect thigh. "Skin's sealed, but it still feels like I've got a burning rod in my leg."

"Gotta love those nanites."

She grabbed the wadded up jeans. "S'pose I should put these on."

"I thought you didn't want to run around the Wildlands in a loincloth." He squeezed the wheel. "Sorry. Car…"

"Yeah…" She kicked her shoes off and pulled the jeans on. "I said pull me in, not rip my pants off."

He squinted at her.

"The belt broke." She flopped the two strands around.

"You scared the crap out of me, I thought you went flying."

Tris leaned on his arm and put the .45 back in its holster. "I did. You saved my ass when you pulled. Gave me a chance to grab the car."

"You didn't scream when you got hit."

She shrugged. "Too much adrenaline. You were all 'we're gonna die.' I was terrified."

"You're pretty hot when you're scared shitless."

"You too."

"I'm not scared."

"Oh, bullshit." She winked.

"I'm pissed. I was supposed to collect 2700 coins for the void salt. Between a thousand for that mess and the 1800 for the meds, we almost made out a tiny gain. Now we're lookin' at maybe a couple hundred coins' worth of repairs… this trip was a loss."

Tris looked over, but whatever thought was at the tip of her brain didn't make it out of her mouth. She bit her lip and looked down. Kevin grumbled to himself. *Yeah… yeah… never should've run drugs. Whatever.*

Silence reigned, save for the whistle of air over bullet holes or the occasional *thump* of the tires striking a crack or pothole in the highway. Whenever a dark shape on the side of the road hinted at potential salvage, he slowed to take a closer look, though everything seemed picked clean.

A little over an hour after bullets stopped flying, he took her hand. "Nice shot. You sure you're okay?"

"Yeah. My leg is pretty much healed." She pulled her hair out of her eyes. "You should probably move those machine guns to the back and get a pair of .50s on the hood."

Kevin chuckled. "Yeah… seems we're gonna be driving for a while longer. Ween had a couple M2s he put back together… wanted five hundred apiece."

"Ouch." She rubbed her leg. "I guess we could've outrun them if they didn't hit the motors. If I had a rifle, it would be easier to make a shot like that again."

He eyed the charge meter, which showed eighty-eight percent. "It's draining too fast for two wheels. If the fucking battery took a hit, I'm gonna be pissed."

"You already *are* pissed. The remaining motors are working beyond capacity. They're used to pulling half the amount of weight. Probably on the far side of the efficiency curve. If the battery took a bullet, you'd have seen a large drop in charge as whole cell clusters went out."

Unbelievable. "Yeah… Yeah. I'm not thinking straight."

Time blurred under the endless repetition of a long, desert drive. A few hours farther west, he pulled over for a quick bathroom break. Afterward, he circled the car while Tris wandered off to have her own chat with Mother Nature. A line of small holes scored from a hand's width above the left rear wheel all the way to the front. Both fenders and the door. Two gouges scored the roof, and both rear-wheel motors had taken several slugs that pierced the tread. Fortunately, the solid bands of rubber held together—the electronics inside the motors, not so much. Kevin popped the hood and walked around front. Dread mounted in the seconds it took him to build up the balls to look, but the giant battery proved intact. One bullet breached the compartment, but only nicked a mounting bracket holding up the ammo box for the machine gun.

Repairs would set him back a couple hundred coins, but the car would survive. *Fuckin' Night Riders. What are they doing this far south?* He slammed the hood and got back in, feeling more optimistic about their odds of reaching Hagerman. *So I run a couple more cans of 'bacco. Nothin' I haven't already been doing.* Tris slipped in and closed her door with a gentle touch, as if afraid of hurting his 'brand new car.'

"I really thought Doctor Andrews had coins to give you. I wasn't lying."

A smile curled the left side of his mouth. "Yeah. I knew you weren't lying. You had no idea what happened there. You think your dad's plan would work? Trying to get the Enclave to open up and help?"

"I'm not sure. The information I had about the resistance implied they thought so." She pulled her heel up on the seat and let her head rest against her knee. "I'm not sure what to think anymore."

"Maybe humanity can't retake the Earth. Sometimes I wonder if we did too much damage and we're all just circling the drain, deluding ourselves into thinking there's something worth hanging on for."

Tris looked at him. "You have your dream. A roadhouse of your own, right? You told me all you wanted to do was serve beer to idiots and stop being shot at for a living... A dream doesn't have to be big to be worth having. It's just gotta be."

"Do you have a dream?"

"Yeah." She picked at her shoe. "Stop the Virus, save humanity from extinction."

Kevin smiled. "So something small."

"I might have the cure in my head. I've got to at least try." She peeled and re-closed a Velcro strip on her shoe in an endless cycle of scratchy noise. "Once I'm done saving the world, maybe I could be happy carrying plates of food to idiots."

He held her hand and smiled. "Bee's an android. You're not."

Tris rubbed her thigh. "Yeah... How long till Wayne's?"

"Probably nine to ten hours at this speed."

She settled into her seat and closed her eyes. "Wake me up if anyone tries to kill us again."

SPARKS

Kevin sat on grey concrete floor staring into the guts of the Challenger's rear left wheel. Three slugs had pierced the tire, though the solid band seemed none the worse for it. Alas, the magnetic ingots on the outer rotating ring had shattered, and several of the copper windings in the middle had frayed. He opened a flap on the front of a cracked compartment and sighed as a crumble of smashed circuit board fell out and snowed to the ground in a flickering cloud. The sudden strengthening in the ambiance of pipe tobacco announced the garage's owner approaching.

"Damn, that's a mess." Irwin sidled up to his right. "Should'a de-rebuilt it back ta Ethanol. I got some parts f'ya want."

Kevin frowned at the dingy brown overalls, crotch level to his face. The man looked as if he wore a corduroy sofa and had an electrocuted raccoon for facial hair. "You try to sell me that old six cylinder every time I show up here. Charging is cheaper, and it doesn't explode if it takes a bullet."

"You lookin' at that thing like you tryin' ta read or somethin'." Irwin spat off to the side.

"You know... I *can* read, right?"

Irwin grumbled, making his mustache and beard dance. "Two new motors'll cost ya eight hundred."

Kevin held his head in his hands. "That's crazy, old man."

"So's not givin' me a cut o' that ambrosia ya got from Gil couple 'o weeks back."

"Yeah, and I get a rep for helping myself to shipments, that's the end of that." He flung a socket wrench to the ground with an echoing *clang*.

Tris, wearing a new belt, rounded the rear end of the car and stepped over the support struts of the hydraulic jack that held it a few feet off the ground. She scooted around Irwin and stopped at Kevin's left. "How bad is it?"

Irwin stared at her chest.

"She'll kill you." Kevin took note of the lack of blood on her jeans. *How much did Wayne charge for the water?* "He wants 800 for two new motors."

"I don't mind if all he does is look." Tris squatted and peered into the wheel guts. "Hm. Looks like a reluctance motor. Synchronous?" She ran her fingers over the magnetic blocks. "Yeah, it would have to be synchronous given the way the poles are arranged. Damn, this thing looks old. No cryonic cooling."

"Uhh…" Kevin scratched his head. "Cryonics? What, like for superconductors? Sorry, we don't have e-tech out here. I scavved this stuff from pre-war heaps. There's some factory parts in Amarillo, and Irwin's got a few left from the old store room… but he's trying to take advantage of—"

"Oh, hush." Irwin's facial hair twitched side to side. "You'd be payin' 800 *each* for them motors in Amarillo."

"Yeah." She pointed at the outer ring. "Why would they put the motors right in the wheels? It's an inverted design where the rotator's on the outside of the stator. That puts all the stress of driving right on the power converter…"

"Which survived up until it hit a bullet." Kevin jabbed a finger at the silicon dust. "Four small motors in the wheels distributes vulnerability. If there was one motor with a gear differential, it would be easier to disable the car."

She leaned forward until her knees touched the ground and stuck her head in. "Hm. General Motors VSSM-43."

Irwin whistled. "Ye know that from lookin' at it?"

Tris sighed. "It's stenciled on the housing. But, yes, I am familiar with it. They were one of the most widely produced sports models after the migration to self-switching gearless inwheel motors. You still get more torque with a centralized engine and transmission but, these will kick you from zero to almost two hundred in a few… painful seconds."

"Two hundred?" Kevin laughed. "Maybe if you can find flat road. And I haven't been able to get this thing over ninety-six."

"Something's not right with it then... This car should've been able to leave those trucks way behind."

Kevin sat back and folded his arms as Tris proceeded to paw and poke at the wheel. She took the end cap off the central housing and gasped.

"Has this ever been cleaned? Look at all this dirt... and half the contacts are burned to charcoal. The power electronics... umm... excitation controller is probably out of calibration."

"Damn." Kevin pinched his nose.

"What language was that?" asked Irwin.

Tris snapped her head back to smile at Kevin. "Guess I'm not just a pretty face."

He laughed. "Saved my life... twice. Yeah, guess not."

"Well." She blew dust out of the wheel's central compartment, waving and coughing. "Technically, I saved both our lives there. Is there a scrapyard around here? I could probably harvest enough parts to rebuild these two motors given enough time... and a little luck."

"You sure you wanna risk old parts? Thems motors I got in the back still in their plastic." Irwin winked.

"For 800 coins, I gotta try. Besides... I trust her." Kevin grunted as he pushed himself upright. "There's a scrap field out behind Irwin's."

She looked at the bearded man. "Do you have a diagnostic machine?"

Irwin shook his head.

Tris thought for a moment. "You think Wayne will let us borrow Bee for a bit?"

Kevin shrugged. "I can ask."

AFTER A FEW HOURS SPENT CRAWLING AROUND CARS FATED NEVER AGAIN TO move, Tris set the last of the components she wanted atop the armload of parts Kevin held. He started the quarter-mile or so trek back to Irwin's, navigating a canyon maze of derelict vehicles stacked ten high. She caught up in a few minutes, tool bag hanging at her side. Her hands clamped on a replacement outer ring and tire tread balanced on each shoulder. He shook his head at the sight of a slender woman lifting two forty-five pound carbon-fiber reinforced steel bands.

Irwin's bushy eyebrows climbed up onto his forehead as she carried them in and lowered them to the floor one after the other as if they were made of plastic. His face flushed, and wandered off to resume working on the same ethanol-eating micro-compact he'd been swearing would outrun anything in the Wildlands for at least the past three years.

"You get the Cooper to start yet?" yelled Kevin.

"Go to hell," said Irwin, from inside the hood.

Tris wiped her face and rested a moment. "Okay, so I'll get going on the wheels while you fix the body?"

"You're makin' me feel inadequate now." Kevin laughed.

"Oh." She walked up and tickled at his ribs. He caught her hands. "Fixing the guts of motors is technical. Working on the skin... that takes love."

Kevin found himself staring into her eyes. "Yeah..."

DO ANDROIDS DREAM

Exhaustion hung on Kevin's back with tangible weight. He slouched over the table, hand pressed into the side of his head, and debated if food was worth staying awake for. Thankfully, Wayne's offered an unusual amount of quiet. After turning in the coins for the damn cube, and paying Irwin for parts and floor space, the trip had wound up costing over four hundred coins. Whatever Tris had done with the electronics had somehow boosted the Challenger, though not quite to the degree she'd predicted. Still, he'd gotten the thing up to 162 on a patch of straight highway to the south of Hagerman. Killed the battery quick, but... at least he could make use of the advantage of being able to run away from another land yacht.

I miss the damn marauder. He daydreamed of his old pickup truck with armor plates.

"You two look tired," said Bee.

Kevin pushed himself up off the table. Tris had her head down on crossed arms. She, too, leaned out of the way so the android could put down two bowls.

"What is this again?" Kevin sniffed a vaguely meat-flavored brown goo.

"Scorpion gumbo." Bee put her hands on her hips. "You two need to clean up. Want me to get the water hot?"

"How much?" Kevin poked at the soup. He'd smelled worse, so he dug in.

Bee tilted her head to the left. "One coin per minute."

He almost choked on the first spoonful, though not from the taste. Once he finished coughing, he squinted up at Bee with the one eye he could open. "That's ridiculous."

"Water's expensive," yelled Wayne from behind the counter.

"Think of it as additional cost of repairs." Bee's face whirred as she smiled.

Tris held up her black-stained arms. "We are kinda filthy."

He grumbled. "Yeah, but..."

"Share a bath?" Tris winked.

"Shower," said Bee. "Extra two coins, I'll even wash your clothes while you're cleaning up."

"Two coins per three minutes," said Kevin, loud enough for Wayne to hear.

Wayne didn't look up from whatever he was doing, though his raised hand indicated acceptance. Bee tottered off to the back room. Tris kept smiling at him as they ate for a few minutes. The gumbo wasn't half bad, though he did cringe whenever something crunched between his teeth.

"As tempting as it would be to enjoy the water..." He scraped clean trails in the thick gumbo coating the bottom of the bowl. "I should've stuck to eth. Those engines, I can rebuild with my eyes closed. Add circuits and chips and crap and game over."

"Well, you got the car put together in the first place. Don't underestimate yourself." She dropped her spoon in her empty bowl and yawned. "I'm not sure I've got enough energy left for anything past degreasing right now anyway."

Bee came by to collect their dishes. "Water heater's up and ready. If you want me to wash anything, leave it in the basket."

Kevin stood and trudged into the little hallway past the bathrooms no one dared use. Soon, his armored jacket stood guard over his boots, shoulder holster, and gun belt while everything cloth went into a metal wire basket near the door. Tris stripped before adding her shoes, katana, and belt to the 'no-touch' pile. Shirt, jeans, and undies went into the basket. A claw-foot tub stood in the back corner of what once appeared to have been a storeroom. Two white PVC pipes came in from the wall to a plastic showerhead controlled by individual valves. Kevin set his .45 on a small wooden shelf near the tub as he got in, next to a bar of yellow pumice soap.

Tris eyed the basket as she followed. "What'll we do if she doesn't bring our stuff back?"

He reached up, grasped both twist valves, and bore the brunt of the ice blast. "Then, I'm going to go have a heart to heart with Wayne."

Within seconds of the water starting, Bee ducked in and grabbed the basket. Clock ticking, he didn't bother waiting for the heat, and set to the task of scrubbing right away. Tris hid behind him until the spray warmed, then got her hair wet. Washing passed as a matter of expedience. Gritty soap scratched up and down his body, chasing off the stains of a long day patching holes and tracing the location of a broken wire. She washed his back and kept going, down over his ass onto his thighs. Her hands lingered there before going back up.

A little while later, he chuckled. "I didn't realize my butt was that dirty."

She grasped his hand and slid the soap into it. "My turn."

The clatter of coins dropping onto the counter played in his mind with each passing minute, though he obliged himself. Kevin pressed the soap against her left shoulder and swiped it across to the right and around her back, working it in a gentle circular pattern. Tris emitted a faint moan of pleasure. Perhaps it was the warm water and pumice, or the lack of a rush, but her skin struck him as softer than he'd remembered it when he'd last been this close to her with no clothes between them.

Black water ran down her arms, carrying car dirt into the oblivion of the drain. He caressed her for a little while longer before she backed into him and reached up behind her. Kevin set his chin on her shoulder as she laced her fingers behind his head.

"Another minute and we won't be able to stop ourselves." She swayed side to side and rose up on her toes, rubbing her ass back and forth over his crotch.

"The rooms aren't too far." He held her for a little while more before putting the soap up on the shelf and cutting the water off.

Tris squirmed around to face him. Her dark blue eyes glimmered with a new light, as if she'd somehow managed to escape the weight of whatever burdened her heart. Her hair matted to her head and body, trails of snowy white only a few shades paler than the skin it adhered to. A droplet of water gathered at her chin and fell into the shin-deep murk.

She stared up at him with an expression that seemed to radiate need, innocence, fear, trust, worry, and hope all at the same time.

She wants something I can't give her... I'm no idealist. He let the air out of his lungs in a slow breath. *I should stop before I do more damage.* He opened his mouth to speak, but closed it as Bee walked in.

"Laundry'll be another oh, ninety minutes." Bee winked. "I'll tell Wayne you used fifteen minutes of water." The android leaned forward and whispered past the back of its hand. "Even though you've been in here for a half hour."

Tris wrapped her arms around him and laid her cheek against his chest. Slight shakes gave away her suppressed laugher.

"I could use another pair anyway. Can you grab some stuff from the store that'd fit? Pants... shirt?"

"Sure thing, boss." Bee pivoted on her heel. "I'll select the less expensive stuff."

Kevin smiled. "Thanks."

Bee wobbled out, closing the door behind her.

"Looks like we got a few minutes," whispered Tris.

He felt a bit like a dust-hopper staring into the headlights of an oncoming war wagon as she leaned up and kissed him. Kevin lifted her and stepped out of the bathtub, setting her on a small oval rug. They kissed for a while more. Tris raked her nails over his chest when he bit her earlobe. No sooner had she reached down between his legs and grabbed hold, than Bee returned. Tris froze, blushing, as the android entered with a pile of folded clothing.

"We had three bottoms in her size. A pink miniskirt, grey dress slacks, and this..." Bee indicated a rolled-up pair of grey-and-white camouflage pants. "Tops in her size, you had a choice between an 'I'm with stupid' tee shirt or this... a tank top. Had a white leather halter with spikes, but you don't have the breasts for it."

"Gee, umm, thanks," said Tris.

"They're not *that* small." Kevin kissed the side of her head, whispering, "What are you embarrassed for, Bee's a robot."

Tris bit her lip and gave him a playful shove.

"You are fortunate, Kevin. I found a pair of black jeans in your size as well as a tee without any holes." The android held up an olive-drab tee shirt with a print of an eagle over a wavy US flag.

"Oh, yeah... perfect." Kevin chuckled.

"Seven coins for the lot," said Bee. "Unless you want to give me another maintenance process. The hip's been acting up."

"Sure." Tris grabbed a towel from the wall. "Morning okay?"

"That is acceptable." Bee bowed at the hip before walking out.

Kevin took the towel when she finished with it, and rushed an attempt to dry off before jumping into the new pair of jeans, fixing the button without zipping it, and gathering the rest of his stuff. Tris pulled on the BDU pants, but covered her chest with the bundle of her shoes, belt, and the unworn tank top as she hurried along behind him to the room they'd rented.

Wayne's roadhouse had rooms… if you can call a bed stuffed in a large closet a room. Kevin entered and dropped his gear on the floor. Tris scooted in and kicked the door closed, bending forward as she flipped the deadbolt with her toes behind her back. Without a belt on, a bounce sent her pants to the floor, and she slithered onto the bed.

Kevin stared at her. *What am I doing?* His gaze traced over every curve from her feet to her eyes, and back down. *Why not? I'm going to hell already.* He shucked his pants and climbed into bed.

A RATTLE WOKE KEVIN FROM A DEAD SLEEP. HE SAT UP, .45 LEVELED OFF AT the door as it opened. Bee froze as soon as she spotted the weapon. Kevin sighed, letting his arm fall into his lap. Tris popped up with the Beretta pointed at the wall and yawned.

"Please do not shoot," said Bee. "I'm bringing your laundry. I did not intend to wake you."

Kevin waved her in. "Don't worry about it. Thanks."

Tris wobbled.

He grasped her hand, removed the Beretta, and guided her to lay back. "Hey, Bee?"

The android set a stack of folded clothes on a tiny table and whirled to look at him. "Yes?"

"Do you dream?"

Bee shifted her weight. "I do not sleep. While I am not technically 'awake' in any sense of the definition of the word, to avoid a cumbersome and lengthy discussion of artificial intelligence philosophy, it will suffice. I am 'awake' continuously, without requiring the break you refer to as 'sleep.' Since your dream process runs while you are engaged in this 'sleep' phase, I am incapable of it."

Kevin pressed the cold .45 to his forehead and moaned. "You could've just said 'no.'"

Bee smiled. "I prefer to give accurate and complete answers."

"Thanks, Bee." He managed a weary smile.

Once the android walked out and relocked the deadbolt from the outside, Kevin relaxed and flopped down. The room may have been tiny, but at least Bee kept the sheets clean.

Tris snuggled up to his side. "What was that about?"

"Mmm?" He threaded an arm around her.

"Asking Bee if she dreams."

He leaned his head to the side, cheek touching her. "It doesn't sleep... at all."

"Mmm." She yawned.

"You do." He squeezed her.

Tris opened her eyes. "What are you saying?"

Here we go. Why didn't I just shut up and go to sleep. "I'm saying I don't think you're an android."

Her hand crept across his chest. He grasped it with his left. "What if I was programmed to act real? Who knows what kind of technology the Enclave has. Maybe I can fake eating and sleeping."

Kevin inhaled the scent of her hair. "You can't fake kissing like that... or those little noises you—gah!" He squirmed as she attacked his sides.

They 'fought' for a few minutes, each trying to keep the other from tickling them. When at last she collapsed on top of him, out of breath, he kissed her on the nose.

"See. You're out of breath."

She went from grinning to sniffling.

"What now?"

Tris laid her head against his chest. "Some spots of my memory don't make sense. When I was in Detention, the cell had no toilet. I remember spending hours on the computer terminal doing e-learns, but never eating, cleaning myself, or even so much as peeing."

"You were probably terrified and blocked it out." He leaned up and kissed her. Several minutes later, he let his head down into the pillow. "You are *not* an android. No robot could kiss like that."

"What if I *do* have the cure in my implant?" She settled down next to him.

"Unlikely. They sent you into the Wildlands as a two-legged bomb. All they had to do was convince you the data existed."

Tris shivered and started to cry. "I had to get this data to Doctor Andrews. If the data's not real, w-what am I supposed to do?"

He brushed her hair out of her eyes and cradled her cheek while staring into her wet eyes. "Maybe you could try just being happy?"

She blinked, sending one tear down her face. Fatigue seemed to overwhelm her. Kevin closed his eyes and tried to let the tension seep out of his muscles. For a few seconds, it felt as if he'd fallen through the bed into a great void, and sleep took him.

A NEW COMPLICATION

Threstart he shock of being alone in bed snapped Kevin from zero to awake in an instant. He squinted up at the dingy curtain made of coarse red fabric, aglow from a midafternoon sun. Dark horizontal threads seemed spaced at random among thinner areas, which turned pink. The deadbolt looked open. Her clothes, weapons, and shoes were gone.

He stared at the empty floor where her things had been for a few minutes. Quiet resignation seeped in as he traced his fingers over the bed at his side. The stained white drop ceiling offered no solace to his aimless gaze. One thumbnail-sized beetle crept across. He thought about his balance, 9,408 coins, dwelling on how he'd slipped farther away from the ten grand he needed. His hand passed over the empty part of the mattress. A roadhouse of his own seemed like such a hollow thing. Four walls, a roof, and perhaps a stream of customers. What if it didn't make him happy?

Kevin looked again at the floor. *She's run off to get that data... but where?*

He swung his legs over the side and held his head. Her laugh echoed from the recesses of his memory. He imagined her arms around him, her breath on his skin. The idea of falling back into bed for another couple hours seemed like a good one.

The car. He sighed. *Wouldn't be the first time.*

One hand on his face tried to hold in his emotion. *Here I thought I was the one gonna hurt her.* He sat up again. *What the hell is wrong with me? I gotta make up for that loss.* A few minutes of pacing around only served to confuse him more. *Why am I not running outside to see if the car is still there?* The empty bed haunted him. He slumped seated on the edge and swiped a hand over the sheet, catching a long strand of white hair between his fingers.

"Yeah… I walked right into it again." He let the hair fall. "S'pose this beats waking up hugging a cactus at least."

He rubbed his face as strange ideas… stupid ideas circled around in his head. Ideas like running off to find *her* instead of the car. *If there is a God, only he knows what I'd do to Morgan if I ever find that bitch.*

Tris walked in, dressed in her new tank top and grey-white camo pants. "Hey."

Kevin stared at her.

She tilted her head. "What's on your mind? You look hung over."

"Nothin'. I… uhh, think I slept too much."

"Wayne's got some food on for us. I packed your spare clothes in the trunk." The katana on her back rattled as she sashayed over. "You okay?"

"Fine." He stood, naked, and sucked in a huge breath.

Tris squinted. "What the hell is the deal with the bathrooms here?"

Kevin cringed. "You didn't—"

"No… my eyes almost melted when I was two steps away from the door."

"Bee won't even go in there." He grabbed his boxers and stepped into them. "Gotta say something."

She covered her mouth. "That can't be healthy."

"Maybe Wayne'll pay you to clean it." He pulled on the eagle tee shirt. "Christ, look at this thing. I'd fit right in if we went back to New Dallas."

"He already paid me thirteen for tuning Bee up again. I've never seen a model like her before, but she's pretty old. Prewar."

"Well, the News didn't put her ass together with toothpicks and rebar." He put his boots on and kicked the toes on the ground.

"Okay. That was stupid." She laughed. "Of course they didn't get Enclave tech."

He smiled, locking stares with her. She bit her lip and looked down.

"I love the way you do that little lip bite thing… it's cute when your face turns pink."

As soon as he said it, she blushed.

"Food should be ready soon." She rolled her eyes with mock irritation and walked out.

Kevin hooked a right out the door and headed to the back porch. He glared at the horizon where heat blur shimmered over the distant expanse of beige as he watered a bush. *It's happening again.* When a scorpion scuttled into view, he shifted to chase it with the stream, but decided against it. *That might be dinner later.* He grumbled. *I didn't think of the car first...* Kevin zipped up. *I'm losing it. Too close. Getting careless.* He held his breath to get past the bathrooms as they tromped down the narrow corridor between the back porch and the dining area. Wayne's old armor hung in a glass-fronted display case between two pale green doors, one with a crude sharpie-marker penis on it and the other with a pair of googly cartoon eyes that were probably intended as tits.

What the heck does she want?

Wayne, two locals, the tall, long-haired New named Alamo, and Bee glanced at him as he entered and made his way to the booth where Tris waited. She'd taken a seat in the rearmost part of the room, facing the door. Alamo offered a slow nod, a sign no bad blood existed. As with everything else, Kevin kept trust at arm's length, though he returned the gesture. Tris scooted in as he joined her on the same bench. Bee dropped off two bowls of scrambled eggs mixed with chorizo bits and green chilies.

He huddled over it, savoring the rare treat of eggs. A couple locals sometimes sold Wayne a few, but he charged through the nose for them. Momentary irritation set in at Tris spending his money when cheaper food would do, but faded under the lump of angst at the beating his ledger entry had already taken. *Hell, maybe she bought it with what Wayne paid her for givin' Bee a reach-around this morning.*

"You sure everything's okay?" Tris looked up from her bowl. "You looked upset when I walked in."

He mumbled over a mouthful of eggs, unable to explain to himself why he was more upset at the idea *she* was missing rather than his car.

She smirked.

"Yeah. Just pissy about the money."

"You'll catch it up." She slipped an arm around him and rubbed his back. "There's no rush on it, right?"

"Only not getting killed before I have enough." He jammed his fork in the eggs and let it stand. "Wayne's right. I'm gonna need more than ten grand. Bunch of crap to deal with. Finding a place. Stockin' up. Havin' a cushion to live on 'till word gets 'round there's a new 'house."

Tris leaned forward over her bowl, keeping her eyes on him while stuffing her face. Something lurked at the tip of her brain, a thought she evidently didn't want to say aloud.

"I know what you're going to say." Kevin stirred eggs until the smell of it got him hungry again and he ate a forkful. "How long will nine grand last? Do I need a roadhouse at all? Why don't we go to New Dallas?"

She stared into her bowl, wearing a slight blush. "I thought it, but getting a house is your dream. I don't want you to give up on it for me."

"Mmm. Why are you blushing?"

"Oh, I dunno." She stirred her food. "You said *we*. As in 'we go to New Dallas."

Kevin chuckled. "You still owe me 980 coins, gonna be 'we' for a while." He felt guilty at the look she gave him. The line between serious and kidding blurred, even to him. As shock began to melt into hurt, he winked.

Tris narrowed her eyes.

"Be right back." He took the bowl with him and wandered to the bar, eating along the way. "Yo, Wayne."

"Damn shame about the Challenger." Wayne shook his head. "Only a true malcontent would put bullets in such a fine machine."

"Think we got 'er back. Barely notice. Got any runs?"

"Not since I trusted a case of refried beans from Arnold. You see that sumbitch, you pop him for me." Wayne's ice blue eyes glimmered as he laughed. "Yeah, couple o' postal runs. Farthest of 'em goin up ta Kennewick."

"What's the pay?" Kevin slowed down, trying to make the eggs last longer.

"Driver's cut'd be forty coins."

Kevin scowled.

"If you're willin' ta play chicken with Infected, there's a run payin' the driver five hundred."

"Define 'playing chicken.'" He set the empty bowl on the counter. "Damn fine eggs, Wayne."

"'Preciate that. Juanita dropped off some sausage two days back. Run's goin' to little hole in the side of the mountain they call Nederland."

Kevin racked his brain. "If it's small…"

Wayne swiped the empty bowl. "With that machine you got, you ain't goin off road, at least not up in the foothills. Best way inta the place is gonna be ta ride north and then take 119 west. Fastest for your speed demon to get there is takin' 25 north through Denver and cuttin' over on 95 toward the area what used ta be Boulder. Terrain's a bit rough if you're thinkin' 'o skirtin' 'round."

"Oh, shit." He pinched the bridge of his nose and rubbed. "Denver's teeming."

Wayne nodded. "Aye. Last word out says so. 'Course, not like you gotta stop."

He glanced at Tris. She smiled. "What's the cargo?"

"Well… s'posed ta be confidential." Wayne hovered close and lowered his voice. "Since I know the odds o' *you* stealin' is slim to shit, I'll let ya in on it."

Kevin put on a flattered grin.

"Three thousand rounds. Mix 'o 5.56, 7.62x39, 7.62x51. 'Bout half is 9mm para."

"Fuck." Kevin coughed. "Where the hell did all that come from? Ween can't make that much that fast."

"Ask your friend." Wayne gestured at Alamo. "Says they found it in some smashed up heap what had fans 'stead o' wheels."

Goddammit. Kevin closed his eyes, thinking back to the little black dot of a hand grenade disappearing under the skirt of an Enclave hovercraft. *I should've gone back for salvage. That much ammo, I could've owned Wayne… and a roadhouse.* He punched the front of the counter.

"Easy." Wayne chuckled. "The Marauder is gone. Ain't nothin' you kin do 'bout it."

Kevin grumbled. "Nah. When I was runnin' Tris up to H-burg, we got jumped by pair of Enclave land boats. Didn't stick around to check for salvage. Son of a bitch."

Wayne held his arms out in a 'what can ya do' shrug. "You got that look in your eye. I'll write you in for it."

"Yeah… yeah…" He walked back to the booth where Tris occupied herself with a cup of black coffee. "Got a job."

"Okay." She took another sip. "Where's it rate on the scale of stupid things to do with a car?"

He flopped onto the bench seat, making her bounce. When Bee looked over, he pointed at her cup and gave the android a thumbs up gesture. "Pretty high, but no drugs." Kevin laced his fingers together to keep them still. "Might be a few Infected."

"Infected?" She grasped his hands. "How bad? You don't need to do it if it's too dangerous."

Kevin smiled at Bee when she dropped off a cup of coffee. "Probably not as bad as it sounds. We won't need to be on foot around them." He explained the route Wayne suggested. "We could try and go around Denver and come in on Boulder from the north, but that area's full of bandit caravans. At least six or seven of 'em, and they're usually shooting at each other... and everything else that gets too close."

Tris picked at the rim of her mug. "Well, Infected don't shoot back."

"And the nomads *might* leave us alone if we don't look like we're making a run on them."

She gave him a skeptical eyebrow lift. "You don't sound like you believe that."

"If the Infected are only supposed to last three months before the Virus kills them, maybe Denver's empty. Risky to run nomad territory."

"Are you sure the roads in Denver are even passable?" asked Tris. "If there are still Infected there, a blocked street could—"

"Be a pain in the ass."

"Okay, let's go around." Tris clung to his side. "You're almost as white as I am. Don't do it to yourself. Phobias aren't funny. Whatever you saw..."

"Naw, it wasn't quite like that." He swirled coffee in his mug. "The bandits dropped me off in this little camp. A pair of survivalists, Eva an' Hemi, took me in. When I was about eleven, they decided to move. I still don't know why."

Tris frowned. "I'm sorry."

"They're fine." He smiled. "As far as I know, they're in a settlement bout forty miles north of Topeka still. Place is too boring, even for Infected. Anyway... When they got in their head to move, we joined up with this group caravanning east. Infected came after us one night. We'd camped too close to some big ass city. No nukes had hit it, so up 'till the Virus came, there had to be a couple hundred thousand people still there."

"Evil." She stared into her coffee as if it could give her absolution for the sins of her ancestors.

"This guy they called Thorn, he got a piece of one up close. Punched its jaw right off. Must've nicked his knuckle on a tooth or something. I saw it, but I kept my mouth shut. Stupid thing ta do, but seein' Infected at all scared the hell out of me. I watched Thorn get sick. By the time they figured it out, he'd gone manic."

"Stage one… still some faculties left, but an overwhelming aggression takes over."

Kevin took a long swig of coffee. "Yeah. Shot up the camp. Dunno how he managed not to kill anyone before they put him down. Two young guys from the caravan we hooked up with went ta bury him. Guess they got blood on their hands and wiped their eyes or something…" He set his coffee on the table. "I don't think they were even seventeen yet. Soon as they realized they didn't have the flu, the boys said goodbye, walked off, and shot themselves."

"Oh, no."

"They had to tie their mother to the bus to keep her from running after them." He looked at her. "So yeah. It left a mark. Sometimes, I think the dreams are worse than what really happened."

"Maybe Nathan was reckless to really put the cure in my head." She spoke in a half whisper. "He knew I had the bomb. What if he was afraid someone would check the data first?"

Kevin frowned and set the cup down. "I'm not gonna bank on the Enclave being reckless."

She let her hands fall in her lap.

He stood, and approached Alamo's table. "Hey."

The man looked up from the silver revolver he had open for cleaning. Tris walked up on Kevin's left.

"Took your run. Ammo to Nederland? Never figured the News would sell ammo *or* have someone else drive it."

Alamo shook his head while chuckling. "We're only selling about a quarter of it. Operating expenses. B'sides, the people of Ned are in a bad way. And they're decent folks."

Dammit. That should'a been my ammo. "Decent folks… Yeah well. Let's get this shit loaded."

"I'm not sure I trust them," said Tris. "These guys tried to grab me twice."

"Old management." Alamo braced the revolver with a thumb and slid in a .44 round. "Since I took over, I found some things." Another round fell in with a *click.* "Raphael had some dealings with Neon in Glimmertown. Seems he wanted exotics to sell." He dropped another bullet in place and turned the cylinder with his thumb. "Not what we stand for."

"You'll have to forgive us if we don't trust easy, but I'm willing to give it a shot. So, where'd you find all that ammo?"

Alamo smiled as he loaded round number five. "So much for confidentiality. Suppose Wayne figures you won't steal since it'd cause too much bad rep for a 'house owner.'"

"Yeah, I'm a real fuckin' boy scout."

"Li'l north of Pueblo settlement. Big ass ol' Enclave transport flipped. We slipped in while the crew mopped up the bandits."

Hmm. Not our kills. I should head back there... "Slick."

Alamo flicked his wrist, seating the chamber with a *click*. "Always. Come to the Bobcat."

Kevin nodded and walked out, jogged down the steps, and headed for the charging panel.

Tris went to the passenger side door. "Bobcat?"

"An old store. Probably used to be a food market." Kevin unhooked the cable and put it away. "News took over the building."

"Oh. If they pull any shit, this time I'm not gonna go easy on them." She yanked the door open and got in.

Kevin grinned, muttering, "I wouldn't expect anything else."

• • •

THE RIDE NORTH FROM HAGERMAN PROVED EXHILARATING, FAR MORE SO than he'd expected. The Challenger purred along at 135 mph effortlessly. Tris had really gotten it straightened out. Still, the threat of an unexpected situation kept him cautious. Temptation gnawed at his brain, causing him to push it to 170 for a few short stints.

Tris occasionally held a hand up and stared at it, as if trying to see through her skin. Sometimes, she'd sit near motionless with her gaze aimed off to the right at the passing nothingness. For a little over six hours, amid the constant vibrating hum of e-motors, Kevin wrestled with the choice of routes. Images of streets swarming with decaying bodies traded places with his daydreamed battle against dozens of little ethanol buggies and feral nomads with axes. Maybe they'd get 'lucky' and run into the smarter ones, the ones with a black flag bearing a single white star. *They have snipers.*

Back and forth, he debated.

"I'm surprised there's anything left here," said Tris. "What with NORAD and all that infrastructure in Cheyenne. You'd think half the nukes used in the war would've been pointed here."

Kevin raised an eyebrow. "NORAD?"

She nodded. "Yeah, it's in a couple historical documentaries." Kevin rolled his eyes. "It was like the brain of the old military."

"Overstated. Was ramped down a lot a couple decades prior to the war. Everything got decentralized."

"How could you possibly know that? You weren't even born yet." She smirked. "The Enclave has all the his—"

"Movies, Tris. They're *movies*. Fiction. They all built that place up to be some kind of military superbrain. Never mind it's so far underground a nuke wouldn't touch it." He shifted his weight, pressing his back to the seat. "Stuff a guy hears running all over the place. People talk. Couple old men with a little hooch in them and all of a sudden, they're right back in the crap... and they talk."

She glared at the road sliding under the hood.

After a few minutes of silence, he squeezed the wheel. "It's running better than ever, like you worked magic."

Her expression softened. "Well... I'm not even all that good at electronics. Every kid gets taught a bit in school. I got a little more training with the resistance before they smuggled me out."

"School?" He blinked.

Tris rubbed her forehead. "You don't know what that is?"

Kevin glanced at her and shrugged. Without thinking about it, he kept going straight on the highway, past the turn that would've taken them far around Denver.

"It's a place where kids go, grouped by age, and learn stuff. Science, math, technology, engineering and stuff. Some start on medical training or advanced sciences when they hit eighteen."

"What did you advance in?" His fingers tightened on the wheel as he realized he drove right at the heart of Denver. *Deep breaths. Don't gotta stop. Don't gotta get out of the car.*

"I didn't go." She plucked a bit of lint from her tank top and flicked it. "I was going to, but when I realized how much of an asshole Dovarin was, I refused to accept the pairing assignment. Instead of university, I got put in Detention."

"I'd feel sorrier for you, but you had food and a clean bed at least." He winked.

She poked him in the side. "Yeah, and an eight-foot hexagonal cell with lights that never turned off. I like it more out here."

Kevin smiled at her, though his mood dropped into his lap. Beyond a gravel patch with train tracks and a slight incline covered in wild grass, the husks of ancient houses stood sentry amid a whirling cloud of ash. Shadows seemed to move in the windows. People? Infected? A trick of the mind? He leaned on the accelerator, pushing the car to 152 as he swerved to avoid taking an off-ramp. At that distance, he'd be long gone before the disease-riddled brains of Infected could process that he was there. Snipers, on the other hand, opportunistic scavs, worried him more, especially on the deteriorated patches of road that slowed him down.

He glided left into the next lane, but jerked to the right again in seconds. Tris wobbled in her seat and put her belt on, giving him a look.

"Thought I saw something moving in those houses. Don't wanna risk getting shot."

Little remained of power lines on the occasional still-standing poles they passed. Scavengers, the war, or who knows what, had long since stripped the wiring. Dead cars littered both shoulders as well as the central median, many scorched or half-melted and layered with grey silt. The rad meter picked up a steady 024 reading, making him think most of them had been caught on the road when war arrived.

"What would make people leave all those parts lying around?" He slowed to sixty when the road grew more debris-clogged. A grass berm came up along the right side, separating the highway from a smaller street.

"Uhh." Tris ran her fingers through her hair. "They look melted. Think people were afraid of rads? Maybe no one dared getting this close to Denver because they heard stories of Infected?"

He stared at a four-wheeled buggy made of aluminum tubing with huge rear tires and rusty armor plates. It looked undamaged, parked by a prewar pickup truck with a substantial lift. "Or the Infected got everyone that *did* try."

Tris swiveled in her seat to look at the buggy as they shot past it. "Not gonna stop for salvage?"

"Might be Infected."

She glanced at him. "I don't see anything."

"Nomads wouldn't have abandoned it. There might be Infected blood on it."

"I could check—"

Kevin squeezed both hands on the wheel, all his focus dedicated to swerving between smashed cars at sixty-four MPH. "Not stopping. Might be a trap. Don't care. It's been sitting there long enough to collect ash. There's a damn reason no one's scavved it."

A dark figure emerged from a cloud of grey fog up ahead, too close and too fast to avoid. With a squishy *thump*, half a human body slid up the hood to the windshield and smashed cheek-first against the glass. Mottled patches of wrinkled skin in purple and brown and a complete lack of hair left the gender up for debate. Black ichor leaked between its teeth as the car's increasing speed crushed its face flatter. Despite being ripped in half at the waist by the Challenger's bumper, the Infected raked and scratched at the windshield.

Kevin stared at it, paralyzed.

Tris slapped a hand down on his arm and yelled, "Kevin!"

His eyes focused on the wreckage of a delivery truck lying on its side coming up fast. He slammed on the brakes and swerved. The gurgling Infected flew off to the left, vanishing into the grey mist. Tires squealed as the Challenger skidded sideways. He corrected, fishtailing the end out. The car passed within inches of a lift gate dangling off the rear end of the truck. Another two Infected bounced off the front end. Bones bumped along the undercarriage.

Ten seconds passed in relative silence, save for a dragging scrape.

Kevin glanced at the floor, picturing a body clinging to something on the underbelly. "Oh, shit."

"It's... following us." Tris stared into the back seat. She blinked, and opened the center console flap to expose the hole for dropping grenades to the road.

A wheezing moan came from the opening.

Tris gulped back a scream and ripped the Beretta out of the holster. Kevin yelled 'fuck' a handful of times as an upside-down city bus emerged from the fog. He made a hard two-lane shift to the left, trying to see past the roiling grey.

"Is it gone?"

Blam!

The report of the Beretta inside the car left his ears ringing. Brass bounced off the windshield and settled on the dashboard. A second later, the rear wheels bounced over something.

"Now it is," yelled Tris.

Kevin stuck his pinky into his right ear and wiggled it. "Shit, I'm deaf." A wall of human silhouettes clarified out of the aerosolized ash particles up ahead. "Fuck this place!"

He flicked the master arm and held down the trigger for the forward-facing M60s. A side-side wiggle of the wheel sprayed the mob. Orange light smears streaked off into the gloom. Stumbling Infected made no effort to evade, and collapsed where they stood.

"That looks just like the blasters in the historical doc—uhh, movie." She smirked.

"Tracers... every fifth bullet." He cringed as the car thundered over what felt like an ocean of corpses.

Infected slapped and smeared at the sides. A dull *clank* rang out as someone's hand detonated on the driver's side mirror. The pounding of his heartbeat in his skull drowned out the screeching and wailing. A mass of Infected filled the rear-targeting monitor, clambering over themselves in an attempt to chase a car on foot.

He flipped the weapons toggle and let off a few short bursts from the rear-firing guns. He didn't care what he hit. Firing at all right now was guaranteed to nail something. Something that used to be a some*one*. Sweat ran in sheets down his face, stinging his eyes.

"Kevin?" Tris pushed on his arm. "Kevin?"

"Yeah?" He squinted at the ash, fighting the urge to slam on the accelerator. *Gotta stay slow. Can't risk crashing into something I don't see coming.* "What?"

"I uhh, think there's blood on the car now." She closed the center console. "You okay?"

"I'll be a whole lot better once I can see more than fifteen damn meters ahead." He coughed. "So glad this is an electric... all this ash would choke an air filter. I *hate* that. What's with the fog and the Infected. So freaky."

"They're drawn to dark places where they can hide. There's nothing supernatural about it."

He risked looking at her for two seconds. "Yeah, but I ain't gotta like it."

Splat.

Something bounced over the roof and thudded off the trunk.

Kevin cringed. "We hit another one, didn't we?"

"Yeah." She winced. "Juicy."

His stomach churned. His breathing grew shallow, and the taste of bile bubbled up into the back of his throat. After swallowing the urge to throw up all over her, he forced himself to look forward. Luckily, the highway remained clear. Roads and streets crisscrossed a blasted-flat area, littered with destroyed pieces of traffic lights and streetlamps. No trace of grass or green remained. The Challenger squealed around a cloverleaf as he rushed the turn onto Route 36. From an overpass up ahead, seven skeletons hung upside down by rope and chain wrapped about their ankles. Each one had a hatchet handle protruding from the skull. The gruesome totems wobbled in the wake of their passage.

Tris gave him a meek look.

"Horsemen." He shook his head. "One of the nomad groups. Bet they've staked a claim on Boulder."

The wipers didn't do much to the layer of red jelly on the windshield, but he ran them for a minute anyway. Tris kept the Beretta in her hands, clinging to it like a security blanket.

"I thought you were vaccinated or something... you look like you're ready to pass out."

She lifted her head, a meek look on her face. "Being immune to the Virus and not being freaked out by rotting zombies coming out of nowhere aren't even close to the same thing."

"Since we're splitting hairs... Zombies are technically undead."

Tris's eyebrows shifted together. "They're decaying, they moan, they want to kill us. Does it make that much difference?"

"Oh, never mind that the Virus was set loose years ago, and it's supposed to kill in three months. Any thoughts exactly what's going on?"

"Umm. Unexpected mutation probably. Viruses sometimes do that." She shivered.

Crap. Now she's wondering if it changed enough to get her. "Maybe they lied. Maybe it's doing exactly what they expected it to do."

She exhaled, fidgeting with the Beretta. "Maybe."

As far as he could see in the ash, the crumbling structures of Old Denver gaped in the wind. Thick haze gathered in narrow channels between some, masking the presence of who knows how many Infected. He imagined them all coming for him, as if a hundred thousand of them possessed a single mind. Kevin relaxed his grip on the wheel ten minutes later. His hands throbbed in time with his pulse. He jumped at every dense region in the cloud, mistaking it for another Infected. Tris remained silent as she stared out at the shattered remains of a once teeming city.

Time seemed to stand still, until finally, the grey miasma thinned enough to see road. A manic grin spread over his face, and he sped up to 110 in seconds. When the air cleared a short while later, he pushed it to 150. The trappings of Denver gave way to open ground on the right and the shadow of the mountains on the left. Abandoned cars streaked by all around them, though were mostly along the edges. An occasional tiny sports car, motorcycle, or truck in his way was easy enough to see coming and avoid without having to slow down.

Ripples formed in the goop on the windshield from the wind trying to push it up. Kevin squirmed in his seat at the thought of Virus covering his car. He drove along a stretch of highway with dirt and open space on both sides. A little less than an hour later, he slowed to a halt where a tangled mess of red and beige steel, glass, and wires had collapsed across the road.

"Goddammit." He stopped, drumming his fingers on the wheel.

"Looks like some kinda bridge so people can walk across the highway between shopping centers." Tris pointed left. "Try there."

He reversed, cut across the median, and took an off-ramp on the southbound side, which led into a lot with a handful of cars scattered about. He didn't trust the large building, probably one of those 'malls' he'd heard talked about, and didn't linger on thoughts of checking it out. Eyeballing the southern end of the pedestrian bridge, he navigated around a narrow, curving road and drove to within hand-grenade-chucking range of the stairs that once led to the crossing. As slow as walking, he drove over about sixty yards of dirt and eased the Challenger back down onto Route 36 on the other side of the tangled mass.

"That's going to be a major pain in the ass on the way out." He grumbled.

Tris shrugged. "We won't be in a hurry then… maybe go way east and cut south?"

"Maybe."

He enjoyed the car's newfound ability to exceed 94 miles per hour, leaving it sliding between 120 and 140 for the next half hour on the way to Boulder. Much to his surprise, nothing moved—not Infected nor Horseman nor other manner of bandit nomad. An ominous-looking brownish red parking garage passed on the right, covered in tattered scraps of cloth someone likely meant as flags. People moved inside, hovering around burn barrels. Some approached the edge, drawn by the sound of their tires on the road, though they moved like normal people.

Kevin didn't feel like sticking around to find out.

Wayne said something about 119 west. They shot under a still-intact concrete overpass, drove straight for a while more. He slowed to 72 mph by the time they reached the city. The place struck him as eerie in the first signs of moonlight. It didn't look much as though a nuclear war had happened, more like all the people had up and vanished.

Tris moved her head around on a swivel. "This is so creepy. This place looks..."

"Abandoned... and normal." He shook his head. "I don't like it. Why hasn't anyone either settled here or scavved it to the bone? Aside from the lack of people, you'd never know there'd been a war."

"Maybe there are and they go to bed early?" She offered a nervous laugh. "Hey, you passed it. Sign saying 119 back there."

He turned around, following her pointing finger onto another stretch of road leading west. Numerous cars littered it, again as though everyone in them had disappeared at the whim of an angry god snapping its fingers. Kevin slowed to a pace he felt sure he could outrun on foot to squeeze between them. Temptation gnawed at him. So many cars... so much possible salvage. *Whatever got these bastards ain't gettin' me.*

Worry of the Virus overpowered worry of ambush when he spotted a white hydrant in the grass on the side of the road by a fenced area leading up to a short concrete stairway. He stopped near it and stared at the handle.

"Hang on."

He pushed the door as wide as it would go before doing the limbo out of the car, afraid to touch any part of it. Once outside, he turned on a flashlight and did a walkabout. The Infected had been so squishy they hadn't dented any of the metal panels, though it looked like he'd driven through the middle of an enormous jelly doughnut. He gagged. As if about to poke a lion in the ass with a sewing needle, he reached toward the back end of the trunk and keyed in the code with one glove-covered finger.

Once satisfied his fingertip had no tainted blood on it, he snagged a wrench, and after about five minutes of effort, got the cap off the hydrant. He snarled at it. No water.

"Turn the nut on top," said Tris.

"Duh. I'm—"

"Freaked out." She rubbed his back. "It's okay."

Soon, water burbled out of it, far from the powerful cleansing stream he'd hoped for. She hurried to the trunk, returning a few seconds later with a plastic bucket.

"Might not be much left. Don't waste it."

While she filled the bucket, he grabbed a smaller pail, and they spent the next half hour washing off the Challenger. Bloody water gathered in puddles on the road. By then, the moon had come up.

"We are *not* going near Denver on the way out. I don't care if we need to take a shortcut through fuckin' Canada."

She took both buckets as Kevin shut off the still-spewing hydrant, and threw them back in the trunk. He stared at the road, terrified of going anywhere near the slime.

"How long is this shit lethal? What if someone comes walking by tomorrow and finds this?"

Tris bit her lip. "Umm. I want to say forty-eight hours in the wild before it deteriorates, but direct sunlight on the road might shorten that... especially when it dries out. You want to camp here and watch the puddle?"

"No." He half started at the car. "Dammit. Infected are walking around an hour away from here. A puddle won't make much difference."

"I got it... stay back." Tris pounced onto the roof, avoiding stepping in the water, and slithered in the window.

She drove the car forward far enough to give him dry land to walk on and hopped into the passenger seat. He stared at the Challenger. Someone else had driven *his* car... and didn't steal it. He trudged around and got in. For a few minutes, he sat gazing into the distance without driving.

"What's wrong?"

"You drove my car. That's like... walking up to someone you never met and grabbing their dick."

"Well, you weren't going to step in the goo." She got ready to pout at him.

He took her hand before her mood could darken. "It's okay. I'm..." Their eyes met. "Trying to accept that it didn't piss me off."

A moment of silence passed.

"It's dark. We should go. How much farther is it?"

He reached under his seat and pulled out an old atlas, losing a few minutes flipping pages while Tris held the flashlight. Eventually, he found the area. Finger to the page, he traced the line over 119 west from Boulder into the mountains.

"Looks like about 17 or 18 miles. Half hour, maybe more if there's something in the way."

Tris yawned. "You're sure the locals are friendly?"

Kevin dropped the book under the seat and accelerated hard. Alamo's strange smile lingered in his thoughts. "If they're not, things are about to get real hot in Hagerman."

NEDERLAND

Unease about what had happened in Boulder dogged Kevin the whole trip along a windy canyon route west. Perhaps a particular feature of the geography of the area shielded it from the effects of nuclear strikes as close as Salt Lake or even Denver. Granted, Denver hadn't taken a *direct* hit… if it had, it'd be like Dallas—a couple of iron girders and some scrap in an uninhabitable slab of glass—but where were the survivors? Why did the place look like a pre-war town where everyone had vanished straight out of their homes and cars?

Tris's posture stiffened. "Roadblock up ahead, two people behind it."

He squinted. *Damn her eyes are good.* "Ain't seein' nothin' but black."

He slowed to below ten MPH. Soon, a pair of large flashlights shattered the darkness up ahead. The Challenger lurched as he hit the brakes a little too hard, and came to an abrupt stop a short distance from the rear ends of two huge dump trucks lying on their sides. Their beds opened to full extension, touching in the middle of the road to form a barrier reinforced by slabs of scrap metal. Each truck had a single figure standing on the side of the cab, half-protected by a dented wall of angled steel welded in place. The person on the right seemed much smaller, though Kevin couldn't make out a lot of detail past the glare of the monster flashlights.

"Nothin' here for you. Turn right on 'round, and git gone." A man's voice, tinged with age, lingered in the chilly mountain air for a few seconds, echoing off the canyon.

A tiny electric motor whined as Kevin rolled down the driver's window. "This Nederland? Got a shipment via Wayne's roadhouse."

"Oh, yeah," yelled a higher pitched voice. They had a girl on the younger end of teen standing guard detail. "Wayne got us on the shortwave. You Earl?"

"Earl's the name'a Wayne's dog what's been dead six years. I'm Kevin."

The man chuckled. "Just checkin'. Give us a sec an' come on in. Emma, git the gate."

In the seconds after the flashlights cut out, a streak of light brown zoomed out of sight behind the shooter's nest on the right-side truck. A figure in a tan duster over flannel and jeans rose to his feet behind the other one. Scraggly, pewter-colored hair hung in spiral strands from under a battered cowboy hat. He offered a brief wave and climbed a ladder to the road on the inside of the gate.

Kevin's hand clenched around the wheel when a large truck engine roared to life. It revved up a second later, and loud scraping from the right side of the gate made him wince. Since the truck lay on its side, 'lowering' the dump bed equated to one of the two large 'doors' moving out of his way. Hydraulic pumps whined at a steady drone until the *clunk* of metal on metal announced it could move no farther.

A slender girl with shoulder-length brown hair, also wearing a cowboy hat, sprinted through the headlight beams to the other side. Soon after another diesel engine grumbled to life, the second truck dragged shut across the paving, revealing the older man standing on the road. He waved Kevin forward. A light touch on the pedal got the Challenger creeping forward. Despite plenty of room between the two behemoths, driving in the Nederland gate made him nervous for his baby.

He eyed the cab on the left. Someone had re-mounted the engine ninety degrees off axis, to sit upright in the flipped truck. Up ahead, the road curved down and to the right. Kevin leaned into Tris and peered out her window. A few dim red glowing spots drifted around a handful of buildings at the end of a dirt road on the right, up in the hills. About two car-lengths from the front bumpers of the trucks, he stopped.

"What the…"

Tris sat up taller. "Looks like people with red flashlights."

The elder sentry walked around the car, holding up a device that resembled a motorcycle headlight mounted to a battery the size of a canned ham. He completed a circle and stopped by Kevin's window, patting a hand on the door.

"Ya had a long ride."

"Yeah."

The engine on the left increased pitch, and the truck bed scraped open again. Kevin's eyes tracked the maybe-thirteen-year-old girl as she killed the engine, crawled out of the cab, and sprinted to the other half of the gate. An AK47 swayed on a strap across her back, too large for its owner. She ducked into the red cab and reached toward the middle of the dashboard area. The second half of the gate bucked across the road with a staccato grinding noise for a few seconds before slamming into the other truck.

"Well, the town knows we're here now." Kevin smiled. "Guess your neighbors ain't the most friendly lot."

"Not rightly, no." The old man gestured. "Take the road ahead until ya hit the circle. Go past it 'till ya see a big orange buildin' on your left on a corner. Park near that."

The second engine cut out, leaving the mountain in deathly silence.

"Got it," said Kevin.

He pulled away, following the same road into a small town that, like Boulder, seemed to have survived the war more or less intact. With only starlight and his headlights to see by, he drove ahead at a modest fifteen miles per hour. A building with a rounded roof similar to old aircraft hangars—though much smaller—passed on the right. The 'circle' the old man mentioned turned out to be a patch of grass in a round curb barely twelve feet across. Kevin chuckled and drove as straight as he could past the hangar-shaped building. A brass sign on the corner read 'mining museum.'

"That looks interesting," said Tris.

"It's probably a pickaxe, a shovel, and a dirt mound." He grinned. "Maybe a nugget of quartz or something."

She rolled her eyes.

"Damn, I'm tired. An hour ago, I wasn't sure if I was going to live to see tomorrow, now I'm making fun of someone who figured mining was interesting enough to deserve a museum."

Tris sighed.

They drove past a dirt lot on the right where some manner of rusting old crane sat. A little further down, on the left, a squarish building with a flattened corner looked like the one the gate man mentioned.

"Is that orange?"

"Uhh." Tris shrugged. "Beige? Tan?"

"Close enough." Kevin turned left and pulled up in a parking space near the double doors. The sheer mundanity of parking in a designated spot made him laugh. "Well, damn."

"What's so funny?"

He pushed the door open and leaned on the button to roll the window up. "Look at this place? It's so out of the way it's like even the war didn't want to make the trip."

Three men emerged from the building. The eldest appeared close to forty, with black hair so short it resembled motor oil smeared on his scalp. He dressed like a relic from the military: full camo. The other two were young enough to be his sons, but looked nothing like him. Both younger men had flannel shirts and jeans. One of the twenty-somethings smiled and waved.

Kevin stood. "Hey. Got that shipment from Wayne's."

"You're a lifesaver." The older man approached in three clean strides and extended a hand. "I'm Bill. This here's Pete and Brett."

The two younger men nodded in time with their names.

"Kevin." He shook. "That's Tris. Nice little town ya got here."

"Eh." Bill let his arm fall at his side. "Isn't what it used to be, but we're managing. Between the zombies and the damn bandits, it's getting rough."

"They're not zombies," said Tris. "Infected are technically alive."

Bill patted a black rubberized handle on his left hip. "If I ram this through someone's chest, do you think they'd care if I call it a machete or a gladius?"

Tris's eyebrows formed a flat line. "That's an oversimplification. You don't need to shoot Infected in the brain to kill them. There are meaningful differences."

"Where'd you find her?" asked Bill. "She sounds familiar."

"Vasquez?" Tris edged closer. "Your hair was longer."

Bill pointed at her. "You're the one they were sending..."

"Whoa." Kevin hooked his thumbs in his pockets. "You two know each other?"

Tris looked back and forth from Bill to Kevin for a few seconds. "H-he was supposed to be with the resistance in Harrisburg."

"I *was* there." Bill glanced at Kevin. "Trunk?"

"Yeah." Kevin leaned into the Challenger and hit the release button before closing the door.

"What happened?" Tris clenched her hands into fists. "We got there and it looked like everyone died."

"I'll explain later," said Bill. "You two look worn out."

"How many boxes is it?" asked Brett.

Tris covered her mouth with both hands, trembling—though she seemed more freaked out and angry rather than frightened.

Kevin held his hands about four feet apart. "One big one."

Pete and Brett followed, extracting the box of ammo after Kevin lifted the trunk lid. They grunted from the weight and shuffled only two steps away before setting it down on the road. Bill walked up as they opened it and did a quick visual check of numerous small boxes of bullets. As often as hand loaders re-used old ammo cartons, he doubted the labels matched the contents.

"Looks good, but we'll need to give it a thorough count." Bill gestured at the two younger men, indicating they should bring the ammo into the building. "You two are welcome to spend the night with me an' the wife if you want."

Kevin squinted at the fast-departing box of ammo. "I'm s'posed ta pick up the payment. 5000 coins."

Bill hooked a thumb on his belt. "Understood. You don't think we'd risk getting on the 'house's bad side?"

Kevin half-smiled and tapped the tip of his boot on the ground. "Ain't the 'house's backside I'm worrying about."

"Heh, fair enough. Guess you aren't too quick to trust people."

Tris folded her arms. "Takes him awhile."

"Was gonna bring out the boxes once we'd finished counting bullets."

Kevin gestured at him. "Why don't we count coins while you count bullets?"

"No need, friend." Bill grinned. "We don't got much use for coins out this way. Most of what we use, we find... what little else we barter for. They're still bank-wrapped. Two $25 boxes of pennies."

"Dammit." Kevin suppressed the urge to snarl. "It's supposed to be five thousand, not fifty."

Tris giggled.

"What?" Kevin stared at her.

"A hundred pennies to a dollar. Twenty-five dollars is 2500 pennies."

"Oh." He rubbed his face. "Damn complicated prewar money."

"Coins are coins. You need some sleep. Head straight on down the road past this place 'till ya see a red house on the left by a row of pine trees. That's my place. I'll be right behind you." Bill jogged past the front doors of the building and pulled a mountain bike away from the wall.

Kevin didn't move until Tris pushed him back to the car. He took a left out of the parking lot, driving deeper into town on the same road they'd come in on. Less than a minute later, a little dirt ramp led off the road on his side, by a red brick house with an angled roof. Lights inside revealed the shadows of at least one person moving around.

He pulled up by a battered garage door and shut down the car. Tris's right leg bounced. She seemed markedly less tired than before. Kevin didn't feel like walking up to a strange house; that's a good way to get shot. Within a few minutes, Bill arrived. The mechanism of his ten-speed emitted a ratcheting *click* as he slowed and pulled up to the porch left of the garage. Kevin got out, giving the door enough of a shove to close with a gentle *thump* behind him.

Bill led the way into a small kitchen where a brown-skinned woman with black hair, about Bill's age, sat at a rectangular table covered with a blue-white checkered cloth. She gave them a cursory glance before cocking an eyebrow at Bill. Kevin looked around, feeling out of place in such a normal setting. Replace the half-dozen candles with electric lights, and it might've been possible to forget a war had happened at all.

A little girl of about nine stood in an open doorway leading into the next room. Blonde and blue-eyed, she looked nothing like Bill or the woman. A threadbare pink tee shirt, sized for a woman, but with the neck sewn smaller to turn it into a nightgown, hung from a bony figure. Her right big toe poked out of a hole in olive-drab socks. The girl stared at him, face neutral, not blinking.

"This is my wife, Ann." Bill gestured between them. "Kevin, Tris... driver who brought in the ammo."

"Oh. Wonderful." The woman smiled. Her English had a trace of Spanish in it. "Have you had anything to eat?"

Kevin's stomach answered for him. "Uhh, no. Not yet."

"We'll give you fair coin for some food." Tris smiled.

"Oh, nothin' doin'." Ann pointed at chairs. "You're guests. Sit. Besides, they'd just collect dust in a drawer somewhere. We don't really use coins here."

"You don't?" asked Kevin, eyebrow up.

Bill grinned. "We don't leave Ned much. No need. That's mostly for inter-town trading and people like you who never sleep in the same bed twice."

Kevin eased himself into a white-painted chair he feared would break if he put all his weight on it. He laced his fingers together and rested his hands on the table. "Food sounds awesome. Thanks."

Tris sat catty-corner to him on the right. The smile she gave him said she had to be thinking about his recent doubts about humanity. "Thank you, Ann." She fixed Bill with a stare as he sat across from her. "So, what happened in Harrisburg?"

The child didn't move from her spot. Kevin locked eyes with her. He shrugged and mouthed 'what?', but the girl didn't react.

Note. Keep the matches away from that one.

"We figured we were relatively safe underground there. The Infected hadn't worked out how to use ladders. Most of 'em couldn't handle the idea of lifting manhole covers. They're pretty stupid."

"Not completely." Kevin rubbed his arm. "One of them knew enough to disarm me once. They understand what guns are."

"I've never seen that." Bill scratched his cheek.

"Might've been recently infected," said Tris. "Still had a bit of higher brain function left."

Bill picked at a gouge in the table. "Anyway, about a day after Nathaniel told us you were on your way"—Tris scowled—"Jeffries stumbled into the command room. He'd been out on sentry watch, and said the floor gave out from under him. His leg was all tore up. Couple of hours later, he crawls to his feet and staggers off down the hall, we think ta hit the shitter, but he kept on going. That old sewer had a street level access point about a quarter mile away. Son of a bitch Jeffries went right to it and tore out the barricades. He opened the damn doors up and let the Infected walk right in."

Kevin shivered.

Bill flicked his gaze up from the Formica to Kevin. "Oddest thing was they were waitin' for him. Like they knew he was comin'.'"

Kevin shivered again.

Tris stared down. "I'm sorry. He probably saved you all... at least the ones who lived."

"How's that?" asked Bill, a touch of a glare in his expression.

"Nathan wasn't trying to help the Resistance. He's probably First Tier administration." Tris's eyes reddened around the edges. "He put a bomb inside me. If you were all still there, it would've killed everyone."

Bill scowled. "Son of a bitch."

"Wait." Kevin tilted his head. "That prick didn't know you were there until you tried to make contact. How would he have known when to set off the bomb? If you didn't get him on that… computer thingee, he'd never have realized you were at the target location."

Tris squirmed. "I dunno. Maybe…"—she clasped a hand behind her left ear—"maybe as soon as they tried to get the data out."

"If I ever see that bastard again, I'll tear his head off with my bare hands." Bill clenched his fingers as if squeezing the life out of the air.

"The Infected didn't kill him?" Kevin raised an eyebrow.

Ann opened an orange plastic container and dumped a brown glop into a pot, which she set on a hot plate. Soon, the smell of beef stew flavored the air.

The little girl continued staring into Kevin's soul. Had she even blinked once?

"No. Damndest thing." Bill shook his head. "They walked past him like he wasn't there."

"He was one of them." Tris rubbed her arms, as if trying to warm her hands. "When he fell, he probably got the Virus in his system where he cut his leg. Unless falling was a lie. If he got too much in his blood fast enough, he might've gone to stage one in only a few hours."

"Stage one?" asked Bill.

"Still in possession of most of his mental faculties, but having lost any sense of humanity. Enough of a brain left to think tactically." Tris shivered.

Kevin put a hand on his stomach, not sure if he remained hungry. "That's some scary shit. You're suggesting the Infected got him, and he knew they were… 'frustrated' at not being able to get into the resistance compound? So they somehow compelled him to open the door?"

"Some of the things we've seen suggests a hive intelligence." Bill leaned back in the chair. "Socrates told me it was one of the reasons the people all migrated here from Boulder about four years back."

"Socrates?" Kevin glanced at him, then at the little girl. "What's the deal with the kid? Or am I hallucinating her?"

"Yeah, they got to callin' him Socrates since he's one of the smarter people around here. That's Zoe." Bill held out an arm as if to invite the girl into a hug. She pushed herself off the wall and approached, rigid—and still staring at Kevin—as Bill cuddled her. "I found her on my way here. Wound up takin' her in."

"Guess she's not much for conversation." Kevin smiled at her, though the child's blank stare remained. He couldn't handle the thought of what she must've seen, and looked away.

"Sometimes." Ann set a steaming bowl of stew down in front of Kevin, and another near Tris.

"Electric stove, nice." Kevin dug in.

"We got some solars scavved outta Boulder. With the ammo you brought in, we'll be able to head up there and collect a bunch more stuff."

"So the Resistance got out?" Tris cradled the bowl to warm her hands. "Are they all here?"

"Nah." Bill shook his head. "Jeffries sorta killed Doc Andrews' spirit. Those that survived scattered to the winds. I honestly couldn't tell ya where anyone of them went 'cept for the handful that followed me here. It isn't a glorious life, but it's rewarding." He smiled at Ann, who sat in his lap.

Zoe seemed to 'tolerate' Bill's arm around her back, neither comforted nor bothered by it. Still, she stared with pale blue eyes at Kevin. Not blinking, not speaking, not smiling, not frowning. He stopped eating for another moment and watched her, waiting for her to blink.

She didn't.

Tris pushed stew around her bowl.

Kevin slid his arm out across the table and held her hand. "Hey…"

"Am I supposed to just give up? Wander around never knowing if the cure is in my head?" Tris's lip quivered. "I believed him. I… really thought I could play some little part in stopping the Virus."

Zoe broke her unending stare at Kevin to peer at Tris for a few seconds.

"There's a guy in Omaha who can probably get at it," said Bill.

Tris's gaze shot up. "Where?"

Ann stood and collected Kevin's empty bowl. "Dear, you should eat that before it gets cold."

"Sorry." Tris shoveled stew into her face.

"Omaha," said Bill. "Far about east of here. Came through it on our way outta Harrisburg. Guy lives inside an old airplane. Whole place is overgrown now, but he's got quite the collection of computer equipment. If I'd seen anyone left on this Earth who might have a chance at getting into your head, it'd be him."

"Got a name?" asked Kevin.

Tris shot him an adoring look.

"Called himself 'Terminal9.'" Bill chuckled. "Probably because that's where he lives."

"What about Infected?" Kevin squeezed Tris's hand. "Omaha was a pretty damn big city."

"Not every city is loaded with them," Tris mumbled around a mouthful of food. "Look at Dallas."

"*Nothing* lives in Dallas... except maybe the cockroaches." Kevin rubbed his eyes. He glanced at Zoe for a second before smiling at Bill. "Sorry... You said something about sleep?"

I'm going to have nightmares about that kid.

Tris got up to carry her empty bowl to the sink, but Ann got in the way. She surrendered it, offering a thankful smile.

"You two can take the loft. I'll get Zoe set up in the spare room." Bill stood.

"No... it's okay." Kevin smiled. "She looks like she's been through enough. The spare room is fine."

"Bed's a little small for two, but if you want." Bill gave Ann a wink.

"It's fine." Tris looked around. "Where?"

Bill showed them to a small room in the rear left corner of the house, adjacent to the bathroom. Pea green walls surrounded a single twin bed, a small nightstand, a desk, and a throw rug decorated with Native American patterns. Zoe stood in the doorway of the kitchen, staring at Kevin until he pushed the door closed and turned around.

He shook his head. "Wow... poor kid."

Tris put her sword between the bed and the wall and stripped down to her panties. Kevin undressed except for his boxers and kept the .45 with him under the pillow. As soon as he settled down, he startled at the sight of the door open two inches. He raised his head to look and found Zoe peeking in. The child stared at him for a full minute in silence.

"Your gun's not big enough," whispered Zoe. She lingered a second more and pulled the door closed.

"Ohhh-kay." Kevin blinked. "So much for sleep."

KEVIN WORKED A PUMP HANDLE, FILLING A TEN-GALLON WHITE PLASTIC bucket. He sucked at his teeth, trying to pry dense nuggets of homemade toast dough from among his molars. Sunlight filtered in wavering patches among the stand of trees that formed a wall to the southwest of Bill's house. Over breakfast, he'd come to learn Ann owned the place. She'd lived in Ned prior to the influx of Boulderites.

His prediction had come half-true. He *had* slept, though not well. Dreams composed of either Infected or creepy-Zoe stalking him played on loop all night. Once, he'd startled awake with the girl straddling him, seconds from plunging a knife into his chest. His scream was real, but the girl a product of his subconscious. The oddity of dreaming that he woke up lingered even now, hours past breakfast. Coupled with his fatigue, he wasn't sure if he really did wake up.

Bucket full, he carried it back around the house to where he'd parked. The windows were dark and empty, though whenever he looked forward, he thought he saw Zoe watching him from one out of the corner of his eye. Each time he snapped his head left, she vanished. *What the hell is wrong with that kid? Am I seeing shit?*

At the corner, he almost walked into Bill coming the other way. Kevin let off a yelp as if the Infected had ambushed him. Water splashed on both men.

"Shit. Sorry." Kevin closed his eyes and tried to calm his heart rate. "Didn't hear you."

Bill chuckled. "Rough trip in? You see anything moving around Boulder?"

"Nah. Empty and eerie. Like everyone just picked up and left." Kevin carried the bucket to the car.

"That's because they did." Bill followed and leaned on the wall next to the garage door, arms folded. "Catchin' nomad attacks from the north and the occasional run by the Infected from the south. Boulder was wide open. Much easier to defend Ned."

Kevin took a small cup and used it to pour water over the tires, cleaning the nooks and crannies of the tread. *I don't see blood, but I don't trust it.*

"Ran one over?"

"Yeah." He stood and twisted around to look at Bill. "What do you think are the odds the data in her head's any good?"

Bill curled his lips in, exposing a thin sliver of teeth for a second. "Hard to say. Our man inside said he thought the data was good. Not Nathan. Someone he didn't know about."

"As far as you know. Might've been all part of the plan." Kevin got down on his knees and threw cupful after cupful of water at the undercarriage. "Don't s'pose there's any chance you got any kind of disinfectant?"

"Got bleach." Bill lifted his right leg, bracing his boot against the wall. "It's possible they were arrogant enough to let it out. They made the Virus, so it stands to reason they know how to stop it, assuming they aren't complete morons. They'd have to plan for the contingency of a backfire, and how to cure their own people if something went wrong."

"Nathan looked that arrogant." Kevin wiped sweat off his forehead with the back of his arm.

"I bet they never thought we'd have the equipment to produce any form of usable medicine from it too."

"Yeah. From what Tris says, they think everything outside their nice little paradise is all a bunch of painted savages running around raping and killing everything that moves."

"Some places ain't too far off from that. Blood Flag nomads out here, and there's a couple bands in the deep woods 'round the Appalachians that'd flip a coin to decide if they wanna eat or try to impregnate you."

Kevin shook water out of the cup and threw it back in the trunk. "Seems like an awful lot of trouble to go to in order to kill 'the resistance.' What's the Enclave afraid of?"

Bill shrugged. "That, I can't answer. You'd have to ask Doctor Andrews."

Tris lifted a large steel bowl off the electric heating element, leaning her face away from the plume of steam wafting from the top. She poured it over the breakfast dishes piled in the sink, loosing the smell of pan-fried ham and eggs in the air. Ann worked a cloth around the table, eventually gathering a handful of crumbs and food bits in her hand as she pulled the rag off the edge. Zoe sat, staring at Tris, still with a half-eaten ham steak in front of her on a plate.

"You really didn't have to do that." Ann glanced at Tris while patting Zoe on the head. "Finish your food, sweetie. There's kids starving out there who'd love to have it."

Tris expected Zoe to say something like 'well they can have it,' but the girl grabbed the meat in her hands and chewed on it. Ann made a face, but seemed content enough that the child ate not to bother her about how.

"You wouldn't let us pay you for the food... I don't want to be a mooch." Tris used a rag that had once been a shirt to wash dishes. "I'm surprised really. It's almost comfortable here."

"We're lucky. Nederland isn't fancy, but it's safe."

Tris looked up as Kevin passed by the window outside, carrying a bucket, white as a sheet. Zoe's reflection glared at Ann, an apparent reaction to 'safe.' *Something's really bothering him.*

"The two of you should consider settling in. There's plenty of unused buildings." Ann tossed the rag on the counter and reached to shut off a circuit breaker where the hot plate plugged in. "Gotta save power. The batteries only go so far, and the wiring goes down every couple of days."

"What'll you do if the solar panels fail or the battery gives out?" Tris handed Ann a clean plate.

Ann dried it. "I suppose it'll be back to wood fires for cooking. Our farm's doing well. People lived long before we knew about electricity. We'll figure something out. It's nice here. A good place to raise a family."

Zoe shoved away from the table and stormed off down the hall, stomping.

Tris watched her until the girl slipped out of sight into a doorway down the hall. "That poor kid."

"She got separated from her father a few months ago. Bill found her wandering alone when he made his way down from the east. Poor thing was half dead from starvation." Ann leaned on the counter, head down. "It's a miracle nothing worse happened to her."

"Yeah." Images from the 'historic documentaries' replayed in her head, hinting at the sort of depravity that the Enclave believed to exist. This little town wasn't part of that world. "It's sweet of you to take her in. I hope she heals."

Ann looked up, seeming sad. "Me too. You really ought to stay here. Pretty, delicate girls like you don't last long out there."

Tris winked. "I'm not as delicate as I look."

EXCEPTIONS

With the Challenger as clean as possible, and the scent of bleach stuck in his nostrils, Kevin carried the bucket of dirty water a short distance away to dump it. Bill hopped on his bike to go check the status of 'the count.' After he stowed the cleaning supplies in the trunk and slammed the lid, Kevin tromped up the small porch and kicked dirt off his boots on the edge of the top step. Inside, Ann and Tris stood by the sink, chatting over dishes. He took a deep breath, filled with the scent of the great breakfast they'd enjoyed, and found himself salivating.

"Bill went to check up on the ammo." Kevin pulled a chair out.

"Oh, no you don't." Tris threw a rag at him. "You're not going to watch the women do dishes. Get your ass over here and help."

He chuckled. "Okay, okay."

Zoe's shrill scream emanated from the back end of the house.

Ann looked in that direction, worry evident on her face.

"I got it. My hands are dry." Kevin shoved the chair against the table. "Probably saw a spider or something."

He jogged into the hallway. Three strides from the ladder leading to the loft, the report of a rifle going off upstairs pounded his ears. Kevin stumbled into the wall and rushed forward. The gun fired three more times while he hurried up the red-painted wooden ladder. Little Zoe, barefoot in a denim dress, knelt by the windowsill of her bedroom, aiming a full sized AR-15 over the sill.

Outside, a man screamed.

Another voice shouted, "Dammit, kid. Drop the friggin' gun. I don't wanna shoot a little girl."

The same voice that screamed in pain shouted, "Kill the bitch."

Kevin grabbed the top of the ladder, about to haul himself into the loft. Zoe shifted left and aimed down at a sharp angle, firing three more times. Spent brass bounced off the wall; one landed in a crystal bowl full of pink barrettes with a *clink*.

"Bad guy inside!" yelled Zoe. She yelped and aimed higher, firing every four or five seconds.

A man in a vest made of tire treads and leather scraps over black military fatigues crept by in the hall right below. He aimed a boxy assault rifle toward the kitchen, and cast a quick glance at the ladder, evidently trying to sneak up on the armed child from behind. At the sight of Kevin, he yelled, "Shit!" and swung his rifle around.

Kevin dove from the loft, tackling the man into the wall and shoving him to the ground. Gunfire *popped* and *snapped* outside, distant as well as nearby. A *smash* announced the front door failing to a boot.

"Don't move, ladies," yelled a different man. "Coins, ammo, and food. Take it easy. We ain't here for women. Hand over the pistol, nice and slow."

Kevin snarled as he wrestled for control of the rifle. The man kicked his legs in an effort to roll over on top, but Kevin reared up and slugged the raider in the head four times, leaving him dazed.

"P-please d-don't rape us," mewled Tris.

Oh boy, someone's about to have a bad fuckin' day. Kevin sat up on his knees and wrenched the rifle away from the semiconscious thug. A second after he knocked the man out with a golf club like swing, a staccato slap of fist-on-meat came from the kitchen.

"*Ay, Dios mio!*" yelled Ann.

Thud.

Footsteps approaching from behind halted with a rapport of a 5.56 from upstairs. Kevin whirled around, aiming out the back door at a twenty-something woman in similar armor made of old tires. She fell on one knee, screaming from a bullet wound in the thigh. Kevin gave her a 'don't' look. *One of these days I'm gonna get killed for hesitating at killing a chick.*

"Drop the gun, bitch," yelled Zoe. The child shrieked as a few gunshots boomed outside.

Snaps and *pops* came from overhead, bullets piercing the wall. Kevin fired over the woman's head, a near miss on the trunk of a tree forced three men to duck—and stop shooting at Zoe.

The dirt-smeared face of the woman less than ten yards from the porch ran with sweat. A rifle went off in the kitchen.

"Zoe!" Ann shrieked and sprinted down the hall to the ladder.

"What the fuck is going on?" yelled Kevin.

The armored woman looked at her bleeding leg for a second before falling face-first to the ground. More men shouted outside, and a ripple of rapid gunshots preceded the *ping* of bullets striking large boulders in the dirt hill behind the house. Kevin jumped to his feet, a quick glance to his right confirmed Tris unhurt and braced against the doorjamb in front, shooting at a target outside with what appeared to be an FN-FAL rifle. Whatever it was, it looked far older than the one Kevin grabbed.

He rushed left, heading for the back door. Bill, Brett, and about eight others including Emma, the young girl he'd seen at the gate, advanced on the pines. The thirteen-year-old crept through the weeds like a trained soldier, AK leading the way. She swiveled at something, fired twice, and made a hand signal at one of the men who scurried in a wide flanking jog.

"I'm okay," yelled Zoe, sounding petulant. "They shot my room."

Kevin ran out the back door, hooked a right, and took cover at the corner of the house. The attacking force retreated back up and over the long ridge. More *pops* and *snaps* echoed in the forest from bullets holing tree trunks or striking rocks. When a beefy figure reared up from behind a boulder as big as a compact car with a grenade in his hand, Kevin fired twice. The bandit shuddered and went over backward. After a six count, and no explosion, Kevin ran up on him, still aiming at the man's head.

The bandit's black fatigue pants had soaked to his right knee, and four tiny bullet holes in the tire vest bubbled with blood. Kevin tilted the rifle to look at the side. A fire-select switch by his thumb indicated '2.' A rifle that fired a two round burst with such speed it sounded like a single gunshot turned his brain into a whirring mess for a second as he tried to imagine how many coins he could get out of Wayne for it.

"Clear," yelled Zoe from high and behind. "The bad guys are running."

Bill jogged over. "You okay?"

Kevin nodded. "Yeah, that woman's not dead." He gestured at the one Zoe got in the thigh. "I think. Could be bleeding heavy."

"Brett, Ed, check her." Bill pointed at the fallen bandit and returned his gaze to the hills. "Bastards must've come in on foot since they can't get past the gate. That's a shitty hike. They must be getting desperate. Guess we're going to have to assign a patrol path out that way."

Tris jogged outside, carrying an all-black FAL with a bayonet. She halted between the two men. "Well that explains that."

"What?" asked Bill and Kevin simultaneously.

"Ann said Ned was 'safe,' and Zoe gave her such a look." Tris stared at Kevin's rifle.

As if on cue, the little blonde girl emerged from the back door, still carrying the AR15 almost as long as she was tall. Kevin squinted at her and picked up the hand grenade. Ann grabbed the kid by the shoulder, keeping her from leaving the porch. Zoe looked up and back at her, but didn't offer much protest.

"What's up with that?" Kevin gestured at her. "Arming a what, nine-year-old? That's gonna make her a target."

Brett and Ed rolled the bandit woman over and tore the leg of her pants open. Ed put a hand on the thigh while Brett collected a pistol and several knives before removing her truck tire armor.

"Kid's not a bad shot." Bill smiled. "She doesn't like killing people, so she aims for legs. In Ned, everyone is responsible for defending the town. 'Course, Zoe *is* a bit young, but I'd rather have her able to defend herself than be at the mercy of whatever makes it inside."

"Someone's gonna kill her." Kevin shook his head. "Giving her a gun is like painting a target on her forehead."

"Who are these people?" Tris glanced at the woman. "Why did they attack your house?"

"Bad luck." Bill pointed at the trees. "The way they came in from the southwest… the trails on the far side of that ridge lead right here."

Emma, now at the top of the hill, made a series of hand signals. Bill waved her back. She moved in a slow turn, surveying the area before lowering her rifle and trudging down the hill.

"Em spotted six people leaving, two vehicles about a half mile away." Bill slung his rifle on a strap over his shoulder. "We got about five more in town coming in from the northeast."

Two of the 'Nederland Irregulars' dragged the man Kevin knocked out from the house.

Bill chuckled. "You one of them pacifists?"

"Yeah right," said Kevin.

Tris winked. "No, he's too cheap to spend the ammo."

He laughed. "I didn't want to get blood all over your nice wall."

"Bandits." Tris edged closer to Kevin. "They were here to steal whatever they could get their hands on."

"You whimper well." Kevin winked.

She smirked, and gave him a light punch in the arm. "Distracted him, didn't it?"

"And you wonder why I don't trust women." Kevin hunted around the rifle. When he found what he thought was the safety, he pushed it, and a magazine fell out of the butt. Rather than bullets, it had a stack of dull brown-orange blocks. "What the hell is this?"

"Looks like caseless ammo." Bill clucked his tongue. "Good damn luck finding more of that out here."

"They must've discovered a crashed Hoplite or something," said Tris. "That rifle's from... uhh, you-know-who."

Shit. Kevin grumbled.

Distant men and women yelled 'clear' at varying intervals.

"Even more reason to sell this thing." Kevin slung it over his shoulder. He narrowed his eyes into the wind, watching the two men carry the shot bandit woman away. "What'll ya do with her?"

Bill shrugged. "If she survives, city elders will take a vote. Depends on what she's gotta say for herself."

"How often do you get attacked here?" asked Tris.

"Once a week... sometimes once every two. Gate keeps us pretty protected against anything big, but every now and then they pull crap like this and sneak in on foot."

"Why don't you counterattack?" Kevin opened and closed his right hand, at last noticing the soreness from punching someone in the skull. "Track 'em back to wherever they come from and take them out."

"Couple of the elders think it crosses the line from being settlers to being a bandit group with a town." Bill lowered his voice to a conspiratorial whisper. "Course, I could pay you a bit to do a *scouting* mission. If it happens to turn into a firefight, well..."

"I'm not a merc. I drive shit around." Kevin sighed. "I usually try to avoid gunfights."

"I'll do it." Tris glanced at Zoe. "If they come back, there's at least two who'll be gunning for her."

Kevin leaned back, staring at the clouds. *Goddammit, why me?* He moaned. "Fine. We'll scout."

Zoe and Ann approached. The kid's denim dress looked like it had been someone's skirt in a past life. It clung to her chest, leaving her shoulders bare, held up by a hand-tied strip of blue cloth looped behind her neck. Take away the rifle, and the shoeless girl would paint a perfect picture of country innocence. She clutched the AR15, index finger straight near the trigger but not on it, and held it sideways, pointed at the ground.

After an appraising look at the boxy rifle he'd acquired, Zoe nodded. "That one's big enough."

"Zoe, please go inside." Bill patted her on the head.

Kevin cringed when the girl turned away, at a trail of blood on the back of her left shoulder. "She's hit."

Zoe shook her head. "I gots a splinters from a bullet hittin' the wall. Ann took it out."

Tris stared at him.

"Okay, okay. Fine. You know this is a bad idea." Kevin stomped toward the Challenger. "I'm too close to my goal. This is going to get me killed, and I will haunt you."

"I'm not asking you to do anything stupid." Tris ran to the passenger side door. "Besides, I'll protect you." She winked and got in.

Oh, that's just great. He slid the rifle in behind the driver's seat, chucked the new grenade in 'the box,' and got in.

"Remember…" Kevin stared at her, half grinning. "I'm going to haunt you."

She pulled the magazine out of the AK to count shots. "I can live with that." Tris slapped the mag in. "Sixteen left. How many in that thing?"

"Not a damn clue." He reversed into a K-turn. "And I don't mean 'creepy footsteps in the attic' or 'shadows in the hallway' kinda haunting. There will be naughty touching involved."

Tris laughed.

FAIR IS FOR DEAD MEN

The Challenger handled the iffy dirt roads in the hills south of Nederland with some difficulty, though the all-wheel-drive arrangement made it possible. Kevin kept it at about twenty miles an hour, wary of ruts and bumps. Bill had given him some brief directions to where he believed the bandit camp was. Trying to figure out what to do when he got there felt like attempting to cut a tomato seed with a knife. As soon as he got what he thought was a decent idea, it slipped out from under his brain.

"What does that face mean?" asked Tris.

He squeezed the wheel, keeping an eye out for tire tracks or any sign of life. "I got some issues going to a place specifically to kill people."

"I understand that... but these 'people' ran into a peaceful settlement and started shooting at us."

"Honestly, I think Zoe fired first." Kevin chuckled, and right away felt guilty for doing so. "One of 'em said he didn't wanna shoot a kid. Yeah, I know, bandits left me alone when I was little... but still."

"Maybe we can convince them to settle in Ned like citizens?" Tris raised an eyebrow. Her expression and tone gave away her lack of sincerity.

"I don't think they're going to feel much like talking."

He spotted lines across the dirt path where tires had crossed and steered after them. The whirr of the electric motors, far quieter than any sound made by an ethanol engine, gave him a little confidence they might pull off an ambush. *Ambush.* Kevin grumbled. *It's going to be at least six on two, probably worse than that.* He thought about standing behind the counter of his own roadhouse, protected by the armor of The Code. An attempt at Wayne's cocky 'king of my domain' smile formed on his face as the fantasy played out. This... this 'assault' mission was as bad an idea as he could've gotten—except for maybe trying to sell void salt in Glimmertown.

His smile faded to a stone face.

Tris pointed. "Look. Scrap of black cloth tied to a tree branch. Go there, left."

Kevin spotted it a few seconds later. About thirty feet off the ground, a strip of fluttering fabric trailed in the wind. The tree it marked stood at the crook of a fork in the path. He eased the car through the turn. After a mild hill, the road dipped down for a long stretch before rising to another, higher, hill on the far end. A handful of rusted vehicles, too far gone to be recognizable, littered the center of a mud pit on the right. Marks on some rocks at the side hinted it had once been a small lake.

He stomped on the brakes as the Challenger crested the distant hill. Down at the bottom of the hill, three bandit buggies had parked by a group of dirt bikes. Over twenty people in tire tread vests and black pants or skirts congregated in front of the vehicles. Another man, in a clean black bodysuit that appeared to be some manner of super-modern light armor, walked up to a huge mohawked man. He carried himself with an air of authority, helped along by slate grey hair and tall, prominent cheekbones.

An Enclave hovercraft about the size of four Challengers put together waited a short distance behind the man in the strange armor. One white helmet protruded from an open-topped turret near the front, which bore a multi-barrel rotary cannon, probably in 7.62mm.

The Enclave emissary approached a stack of long, grey boxes, and shook hands with the large man. "A pleasure, Golem? Is it?"

"You one strange dude," said Golem. "You say we ain't gotta give you nothin' for this shit?"

"No payment is necessary, friend. All we ask is that you keep doing what you have been doing, and we will continue to bring you weapons."

"Works for me." Golem grinned.

"We'll see you next month then." The Enclave man shifted to walk back to the hovercraft, but stalled when he faced the hill—and the Challenger.

Kevin flicked the master arm switch.

The man in black gestured at the car and looked at Golem. "It appears we have a guest."

"What are you doing?" asked Tris.

Servos in the M60s on the hood chirped to life.

"Trying not to fuckin' die." Kevin sucked in a breath and held it. "Turret boy's all yours."

He pressed his right thumb into the button mounted on the steering wheel, causing both guns to breathe flame and lead. A second after opening fire, he let off the brake and weaved the car side-to-side as it rolled down the hill. Bits of retread went flying, as did blood and flesh. Bodies spun and collapsed. Ethanol tanks on the dirt bikes burst into flames, throwing off brief orange flashes and loud *whoofs*.

Tris slithered half out the passenger window; a second later, she fired. The rotary gun started to spin up, but slowed to a halt as the helmet rocked back and fell out of sight. Kevin let off the button and the M60s went silent. She sat on the side of the door, keeping her AK trained on the pile of bodies. Kevin brought the car to a stop, threw it into park, and got out.

"Guess we're not talking," said Tris, over the roof.

Kevin approached the carnage, .45 out. The level of similarity in the bandit's clothing unsettled him. Too much like uniforms. *Enclave bastards are feeding it... hoping we kill each other.*

"Kevin!" yelled Tris, a second before two near-simultaneous gunshots rang out.

He took a lurching step forward, twisting with a hit as if someone whacked him in the back of the left arm with a pipe. A grunted "oof" came from behind him, followed by the whir of the rotary cannon spinning up again. Kevin whipped around, raising the .45 to the rear as a gout of orange burst from the front of Tris's AK. The white helmet in the turret fell out of sight for the second time. The Emissary seemed stunned from the effect of two 7.62 bullets mushroomed into his chest; a fancy plastic-bodied pistol dangled from his hand.

Kevin lined up a shot at the Emissary's exposed head as the man gasped for breath. He flopped to the ground the instant Kevin fired, as if something warned him. Before Kevin could fire again, a spray of dirt from approaching bullets made him duck behind bodies.

"She's supposed to be dead," wheezed the emissary. "Kill her!"

Tris swung the AK away from the hovercraft at the Emissary, but wound up diving to the ground as another man in the same thin armor whipped around the rear end of the hovercraft and squeezed off a burst from a compact rifle at her. She landed on her front, clutching a bullet hole in her right arm.

"Shit." She made a noise halfway between whimper and growl.

Kevin popped up, managing to fire twice at the man who shot Tris. One slug hit in the chest with a loud *slap*, the other caught him in the throat and knocked him over, gurgling. A third man exited a door on the right side of the hovercraft, training a compact rifle on Kevin at the same time the Emissary raised his pistol. Kevin jumped into the pile of bodies, pulling Golem up as a human shield. A handful of rounds, plus three pistol shots, struck the big guy's chest. Two bullets made it all the way through Golem with enough force to smash painfully into his armored jacket.

Tris's AK went off again, and a small explosion came from the hovercraft, accompanied by the muted sound of an alarm leaking from an open hatch.

Boots scuffed, at the speed of a run.

Kevin peeked up, but ducked another spray of fire that kept him pinned until the roar of hovercraft fans started. He counted three seconds and looked again. The Enclave soldiers had gone back inside, and a dense whorl of greasy black smoke emanated from a patch of ventilation slats near the left rear corner. With a grunt, he heaved himself upright and ran to Tris. She struggled to her feet, AK hanging limp in her arm with her left hand clamped over her right bicep. Blood streamed between her fingers.

"I'm okay, it's a clean through. Don't let him get away!" She climbed into the car window.

Kevin ran around and got in. The hovercraft's air cushion inflated, and seconds later, it zipped away in reverse. The smoking corner seemed less high off the ground than the rest. He jammed on the accelerator, steering after it while Tris forced breaths in and out past clenched teeth. The AK lay across her lap, wobbling about with the bumpy terrain. The hovercraft ducked past a rocky outcropping, sliding along a curvy road flanked by trees and canyon-like walls, which gave him little chance to open up with the guns. Each time he tried to line up a clear shot, another natural barrier got in the way.

"What the hell is a Gladiator doing this far east?" Tris lifted her hand to peer at her arm and the already-intact skin. "One good thing about a tank top, he didn't rip my shirt."

"By that logic, you should consider the loincloth thing again."

She held up a bloody middle finger.

Kevin grumbled as he pulled a tight left turn. "Giving away guns to local bandits, that's what they're doing. Probably their 'Plan B.' Virus isn't killing us fast enough, so they're stirring the pot."

"Kevin... you can't let him get away. He recognized me. If he gets back to the city..."

"I'm trying... I'm trying." He drove a little faster than he felt comfortable with given the treacherous turns. Tires skidded in the dirt as he took a hairpin right. "Gonna have to get in front of that monster and do the grenade trick. The 60s aren't going to bother its armor."

"Right." She winced.

Ten minutes later, the road straightened as the terrain leveled a bit. Dirt gave way to paving. He leaned on the accelerator, nudging the Challenger up past 130. The enormous hovercraft went from leaving them behind to rushing up on his front bumper.

Crap, the big ones aren't so fast. He flashed a manic grin. *If I had real guns on this thing, I could go hunting.*

At both rear corners, boxy pods extended and flipped over, revealing a quincunx of holes containing bright red warheads. Kevin slammed on the brakes and swerved to the right, skidding into the dirt and throwing up a huge cloud of dust. He looped in a circle once to kick up more before straightening out and flooring it back the way they came.

"Where are you going?" yelled Tris. "He's getting away!"

Kevin looked back and forth from the windshield to the rearview screen for about six seconds, until the Challenger slipped behind a wall into the swerving roads. "Missiles, Tris. They have missiles as big as my leg. This car isn't equipped to deal with shit like that."

She grabbed his right arm with two hands, shaking. "They're gonna know I survived. Nathan's going to come after me." Tears ran down her cheeks. "Please... we can't let them go. Do you like your car more than me?"

Yes. Wait. Do I? He pondered losing one or the other, and couldn't decide which one would suck more. *Wayne's right. I'm screwed.*

He put his left hand on top of hers. "Tris... Missiles. If they hit us with one of those, there won't be anything left of you *or* the car... or me."

Her lip quivered.

"If I thought we had any chance in hell of taking that thing out... it's like twice the size of the hoplites."

She covered her face in her hands and sniffled.

That's not manipulation. She's scared shitless. "Hey." He slowed to a stop and took her hand. "You said yourself they won't go too far east, right? We can lay low for a while until they give up. Besides, they'll have no way to find us. There's a lot of land to cover and they got nothin' to go on once we get the hell out of here."

"What if I've got like a tracker inside me?" She swallowed.

"If that was true, it wouldn't have surprised them you were alive."

Tris exhaled, seeming calmer. "True. Okay."

The drive back to the site where they'd ambushed the bandits seemed ten times longer than the chase. All the while, the Challenger bucked and bounced over the uneven road, Tris fidgeted with the AK. She didn't look up until the clearing full of bodies came into view. Kevin parked by six identical boxes stacked in a pyramid. For a moment or four, he stared at the dead.

They'd have thought nothing of killing the two of us. He clenched his right hand. *Dammit, this is exactly what the Enclave wants.*

"It wouldn't have been much of a fight the other way either." Tris slipped her fingers around his fist. "You had to."

"Yeah... he who fights fair dies first." He shoved the door open and climbed out.

He undid two plastic clamps and lifted the lid of the topmost box. Inside lay six rifles of a type he hadn't seen before, packed in foam. Kevin pulled one out and looked it over. A straight magazine descended from the butt, behind the trigger. Boxy housing encased a thick barrel and included an integral scope. At first, he thought it useless due to there being no crosshair, but when he sighted through it, a red dot appeared in the middle of the lens. He swiveled and trained the weapon on trees and rocks; the scope zoomed in and out as if sensing the range to the target on its own. The effect kept the perceptible relative distance the same whether the target was thirty or three hundred yards away.

"Holy shit." He popped the mag out to examine the ammo, but it was empty. "Crap."

Tris's hair trailed off to her right as she walked around the front of the car and stood nearby, casting a mournful glance at the former bandits. Kevin unstacked the crates, checking each. The sixth box contained ammunition, which appeared to be standard 7.62 x 51, and fit the fancy rifles. He closed up the cases and stared at the Challenger's trunk.

"Aw, crap."

"What?" Tris, squatting amid the dead, paused from her rummaging to look at him.

"This shit ain't all gonna fit in the car." He grumbled. "Screw it, don't need the boxes. Padding takes up too much space. Anything useful over there?"

"Should I pull a Bee?" She tilted her head.

Kevin opened case one and plucked the rifles out. "What does that mean?"

"Strip them and collect every scrap of everything?"

"Nah. I don't wanna be out here too long. Plus they're a damn mess. Weapons, tools, useful stuff. We can tell Bill where this is if he wants to send people to take their skivvies."

"Okay."

A little under an hour later, Kevin set the last box of ammo in the trunk and eased it closed. He lifted his weight up on his hands to force the latch to click. Fifteen of the rifles wound up in the back seat, tied down with seatbelts. The rest, and the ammo, filled the trunk. Kevin smiled and dusted his hands off. *There's my roadhouse.*

Tris came up behind and wrapped her arms around him. He turned to face her, unsure what to say to the mixture of horror and fear in her eyes. She clung to him for several minutes before trembling faded to slow breaths.

"Needle in a haystack." He kissed her on the lips.

"Yeah. Let's hope."

Reluctant to pull back, she held on to him, fingers clutching the thick sleeves of his jacket. His confidence the Enclave wouldn't bother with her seemed to soothe her eventually, and she let go. He cast another glance at the buggies and bikes, all ethanol-eaters, and not a scrap of space in the Challenger for salvage.

Damn, I miss the Marauder.

Kevin drove back to Nederland in silence, pulling up to the dump trucks fourteen minutes later. At that hour of the day, four men and two women stood watch. One person on each side climbed down. Soon, both trucks started at the same time and the heavy gate opened. He waved in greeting at them and drove straight to the red house.

Bill emerged from the front door, rifle over his back, and walked up as Kevin shut down the car and got out.

Kevin set his hands on his hips. "Good news and bad news."

Zoe crept to the edge of the porch, half hiding behind a strut that used to hold a screen, and curled her toes over the first step. She'd traded the rifle for a battered teddy bear. Kevin felt a little better inside that the kid wasn't armed.

"Alright," said Bill.

"Seventeen bandits won't be bothering you anymore. We stumbled into a deal of some kind… with the Enclave." He smiled. "That's the bad news."

Bill covered his mouth.

Tris, arms folded, trudged over. "They had a Gladiator. Enclave got away."

"That's a lot of hardware for a meeting with nomads." Bill whistled.

Kevin kicked at the ground. "Yeah, they were handing over weapons. Probably hoping 'the unclean ones' kill each other."

Tris blinked. "Why don't we leave the rifles here, these people need them more than we do."

Bill raised both eyebrows.

Kevin held up a finger in a 'one moment' gesture to Bill and turned to Tris. "What's sitting in the car right now is enough hardware to pay off the rest of my roadhouse."

She waved an arm at the town. "But… these people need help defending themselves from bandits. Six of them died yesterday."

"That's tragic." He exhaled out his nose.

Tris focused her dark blue eyes on him. The look on her face questioned what kind of person he was. A tear running down each cheek made him look away, right into wide-eyed Zoe staring at him. He couldn't reconcile the innocent blonde sprite with the memory of her shooting at bandits—and nearly being shot herself. Would owning a roadhouse be worth it without Tris?

What the hell is wrong with me? Old daydreams played in his head, showing him the future he'd wanted for so long. *I expected to wind up like Wayne. Old and only a wobbly android for company.* Tris sniffled. He looked at his boots. *The stubborn coot's happy like that.*

Kevin grumbled. "Alright, alright. But I'm keeping one." He grinned like a little boy. "That scope is too damn cool."

THE WHOLE CONSCIENCE THING

An hour past sunrise, forks scraped over a few minutes of silence. Kevin stirred the dust-hopper hash into the fried potatoes, mushing it all together. Ann, sitting across from him, had spent the past few minutes going over details of the Nederland farm project with Bill. She'd been entrusted to manage the entire food production effort of the town and supervised a team of nine people. The oversized jackrabbits had become a nuisance when they chewed in through a retaining wall and attacked the crops, though it had made hunting them easier.

Zoe, at the right end of the table, mimicked his mash-up of the food and continued staring at him. She'd traded the denim dress in for a torn green tee shirt and shredded black jeans, which let both of her knees show. Kevin made eye contact with her, but she didn't show any noticeable reaction.

Tris, at his right, kept glancing at him as if she wanted to say something, but only smiled. He couldn't help but grin back at her. Charity had, in the near term, made for a fun night—though keeping it quiet enough not to disturb their hosts had been a challenge.

"What?" he asked, low.

She pushed hash and potatoes around her plate for a few seconds. "I... do you think we could check out Omaha?"

His mood plummeted. "I dunno. Major city… Infected… seems like a suicide run with no guarantee there's anything worth finding."

Zoe shifted her gaze to Tris for a second before looking back at him.

"What if it's really the cure?" She sulked at her plate.

"There might be some coin in it for you," said Bill.

Kevin gave him a disbelieving look. "How's that?"

Bill glanced at Zoe. "Omaha is sort of on the way to Chicago."

The little girl shrank in on herself. A second later, she crossed her arms on the table and put her head down.

"Oh, no…" Kevin shook his head. "I am *not* escorting a little kid into an area overrun with infected."

Zoe sniffled, making noises like she wanted to sob, but fought to keep quiet.

Tris leaned over and patted her back.

"Of course not." Bill scooted his chair back and stood. "She's safe here. I'm not about to put her in harm's way. Her dad and older brother are stuck in Chicago and looking for help getting out."

Kevin propped his head up on one arm and tried to force visions of city streets teeming with rotting bodies out of his head. Bill walked off, deeper into the house. Ann got up and moved around behind Zoe, also trying to comfort her.

Tris gave him 'the look.'

"How long ago was that?" Kevin shrugged at her. "We don't even know if they're still alive."

Zoe lost her war with silence and sobbed.

Asshole. Yep. That's me.

Bill returned carrying a sheet of blue-lined paper with several folds. "Found this note in her jacket pocket. Her dad's in Chicago, offering a thousand coins to whoever protects Zoe… and another thousand for someone to get him and his son outta there."

"How long ago did you find her?" asked Kevin.

Zoe shifted, and clung to Ann, sniveling.

"'Bout two months ago on my way outta Harrisburg. Came across a flipped bus on the far side of Des Moines, so we decided to check it out for anything useful. Was a goddamned bloodbath inside. Not much to see but a couple pieces of luggage. Found her hiding in a suitcase."

Tris gasped.

"What happened?" Kevin blinked.

"No idea." Bill settled into his chair with a defeated look. Air flapped past his lips. "She won't talk about it."

"You drove me to Harrisburg for a thousand…" Tris winked. "Chicago's closer."

Kevin wrestled with the idea of Infected. Harrisburg *still* haunted his dreams, and the ride in through Denver hadn't helped. "I'm not sure it's worth it… and I don't mean money. What if we get out there and…"

Tris cringed.

Zoe sniffled, and pulled her face out of Ann's shoulder. She stared at Kevin for what felt like an hour and wiped her eyes. "Daddy said I hadda get on the bus. They didn't even want me 'cause it was full. Dennis made them take me since I'm small."

Bill blinked. He leaned over the table, wide-eyed, and took Zoe's hand. "Dennis?"

"Yeah." Zoe continued to stare at Kevin. "He like tells everyone what to do. They all listen to him. Cody an' Daddy couldn't fit on the bus, but Daddy made me get on." She succumbed to crying again. "I didn't wanna."

Ann rocked her, making comforting sounds. It took the girl a moment to collect herself enough to speak again.

"I was sleeping, an' this man dumped all the stuff outta this box and put me inside it. He told me to be quiet and don't move. He said they'd let me out when it was safe, but no matter what I heard, I wasn't s'posed ta open it…" She gazed into nowhere. "There was shooting and screaming, and someone pushed me around, but no one never opened it."

Kevin looked at Bill. "Had to be Infected. Bandits would've checked for salvage. Surprised they couldn't figure out how to open a suitcase."

Tris bit her lip. "They can't climb ladders…"

"I couldn't get out, but I was too scared to yell. He opened it." Zoe reached for Bill.

He lifted the girl from Ann's lap and held her. "I can't say for sure what happened there. We found the bus, but didn't see any bodies."

They got up and walked away. "I can guess." Kevin ran a hand over his hair, trying to find a strand of courage… the kind of courage that got his dad killed. "Thousand coins huh?"

Bill dropped the handwritten note on the table. "Yeah." He kissed Zoe atop the head. "You can even have the thousand he offered to whoever took care of her if you'll do it."

Zoe looked up at Bill, shock on her face, and clung to him. A few seconds later, she squirmed around enough to stare into Kevin's soul.

Kevin pursed his lips and studied his lap. "I just have 'sucker' written across my forehead, don't I?"

Tris squeezed his arm.

"We'll go to Chicago." He looked at Zoe, thinking of saying something about there being no guarantee her father or brother still lived, but couldn't bring himself to spit it out. "Gotta swing by Wayne's first, and drop off the payment for the ammo."

"Of course." Bill handed Zoe back to Ann. "Meet me at the town hall, I'll bring it out."

"Thank you," whispered Zoe.

Bill walked out.

Kevin trudged outside, two steps behind Bill, wearing a smile until the child could no longer see his face, then worry reigned. *I'm walking into a goddamned death trap.* Bill went for his bicycle. Kevin fell hard into the driver's seat of the Challenger and pulled on his gloves. Tris got in, grinning from ear to ear.

"What are the chances you'll stop in Omaha?"

He glanced at her with a mischievous grin. "About as good as the chances of me getting some head right now."

She stared at him, aghast.

"Kidding." He flicked the switches on, filling the car with the low hum of active electronics. "I love that face you made." One hand gripped the wheel and he glanced at the rearview screen. "'Course, I wouldn't object if you wanted to."

Tris punched him in the arm, laughing.

"Two big cities…" He shook his head. "I dunno."

She stopped smiling.

A short distance later, he pulled up alongside the orange building. Bill, Brett, and Pete waited with two cardboard boxes marked with red letters: "$25 Pennies."

Kevin stopped and hit the trunk release before getting out. They handed over the boxes one after the other and he set them in the trunk.

"Bill… tell me about Omaha. How bad is it?"

"Well, you only need to get to the airport. It's on the northeast part of the city, mostly surrounded by water. Closest bridge is north a ways of it, but if I remember right, there's a road that runs along the edge of the river that should let you skirt most of the interior. For what it's worth, we spent a couple days at the airport terminal and didn't see one Infected."

"They don't like water," said Tris, behind him. "Virus causes hydrophobia."

Kevin chuckled. "Well, it's on the way. Suppose we can at least look." He shook hands with Bill. "Assuming we don't die in Chicago, see you in a couple weeks either way."

"Don't do anything stupid." Bill winked.

"Too late." Kevin gazed up at the clouds. "Already agreed to do this."

Bill chuckled. Tris smirked.

Zoe came running down the road, carrying a cloth bundle larger than her torso. She raced over and held it up to him.

"What's this?" Kevin accepted it; he peeled open a few layers to find what appeared to be dust-hopper jerky and a folded paper with childish writing on it.

"It's food for your drive." Zoe took a step back, clasping her hands in front of her. Hope radiated from her eyes. "An' a letter for my Dad an' Cody."

"Thanks." He looked at Tris. "Might as well get going."

After they got in, he took a breath and dropped it in gear. Zoe lingered in the rearview, a tiny staring figure growing ever smaller as the car approached the gate. The eager hope on her face crushed him; he knew he'd come back with bad news—if he came back.

Kevin sighed. "This is what killed my dad…"

"What?" Tris looked up.

Kevin wrung his hands on the wheel. "This whole 'conscience' thing. Why am I even doing this? I'm an asshole."

Tris rubbed her wrists. "Yeah… you are." She winked.

TERMINAL

M uch to Kevin's surprise, the handoff of coins at Wayne's came with no surprises. Alamo kept truc to his word. IIe'd restocked some 7.62 for the M60s, traded in the odd boxy rifle with the tiny bullets for more .45 ammo and some 9mm for Tris, as well as some provisions. With 9804 coins to his name according to the ledger, the notion of driving to Chicago felt like the worst possible idea in the world. Whenever he came close to forgetting the whole thing, Zoe's face would appear, and he'd grumble. Bad enough he had Tris making doe-eyes at him about the Omaha situation... as pretty as she was, her powers of guilt-fu had nothing on a nine-year-old who'd managed to survive an Infected attack.

By the grace of a suitcase. Maybe I should carry one around big enough for me...

The ride from New Mexico to Nebraska had been quiet. Quiet being a relative term. Two buggies, a rust-bomb of an old Ford van, and a pack of five biker-bandits later, hints of Omaha started showing up on the mangled remains of street signs. He pondered the lack of bullet holes in the metal; the farther west one went, the more shot-up the signage got. *People have more reason to save ammo in the east, I guess.*

Tris sat rigid, kneading her hands in her lap and looking as frightened now as she did in the moments after the Enclave guy eluded them. She'd put her leather shirt back on, as well as the original pair of jeans he'd bought her from Wayne's. Her black shoes sat unworn on the floor in front of her. For most of the morning, she'd had her feet up on the dash, letting them 'breathe.'

He slowed as they approached the river. A grid of pea-green ironwork surrounded them, enshrouding both lanes of a split bridge spanning the water.

"You okay?" He slalomed a maze of smashed cars repurposed into barriers.

She slipped her shoes on. "Looks like someone started setting up defenses."

"Probably pre-Virus. Big cities used to have substantial survivor populations. Looks like they wanted to slow down approaching vehicles to make them easy targets. Not that unusual. Same thing at Glimmertown."

The road cleared after forty meters, letting him up to about seventy on the bridge. No defenses had been installed on the inside, leaving the road wide open.

He squinted at a sign marked 'Eppley Airfield' over an off-ramp right after the bridge gave way to solid ground again. "Well, I don't see any giant buildings yet... so maybe we have a chance."

"Thanks." She grabbed his arm. "This means so much to so many people."

"Yeah..."

He shook his head as he blew past a stop sign at the end of the ramp, turning left and zooming under an overpass. Twenty yards later, a little green 'airport' sign with a silhouette of a plane caught his eye soon after, and he hooked a left. A tall, narrow building passed on the left, brick red and shaped a bit like a barn. Numerous cars littered a grassy island between two lanes. All their windows had been smashed, doors taken and seats gone. *Probably got all the engine parts too.* As irritating as it was to see nothing he could scavenge, that people had been here to loot the wrecks at all made him feel better.

He followed the road around a slight left, passing what appeared to have been an electrical substation on the right. Someone had already ransacked it and tore the place to scraps. The giant green metal shape of the bridge he'd crossed moments ago loomed up ahead, though the road he followed headed to a T intersection abutting the water. A left turn would take him under the span, but he had a feeling the airport was in the other direction.

A huge silvery metal warehouse took up most of the view on the right as he accelerated down a two-lane road parallel to the river. The building had no windows and no signs of life or activity. His heart beat faster at the thought the massive structure might be full of Infected, who wouldn't care much about the barbwire tipped fence around the place.

The road continued for some distance, surrounded by the resurgence of nature overwhelming the remnants of humanity. Grass as high as the windows swayed on both sides, with the occasional house trailer visible on the left among thick trees. If anyone still tried to live there, he couldn't tell. A small sign reading 'J Pershing' went by on the left, soon before the road took a sweeping left curve.

A red and white gas station on the right attracted Tris's attention. "There's a little store there… petro something?"

"I don't want to waste battery. Last thing I wanna do is get stranded over a couple of damn Twinkies."

"What's a Twinkie?" She blinked at him.

"Accordin' to Wayne, it's some kind of alien ration. Back in the 1950s, the government made contact with aliens at Roswell, but they kept it all quiet. They gave us some technology stuff, like food that never goes bad. Sometimes you find them here and there and you can still eat it even a hundred years later."

She stuck her tongue out. "Eww. What the hell do they taste like?"

He shrugged. "Sweet. They don't taste like much but sweet."

"Sounds like nice aliens… they gave it away?" Tris raised an eyebrow.

Kevin shrugged. "Wayne said they had a thing for cows. Took some in trade."

She frowned. "I think he was teasing you."

"What, you don't think some civilization from another planet drove flew gajillion miles for a good steak dinner?"

"Not really."

At the end of the curve, the land on the right of the road looked scorched to bare dirt. The rad meter ticked up all of a sudden to 055. Kevin stomped on the accelerator, going up to almost ninety past a structure resembling an old quonset hut, covered in rust. Smashed warehouses occupied both sides of the street as it opened into an industrial campus. Parking lots crammed with melted cars drew a gasp from Tris.

"People were working when it happened. They never even saw their families again."

"Yeah..." Kevin cringed at the damage to the upper floor of the building; the second story lay exposed, no trace whatsoever of the roof. "At least they didn't feel anything."

He slowed to fiftyish and skidded around a left turn when the road ended at another T. An 'airline terminal' sign pointing left was all the prodding he needed to pick a direction. The rad meter had ticked back to 018 by the time the airport field came into view on the left a minute later. He steered across lanes intended for oncoming traffic and drove over a collapsed chain link fence onto the tarmac. A handful of planes clustered by a terminal building covered in green leaves and weeds. Gaping holes in the walls brimmed with vegetation that seemed to be tearing the airport down in geological time.

"Any idea where this guy is?" Kevin slowed to a jogging pace, leaning to the window to peer up at the tail ends of airliners going overhead.

"Look at that..." Tris pointed.

At the end of the row of planes, a massive quantity of techno-scrap gathered in piles. Airplane parts, computers, unidentifiable machine bits, and even a few android limbs jutted out of row upon row. Someone had organized a junkyard out of high-tech detritus. He would've been excited to find so much apparently-useful stuff, if not for most of the world having no use for anything of the sort these days. A giant airliner, the last in the row and closest to the scrapyard, showed signs of life—light in the windows near the front end.

"There we go." Kevin looked around, gut tightening at the idea there may be Infected waiting out of sight, ready to pounce as soon as he let his guard down. "This is... too easy."

"They're not supposed to live long, remember? Maybe the Virus worked correctly here."

He studied the plane. The only way in appeared to be a boarding gate, which extended from the main airport building. Accordion fold sides had stretched almost to the point of tearing, but the cushioned collar on the front end kept a tight seal against the hull.

"Shit. Looks like we've got to go into the building." He stared at a white sign bearing 'A9' on the side of the boarding tunnel. "Remember A9."

"Okay." Tris secured the Velcro fasteners on her shoes.

A few minutes of driving later, Kevin found a side door into the terminal building by a pack of baggage carts. He parked, shut the car down, and grabbed his new rifle with the automatic scope. Infected weren't so scary at three hundred yards.

The door led to a room full of conveyor equipment. A jumbled pile of suitcases at one end lay where the machinery dumped them. Printouts, yellowed and wrinkled, adorned the cinderblock wall to the left. It took him a minute to grasp what the images showed, but soon he realized they were X-rays of strange or embarrassing items inside luggage. Phallic-shaped devices, handcuffs, live animals, and some unidentifiable things he couldn't begin to guess at their purpose.

"These people must've been bored." He sighed and pushed open an interior door that led to a space behind a counter.

Four ancient computers sat dead on the red linoleum, one monitor knocked to the floor. He moved left, through a white door on two-way hinges that let it swing in both directions. A few steps deeper in, a skeleton lay in a pile of rot. Recognizable vestiges of a blue uniform with a skirt bore the same logo as what adorned the counter behind him. Here and there in both directions, more skeletal remains lay. Though, so much time had passed, the air smelled only of sickly mustiness.

"Panic..." Tris squatted by the dead employee. "I bet they trampled her trying to escape the fireball." She sighed. "Can you imagine? Being thousands of miles away from home when the world ends..."

"I don't think there really is a good place to be in that case." He looked around, trying to orient himself. After spotting a sign for terminal A, he walked in that direction.

Tris caught up, AK held in one hand, and threaded her left arm around his right. "With the people you love."

Hey now... Don't get ahead of yourself. I'm only putting up with having a woman around because you still owe me like 800 coins. He smirked. *Okay, the sex isn't bad.* He sighed. *Okay, maybe I would miss her.* "Yeah... I guess."

The trail of trample victims continued along the length of a wide concourse that brought him to an area full of seats and huge, dark display boards. Painted letters mentioned 'arrivals' and 'departures,' but none of the parts that lit up with information held anything but dead flat panel monitors. Terminal A was easy enough to find from there, and the boarding tunnel of Gate 9 glowed yellow from the effect of the sun on the thin material.

Kevin raised his rifle and advanced with caution. "Hello? Is anyone there? Heard there was a computer guy around here somewhere?"

"We're not a threat," yelled Tris. "We need help."

After twenty seconds of no reaction, he walked forward again. At the end of the docking tunnel, the airplane door sat closed. Where once a window had been, a panel of metal and wiring had been installed, with a little eight-by-eight-inch screen. Kevin edged up to it, looking for a button or something.

"Where's the doorbell?" He chuckled.

The screen buzzed and crackled to life, displaying a monochromatic green face: a low-res image with dark lines banded across it. Sunken cheeks and heavy goggles coupled with the grainy portrait left age a matter of debate, though the figure seemed male, and at least adult. "Who goes there?"

Kevin glanced left and low from the screen, at a naked two-inch speaker hanging on wires. "Heard you're good with computers and stuff. We need someone who can access data from an implant."

The face grew in the screen, as the man hovered closer to the lens. "Interesting... what sort of data?"

Tris moved up. "I escaped the Enclave. I'm carrying data for the resistance that might have the cure for the Virus."

"Wow. I haven't seen one of you in a couple years." The man leaned back. "I didn't think they made your series anymore."

Kevin glared.

"Made me?" Tris raised an eyebrow.

"You look like a Persephone infiltrator. Assassin androids developed a few years before the war." The green face moved up and down as if examining her. "Remarkable."

Tris shivered. "I-I'm not an android. I have cyberware."

"I'm curious enough to risk opening the door," said the man. "You should know... and this is *not* a bluff... I am wearing a bio monitor which will trigger a release of nerve agent if my heart stops."

"We're not here to hurt you." Kevin smiled. "We just want some answers."

"Come in. Turn right and go to the stairs."

The door buzzed and clicked. He slung the rifle over his shoulder and grasped the corner of the metal window plug. A light tug pulled the curved slab of airplane to the side, letting cool air blow out the gap. Kevin ducked in first, coughing on the overwhelming smell of instant ramen and unflushed toilet. The cabin, at least by the entrance, had been converted into storage space. Boxes upon boxes stacked up in the seats. He moved past them, not curious enough to rummage.

Tiny orb cameras, smaller than a fist, swiveled to follow them as they moved down the aisle to a narrow spiral stairway up. Tris seemed barely able to resist shaking as she followed him to the second level, where a thin man in a black tee shirt and Hawaiian-patterned shorts waited for them near a bar counter. He was as short and scrawny as Kevin expected, with oily brown hair draped to his shoulders.

The area resembled a college dorm room more than the lounge/bar of a jumbo jet. If passenger seating had existed in here, this person had replaced it with sofas, a coffee table, and more pieces of random technology than Kevin's brain was able to deal with. Wires, monitors, and circuit boards occupied every available surface, as well as the floor.

Kevin whistled at the gathering of tech. "So, uhh… whatever your name is… you can get at the implant in her head?"

"Call me Terminal9, and maybe." He made no effort to conceal his interest in Tris's chest.

"Wow, your parents must not have liked you much." Kevin chuckled.

"It's an online handle." The man frowned. "Not my real name."

"I'm Kevin. What do you mean online? There is no 'online' left."

Terminal9 flashed a patronizing smile. "Oh, there is… but it's pretty small. A scattered collection of radio terminals, repeaters, and servers all over. Couple hundred users."

"Great," said Kevin. "So, can you read her head or what?"

"Let's have a look." Terminal9 approached Tris.

She pulled her hair aside, exposing a tiny silver plug behind her left ear. The techie hovered close, as if trying to peer into it like a peephole in a door. Tris made a gagging face. Kevin looked away to hide his amusement.

"Yeah. I think I can get at whatever's in there." He looked at Kevin. "This unit's in remarkably good shape. Where'd you find it?"

Tris gazed at the floor.

Kevin grabbed his shirt, pulling the little man up on tiptoe. "*Her*. Tris isn't an android."

"Self-repairing body? Superhuman reflexes, strong, doesn't get tired?" Terminal9 tilted his head.

"She also bleeds red." Kevin narrowed his eyes, but let the man down. "And I've seen her get tired."

"Of course. What good would an infiltrator be if it was obviously fake?" The techie headed for the cockpit area. "This way…"

The next segment of plane appeared to be the 'master bedroom,' where

Terminal9 had cobbled together an enormous sleeping platform from three twin beds. Screens flashed images of pornography here and there between hanging posters of nude or bikini-clad models. Much of the scenery depicted cartoony women in various states of molestation by tentacles, and the printouts looked ready to fall apart at a stiff breeze. The techie continued past it all down a short stretch between rows of first-class seats, and opened an armored door to the flight deck, allowing brain-tenderizing noise to flood the room. Kevin and Tris cringed, holding their ears until the din ceased.

"What the hell was that?" yelled Kevin.

"All That Remains," said Terminal9. "Metal. You know… music?"

"All what remains?" Kevin stuck his pinky finger in his ear and wiggled it.

"It was a group." Terminal9 scoffed. "Don't you have any appreciation for culture?"

"What were they doing to that man?" asked Tris.

"He was singing." Terminal9 flailed his arms. "Oh, forget it." He pointed at a chair by a stack of electronic components. "Sit there and take off your shirt."

Tris squinted, looking unsure. "Is that necessary?"

"Not procedurally, no… but my fee for helping you is a few tittie pictures."

Kevin took two stomps forward before Tris raised her hand.

"Okay… but if you touch me in any way other than connecting a wire, I'm going to twist your head off."

"Tris…" Kevin stared at her.

"Let him look. He's maybe one of four people left in the world capable of accessing this data who isn't Enclave." She handed the AK to Kevin.

"Easy," said Terminal9. "Nerve agent."

"And you think I'm an android, so why should I be worried about nerve gas." Tris pulled her shirt off over her head.

The techie seemed to get weak in the knees at the sight. "Perfect…"

Kevin looked away from the man's obvious enthusiasm. "I can hold my breath for a long time."

Tris sat in the chair. When the techie reached for a camera, she folded her arms over her breasts. "That happens *after* we have the data."

"F-fine…" Terminal9 smiled. With shaking hands, he uncoiled a wire and connected one end to a device the size of a stereo component. He handed her the other end. "Whenever you're ready."

She looked at the silvery plug. "Looks like the right type of connector." After a nervous breath, she leaned her head to the side and connected it, shuddering. "I hate the way that click vibrates my skull."

Terminal9 raised an eyebrow. "Interesting. Okay, hold on."

The man flopped in a seat and swiveled around with his back to her. Four computer monitors flickered to life in front of him and he poked his finger at a few icons before typing like mad on a keyboard. Kevin, wearing the fancy assault rifle over his back and holding her AK, stood as still as he could manage. He looked anywhere but at Tris or Terminal9; catching sight of either of them made him too angry. One of the side windows had been smashed out, allowing a thick bundle of duct-tape-wrapped cables in from the outside, which snaked through the copilot's flight yoke before breaking up into individual strands that went to individual components. The techie hovered over his screen, swiping his hand over a trackball to navigate a menu composed of green bars and blue spheres.

"Okay, there's a file in there." Terminal9 held up an imperious finger, which he drove downward into the rubberized keyboard. "Downloading now."

"It's getting warm." Tris kept her arms folded over herself. "Feels strange."

Terminal9 spun his seat around, squeaking. "I'm pulling the data out a little faster than the hardware was meant to handle. It'll feel hot, but it shouldn't hurt anything."

At the sight of Tris shivering, Kevin took a knee by the chair and offered a hand. She took it.

Terminal9 leaned forward, staring at the exposed breast. "Fascinating. I've never seen one this close before."

"No shit," said Kevin. "I got that feeling from your wallpaper."

The techie frowned. "No, asshole, I mean a Persephone. I almost can't even see the seams."

"Wait, so you think she's a robot but you still wanna take pictures for your spank bank?"

Terminal9 smiled. "Hey, she's realistic."

Tris curled into Kevin's side.

"Tris is *not* a goddamned android. She *is* real." Kevin set the AK on the floor so he could put an arm around her.

"Oh boy. You're sleeping with it aren't you?" Terminal9 shook his head. "Now I understand the defensiveness. You don't want to admit you're getting jiggy with a toaster. Got some balls givin' me 'tude about my anime ladies."

"I'm gonna fuckin' kill this little prick." Kevin stood.

Tris pulled him back. "No. Don't."

The machine beeped. Tris flinched at the same instant.

"File transfer completed." Terminal9 kicked off the floor, spinning his chair in a graceful twist before a bare foot on a file cabinet stopped him. "Let's see what we got."

A list of text scrolled down the screen. A few seconds later, music blared out of the speakers. Terminal9 pushed himself back around, hand over his mouth. He sat still for a moment, before pulling his fingers away and smacking his lips.

"Never mind about the tittie pictures... I can't..."

Kevin handed Tris her shirt. "What? What is it?"

Tris bit her lip, bundling the leather garment in her lap as she leaned forward. "What is it?"

The hacker exhaled hard. "Well... you were almost correct. She does have The Cure in her head, but... not for any virus. Her implant is carrying Mp3 files... the entire discography of a band named The Cure." As soon as I opened the file, it had a script that forced a particular song to play... uhh, called 'Burn.'"

"Wow..." Kevin stared at the wall. "Nathan really is *that* kind of asshole."

"No..." Tris slouched and sobbed.

Kevin unplugged the wire and pulled her shirt over her head.

"I'll, umm... leave you two some privacy." Terminal9 stood. "Please don't touch any of the equipment? Thanks..." He slid past them and scooted out to the bedroom area.

Tris cried for a few minutes before flopping back in the chair like a marionette. No strength seemed to exist in her limbs. Kevin reached up under her shirt and threaded her arms into the sleeves, dressing her like a toddler.

"You said it was bullshit." She continued gazing into space. "I was so convinced I had the cure."

You, uhh... did. He cringed. "It's okay. It didn't cost us anything but time to come here."

She sniffled. "It's hopeless. The Virus is going to wipe everyone out. Doctor Andrews... we were supposed to stop them."

Kevin looked around, wanting to smash something. The way she seemed... dead... clawed at him, making him feel helpless to do anything about it. He squeezed her hands and tried to pull her to her feet. "Hey, come on. Zoe's counting on us to find her family."

Tris continued to stare into nowhere. "Why? They'll only get sick and die like everyone else. How could I have been so stupid?"

Kevin shook her by the shoulders, but she remained limp. *Great. I knew this was a damn mistake.* He looked at the door. "Hey, Term... how do you shut this shit off? I can't hear myself think?"

He closed his eyes and let his forehead rest on her shoulder.

JUNK

Nothing mattered anymore. Tris lost herself to memories of home. She tried to think back to growing up, of being a child with two loving, albeit surrogate, parents. All that came to her were fleeting glimpses that felt a little too much like purposefully arranged 'memory bytes' designed to create an illusion of a life. *Did I really have a father? When he 'died,' and I got reassigned to a new family... were they the ones who bought me?*

"Tris?" Kevin jostled her. "It's not the end of the world. That already happened. Come on, come back to me."

She focused on the image of an older man, thin, with long white hair. *Daddy.* He had to be sixty... how could he be her father? *That's the man who made me... I'm a robot. He was the designer.*

Kevin tried to drag her upright, but her legs held no weight. She slumped to her knees. "Tris, knock it off."

"It's all a waste of time. Humanity is doomed. The Enclave already won."

He lifted her back into the chair. "Don't make me slap you. Come on."

"That's why my cell had no toilet. I'm a robot. The little guy's right. I'm... That's why they want to kill me so badly. I'm probably top secret. They knew the data was fake."

She slipped into old memories again, hours upon hours of being confined in a tiny octagonal room for refusing to have children with a man she detested. *Is that a lie too?* The more she tried to picture Dovarin's face, the more indistinct he became. *Was he real? Maybe he was one of the programmers... a convenient face to insert into fake memories.* She gazed at the time display hovering like a cyan specter at the corner of her view. *I don't have an optic nerve. I'm a machine.*

Tris felt herself crying again. She made eye contact with Kevin. He looked frightened and clueless, like an overgrown boy lost without his mom. *He doesn't want me anymore. He's horrified at what I am.*

When she turned, he grasped her chin and made her look at him again. "Tris. Don't let that bastard win. Nathan's an asshole. He used you. I told you all along the data was horseshit. They'd never let it out. *You* didn't fail. It never was."

He thinks I'm a monster. She shied away from him, staring at the stack of electronic components. *Maybe those are my family.*

"Tris!" He grabbed her arms and pulled her standing, supporting all her weight.

She sniveled at the look he gave her. Hurt. Maybe he had loved her, but who could love a toaster. "Go on... I can't."

"Tris," he whispered. "This isn't you."

"Leave me alone. I know I'm an android now... I don't need you to feel sorry for me." She yelled and pushed away, falling back into the chair. "Go on... go get your coins and roadhouse and sell shitty beer to idiots. That's all you ever cared about anyway."

He sucked air in his nostrils. A sudden motion made her flinch, expecting a slap—or fist, but he stormed out without laying a hand on her. At the *thuds* of his boots on the airplane floor growing quiet, she cringed, curled tighter on the chair, and sobbed.

Silence lasted for some time before Terminal9 risked walking in. "Hey... Uhh, what happened?"

She stared at the floor.

"Guess you had him fooled huh? Hey, I have no issues with cross-species mixing... Since he's gone... if you uhh, get lonely or anything..."

"Nerve gas will come out if you die, right? Since I'm an android, it won't hurt me, right?"

"Most people would just say 'no thanks' or maybe 'go fuck yourself.'" He chuckled, raising his hands. "Take it easy."

Kevin...

Tris grabbed the armrests and leapt up, causing Terminal9 to yelp and scurry away. At the sound of electric tires peeling out, she ran across the bedroom, down the stairs, and down the length of the plane. She flung open a door near the tail, teetering on the edge and staring at a receding plume of dust. The Challenger, a tiny black dot at the head.

He really doesn't want me anymore. She slumped to the floor, sitting with her feet dangling. Out below her, miles of scrap and junk stretched as far as she could see. A rattle caught her notice a moment later, from a metal chain ladder that must have fallen when she shoved the door open. Terminal9 kept his distance, not having bothered to leave the safety of the upstairs.

Tris stared at the car until the ever-shrinking black dot vanished amid the terrain. She pressed a hand to her chest, feeling every beat of her heart... or every simulated sensation fed to an electronic brain trying to convince her she had one.

Images of being carried into Wayne's, bound hand and foot, returned to her mind. The tightness of phantom rope gripped her skin. *If I'm an android, why couldn't I break free?* She stared at her wrists, wiggling her fingers around and watching what appeared to be tendons move beneath the skin. *I am as strong as a big man... too strong for this little body. Not superhuman. Easier to hide.*

She replayed killing Neon's bodyguards. Four men dead in seconds. Tactical computer coupled with neural accelerators and dexterity boosts? Or did she have electric muscles and a computer between her ears?

Desks appeared in her daydream. Thirteen years old, sitting in school and surrounded by other children her age. All but five with white hair too. The teacher, a pleasant-faced older man in a crisp black jumpsuit, wandered back and forth while rattling on about advanced artificial intelligences. He explained how they evolved to a point where they could pass something he called the *Turing Test,* capable of emotional mimicry, empathy, and sentience. Her vision focused in on the tip of a pen in her fingers, doodling a silly, smiling anime catgirl head. School had been boring. Most kids hated being there, and she didn't remember being any different.

Tris looked up at the horizon. No dust. No Challenger. No Kevin.

With a lethargic shove, she shifted around and climbed onto the ladder. Chain and aluminum tubes rattled as she made her way to the ground below the plane. *I eat.* Nanites needed raw materials. Maybe whatever she didn't need came out? An 'infiltrator model' would have to pass as human in every way.

She remembered her first bath with Kevin. Her first time with him.

Tears blurred her vision. *I'm such an idiot. Why did I call his dream stupid?* She sniffled. *He was only looking for an excuse to get rid of me... I didn't have to make it so easy.* Shame fell heavy on her shoulders as she imagined his horrified expression. Every memory she had of making love to him changed as if she'd turned into Bee in the middle of the act. The look of utter repulsion on his face drove her deep into sobs.

When no more tears came, she stumbled to her feet and trudged in a random direction that brought her into one of the corridors formed by stacked junk. Microwaves, computers, monitors, security equipment from the airport, X-ray machines, and android parts surrounded her in rising walls that felt as though they could fall in and engulf her at any moment. She wandered the maze for a little while, until she found a dead-end ringed with arms, heads, and legs. Some resembled Bee, a few looked more advanced—though none were as high-tech as her. Not one of them would fool even the most idiotic dweller in the Wildlands into thinking it was a real person.

These are my ancestors. She walked over to a small body that resembled a tween girl, with a bundle of wires hanging out of its open mouth. Plastic eyes lolled back in its head like one of those dolls whose eyes closed when you tilted it back. Rich black hair fell in curls around a face marked with thin seams. She traced her fingers over the cheek. Hard. Lifeless. Artificial.

A few feet away, an artificial torso made to look like a twenty-something man jutted out at a horizontal angle. Blond, short hair sat atop his head like a sponge, impervious to the world. He wore only the smile one might expect from a person trying to sell something to someone for more than it was worth. Fortunately, no attempt had been made to include *all* parts. He remained as featureless as the department store mannequin he resembled.

Tris sat on the mound of junk and slipped a hand down her pants, surprised at not feeling smooth nothing. She got no thrill from the contact, only revulsion at the thought she'd been made *too* real. A memory of Kevin's scruffy face sliding around between her thighs brought another wave of sniffling.

She withdrew her hand and curled up on her side. The couple to which she'd been reassigned at nine years old treated her like their own daughter. They never once spoke of the man she thought of as her father. To them, she'd always been theirs. Had they been right? Was the old man a daydream?

Why did she have memories of being little and having such an old man for a caretaker?

Why did she want to run home to those 'parents' who may not have even existed?

Why did she feel terrified at the thought she couldn't go home because Nathan would kill her.

A vague memory of a bedroom, a child's safe haven, came and went. Did she cease existing to them as her real father had the minute she'd been detained?

The Enclave wasn't my home.

She crunched herself up in as tight a ball as she could manage, and closed her eyes. Androids didn't need food or water... or anyone to love.

I'm where I belong. Another broken machine no one wants.

A THOUSAND COINS

Mile after mile of road slid under the Challenger's nose. Kevin hadn't thought about much but driving. Tris's shouting voice played in his brain, running an endless loop. *All I ever cared about...* He snarled. *Yeah, I'm an asshole. So what? People who don't chase their dreams lose them. Am I wrong?* For some reason, he still headed north. *Two thousand coins to give some idiot a ride out of Chicago.* He grumbled. *Guy is probably dead already. I could kill a few days, go back, and say I couldn't find him.* He flicked at the wheel, imagining the horrified look Tris would give him for suggesting that.

"Damn women." He shook his head. "All she wanted to do was get that damned data out of her head. I told her it was bullshit." He gestured at the windshield. "I *told* her it was a lie. Did she believe me? *Nooo.* Of course not. I've got a dick. I know nothing."

He huffed.

Five minutes later, the weight of the empty seat to his right gnawed on his mind. Whenever sunlight flickered off the passenger side mirror, he glanced at the flash, expecting to see white hair.

"Fuck it. Wayne's alone. He's happy." Kevin shifted in the seat. "She *told* me to go away."

Five minutes later, he glanced at the empty seat again.

"I didn't even want to go to Chicago. I know this is a damn suicide run." He slapped at the wheel and tapped his left foot, attempting rhythm—poorly. An imagined Zoe pouted at him. He sighed, feeling even more like an asshole.

Red light caught his eye up ahead. A roadhouse sign. Kevin eyed the charge meter, a little over forty percent. *Better to be sure.* He took the off-ramp to an old highway rest stop. *That's a damn good idea. I wonder if there's any abandoned rest stops up on 80 I could take over...* He parked by the front and hooked up the charging cable, noting the numeral 2 over the plug.

A skinny old man who looked like beef jerky bestowed with sentience clung to the back of a glass counter inside. Wild grey hair exploded in all directions from his scalp and face, somewhat contained by a floppy, wide-brimmed leather scrap that resembled the bastard love child of a sombrero and a ten-gallon hat.

Above him, an old menu bar listed various items, mostly fried chicken and burgers with prices. Kevin's eyes almost popped out of their sockets. *This old bastard better not ask me for 599 coins for a burger.*

"Need a charge on port two, and do ya got any hot eats?" Kevin leaned on the counter.

"Whazzat?" asked the man, hand by his ear.

Kevin repeated himself, at a shout.

"Ah, got ya. Too much shootin' ya know. Ears ain't what they used to be."

"No problem."

"Whazzat?"

Kevin sighed. "How much?"

"Two fer'a charge. Got some hopper skewers. 'Nother two."

"Done," yelled Kevin.

The proprietor shuffled to a circuit breaker box to the right of the counter and threw a switch. Every light in the place dimmed for a second. Kevin glanced over his shoulder at the window, terrified he'd find the Challenger on fire... but it looked okay. As the man teetered off to cook, Kevin pulled out four coins and set them on the glass counter. Old red and white paper buckets lined the topmost shelf, though they were empty of everything but dust.

'Whazzat' returned in about four minutes, with a pair of metal skewers loaded with flat bits of meat basted in a dark sauce. Kevin pushed the four coins over the glass and took his food. The fragrance of barbecue sauce—or something making a decent attempt at it—flooded his nostrils. He walked to a tiny red table by the window where he could watch his car and settled in a plastic ass cup someone had the nerve to consider a chair.

He nibbled on the dust-hopper, and couldn't help thinking about Tris going savage on the one he'd cooked the first time they'd camped. For most of that day, he expected she only wanted to get him off guard long enough to steal the car. Untying her ankles had been sheer laziness, since he didn't want to carry her. Cutting her hands loose had been a matter of survival. He couldn't drive, dodge a machine gun grenade launcher, *and* drop a hand grenade through the slot at the same time.

Even after they'd stopped to sleep, he couldn't settle down. He remembered the sorrowful face she'd given him when she offered to let him tie her again so he could feel safe enough to sleep. Tris hadn't flinched when he grabbed rope. She'd even talked him into taking his armored jacket off and given him a back rub. He closed his eyes as phantom fingers kneaded his muscles.

I'm a sucker, just like dear old dead Dad. He gnawed on the tough, stringy meat. *She didn't steal the car.*

"She's too whiny." *Chomp.* "Soft-hearted... that gets you killed out here." *Chomp.* "Probably *is* a damn android. Humans aren't that caring."

His newer daydreams haunted him. Working the counter of his own roadhouse while Tris waited tables... or he waited tables and she cooked. Or he cooked and she worked the counter... or they worked on cars for people together—in his roadhouse. *Their* roadhouse.

Not alone.

Kevin dropped the empty skewers on the table. *It's Morgan all over again. I got too attached.*

He caught a catnap at the table until a sharp *buzz* from the circuit breaker startled him awake. 'Whazzat' ambled over and flipped the switch. Kevin waved, stood, and made his way down the length of the rest stop to one of the bathrooms. After adding a little more stench to a urinal that hadn't seen running water in fifty years, he returned to the car.

For a few minutes after getting back in, he stared at the fake bricks a few feet in front of the bumper. His gloves creaked on the wheel. He pressed his thumb down on the main power switch and swiped it across the five others in a practiced gesture. Within seconds, the Challenger was ready to drive. The battery meter read 98%; the rad meter showed 000.

He backed around in a semicircle and stopped with the car pointed at the exit to the highway. Another two minutes of staring through the windshield passed. He dreaded what waited for him in Chicago. A look to the rear seat at the bundle of jerked dust-hopper and a handwritten letter slapped him with guilt. He grasped the corner of the empty passenger seat and squeezed.

"I *am* an asshole."

Kevin stomped on the accelerator and took off—headed back to Omaha.

TWO HOURS AND ELEVEN MINUTES LATER, THE CHALLENGER SKIDDED TO A halt under the tail of Terminal9's 747. Hard driving had left him covered in sweat from more than a few close calls with wrecks, curbs, and grass-covered islands. He flung the door open with one hand while shutting down the car with the other.

Kevin made it three steps into a jog for the baggage room door when he spotted a chain ladder dangling from the far side of the plane, nearer the tail. Marks in the silt collected on the tarmac led into the junkyard.

Oh, shit. What did she do?

He ran as fast as he could while keeping one eye on the footprints. Countless tons of tech junk passed on both sides. Left turn, thirty yards straight down a row of computerized coffee makers, right turn, unrecognizable high-tech crap—probably from aircraft—surrounded him. Gold panels, little dish antennas, and circuit boards blurred as he sprinted along her tracks.

Android parts became more prominent in the mess by where her footprints took a turn. He whirled around the corner and skidded to a halt on his heels. Tris curled up amid the trash, as if she'd made a nest. A few strands of her hair wavered in the breeze, though she seemed asleep. From the red around her eyes and water on her cheeks, she'd cried herself out.

I am such a dick. He crept closer, taking a knee and grasping the edge of the shelf of debris she lay on. Seeing her alive chased away the fear that had dogged him the whole ride back. Each time he thought she might have hurt herself, his worry added another fifteen miles per hour. *One-ninety-eight... and it didn't rattle apart.*

"You did good work."

She stirred. Her eyes opened. Tris gasped.

"I'm an asshole." He gazed down. "You're ri—"

Tris jumped on him. Slender arms with too much strength in them forced all the air from his lungs as she hugged him. Her cheek against the side of his neck felt warm. She gave a final intense squeeze and leaned back to stare into his eyes.

"Sorry. I shouldn't have said that… about you not caring about anything. It's not true. I thought you didn't want an android around." She sniffled. "What are you doing back here?"

Kevin flashed a pirate's grin. "I can't leave you here… you still owe me a thousand coins."

She clamped both hands over her mouth and laughed past her fingers. He slipped one arm under her knees, one behind her back, and lifted her. Happy tears rolled down her face as she clung to him.

"You left the rifle behind…"

He glanced in the direction of the tailfin protruding up over the wall of debris. "Yeah. Hope ol' Term isn't thinking he's keeping 'em."

"Hey." Tris pointed. "Look. That's the same type of android as Bee."

Kevin set her on her feet. Tris hurried to the wall and dragged a half-body out of the pile. A bit of metal spine, hips, and most of two legs clattered to the ground. Not much remained of the fake skin, though the inside parts appeared to be in good condition. Tris examined the mechanism.

"We should bring this back to Wayne. I wonder what he'd pay us to fix Bee's hip for good." Tris winked.

Kevin chuckled. "Probably not all that much, but Bee would be grateful."

Tris lifted the part with ease. "Least we can do… a roadhouse man needs his android."

He stared at her, took a step closer, and cradled her head in both hands. Forehead to forehead, he gazed into her sapphire eyes. "I don't for a minute think you're an android."

She leaned up and kissed him.

WATERING THE BUSHES

Kevin glared at a plastic bag dangling from the glove box, filled with empty camouflage-green bottles. The road wound through a pastoral expanse of trees, the last thing he ever expected to see so close to a huge city like Chicago. Tris reclined in the passenger seat, right foot up on the cushion, head back, staring up at the sky over the passing branches. She seemed strangely happy given the revelation the data she'd hung so much hope on had turned out to be not only useless, but a cruel twist of the knife.

Pressure between his legs grew too strong to ignore. He glared at a couple of empty plastic bottles on the floor. "Damn these L-rations."

"If you hate them so much, why do you buy them?" She smiled.

"Wayne sells them cheap." He shifted, unable to get comfortable. "Military came up with them so soldiers didn't haveta shit so much out in the field. Easier to piss... even if you're doing it every ten goddamned minutes."

Tris frowned. "Easy for you to say."

"You could turn one of the towels into a loincloth." He winked. "Maybe go topless while you're at it."

She slugged him in the arm.

After a brief silence, they both laughed.

"Almost there..." She leaned forward to peer ahead. "I still don't see any skyscrapers. Hey... you know pissing sounds like a good idea."

"Done." He slowed and stopped.

Kevin got out and walked to the side of the road a few paces from the car. Tris headed into the trees. He shot her a quizzical look as he let fly. "Wandering off? You weren't shy about much last night."

She paused, deep enough in the shrubs that only her head peeked out. "That's entirely different. This is… just… no."

"Be careful," he yelled.

Kevin closed his eyes, enjoying the feeling of unburdening his bladder.

TRIS PUSHED THROUGH THE THICK UNDERBRUSH UNTIL SHE COULD NO longer see the road. Kevin's idiotic muttering, what he called singing, remained close enough to add to her feeling of safety. Confident she had no audience, she slipped her jeans and panties down and assumed the position. The awkwardness of finding a way to situate herself to keep her clothes dry made her scowl at the clouds. If humanity had been created by something it still had yet to understand, why had taking a whiz in the wilds been made such an ordeal for women? She scowled. *I haven't worn a dress since I was… fifteen?* The feeling of relief from a shrinking bladder couldn't be anything programmed into an AI. Why would they bother? Software had no conscience unless it was programmed to have one. If an android needed to impersonate a human, why would the people who made it have to fool the android into believing it was human? It could lie without remorse.

The simple act of urinating left her brimming with hope.

I'm alive.

Finished, she grabbed the bundle of cloth and made to stand. A rock rolled out from under her heel as she wobbled in an ungainly duck walk in an effort not to step in wet.

Hiss.

Something whizzed past her head.

Boom.

Tris landed on her back, as a distant rifle report echoed in the trees. A split second later, she flipped over onto her hands and knees and crawled, pants still around her shoes.

Boom.

An explosion of splinters showered over her from the right. Rocks and twigs ground into her knees. Low hanging vines pulled at her shirt and scratched her bare legs.

"Tris?" yelled Kevin.

She wanted to yell, but whoever was shooting at her might hear it too. Her fingers dug into moist soil and dead leaves in a desperate hurry to find somewhere safe. As soon as a downward grade opened to the right, she dove for it and rolled flat on her back. Dew-laden foliage caressed her ass with icy fingers. In the momentary reprieve, she shook debris out of her pants and pulled them up.

"This is supposed to be a damn metaphor," she whispered.

Another shower of tree bark and wood rained on her, followed a split second later by a heavy *bang*. She crawled farther down the hill and scooted behind a cluster of big rocks, huddled as low to the ground as she could get. Several minutes passed as she listened. Leaves and twigs crunched behind and to the right. Hoping it was Kevin, she peeked. A figure in light black armor, similar to that worn by the Enclave emissary, pointed a five-foot long rifle in her direction.

Tris leapt flat on her chest before the massive weapon discharged.

At least he let me finish. She pulled the Beretta from her hip. "The last thing he's going to expect is for me to pop straight up."

Tris crawled for a few feet while searching in vain for the nerve to risk presenting a target.

"Tris!" shouted Kevin.

Boom.

The sound seemed different. Not aimed at her. She shoved herself up with all the power she could force out of her arms. Compared to her body weight, her strength launched her off the ground. She landed on her feet and yanked the Beretta out of its holster. The sniper aimed at something to the left. At over a hundred yards' range, the trajectory line created by her cyberware looked more like a rainbow than a bullet path. She raised her arm at a near forty-five-degree angle and fired four shots in rapid succession, each going off before the muzzle flash of the previous shot faded. Four copper-jacketed slugs spiraled through the air, inches apart. The sniper whirled, not trapped in slowed time. Tris threw her weight to the side.

Boom.

A large, pointed slug drilled toward her while her bullets dive-bombed the sniper.

Four slugs mushroomed into the distant figure's chest, almost on top of each other. The incoming round tore a slice across her ribs, three inches under her right armpit. Tris hit the ground on her left side, clutching the wound. The sniper fell to his knees; nothing pierced, though it seemed the wind had been slammed out of him.

Ignoring the pain, Tris got up and ran. Searing pain melted to furious itching as the Nanites in her blood got to work on the cut. *I'm alive. Fuck you. I'm not an android. I'm not going to die.* She let go of the bloody rip and pumped her arms and legs in a sprint trying to put as much distance as she could between her body and a sniper's bullet. The Beretta stayed in her hand only because putting it away at a full run was impossible. It couldn't kill the sniper through the laminate composite armor. Hell, her AK wouldn't even breach that stuff, though the slug would at least break ribs.

Kevin's voice rang out in a brief yelp. Her heart skipped a beat, but it sounded more like he'd tripped than been shot.

She daydreamed about pumping fully automatic fire into the asshole trying to kill her, grinning with psychotic glee at the thought of inflicting so much pain on someone. Her long strides devoured the terrain, and she headed for a hill that led to the road.

Or so she thought.

At the top of the hill, more forest waited. Trees in every direction, and somewhere nearby came the rushing sound of water. Somehow, Kevin had found an entire forest southwest of Chicago.

Bang. Bang.

Tris screamed and hit the ground. Nothing struck close by, and she realized the rapport was too quiet to have been the sniper's rifle. Fearing another shot any second, Tris clambered to her feet and surged forward, seeking low ground and cover. The thick woods masked the sun, or maybe she was too scared to find it. She darted in a random zigzag pattern around trees and shallow channels between mounds, hunched over in an effort to present a low profile.

One thought took over her mind—hide.

HUNTING THE HUNTER

"Tris!" screamed Kevin.

He leapt off the side of the road into the woods, racing toward the *crack* of a heavy rifle firing. Arms raised to deflect branches and vines, he ran toward his best guess of where someone crashed through the underbrush. The downward angle of the hill flattened out for about twenty yards before he struggled up a sharp incline for a couple feet before it leveled off again.

Kevin stumbled on loose dirt at the top of the hill, grabbing a tree to keep from falling as a vine running over the ground tangled his feet. A glint caught his eye; he looked up at a slim black-clad figure in an Enclave body suit and full helmet less than fifty yards ahead of him, pointing a massive rifle at his face.

A short burst of gunfire would've wet his pants if he hadn't already dealt with that. The sniper's body blurred, huge rifle going from pointed at him to ninety degrees left in an instant. Fire belched from the muzzle break. A wicked *slap* rang out, echoing in the forest, and the sniper fell to his knees, sagging forward as if he couldn't breathe. Copper spots appeared on his chest—bullets.

Kevin surged ahead, running at him.

When the rifle whipped up, he let off a yelp and dove behind a tree. He crouched against the base of a trunk wide enough to hide him, and probably stop a bullet. Once footsteps crunched, jogging away, he risked a peek. The black-clad figure rushed off to his relative northwest, though for all he knew at that moment it could've been south. Kevin let the sniper get far enough away where he hoped he could remain undetected, and slipped out from cover.

One hand on his .45, he hurried along in a gait not quite running and not quite stalking. The sniper took a sudden left. A splash of white drew his attention to Tris, so far away she appeared only inches tall. She'd emerged at the top of a hill, and spun around, clearly lost and disoriented.

The sniper swiveled and raised his rifle at her.

Kevin tore the .45 from his hip and squeezed off two quick shots. The thin man spun and leapt to the right, diving out of sight into the trees. Kevin glanced in the direction he'd seen Tris, but the thick mass of green branches had engulfed her. Gun up, he rushed ahead to where the sniper had gone down.

I think I hit him at least once.

He hesitated by the tree where the man had paused to aim at Tris. After a two-second breath, he jumped around and aimed at… open ground.

Fuck.

Kevin froze, looking for the gun about to kill him moving only his eyes. Finding nothing, he crouched behind the nearest tree and tried to remember how to breathe.

"Pathetic," said a female voice. "You're not even worth a bullet."

He jumped back as half the tree he hid behind shimmered and went from bark texture to flat black. At this range, the sniper seemed no taller than Tris. She lacked a rifle, but pointed both fists at him. Sparks crackled over her forearms as a rapid series of spitball like noises broke the silence.

Sharp points stabbed all over his chest and face. Lightning exploded across his vision as every nerve fiber in his body seemed to ignite at once. The next thing he knew, he lay flat on his back, unable to move or breathe.

The sniper took a step to the right and dug the long rifle out of a pile of leaves. Kevin moaned. She sighed and poked a finger into her left forearm. Another wave of crackling pain danced over his chest.

Blue sky became purple.

Blackness.

WITH FRIENDS LIKE THESE

Tris leapt over a series of head-sized stones spanning a wide, but shallow creek. She slipped in the mud on the far bank, windmilling her arms to keep balance while careening around a rapid turn. After another few minutes of running and weaving among trees, she couldn't bear the thought of going another inch. Her gait came to a loping halt. She spun in a quick circle, seeing nothing but forest. Panic refused to release its grip on her brain, and she stumbled ahead for another thirty or forty yards before collapsing on all fours.

Her lungs burned; she lost track of how long she'd been running, but her body refused to go on. The irony of it bubbled up in a laugh, which she clamped a hand over her mouth to arrest. *An android wouldn't get tired.* She crawled a few feet more and took cover in a spot where three trees sprouted from the ground at almost the same place. Not wanting to risk her stark white hair giving her away, she rolled flat on her back and tried to gasp for air while making as little noise as possible.

Pain along her side had faded to a mild itch. She hid her face in the crook of her right elbow, focusing on getting her breathing under control. Eventually, she went from 'someone shoot me' to merely exhausted. Aside from the chirping of a few birds, the woods remained deathly quiet. Tris didn't dare move. Kevin had stopped shouting, though the sniper had also ceased firing. She hadn't heard a gunshot in enough of a while to entertain the thought she may have gotten clear.

No. I don't trust it. Stay down.

A snapping twig made her jaw clench tight. She kept still until indistinct furry figures emerged from the trees. Tris sat up with superhuman speed, Beretta raised at a stocky, dark-haired man wearing a tunic and shoes made from what she guessed was bear fur. A thinner man of fairer complexion, with light brown hair stood a little behind and to his right. Both carried machetes and stared at her as though she'd make a fine dinner or wife.

Her finger tensed on the trigger, but she hesitated. A gunshot would give her away. "Go away," she whispered.

"Jeeble, Marvin, and Joseph," said the stocky man, hand over his chest. "Ya dun scared the beshibbits outta me."

"Easy, Miss." The thin one raised a hand. "We ain't gonna hurt ya."

Tris squinted. "Like I've never heard that before..."

"Serious. You lookin' in a bad way." The larger man smiled a half-toothless grin at her. "You need help or anythin'?"

"Where am I?" She kept the Beretta up.

"'Bout a mile an' a half... maybe two miles from the stone place." The thin man pointed behind him. "You don't wanna go there though. Bad, bad, bad."

"Yeah." The heavier man nodded. "Stone place full'a stupid dead. They ain't know they dead, so they keep on livin'."

She tried to remember the road Kevin had been on. "How do I get to... Street 107?"

Both men shrugged.

"There's a big lake right next to it."

"Oh." The big man pointed a little to his left. "Head that way. South."

"Hey, D... if'n she's got a gun... what's she runnin' from?" The thin one squinted.

"Aw shit." The other man pointed. "Bigger gun."

Both men hit the dirt.

Tris didn't bother looking and took off at a full sprint an instant before a rifle shot rang out. *Dammit.* Weary muscles protested after only a few seconds of running. She navigated a steep but short downhill, fell into a somersault that bounced her right back onto her feet, and kept following a tunnel-like section of trees with a heavy canopy for about sixty yards. A spray of red flashed in front of her seconds before she heard the shot.

Boom.

The taste of dirt filled her mouth. Her brain processed the flavor and texture of soil before the pain in her back registered. An attempt to breathe filled her mouth with the metallic taste of blood. She dragged herself forward a few inches before her body quit, and her cheek hit the ground. A dull throbbing ache accompanied the sensation of cold air entering her body from a hole that shouldn't be there. The bullet had passed clean through her chest, though by some miracle missed her heart. Short-lived relief died as the horrible internal itch of Nanites swarming around her left lung triggered a scream in her mind.

Leaves crunched behind and left, growing louder.

She tried to gasp 'please don't' but only spat out a bubble of blood.

Black boots and the tip of a rifle moved into her vision. "Damn, you're actually a lot prettier than I thought you'd be. Shame."

Tris coughed and rolled onto her back, staring up at a slender figure standing over her. A smooth black helmet covered the head, gleaming with the reflection of sky and trees. Scuff marks on the chest hinted at where 9mm rounds had failed to penetrate. "W-why? Please… don't. It's…"

An electronic *chirp* emanated from the sniper's general vicinity, and the helmet disassembled itself into several dozen segments—bands and panels that disappeared behind her head into the armor's back plate, revealing a jet-haired woman likely in her early twenties. She had the same paper-white skin as Tris, but her amber eyes glittered with annoyance.

"You don't have to…" Tris clutched her hands to her chest, an inch below her left breast where the bullet had exited. Pins and needles *inside* grew maddening. She screamed, forcing blood to ooze between her clenched teeth. "Data is fake."

"I'm not here to ask questions." The woman squatted and laid the rifle on the ground. "It's an awful waste of ovaries, but I've got to take your head back to the Enclave."

"No… there's no data in my head. It's bullshit." Tris coughed. "It was music. A band called 'The Cure.' Nathan's a sadistic bastard. I have nothing that's a threat to them."

The woman gazed into the trees. "I can't stand being out here in the goddamned sticks. The sooner I finish my job, the sooner I can get back to civilization."

Tingling gave way to burning. Tris grew dizzy trying to breathe with one collapsed lung. Red foam slid down her chin. She propped herself up on her elbows, but between choking on her own blood and having run her muscles to jelly, her body refused to move.

"Can you maybe act a little less pathetic? This isn't exactly easy for me either."

"How can you want to go back there? It's not as bad as they say it is out here." Tris fought for a few rapid breaths. "They need to open the doors. Why would you want to be told who to marry?"

The sniper shrugged, not quite looking at Tris. "I'd rather have healthy children than pick some guy I fall in love with now only to have that fade to disinterest or resentment later. The way we do it is better. Neither of us goes into it with any expectation beyond propagating. Love? That's what affairs are for."

"You…" Tris cringed as electric tingles wrapped around her lung, as if fingers of lightning squeezed it. Tears leaked out of her eyes. "Oh, God, it hurts so much." She gasped. "Do I know you?"

"We were in fifth through tenth grade together. You sat at the desk to my right." The sniper stared at the ground. "Your nanites are getting close to finished. I better get this over with before you get up and start running again."

"Zara?" *Friends* was a bit of a stretch, but she remembered trading text messages during class with her. They'd both have gotten in trouble, but somehow never managed to get caught. As if the Enclave couldn't stand people having friends… or emotions. Tris's arms gave out, and she fell flat on her back amid the damp leaves. *That's gotta be Nathan… made* her *come after me.* "People out here aren't hostile to technology. Think of all the good the Enclave could do for the world. It's the seed of civilization. They should be spreading it, not keeping themselves shut off. They're misguided. If the doors stay shut, they're dooming humanity."

"We're safe inside. I… I just do what they tell me to do." Zara grabbed at her right hip and drew a fourteen-inch blade from a thigh sheath. "Sorry, Tris. This philosophical stuff is way over my pay grade."

She grasped a handful of Tris's hair and lifted her head to expose her throat.

"Don't." Tris shut her eyes.

Bang. Bang. Bang.

A noise like a punted goose came from Zara, and she collapsed.

Leaves crunched. Tris forced her head up. Kevin stormed over, .45 pointed at the sniper's inert body.

She'd never seen him looking that infuriated. She held her side and whined.

"Guess I'm over feelin' bad about shooting women." Kevin took a knee at her side. "Tris... Shit... are you okay?"

"I..." She gasped, swallowed blood, and managed a weak smile. "Ow. Looks worse than it feels." She coughed. "No. I lied."

Kevin glanced at the inert sniper. "Feels like I should say something here... You know, like in one of your 'historical documentaries.'"

Tris reached a hand up. He took it in his left, keeping the .45 pointed at Zara.

"It hurts so much... I'm alive."

At the sight of a tear on his cheek, she tried to sit up and hug him. He held her down. "Wait. You're in no shape to move yet."

"Okay." Tris closed her eyes, listening to her racing heart. "I'm not gonna die, but I could eat a whole dust-hopper right now."

42

SECOND CHANCES

Kevin leaned down and kissed her on the forehead. "Guess what. You're not an android."

"Yeah." She wheezed. "I figured that out while pissing." Zara moaned.

Kevin stood, and shot her again. The slug hit armor between her shoulder blades with a loud *slap* that echoed back over the gunshot and then bounced off the trees. "Son of a bitch."

He leapt up, took a step, and kicked her over on her back, pointing the gun at her unarmored face.

"Stop!" Tris's attempt to yell sounded feeble. "Kevin…"

"Sorry, Tris. You're too damn nice."

"I went to grade school with her. Please don't make me watch."

"So close your eyes."

"Kevin…" She whined.

He lowered his arm—and shot Zara in the chest. A little blood seeped from the woman's lips. "Damn armor." Kevin plucked another one-inch metal cross with sharp barbs at each end from his arm. Where the two barbs met, a small antenna sat in a tiny pit of glowing violet gel. He flicked it into the weeds. "I hope that hurt. What I'd love to do is cover this bitch with those fucking lightning spider things and spend an afternoon hitting that button over and over again."

Tris rolled onto her side. "If we kill her, we're no better than they are."

He sighted over the .45, trying to decide which of her eyes to put a slug in. "I never claimed to be."

Rustling behind him made him look. Tris, grunting, wobbled upright. He whirled back to finish off the sniper, but Tris threw her weight onto his arm, causing another slug to hit the woman in the gut. Zara's eyes bulged.

"Where was this high-minded idealism with Neon?" He shifted Tris to his left arm and helped support her weight.

"That piece of shit was a slaver. He deserved both bullets I put in his head." Tris wheezed.

Kevin grumbled. "I thought I was the one that's supposed to have issues hurting women."

"She's still young. She can have kids. Humanity can't afford to lose her."

"So what the hell are we supposed to do with her then?" asked Kevin. "Next time, she's going to hit you in the head, not the chest. Can your Nanites fix brain tissue?"

Tris dug her fingers into his jacket. "No… Look, she didn't really want to kill me. If she did, she would've shot me in the head or cut my throat without saying a word. Let her go back to the tech she loves so much."

Kevin pumped another round into Zara's chest. "She didn't shoot you in the head because she's supposed to take your implant back."

Tris jumped. "What was that for?"

He shrugged. "Felt like it. Ain't killing her, is it? She's got the same nanite shit you do, right?"

"We all have it. Universal medicine." Tris's stomach growled. "I'm sorry I ran the wrong way. I got turned around."

"It's okay. I don't have a goddamned idea where we are either."

She looked at him with horror all over her face.

Kevin smiled, pointing the gun to the rear over his shoulder. "Teasing. We gotta go that way." He stared at Zara. "You are absolutely sure you don't want me to kill this bitch for trying to cut your head off?"

Tris leaned on him. "Yeah."

"Wow. I don't even know what to say to that." He shot Zara in the chest again, laughing at the stepped-on goose noise she made. "This is kind of fun actually."

Zara gurgled.

Tris pulled on his arm. "Stop that!"

"She's either got a really low pain tolerance, or she's faking." Kevin aimed at her face again. "Maybe they'll kill her for failing?"

"No way. The Enclave doesn't have that many people. They can't afford to lose anyone, especially anyone 'uncontaminated.'" Tris shoved at him, trying to get him away from Zara. "She took her helmet off. She showed me who she was, wondering if I'd remember her. Please don't kill her."

Kevin pressed his hand, and the side of the .45 to his face, eyes closed, and moaned in his head. "So, what do you wanna do with her?"

Tris smiled. "Do ya trust me?"

43

TWO HOURS

Driving away from Chicago again was not bringing him any closer to clearing his conscience, though Kevin couldn't help but feel more comfortable with each mile that went by. Chicago was undoubtedly full of Infected, so anything that delayed his arrival was welcome. Tris had the pack of jerked dust-hopper in her lap, having inhaled enough for three normal meal portions. Her leather shirt looked a bloody mess, but she seemed tired. Perhaps Chicago *should* wait a bit.

He glanced over his shoulder into the back seat. Zara, stripped to a black sports bra and panties, sat behind Tris, arms bound behind her back and legs tied at the knees and ankles. "Not bad, most of the bruises are already gone."

Zara glared, though didn't try to speak past the duct tape over her mouth.

Kevin shook his head. "I officially give up on understanding *anything* about women. One minute, she's trying to kill you, now you're like old friends… in a sort of quiet, tied up, and gagged way."

Tris rolled her eyes. "We *did* go to school together."

"Were you two friends?"

"I'm not sure anyone actually had *friends*. We all went home after school. No one really hung out with anyone but their parents. We weren't allowed to socialize on school grounds either."

"That's only a *little* strange." Kevin glanced at her. "Little creepy too.

Almost sounds like they don't want people thinking too much on their own."

Tris remained silent, lost in thought. She took another piece of jerky out, stared at it, and dropped it back in the box. "Yeah... I think you're right. The Enclave's up to something."

"So why'd they send an assassin after you if they knew the data in your head was old music?"

"Like I know that?" Tris closed the package of food.

"I wasn't asking you."

"Tape." Tris shook her head and reached into the back seat. "Sorry. Quick hurts less."

Rip.

"Ow," said Zara, sounding bored.

"Well?" Kevin shifted left one lane to avoid a smoldering motorcycle. "So, where's your vehicle?"

"I got dropped off by an air unit. Is it really necessary to make me sit here in my underwear?"

Kevin shrugged. "You're the one who didn't have anything on under the armor. If I shoot you again, I want you to die. So... since I've somehow been talked into not killing you, the least you can do is explain some shit."

"I have no idea. Maybe they wanted to keep up appearances?" Zara eyed the box behind his seat.

"You wouldn't set off a hand grenade in the car, would you? That would kill all three of us." Kevin made a *tsk tsk* noise.

"She can't. Even if she gets her hands loose..." Tris held up a roll of duct tape and grinned. "I gave her mittens. And bullshit. What illusion? It's not like they need me to do anything anymore." Tris shifted to stare into the back seat. "Zara... come on. You didn't really want to kill me. What's going on?"

The woman sighed. "I don't really know. It's not healthy to ask questions. Maybe they're afraid of what your father might've told you."

"My dad died when I was nine. He never told me anything strange or secret-sounding. I got reassigned to a new family, and everyone acted like he never existed."

Kevin eyed the side door mirror. A lone motorcycle came racing up in the next lane left, the driver waving. From the high-pitched whine, he assumed it an ethanol-eater. "What the hell?"

He rolled down the window, staring at the flailing man in a flapping denim jacket. The 'hey wait' act came to an end as the bike pulled up alongside. The rider produced a glass jar of clear liquid with an unlit wick and raised his arm as if to throw it.

"Hey," yelled Kevin, pointing. "Your Molotov ain't lit."

The rider glanced at it, blinked, and peered back at Kevin with a confused, cross-eyed expression.

"You gotta light it first," yelled Kevin. "One sec, lemme help you with that."

He reached up and pulled the cord over his head. With a heavy *whoosh*, the incendiary sprayer roared to life, dousing the biker in burning gel. The odor of ethanol and grease filled the car. A screaming fireball veered off the road and went tumbling end over end into the grass. Three spins later, either the Molotov or the fuel tank detonated in a red-orange fireball.

Kevin rolled up his window. "Moron."

Zara shivered. Her calm veneer showed a crack. "Okay, you win. Let me go. I swear I won't come back. I can't stand it out here. It's so... dirty."

Tris took a piece of jerky out of the box and held it up. "Hungry?"

"Don't waste food." Kevin rolled his eyes. "That's for us. She tries to kill you, now you wanna feed her too?"

"Well if you didn't shoot her nine times... nanites hurt when they're hungry." Tris squirmed.

"Good. You should've let me zap her with that... that... spider zappy thing." Kevin rubbed his chest. "That felt like my skin peeled off and I got rolled in salt."

"Capacitive coupling based neural stunner," said Zara. "They sync up with the electromagnetic frequency in your nerves and overstimulate them. Supposed to knock someone out for at least an hour. Armored jacket?"

"Yep." Kevin kissed his sleeve.

Tris waved the jerky at Zara. "Say something useful?"

Kevin mouthed 'ooh, bitch' silently.

Tris winked at him before staring into the back seat again. "They had to tell you something to talk you into hunting me down. I saw you hesitate. You really didn't want to do it. What did they tell you?"

"Your dad was a radical thinker. He and his associates... They wanted to break away from the Enclave. Almost started a coup. The radicals planned to reintegrate with the outside, not destroy and replace. Your father tried to stop the Phoenix project. He didn't want them to let the Virus into the wild. He was sure they wouldn't be able to control it."

Tris stretched into the rear and slipped back into her seat without the jerked jackrabbit. Zara mumbled something.

"Hold it with your lips while you chew," said Kevin.

Tris gave him that wounded puppy look he loathed so much.

"What?"

"My father… Nathan is *that* kind of asshole. He probably matched me with Dovarin on purpose knowing I'd refuse him, get arrested, and then he could use the daughter of the man who started the resistance to destroy it. And he probably picked Zara to come after me because we knew each other… sorta."

"Wow." Kevin raised both eyebrows. "I think I owe that man a beer. He's raised asshole to an art form. I could take lessons."

"Bastard!" Tris shouted and punched the dashboard, leaving knuckle dimples in the glove compartment lid.

"There'd always been a cloud of suspicion over you," said Zara. "Sometimes people thought you knew about it and were trying to help the resistance from the inside, even though you were a kid like the rest of us. When you started spouting off about opening the gates back there, I thought they were right."

"It's wrong." Tris scowled at her. "All those 'historical documentaries' are lies. The world out here isn't as bad as they think. It's not all contaminated and deadly. There are a lot of good people left."

A little over two hours after they'd resumed driving, Kevin steered across the grass divider and into oncoming lanes of highway. He drove down the 'exit' ramp of the rest stop and pulled up to the same space he'd used last time. "You carry your friend." He hopped out and plugged in the charger.

While Tris dragged Zara out of the car, he collected her sniper rifle and armor from the trunk. It flopped about like a rubber suit with rigid panels in spots and didn't feel near as heavy as it looked. *Tris should keep this. She's too damn nice for her own good.* Kevin made a funny face while mimicking her predictable reply of, 'but they'll know something's wrong if she goes back without it' in his mind.

Tris heaved Zara over her shoulder. The woman wriggled, unable to attack the rope with her hands in duct tape cocoons.

He wandered past a few empty parking spaces and entered the rest stop with Tris close behind.

"Hey, Wazzat?" yelled Kevin.

Tris blinked. "What kind of name is that?"

Kevin smiled.

The old man emerged. "Whazzat?"

"Need a favor."

"Whazzat?" The old man put a hand to his ear.

Tris rolled her eyes. "Oh, that kind of name."

"Need a favor," yelled Kevin. "This one tried to kill us, but my friend here's too nice for her own good. We can't keep her with us, and I don't trust her enough to let her go right away. Can you watch her for like two hours, then cut her loose?"

Whazzat flashed a toothless grin at Zara's ass. "Ah shure kin' too."

Tris set the woman in a chair. As soon as she got a look at the old man, she wobbled back to her feet, face red.

"No way. You can't leave me tied up in my skivvies with that creature."

"Whazzat?" asked the old man.

"Oh, he's harmless." Kevin shook the armor at Tris. "Are you sure you don't want this stuff?"

"You told me to get rid of the black jumpsuit because it screams Enclave." She folded her arms. "Besides, it's hers. If she goes back without it—"

"Yeah, yeah. The jumpsuit doesn't stop bullets. Who cares if they think you're Enclave if they can't kill you?"

"Cut 'er loose two hour?" yelled Whazzat.

"Yes," yelled Kevin. "Give ya four coins for babysitting."

The old man nodded.

"No. Look, you could've killed me." Zara squirmed and fought the rope binding her arms. "I respect that. Really, I do. I won't come after you again. All I want to do is go back where it's clean and disease free and I won't get ten infections from my bare ass touching a plastic chair."

"You can stand," said Kevin.

"Okay," said Tris. "We'll cut you out right away, but we keep the rifle and the armor."

Zara bit her lip. "I need the armor to get home. There's a radio in the helmet."

Tris folded her arms, showing no sign of backing down. "You really believe they're going to come back for you, don't you?"

"What?" Zara squinted.

"You're too far east. They won't come out this far to pick you up." Tris loomed at her until she flopped in the chair again. "Did the Council of Four send you out here, or was it Nathan?"

Zara stared at her feet. "Nathan."

"You're already written off," said Kevin, sounding like he knew what he was talking about. He hid the cheesy smile before Zara looked up.

"Don't leave me helpless. Better you killed me."

"Two hours," said Kevin.

"Whazzat?" asked the old man.

Kevin held up two fingers and handed Whazzat four coins.

"Cut 'er loose in two hours." The old man checked a wristwatch under three sleeves.

Kevin noted it hadn't been wound and wasn't moving… but kept his mouth shut.

"Fine." Zara gazed with longing at her armor. "But do I have to stay out here where everyone can see me?"

"Whazzat?"

Kevin translated into yell. The old man waved and pointed into the back. Tris carried Zara into a storage room. With great reluctance, Kevin handed the armor and rifle to the old man.

"Those are hers."

The old man shook hands and hid the stuff behind the counter.

Kevin looked at Zara again, thought of Morgan, and put his hand on the .45. *She's playing us so damn hard. I oughta settle this for good.* Tris leaned on him.

"Hmm?" He glanced down at her.

She kissed him quick on the lips. "Thanks. I suppose it was about time for you to save my ass once, since I keep havin' to save yours."

He laughed. "You sure you trust this one?"

Tris stared at Zara. "No. No, I don't. But… killing everyone that pisses you off isn't the answer."

"I tend to make exceptions when they shoot first… and use tiny metal spiders from hell on me."

"I can't." Tris sighed.

"Yeah… I know." He walked out. "She gave you almost the same look you gave me back at Wayne's."

She hurried after him. "*I* didn't try to kill you."

"No… no, you didn't. Good thing too. I'm not as forgiving as you are."

Whazzat closed the storeroom door.

KEVIN RUMMAGED A SCRAP OF PAPER NAPKIN OUT OF A CUP HOLDER AND handed it to Tris. An extra four-hour detour would give them less than two to find Zoe's family before darkness settled in. He had half a mind to spend the night at Whazzat's roadhouse and go in the morning, but between Zara and an odd feeling he'd have to explain to a little girl how a matter of one night's sleep killed her family, he decided to go. Assuming, of course, her father and brother hadn't died within hours of her leaving.

Tris took the napkin and covered her mouth while coughing. The paper came away bloody. She cringed, folded the paper over the discharge, and coughed into it again.

"You okay?"

She clamped the napkin over her mouth, coughed again, and nodded.

"Doesn't sound like it. That's blood." He slowed at the sight of a black smoke trail ahead.

"Yeah." She breathed in and out hard, triggering another few coughs. "Leftover blood in the lung. It's uncomfortable and annoying, but I'll be alright."

Kevin chuckled as he stopped by the side of the road. "Damn, I need to get some of those nanites."

"They can be problematic out here too." She crumpled the bloody tissue in her hand and let her arms drop in her lap. "Increased food requirements wouldn't be too popular in situations where it's scarce." She glanced out the window. "What's that?"

"Remember the idiot with the Molotov?" Kevin got out. "Gonna see if he has anything worth taking."

The crash left an obvious trail in the waist-high grass, which had fortunately been wet enough not to trigger a brush fire. He found the rider's corpse a short walk from where the bike detonated. Incendiary gel had melted the man's clothes to his flesh, leaving them unsalvageable. Kevin grabbed a Glock-17, which went into the empty holster under his left arm. *Damn, I miss that Sig.* Two knives, fifteen coins, and a crowbar survived. He collected everything and headed back for the Challenger, where Tris knelt by the right front tire with the black AK.

She stood when he got back to the road, and they got in at the same time.

"If we weren't in such a hurry, I'd start looking around for a trail or something. This guy probably had a cache of stuff… maybe a cabin out here somewhere." Kevin accelerated hard enough to spray gravel.

Tris gave him a quizzical look.

"Don't usually see motorcycles alone. Makes me think he's a hermit or something, saw us as a target of opportunity."

"Either that or he's the prospect." Tris chuckled.

"Heck is that?"

"Motorcycle gangs usually have an initiation period before they let someone in. An applicant that's trying to earn favor with the club."

"Historical documentary?" Kevin raised an eyebrow, grinning.

"Yeah." She squinted. "Does that mean it's fake?"

He shrugged. "No idea. His stuff was too charred to tell if he had any markings."

"So… have you thought about how to tell Zoe her family's gone?" Tris stared into her lap.

He exhaled, hesitated a second, and shook his head. "Nope."

A few minutes passed, silent but for the mesmerizing drone of tires consuming road.

"Hey. You're supposed to be the optimist here."

She almost smiled. "Is it better to be a disappointed pessimist or a satisfied optimist?"

"That's above my pay grade."

Tris slugged him in the arm.

"What?" He blinked.

"Zara said that to me right before she was going to cut my head off."

"Hey." Kevin pointed at her. "*You're* the one who told me not to kill her. I still don't know how she went down so fast."

"Possum probably." Tris twirled a strand of hair around her finger. "Her head was exposed. Playing dead hoping you turned your back on her."

"Are all women like that?"

Her eyebrows drew together. "Like what?"

Deceitful, lying, bitches who expect men to let their guard down when they flash the innocent face. "Uhh, beautiful and deadly."

"That sounded like manipulative and cunning to me." She winked. "And when we have to be." Her expression darkened. "Shit. I should've asked her…"

"What?" He turned onto the same road where they'd stopped to piss before.

"If she has any idea why some of my memories don't make any sense."
She stopped twirling her hair.

"Is that why you thought you were an android?"

"Part." She laced her fingers together. "Why did Terminal9 call me
Persephone?"

He tilted his head toward her, smiling. "Had to be a combination of
white hair and stunning beauty."

"Now who's being manipulative?" She grinned. "You've never said
anything like that to me before."

"What? A guy can't tell a girl she's pretty?"

She put a hand on his leg. "It's nice, but you… I dunno. You're always
so suspicious and focused. Sounds strange to hear you say something like
that."

"Good strange or bad strange?" He leaned forward, eyeballing the
treetops. *Whatever thing dropped that bitch off might still be out there.*

Tris rubbed his thigh. "Good strange."

Minutes later, forest gave way to the ruin of a great city. Skyscrapers
and concrete dominated the landscape, overgrown with vines and green.
Cars and trucks collected against walls and barriers here and there as
though they'd been debris picked up by a massive river and deposited as
part of a flow. Many looked like electrics, with similar in-wheel motors to
the Challenger. The parts appeared unsalvageable, having sat in the
elements for half a century.

Navigating the strewn wreckage forced him under twenty MPH. Slow
speed coupled with no sign anyone had attempted to scav these vehicles
for parts left his knuckles white. He decided to go left onto a north-south
street, heading for the largest collection of tall buildings. The exact *last*
place his instincts told him to go.

"What are we looking for?" asked Tris.

"Your guess is as good as mine." Kevin gazed up at a blown-out
building. An old bank sign, letters of mangled aluminum, swayed back
and forth along where the third through eighth stories lay exposed. What
had once been wall now littered the street in chunks. "This place is dead.
I'm not expecting to find anything here."

"Then why did we come?" She twisted around and stuck her hand in
'the box.'

"You know how certain things counteract each other? Acid to base for
example? Positive to negative?"

"Yeah." She slipped back into her seat with the folded paper from Zoe's jacket.

"Well. The way that kid stared at me... it's like anti-asshole radiation."

Paper crinkled. "You try so hard to hide it, Kevin... but you're a good man."

He felt heaviness spread over his chest. "So was my dad."

"Sorry." She smiled at him, half her face hidden by hair. "But you are your father's son."

"Yeah well. Don't let word get out, or everyone will use it against me." He stopped in a large intersection where six lanes crossed four. One skeleton, a rusted chain around its neck, dangled from a traffic light in the middle. A cluster of arrows protruded from the ribs, shot from multiple angles. Everywhere he looked, devastation. To the west, a few of the skyscrapers appeared to have fallen over like limbless trees in the face of a great blast. "So, the Virus is supposed to kill in a couple months. In theory, Infected should languish around for a while and drop dread."

"Yeah. Hey... this smudge looks like it was writing." Tris held the paper up to the light. "I can still see the indentation from the pen... What's Fuller and Akeview?"

"Names?" asked Kevin.

"Corner Fuller?" She glanced at him. "That's an odd name."

Kevin stopped the car and reached under his seat for the atlas. "Street names... Keep an eye out for anything moving."

Tris shifted onto her knees and proceeded to look around.

He flipped pages to Chicago and skimmed a finger back and forth down each street. After a few minutes, he spotted a 'Lakeview Avenue' and traced it up and down until it crossed another line labeled 'Fullerton Pkwy.'

"Tris? Any chance that might say corner of Lakeview and Fullerton?" He kept his finger on the spot and looked at her.

She held the sheet of notebook paper up to the sun, tilting it. "Could be. Hard to say. The paper's been through a lot."

"More than we got." He looked around for street signs. "Wow, almost tripped right over it."

After orienting himself, he dog-eared the page and stuffed the Atlas back under the seat. A short ride to a right turn put him on Fullerton. Vines and holes covered the walls of a canyon of concrete, steel, and glass that blocked most of the view. Several buildings bore spray-painted lettering calling on people to 'repent,' while other impromptu artists were less theological. 'We're fucked,' 'bend over, here it comes again' and anarchy symbols were among the most common. As more high-rises passed, graffiti about a zombie invasion took over, painted over the scrawled writings of the Armageddon prophets.

"Oh, this has bad idea all over it."

"Look." Tris pointed ahead.

On the next corner, a plain rectangular grey and glass building showed signs of habitation—lights in the windows about halfway up the length of a tower with thirty-ish stories. The ground floor walls sat recessed behind a series of exterior columns, ten or twelve feet in from the outer perimeter. Sandbag barricades occupied the space under the overhang, spattered with dried blood. Brass shell casings decorated the sidewalk around the building like confetti. All the glass of the first four levels was gone, and more razor wire clung in patches to the lowest three floors.

Orange in the sky worried him. It would be dark too soon.

"Virus doesn't spread by air, does it?" Kevin pulled to a stop by a gap in a short brick wall near the building, which appeared to open into a parking lot.

"Only the initial weaponization did. After ten years, if there were any traces of it left, they'd be dead and harmless. The stage two Virus is only communicable via bodily fluids."

A dark skinned woman on the fifth floor moved up to a bashed-out window. She pointed at them and said something too quiet to hear. Kevin squinted at her. Beige shirt, healthy looking skin, a sense of higher intelligence in her eyes.

He pulled the rest of the way in and parked a few paces from the side of the building. Another woman, Asian, and two men appeared flanking the sentry who spotted him. He got out and waved.

"Man, you got lucky," yelled the dark woman. "Get yo' ass up here 'fore they come out."

She pushed a flexible ladder off the windowsill, which unrolled on the way down. The last rung hovered at about hip level. Kevin looked at the deepening shadows in the streets. *Climbing doesn't seem like such a bad idea.*

"Minute," yelled Kevin. He leaned back into the car and swiped a finger over the row of switches, shutting everything down before grabbing his fancy new rifle. "Come on. We're going up. Bring the note... and Zoe's letter."

"You have no idea who these people are." Tris stared at him.

"I know they're alive. You know that whole 'banding together to survive' thing? This is it. They don't know us either and they're inviting us in." He shoved the door closed and typed in the code to lock the car down as soon as Tris opened her side.

Tris slung the AK over her shoulder, gathered a few things from the back seat, and closed the door with a *thunk*. Kevin hauled himself up onto the ladder and made the swaying climb to the fifth floor. The two men at the top helped him over the edge into a grey-carpeted room with a twenty-person table and a dark wall-mounted TV.

"Hey." Kevin nodded at them.

"Well now." The dark-skinned woman regarded him with obvious interest before smiling. "Kinda unusual to have someone show up around here."

Tris climbed in. "Thanks."

"No problem," said a somewhat older, bald man.

The two men pulled at the ladder, drawing it back inside.

"Yeah." Kevin took the note from Tris and offered it to the woman. "Got a note about some guy wanting a ride. I'd say meter's runnin', but I'm not sure I want to be on the ground level after the sun goes down."

"Nope. Fo' sure you don't." The woman glanced over the note. "Well, I'll be damned. Name's Patricia."

"Kevin... That's Tris."

Patricia started toward the door and waved him to follow. "Come on."

44

SUNSET

S tretched rectangles of orange sunlight crawled up the walls of a long corridor past offices-turned-bedrooms. Patricia walked to a stairwell filled with the smell of dust and piss, and up another six stories to the eleventh floor. Half a hallway down after exiting the stairs, she passed a double door on the left with some medical looking symbols on it. The corridor opened on the right, to a space with two elevator doors and frontage for three offices. Patricia ducked past an aluminum frame that likely once held a massive window, though no trace of the glass remained.

Inside, a crowd sat around folding tables. Most had plastic plates with meager helpings of vegetables. Clusters of candles had been set out in preparation for dark. People looked up as Patricia led their group in. The survivors ranged in age from six to their sixties, at a guess. The smallest, a girl with deep brown skin and wild curly hair, smiled at him. A woman next to her, obviously the child's mother, also seemed happy to see them. She looked a little older—later thirties or early forties—and wore a denim shirt over some other tattered garment.

Aside from the little girl, the only other child was an adolescent brown-haired boy, his too-thin body lost in the folds of a man's coat. Unlike the casual notice and disregard of rest of the people here, his reaction to Kevin and Tris took the form of an intense stare.

"Yo, Dennis," yelled Patricia.

An athletic older man with short greying hair looked over. His expression of curiosity shifted to mild annoyance, then resignation. He stood, carrying a plate with a potato and carrot on it, and walked over.

Tris scrunched her eyebrows down, mouth open.

"Hi." The man offered a hand to Kevin. "I'm Dennis... I guess you could say I'm sort of in charge here."

"Kevin." He shook hands. "Look, I ran into this little girl who said her daddy needs a ride. Has a brother too?"

The boy tripped twice trying to get up from the table and zoomed out a back door yelling, "Dad... Dad..."

"Guess that's the brother," said Kevin.

Tris pointed at Dennis. "Have we met? You seem *so* familiar."

"I guess I have one of those faces." Dennis smiled. "Stranger things have happened."

"Doctor Andrews?" Tris blinked.

Dennis's eyes widened. "You... you're the one they were sending. I believe we spoke via video chat."

"I'm sorry..." Tris whirled on Kevin, burying her face against his shoulder and sobbing.

"Uhh..." Dennis exhaled.

"The data in her head turned out to be bogus. Nathan set her up. He's trying to destroy the resistance, not help it. She did bring you a nice little bomb though... of course, she had no idea."

"Damn." Dennis pinched his nose. "Not that it matters anyway. We got overrun in Harrisburg."

Kevin ran a hand up and down Tris's back, trying to be comforting. "Yeah, we were there. Bill told us what happened."

Dennis laughed. "You met Bill? How is the stubborn bastard?"

"Not bad. Found him in Ned. Had a li'l girl with him."

The boy returned, sprinting past the tables to Kevin. A man in his early thirties who looked like an older version of him followed at a jog. His red and white flannel sported numerous bloodstains, though they didn't look to be from any recent wounds, probably not his.

"Whoa. Hold on." Kevin held his hands up. "There's only supposed to be one brother."

"I'm Paul." The man trembled with emotion. "You... you've seen Zoe? She's my daughter."

"You're the father?" Kevin glanced at the boy. "Damn, you got started young."

Paul chuckled and threw an arm around the boy. "We had Cody at nineteen."

"My sister's okay?" asked Cody.

"Yeah. Bit psychotic, but fine."

Tris punched Kevin in the shoulder and sniffled.

Most of the color drained from Paul's face. Dennis raised an eyebrow.

Kevin cringed. "Long story."

"She's not psychotic," said Tris. "Sad and frightened."

Dennis gestured at a hallway. "Let's talk."

Kevin, Tris, Dennis, Paul, and Cody filed into a small conference room with a round table. Dennis lit a candle in the middle before sitting. Over the course of the next half hour or so, Kevin told them about how he'd stumbled across Bill and Zoe, the bandit attack, Zoe participating in the gunfight, the creepy stare, the story of her surviving by hiding in a suitcase, and how he'd come here to pick the two of them up.

Tris handed over Zoe's handwritten letter.

Paul unfolded it and wound up crying in seconds. He slumped in the chair, elbows on his knees, and muttered thanks to no one in particular for keeping his daughter alive. After a few minutes, he collected himself and smiled—though tears continued to fall. "She says she's not mad at me an' Cody for making her go on the bus, but she won't forgive us if we're dead."

Dennis leaned back.

"Zoe's safe." Kevin tapped his fingers on the wood-patterned table. "Nederland is well defended. We can get out of here as soon as the sun's back up."

"Uhh…" Dennis pursed his lips. "It's not only Paul and Cody. There's twenty-eight of us who need to get the hell out of here. Everyone. Danielle's got a garden going on the roof, but it's not going to last forever. I give us a couple weeks… if that."

"Not happening." Kevin stood.

Tris grabbed his hand. "Where are you going?"

"Back to Wayne's."

"Through Chicago at night?" She pulled him closer. "We can't leave these people here."

Kevin fell hard into the chair and grabbed his head in both hands. "Are you forgetting that we've got a sports car? Six half-starved women was pushing it to the limit. We might be able to get eight if they're small… or intimate." He slapped his hand on his knee. "It's not physically possible.

Paul's note askin' for a ride said nothing about 'bring a goddamned semi truck.'"

"There's a bus depot a little ways across the city. We checked it out a couple weeks ago, but none of them work. Most people who have running vehicles are pretty handy with mechanical stuff. Think you could get one of those old beasts moving?"

Kevin sucked on his teeth. "Never tried to fix anything bigger than a pickup. Why don't you walk outta here? Ain't that far to the woods. You should be able to make it before darkness."

Dennis shook his head. "The Infected aren't harmed by daylight. They dislike it. Part of the psychological warfare effect of the Virus. Whatever psychosis drives them to attack people who are not infected overpowers that fear."

Paul broke down in sobs again while Cody glared at the floor.

"Sorry," whispered Kevin.

Paul gathered himself and wiped his nose on his sleeve. "We… uhh, found that out the hard way. Half of the people we got left are alive because of Michelle."

Tris looked at Paul. "I'm sorry."

"It should've been me," said Paul. "I was carrying Zoe. Michelle had the rifle… she never saw the ones coming from the alley."

"She bought everyone time," said Dennis, in a firm tone. "We need to get out of here."

Kevin shifted his gaze to the right. Tris stared at her lap. *She knows if she looks at me I'm going to think she's trying to guilt me into this.* He shivered. *Fuck infected.* At the sight of his hands trembling, Tris reached over and held one.

"I'll check the bus yard, but I can't promise anything." Kevin squeezed her hand.

"If it doesn't work out." Dennis stood. "You take Paul and Cody and get the hell out. Maybe send back something bigger."

"I'm not running and leaving everyone behind," yelled Paul. "It's bad enough we shipped Zoe out on her own. She almost…"

"This isn't your responsibility, Paul." Dennis offered a handshake to Kevin. "I appreciate you at least trying. The man's right. He's only got a small car. There's no way we're all getting in it. I'll ask for some volunteers to go with you to the bus lot. If you follow me, I'll show you a spot where you can sleep."

Paul and Cody wandered back among the tables in the 'cafeteria,' and

Dennis headed again to the stairwell. He went up one floor, down a short corridor, and through a frosted glass door bearing a logo of a blue and cyan diamond hovering over a field of little squares above the name: "Software Concepts."

"Got a cube farm in here." Dennis pointed at two hallways leading out of a reception area. "Feel free to set up in any empty. A lot of them are uhh, available now."

"Yeah." Kevin smirked. "I know how Infected work."

"Doctor Andrews?" asked Tris. "I thought the Virus was supposed to kill its victims after about three months. Do you know why they're not dropping? Or what that serpent thing is?"

He grumbled. "An effort was made in an attempt to increase the usefulness of the cleansing agent, involving a weaponized version of Nanites."

"Oh, shit." Kevin scowled. "So the damn things regenerate like Tris?"

"Well... in a manner of speaking, yes." Dennis folded his arms. "Though, a brain wound is not repairable, and only the most minor of injuries to cardiac tissue is survivable. The symbiote, which you refer to as the serpent, discharges nanites into the host's tissues and perpetuates a constant state of repairing some of the cellular degeneration caused by the Virus. Drones deposited these symbiotes in selected areas, and by now, given access to basic materials, they have reproduced."

Tris gaped at Dennis. "They're in agony... It felt like my lung was on fire when I got shot."

Dennis nodded. "The symbiote suppresses pain signals for a short time following a kill. This, of course, increases their motivation to attack anything that moves."

"Son of a bitch." Kevin shook his head. "So these things really are unstoppable." He looked up. "Wait... radiation."

"Might damage the delicate circuitry within the symbiote and toast its AI." Dennis nodded. "An electromagnetic pulse would wipe them out... or at least allow the normal life cycle of the Virus to run to completion, which would bring about tissue degeneration in approximately three to six months after infection onset."

"Sorry, I'm all out of nukes." Kevin chuckled.

"EMP doesn't necessarily require a nuclear detonation," said Dennis. The Enclave has some devices capable of generating only the electromagnetic effect. Anti-technology weapons."

"There are no infected in Dallas." Tris perked up. "What effect would latent radiation have on the virus itself?"

Dennis rubbed his chin. "That was something we didn't test. The Council wasn't comfortable with us handling radioactive material. My guess is it may neutralize the virus or it suppressed the symbiotes, thus allowing the Infected there to die off as designed."

"Doctor." Tris bit her lower lip. "Do you have any idea why my memory would have strange patches? Did you know my father?"

"I worked with Doctor Jameson for a few years yes. I'm afraid most of what you've heard about him is probably true. He was an advocate for 'opening the doors' and *rejoining* society rather than 'overwriting' it. They caught him attempting to sabotage the Virus drones before they could launch. I... never saw him after that."

Tris glared at the empty white reception desk. "I know he's dead."

Dennis cringed. "Probably."

"She's hoping to be a disappointed pessimist." Kevin offered an arm.

She leaned against him. "Not this time. They went out of their way to act as if he never existed. No one planned on him coming back."

"As for your spotty memory?" Dennis pointed at a small plug behind his left ear. "Some of what you remember might be uploaded, or an attempt to implant other memories might have interfered with real memory."

"They can do that?" Kevin blinked. "Take your memories away?"

"No." Dennis shook his head. "As far as I know, they can only write new data, but the process is not perfect and occasionally, there are collisions."

"The resistance plugged me in to virtual reality to train me before they sent me out. 'Uploading' usable skills doesn't work right. It turns people into robots doing tasks, without thinking or improvising. Simulating the training in VR is the same as really learning. It felt like eight months went by, but it was only two weeks for real." Tris shivered. "What if... oh, no. That's it. The... I never woke up from the egg harvesting. 'Detention' was VR. It had to be."

Kevin rubbed her shoulder. "How did you go from a holding cell to the underground?"

"Nathan hacked the door open." Her eyes widened. "That was real. That's why my hair was wet. Somehow, they moved me from a VR prison to a real holding cell when I was asleep so they could make me think I escaped."

"Well, I suppose it does make a degree of sense." Dennis started for the door. "I need to get back downstairs. Prisoners in VR don't take up as much space or need as many nutrients."

"Stacked up like junk in a closet." Kevin put his hands on her shoulders.

She gave him a stare laced with hope and vengefulness.

"Not my circus; not my monkeys." He shook his head. "We'd have to raise an army to stand up to the Enclave, and even then it's pretty much suicide. You said it yourself… if they don't open the doors, they'll die off anyway."

"What about the Virus?" She frowned at the floor. "Or everyone else left alive?"

Kevin wandered down the hallway on the left. "I dunno." He selected an open cubicle and settled in on a mattress made of sofa cushions, after leaning the Enclave rifle against the grey, fabric-covered partition. "I'm sure you'll come up with something."

———————

For half an hour, Kevin's snoring played backdrop to Tris's roaming mind. Whenever she closed her eyes, she'd see her father, the replacement family, or a sterile schoolroom with all the kids in black. She remembered the bright floor with lights under opaque white tiles, but not why anyone felt the need to put lights overhead as well as below. It all had a dreamy, surreal quality to it that made her question everything.

When she'd been with her father, she had memories of crawling around among wires and hoses and getting filthy. He was always in his 'secret workshop' in the basement. Their house in the small part of the Enclave territory that permitted freestanding dwellings had been a mark of station. Daddy had been important before he 'turned traitor.'

She slipped into a dream of walking down a beige-carpeted hallway in the middle of the night, a clingy black 'sleep suit' covering her from throat to knees, and elbows. Nine-year-old Tris opened the door at the end, squinting from the glaring sun. She glanced back at the hallway, at the windows that had a second before been pitch dark.

Two women in black security uniforms smiled at her. That patronizing smile of people who treated all children like two-year-olds.

"Get dressed, sweetie. You need to come with us. Something very bad happened, and we don't want you to get hurt."

Everything after the two women in black felt fake. The family who didn't believe her father existed, years of school where none of the children spoke to each other or made friends, and finally Dovarin. An asshole so severe she preferred Detention. Nathan's face appeared, dirty and disheveled, a fake hacker working for the resistance. He opened his mouth to speak, but Kevin's snoring came out of it.

Tris sat up and rubbed her face. Faint moans from the window reminded her why they were hiding high up in a building with no way in from the ground level. She peeled the blanket off and frowned at her leather shirt and jeans. *Maybe that's why I can't sleep... but who knows what'll happen here. Too dangerous.* She slipped her shoes on and crawled away without waking him. *I need some air.*

Someone had covered the stairwell walls with black sharpie marker from the fourteenth through twentieth floors with writing taken from the Bible, as well as crude attempts to draw some of the scenes. She trudged without looking at much more than her feet until the stairway ended at a black metal door, which led to the roof.

Around a central structure that probably contained the remains of HVAC systems or elevators, stood numerous grow troughs made from anything and everything they could get a hold of. The larger ones looked like metal awnings taken from industrial stoves, flipped upside down and packed with soil. Some were giant flowerpots, probably once used to hold tiny trees in various offices. Water cooler jugs with the tops cut off hosted clusters of beans or onions. The lot of them overflowed with vegetables, though some didn't thrive.

She passed a twelve-foot steel awning full of tomato plants on her way to the roof edge. The sky ranged from dark blue-black straight above to royal blue tinted with red-orange at the horizon in the west. *A few minutes left of sunset.* Tris approached the wall at the edge and leaned on her folded arms. Flickering candlelight needled at her attention from her peripheral vision.

At the corner of the roof, a shack made of sheet metal and stacked cabinets played home to the mocha-skinned woman and the little girl she'd seen earlier in the cafeteria. The woman sat cross-legged on the floor next to a cot, reading a bedtime story to the half-awake child. Tris offered her best 'don't mind me' smile and turned her gaze back to the sky.

Her hair danced in the wind. Thirty stories off the ground, the city didn't seem so frightening. Aside from the occasional fleeting shadow in the street, it looked peaceful. The woman approached a few minutes later, shoes crunching over the roof.

"Heard you an' your friend were gonna try and get us out of here?"

"He's thinking about it." Tris let her head sag. "You must be Danielle?"

"That's me. Guess knowing my way around a garden came in handy. Soil's tapped out, though. Sometimes, a couple people volunteer to go harvest more or get water, but no guarantee they come back."

"Doctor Andrews mentioned the garden was failing." She twisted her head so the wind pulled her hair out of her face, and smiled at Danielle. "I'm not going to let him leave you all here."

"We've lost too much already. I never should'a listened to Carl. That man always said we'd have strength in numbers, only them numbers keep on dwindlin'."

"I'm sorry."

"Well. I learned a long time ago, ya can't be angry all the time. You one of 'em, ain't cha?" Danielle raised an eyebrow. "Enclave?"

"By genetics maybe. Not in spirit." Tris pushed off the wall and stood upright. "I was just a kid when they let it out."

"Now that?" Danielle put a hand on Tris's shoulder and squeezed. "That's guilt you don't need. It ain't got no claim on your soul. No more 'an Star could be to blame for anything that man Dennis decides."

"Star's your daughter?" Tris leaned to the side to smile at the sleeping child. "Pretty name."

"Thanks. Only damn good idea Carl ever had." Danielle chuckled. "I guess you don't need me heapin' on no more guilt."

"Mind if I ask why you're living in a metal box on the roof?"

Danielle shook her head, a somber expression on her face. "This building used ta be full. Damn near four hundred of us. Was a time no one had any privacy. I got settled in up here, no point movin'."

"Damn." Tris cringed. "All that stuff on the walls… I hope it's true. I hope whoever made the Virus has to answer for it."

Squeak.

Tris glanced to her right at the scrape of a metal door moving. Seconds later, a sleepy-eyed Kevin emerged from the corner with his hands stuffed in his jacket pockets. He offered a lazy smile to Danielle and sidled up on Tris's left.

"Hey… couldn't sleep?"

She looked down. "No. Bad dreams."

"Me too." Kevin closed his eyes and yawned. "Keep seeing Infected coming after me."

As if on cue, a moan rose up from the street level.

Tris stared at the wavering tomato plants for a few seconds as the breeze picked up.

Danielle sighed. "Star thinks they're sick, and they're not getting better because the factories that made band-aids are all gone."

Kevin sent an awkward smile at the roof. "Okay… we can't leave them here. This pathetic little garden won't feed them much longer."

"Aw, you go ta hell." Danielle laughed. "Pathetic my ass."

He grinned.

"Mommy," yelled a small voice. "They're coming up the stairs."

Danielle whispered, "Sorry," and hurried off to the little shed to calm the girl.

Kevin yawned and rested a hand atop the wall at the roof's edge. Tris wrapped herself around his right arm and leaned her head on his shoulder. They gazed westward until the last traces of light sank into the horizon.

"Are you scared?" asked Tris.

He held up his left hand, which no longer shook. "Used ta be, the only thing I'd ever truly been afraid of was turning into one of those *things.*"

She slid a hand up his chest, under his jacket. "Used to be?"

"Yeah." He pulled her close. "Now I'm afraid I'll lose you."

Tris sniffled. Emotion welled up inside, leaving her unable to decide between smiling and crying.

"For a while there, I was sure you were waiting for a chance to sneak off with my car." He leaned down, close enough for his breath to fill her mouth. "You did steal from me, but it wasn't my car."

"Kevin…" She closed her eyes and kissed him.

The wind blew his hair into her face, hers back in a wild spray of white. She kissed him as if tomorrow would be their last day on Earth. She trembled.

"What's wrong?" whispered Kevin, into her ear.

"I don't want to lose you."

He smiled as if he tried to sell her a used car that would fall apart an hour after it drove off the lot. "I promise I won't do anything stupid."

"You already have." She clung to him and closed her eyes. "We should try and sleep."

"Yeah… try."

He stooped and picked her up. Tris grinned at the memory of hopping after him with her ankles tied together. How had she gone from wanting to beat the shit out of him to feeling like she couldn't live without him? Maybe humanity *did* have a chance.

Strange things happen. That's what Doctor Andrews always said...

45

BATTERIES NOT INCLUDED

Kevin's eyes popped open. Early morning sunlight striking the tinted office windows turned the drop ceiling tiles pale blue. Tris, naked, lay half on top of him, face down and one leg up. She'd been right. Her suggestion for a way to be able to sleep had worked perfectly. Aware that at any moment, someone might walk by, he jostled her awake.

"Get dressed," he whispered.

Tris yawned and stretched before crawling over his body again and kissing him.

Kevin wrapped his arms around her back and held her as she nibbled at his lips and entwined her tongue with his. He slid his hands down her back and cradled her ass. Time lost meaning as they writhed together, kissing and fondling. Whenever he played with her breasts, she bit him to muffle her squeals. Sensing weakness, he gave her nipple a light pinch and tickle.

Kevin gasped as her teeth nearly drew blood. "Aaaah."

She moved her mouth to the base of his neck and kissed there.

"We're out in the open," he whispered. "They're expecting us to head out first light…"

Blushing lent a touch of color to her face, darker around her nose. She bit her index finger. "I don't care if you don't care."

Kevin shrugged.

With that, she adjusted her position and lowered herself onto him. Kevin tried to stifle gasps and moans as she raised and lowered herself. She bent forward, grasped his shoulders, and stared down a tunnel of snowy hair into his eyes. They spent a few more minutes kissing before she sat up straight again and moaned. Kevin held her by the hips, thrusting upward in time with her gyrations. Eventually, she threw her head back in a waterfall of white. He slid both hands up over her stomach and cradled her breasts, squeezing her nipples between his fingers.

Tris shuddered. His eyes rolled up into his head as his body convulsed out of control. Once the moment of ecstasy passed, she fell limp on top of him, out of breath. He stroked her hair for a little while until the *bang* of a metal door in the hallway startled her into motion.

She leapt off him and raced to get her panties on. Kevin pulled his boxers in place before standing. Tris grabbed her jeans and jumped into them while Kevin stretched.

Dennis stepped around the cube partition and froze with his gaze on Tris's bare chest. He coughed, whirled around, and ducked out of sight. "Sorry."

"My fault." Tris cringed at the sight of her bloody leather shirt, but put it on anyway.

Kevin slipped into his eagle tee and covered it as fast as he could with the armored jacket. "All clear."

Dennis approached, keeping his gaze on the floor. "Sorry about that. I should've expected you two would, umm, yeah. Anyway... Three volunteers offered to go with you."

"Your eye twitched," said Tris. "What are you hiding?"

"Sharp." Dennis chuckled. "Nothing much. There were five, but I asked Paul and Cody to stay here. They're not in a good state of mind."

"No way on the kid," said Kevin. "You think Paul's unstable?"

"Not really. My sentimental side. I'd rather he be alive to get back to his kid. It wasn't easy on him putting her on that bus. It's been killing him ever since."

"Yeah." Kevin grabbed the Enclave rifle. "Faster we get moving, faster we get outta here."

Dennis led the way downstairs to the cafeteria area where all twenty-eight survivors gathered. Paul came rushing at them, red-faced, finger poised.

Kevin intercepted him before he could get to Dennis. "I'm sorry, Zoe. Your father's dead."

Paul stared at him as if he'd whipped it out and pissed on him.

"Exactly," said Kevin. "Because I *don't* want to have to say that, your ass is staying here."

"Look." Paul seemed to calm a little. "I can't just sit here like some little child myself and be saved. What kind of dad wouldn't do everything he could to get back to his kid?"

Kevin looked at Dennis and shrugged. "Whatever, man. Come on. You got a weapon?"

Paul ran off. "Yeah, be right back."

Danielle brought over two plastic plates of tomato slices and green beans, handing one to Kevin and one to Tris. After the meager, but welcome offering, Kevin headed for the stairwell and down to the fifth floor, where they'd climbed in the window. Patricia, as well as the two men who'd helped him climb in, stood guard in the windows while three other men sat at a long folding table and checked over weapons.

A bony guy with short black hair and a thin mustache in a tank top and camo fatigues loaded a 40mm shell into a grenade launcher attachment on his M-16. At his right, a stocky man with long brown hair snapped buckshot shells into a SPAS-12. The pockets of his olive drab trench coat swelled with extra ammo. On the near side of the table stood a dark-skinned man with an afro many months devoid of any attempt at maintaining it. His ordinary sneakers, jeans, and plain white tee shirt made him seem like he'd fallen through a time hole from before the war. Only the silver Desert Eagle on his belt seemed to belong in this damned new world. A leather bandolier over his chest held about ten more magazines. He looked up at them and offered a nod.

Dennis moved past Kevin and spun to face him. "I can't tell you how grateful we all are that you're willing to do this for us. It's been... hell being stuck here. We're all hoping you can get one of those old buses to work."

"Gee... no pressure at all." Kevin smiled.

"Heh." Dennis chuckled. "This is Gene." The man with the M-16 waved. "Martin." The long-haired man flared his eyebrows up twice, with a manic 'lets do this' expression. "And Rod." The man with the Desert Eagle nodded. "Rod was with us the last time we went to the depot. He knows the best route."

Kevin hurled a playful accusatory glance at Tris. "I'm sure you all have been dealing with these damn things for a long time too, but I'd appreciate it if we tried to stay as quiet as possible. If we see Infected, but they don't see us... don't blow their heads off. Gunshots will attract more."

Paul ran in holding an Mp5, with a black hip satchel clattering at his side. He'd changed into an almost complete grey-white city camouflage uniform.

"Paul." Kevin shook his hand. "Bear with me here; I'm saying this to make myself feel better. The Infected are not undead. They are alive. One bullet to the heart will put them down."

The men offered murmurs of agreement and nods.

"Sometimes when you've got a choice between shitting your pants and going full auto, full auto happens," said Paul.

Kevin walked to the window. "Yeah, I understand that. I'd prefer we got there without a shot being fired."

Marty racked the pump grip on the SPAS, and locked it forward. "You know that ain't happening."

"Didn't you hear? I'm an optimist." Kevin held his hands up to the sides and winked at Tris.

He slipped up and over the windowsill amid subdued laughter. The flexible ladder rattled and swayed on his climb to street level. Before anything else, he paced a circuit around the Challenger and breathed a sigh of relief that nothing had bothered it during the night. One by one, the others came down and formed up in the small parking lot.

Tris tugged on the handle to the passenger door. When it didn't budge, she flashed an expectant look. Kevin walked up to her and hovered nose to nose with her, smiling.

After a light peck, he kissed her ear, and whispered, "4-1-9-4 to open. Push 0 and 9 together to lock it."

She gave him a quick hug. Kevin swallowed a tiny hint of fear that he'd set in motion a chain of events that would culminate with being tied naked to a cactus again, without a car. He forced the worry out of his mind and jogged over to Rod.

"What's the best way there? Long enough to drive it?"

Rod frowned. "The roads got junk all troo 'em. A bus'll push crap out its way, but that nice ol' car o' yours ain't doin'. We make it on foot jus' fine. Take 'bout forty minutes."

Thump. Kevin looked up as the car door closed. Tris jogged up to the huddle with her AK across her back on its strap, and the katana out.

"What?" She shrugged. "You said you wanted quiet."

Marty loosed a wistful sigh. "I used to have a claymore."

"Damn stupid to get close to them." Gene held the M-16 up in one hand. "Prefer working at a distance."

Kevin bowed to Rod. "Your show. Lead the way."

Rod walked out of the lot and crossed the street, headed generally south and west. Despite his request for quiet, Kevin held the Enclave rifle at the ready. The ghosts of a once-thriving city echoed in the back of his mind as his brain tried to fill in for the lack of noise. He imagined a place like this would never have been so quiet, even in the dead of night. Hundreds of cars littered the streets, undisturbed since their former owners last touched them before the world went up in flames. Windows coated in rain-hardened silt hid whatever secrets lay within under a shell of death.

He edged away from the sides of the road and walked the centerline. Any of that muck could've been nuclear fallout. Heck, most of it probably was. Fifty years didn't seem like a whole lot of time for radiation to go away, but Wayne had seemed convinced the danger of fallout particles abated after only a couple weeks. *What the hell happened in Dallas then?*

Marty swung his shotgun left and right as they passed side streets and alleys, looking eager to kill something. Paul started off bringing up the rear, but Gene faded back enough to give him some protection. After fifteen minutes of walking, Tris slid the katana into the sheath and flexed her hands.

The eeriness of an empty city seemed to press in on him. Dripping water and the rustle of unseen small animals kept everyone jumping and spinning at the slightest noise. Rod took a right turn, following another street west until tall buildings gave way to a more residential looking section with nothing over four stories. Minutes later, he went south again onto a road littered with cars. Some had been flipped upside down, others lay on their sides, and many had hundreds of bullet holes in them.

"What the fuck?" whispered Kevin.

Gene quickened his step, getting close enough to speak in a low tone. "Pre-infected territory war. Three gangs went at it for about two years. Ugly time. Course… makes ya wonder if it's better than this."

"Turf war is easier to deal with than Infected." Kevin jumped at a moving shadow in a trash-strewn alley. "City's so damn big, what was the point of fighting?"

"People who have power always want more," whispered Tris.

Gene chuckled. "Nah, nothin' that highbrow. I think someone tried to put ketchup on a hot dog."

"Huh?" Kevin blinked.

"Aw shit." Gene laughed. "You ain't from around here are ya?"

"Nope. New Mexico."

"Damn. What the hell made you come all the way out here?" Gene whistled.

"A blue-eyed blonde." Kevin glanced at Paul. *And two thousand coins.*

Rod climbed over a roadblock of orange plastic construction barricades, causing sand to leak out of numerous bullet holes. The others followed. Minutes shy of an hour after leaving the building, Rod came to a halt at a corner and pointed at a wide chain link rolling gate at the end of a short section of road. Two coils of razor wire ran along the top, connected to a tangle of more razor wire perched on a security guard's booth at the left side of the driveway. Beyond the fence, eleven white metro-buses parked in a neat row in front of a one-story Transit Authority building. Solar panels covered the roof, and all three garage doors were closed.

"We're here," said Rod. "I'm impressed. Quiet worked."

"We didn't see anything to shoot at," said Marty, sounding disappointed.

Kevin jogged down the approach road, weaving between rows of water-filled barrels set up as a defensive fortification. With any luck, one of the flat-fronted e-buses could push through them. As expected, the outer door on the security booth was locked. He jiggled the knob out of annoyance and hit the blue painted metal door with a light punch. "Dammit. Rod, how'd you get in last time?"

"Door was open last time. We slammed it runnin' away from Infected." He offered a weak smile.

"Wonderful." Kevin sighed at the clouds.

"Break the window out?" said Paul.

"I got it." Tris took a knee by the door and fiddled with her left shoe. She pulled a pair of small metal rods out of the heel and stuck them in the keyhole. "Try to stay quiet so I can listen."

"You're full of surprises," whispered Kevin. "Where'd you learn that?"

Tris emitted a sad sigh. "I was trained for the resistance, remember?"

She picked the lock in about forty seconds and stashed the tools back in her shoe sole. As soon as she opened the door, a rotting body in a security guard uniform moaned and reached for her from the ground.

Tris's arms blurred. The katana went from the scabbard on her back to pointing down and to the left in the span of a camera flash. A severed head hit the ground with a hollow *clonk*. She'd cut it at the level of the mouth, leaving a bit of chin and jawbone attached to the larger portion of corpse.

"Fuckin' A," said Marty.

"What was that?" asked Paul. "She some kinda android?"

"No. Don't call her an android again, or she'll cut your balls off." Kevin smiled.

"I will not," Tris muttered while wiping blood from the blade on the dead man's shirt. "Don't touch the blood."

"No kidding." Kevin took a long step over the body.

The interior door of the booth opened with ease, and he jogged up to the first bus in line. Over the next hour, he went from bus to bus, finding them all stone dead. The massive vehicles filled him with daydreams of creating the Marauder II. The tires came up to his chest; he thought of all the armor he could pile on a beast like this. Nothing would stop it once it got rolling. He'd be a wildlands juggernaught. As awesome as it could be, he'd still rather 'sell fried potatoes to morons.' Some looked as though they'd been pressed into service during the gang warfare, and bore numerous scars from pipe bombs, bullets, flames, and full-on collisions.

Kevin surveyed all eleven buses, disregarding four off the bat as unrecoverable. Of the three in the best outward condition, one had a small army of dead Infected hanging on spiked armor plates all the way around it. That one, he wanted *nothing* to do with. The next best bus, in terms of lacking outward damage, turned out to have taken a hit from an explosive in the left rear, which exposed most of the inner workings of the biggest in-wheel motor he'd ever seen.

His last, best, hope had four intact wheels, but the ass end looked like a work of modern art. No less than ninety silver circles surrounded finger-sized holes where black paint had flaked away at the impact of a bullet. Cringing at what he'd see inside, Kevin grabbed the hatch release and opened the rear panel.

The battery cluster had long ago ceased oozing whatever chemicals they put in it. He knew enough to understand it should contain pale blue gel, not bright green foam. Odds were decent that between the other nine buses—he disregarded the existence of the one covered in Infected bodies—they could find enough serviceable battery modules to make one full array. If the only thing wrong with this one was lack of power, they might have a chance.

He waved everyone over.

"Okay, I think this is our winner."

"That don't look like winning," said Rod.

Gene chuckled.

Kevin smiled. "Looks bad, but it's actually in the best shape of the lot. All we need to do is replace the batteries. I know it's hard to see through this crusty foam shit, but there's sixteen battery modules in there. Each one is about ninety pounds. We're going to have to take them from the other buses and put them in here, then charge it up. Tris, can you check the solar panel controls? Before we start busting our backs, might as well make sure we're not wasting time. Paul, go with her in case there's shit inside the building. Everyone else, with me to the garage."

Tris nodded and jogged off. Paul hurried after her. Kevin strode up to one of the rolling garage doors and hesitated long enough to watch her disappear inside the office portion. He squatted and got his fingers under the rim. Rod, Marty, and Gene followed suit. The four of them grunted and lifted, flinging the cumbersome barrier into the air with a great rattling of counterweight chains.

Unfortunately, the garage contained no intact bus waiting to be driven with zero effort. It did have three massive lifts that called out to the little boy inside him who wanted to play with something that cool. Kevin resisted the urge and pointed at four machines resembling the bastard child of a pallet jack and forklift.

"We're good," yelled Tris from an open window. "Panel array is online."

"Grab those battery lifts. Should be self-explanatory how to use it. There's rails near the top of the battery for those prongs. Slide it in and pump the handle. Lift the battery an inch and pull it back." He grabbed appropriate-sized socket wrenches and handed them out. "Each battery is wired in a sequence with two contacts. Unscrew it, clear the wires, and pull it out. We'll need sixteen intact packs. The stuff inside should be sky blue. If it's any other color, don't bother with it."

Kevin picked up a crowbar and a socket wrench before jogging back to the chosen bus. He got to work on the foam crust, bashing and stabbing at it to clear away the batteries underneath. Greening in the metal gave some evidence of an electrogel fire, though the real damage looked confined to the plastic battery casing and anode/cathode plates. Once he got the debris out of the way, he attacked the nuts holding the wires in place. All the while he worked, the grating sound of hard wheels on paving announced the arrival of battery module after battery module. At one point, he looked up at a shocked noise from Marty, at Tris lazily pulling a battery cart along with one arm. She didn't bother pumping it down, rather pulled the battery off the rails with her hands and set it on the ground.

"You know, they made those so people don't throw their back out." Kevin winked. "Work smarter, not harder."

"It takes too long." She sighed.

"I'm tellin' you, she's gotta be an android," whispered Marty.

The locals discussed androids and Enclave cyberware with Tris while collecting the remainder of the replacement batteries. Gene pointed out that Tris was sweating, something an android couldn't do. A few times, Kevin had to resort to bashing the socket wrench with the crowbar to crack through the crud on the nut. *So what if I break a bolt. Not like we need this bastard to run for the next twenty years.*

Once the last of the bad battery units came free, the entire group descended upon the bus. It took them about twenty-five minutes to de-load the smashed batteries, drop them, and slide the scavenged ones in.

Kevin wiped sweat from his forehead with the back of his arm. He tossed Tris a wrench. "I could use a hand with the nuts."

Marty laughed.

Tris raised an eyebrow. "Right here? Now?"

"I'm half tempted to call your bluff." Kevin slipped the first contact over the bolt post and set to the task of tightening it. "How's the panel array?"

"Operational. A few of the capacitors are blown, but that won't be a problem unless we're charging all eleven buses at once."

He smiled. "Maybe the extra power will get us out of here faster."

Between her superhuman dexterity and enhanced strength, she secured four to five contacts for every one he tightened. Before long, the bus looked ready to go.

"Okay, now for the shitty part." Kevin chuckled.

"There's a shitty part?" asked Gene.

Kevin grinned. "See where this bus is?"

Everyone nodded.

Kevin pointed to an island on the opposite side of the bus yard that resembled a tiny gas station with a covered awning. "We have to push the fucker over there to charge it."

"Great," said Marty.

Paul shook his head. "Wonderful."

"Shit." Gene spat.

Rod whipped the Desert Eagle off his hip and aimed. Everyone froze, and turned in a gradual spin to stare where the pistol pointed. A lone Infected, a heavyset bald man in a coral pink shirt, wobbled across the street by the gate. He sniffed around the security booth. Milk white eyes gazed over the group, though he didn't seem to notice them.

Kevin mouthed 'nobody move' without giving voice to it.

The pudgy, rotting man crawled through the booth and shambled into the bus yard. His left arm tucked up like a bird with a broken wing while he dragged a right leg that seemed incapable of bending at the knee. One of his cheeks hung open, a swaying flap of skin exposed bright red muscle underneath, roiling with maggots.

Tris eased the katana out.

Kevin put a hand on her shoulder.

"If we shoot it, there'll be fifty more." She eased up to the corner of the bus, sword held down.

Paul broke out in a cold sweat and raised his Mp5. Gene waved him off. Paul moved his finger off the trigger and nodded. The Infected bobbed his head, as if somehow waving it back and forth would help him smell or hear. Everyone huddled behind the bus. Kevin crouched at Tris's side and grabbed the back of her belt.

She squinted at him. "I'm not an idiot."

The Infected swung itself around in response to a distant *clank*.

At almost the same instant, Paul rasped, "What are you waiting for?"

Kevin cringed.

The decaying man whirled around and hobbled closer, emitting eager grunts and sucking noises. Kevin released her belt. *She's immune. She's immune.* Tris flexed her knees. When the Infected reached the front end of the bus, she ran out.

Another distant *crash* got its attention, and it spun away, drawn by the louder noise. It took one step toward the gate before the crunch of Tris's shoes on the paving got its attention. The Infected sucked in air, preparing to howl. She rammed the Katana into its chest to the hilt, raised her right leg, and stomp kicked it while jerking the sword free. Gurgling, the dead man fell over backward with a sickening *splat* of semi-rotten flesh striking asphalt.

Everyone exhaled at once. The group fanned out in a V, aiming weapons at all possible points of entry to the yard they could see. After a few minutes of nothing, Kevin patted Gene on the shoulder and pointed at the bus.

"You steer, you're the scrawniest."

Gene let off a dry chuckle and slung his M-16 over his back. "Won't get an argument outta me. You sure you don't wanna let the chick drive?"

"Tweet. Tweet," said Tris. She jogged to a spigot on the wall and washed off the blade.

Rod chuckled. "She's probably stronger than any of us."

Kevin ran to the back end of the bus and slammed the battery housing cover. With Tris at his side, Rod, Marty, and Paul pushing as well, he grunted and heaved. They may as well have been attempting to move the building. After a few futile seconds, Gene appeared at the corner.

"Sorry. I'd have yelled, but… yeah. Took me a minute to find the parking brake. Gimme ten seconds and try that again."

Kevin sighed.

Soon, they shoved again, and the massive vehicle crept forward. Once clear of the row of parked buses, it turned to the right, and a laborious minute later, they got it close enough to the charging station for a cable to reach. While everyone collapsed to catch their breath, Gene ran around and plugged it in.

"Awesome," said Marty. "This is gonna work? Be awesomer if I got to pulp something's head." He rattled the SPAS.

"Awesomer isn't a word, dumbass," said Rod.

"Two words." Marty tapped index and pinky finger under his eyes before holding up 'metal horns.' "Nuclear fuckin' war."

"Isn't that three words?" asked Gene.

"Naw man. The 'fuckin' don't count. It's like a modifier or something. Who gives a rat shit about grammar now?"

"There's always one," said Tris. "Always."

"So… how long?" asked Rod.

Kevin stood. "Well, nothing's caught fire yet, so that's a good sign. Means I got the wires hooked up right. If the cells were stone dead… we're looking at six to eight hours. Maybe half an hour before I know if we're going to get a charge at all."

"That ain't good man." Paul paced in a tight circle. "Gotta get out of here."

"Chill, man." Rod patted his arm. "We got at least seven hours of sun left."

Tris walked out of sight beyond the corner of the bus.

Kevin went the other way, heading for the door. He jogged up the steps and flopped into the driver's seat, staring at the blank instrument panel. *So strange being this high up off the road.* The cushioned seat felt wonderful, even if it did smell like an old sweat sock. White hair drifted by the window. He leaned up to watch Tris root around inside the wheel. She shut the cover in a few minutes and moved past the front to the other side.

Kevin closed his eyes. The next thing he knew, a light *ping* noise happened, making him sit bolt upright in the chair. The instrument panel lit up with blue and green glow. A square sub-panel near the speedometer scrolled with a boot process, the battery charge meter showed 8%. Another panel displayed a number of maintenance alerts.

Tris bounded up the steps. "We have a problem."

"Shit. How bad?"

"I think there was a surge when the previous battery got shot out. No way to know for sure but to try it, but if we turn this thing off, it might not come back on again without replacing the power management board and maybe a third of the wiring. There's melted insulation on most of the lines going to the wheel motors."

"How long?" He rubbed his face.

"Two or three days, maybe four… with a crew of trained mechanics and parts on a shelf. Double that if we have to scav it from the other buses. Also, the rear wheel fuses melted. I can replace those easy though, plenty of spares in the other buses."

"Damn, and I was about to get happy it turned on at all."

She shrugged. "It *might* come back on."

"So what you're saying is if we turn it off, we're probably going to kill it… so we gotta drive outta here today."

"I'm saying it's very likely that this thing will become a brick if we try to shut it down for the night."

Kevin glanced at the roof. Two plastic-domed skylights, one near the front and one closer to the back, gave him an idea. He jumped up and ran outside, waving at the others to gather. Tris jogged over to the next nearest bus and opened the wheel cap, gripping at a cylinder fuse the size of a pair of beer cans stacked on end.

"What's up?" asked Rod.

"Tris found an electrical problem with the bus." He held up a hand as the groaning started. "The bus may or may not turn back on if we kill the power. I don't really want to walk back and pick this bastard up in the morning. Be just my luck some idiot finds it and takes off. There's roof lights we can cut out and make holes. What say we get some metal welded on over the side windows, open those hatches, and pick everyone up through the roof?"

"What like drive up under the ladder?" asked Gene. "Might work. Though, the bus ain't that tall. Infected could climb over each other and might reach."

"A couple of us on the roof can hold them off." Marty stared into space, clearly daydreaming about a ride of glory with his shotgun.

Rod made faces. "I dunno. Rushing is risky. We could spend the night here."

"In a lit up bus?" Kevin cringed. "Infected would be on us like moths on a headlight."

"Can't you shut down the lights?" asked Gene.

"I couldn't find a switch. If the power's on, the interior lights are on." Kevin tapped a finger to his mouth. "I suppose I could take the bulbs out."

"If we don't go back, they might think the worst happened." Paul flicked a switch back and forth on the Mp5, making a continuous clicking.

"I honestly don't think it will matter." Kevin pointed at the gate. "When we drive this monster out of here, it's going to make noise. All that crap in the road. The gate... grinding metal. Dark or not, we're going to be up to our eyeballs in them."

Tris trotted back over with her prize and looked toward the city. "Light may make them hesitate and buy us a couple of minutes."

"How much chance is there something else could go wrong?" asked Rod. "If we sat on this bus overnight?"

"Gamble either way." Tris shrugged. "The electrical system on that thing might tolerate holding a full charge all night... or we come back to a bonfire."

"I haven't got any experience with a vehicle this big," said Kevin. "But... there's a roadhouse about two hours away. It should have enough juice to make it there. If it drops dead then, no big deal. Place will have food and beds, and we can worry about running everyone back and forth a couple at a time... no pressure."

"Uhh, Kevin?" Tris poked him in the side with the fuse. "Are you gonna drive that bus at 110?"

"Shit." He held his hands up in surrender. "Okay, make it four hours."

"Fuck it." Rod glowered. "I'm gonna head back to the building and get everyone off their asses, ready to move out fast. We do this tonight." He looked at Kevin. "Think you can find your way back?"

Kevin scratched his head. "Quick map might help."

Tris jogged off. "There's some paper and pencils in the office."

"No problem," said Kevin. "Got the feeling you wanna head out tonight."

"Yeah, man." Rod shook his head. "Fuck this shithole. I'll have everyone ready to move. Drive this pig back as soon as you think it'll make it to that roadhouse."

"Got it." Kevin waved at Marty and Gene. "Gimme a hand with some welding."

Tris returned with a yellow pad and a standard pencil before heading over to replace the fuses in the back wheels. Rod sketched out a crude map of lines and arrows ticking off how many side streets to pass before turning right, another handful and a left, then a right on the next street.

"Y'oughta know where you are then." Rod handed him the paper.

Over the next several hours while the bus batteries charged, they affixed slats of scrap metal to the windows. Marty, claiming the only protective mask in the garage, appointed himself "King of Weldonia" and ran the acetylene torch after a quick lesson. Kevin got up on the roof and tore open the skylights, creating two square holes big enough to accommodate a person with ease. Inspiration hit him, and he dragged a pair of stepladders into the bus and had Marty weld them in place by each opening. Once they exhausted available scrap metal, and the oxy tank ran dry, Gene muttered something about taking a piss and walked off, headed for the rear of the garage. Marty tossed the welding mask, collected his SPAS, and followed.

SEVENTEEN PLUS ONE

Kevin relaxed in the driver's seat, studying the map he'd hung on a suction cup clip to the windshield. Late afternoon sun made the yellow paper glow. He smiled, tapping a finger over the charge meter, which read 72%. The dash clock claimed the time as 6 p.m. He spun around to face the interior, feeling confident about the irregular zigzag of metal banded across most of the side windows. An occasional gap where a bar fell off or never existed didn't bother him much, being too small for a body to squeeze through. *Marty wasn't getting graded on being 'neat.'*

Paul leaned in the door, grasping the railing on both sides of the steps. "How's it look?"

Kevin smiled. "It's holding a charge. How much time do we have?"

"Sun'll probably go down about eight or so." Paul looked at the sky. "Yeah 'bout that."

"I'd like to give it another hour before—"

Bang.

"Oh, shit." Paul took off running for the garage area.

Gene's screaming echoed out of the hollow garage followed by a series of rapid gunshots. After nine or ten sharp *bangs*, a heavy *boom* sounded.

"First wave," yelled Marty.

Kevin snagged the Enclave rifle from where he'd rested it against the wall under the side window, and ran after Paul.

"Fuck! Run!" yelled Gene from inside the garage.

"I got this!" shouted Marty, right before three heavy *booms* went off in a staccato ripple.

Tris came running from the office door, swinging the AK off her shoulder. Paul tucked up to the open garage door and aimed inside. He fired two shots, swiveled a bit to the right, and fired again. His Mp5 sounded feeble next to Marty's portable howitzer.

Kevin ran in a rightward circle from the charging station to get a firing angle in the garage door. He took a knee sixty-some yards away. The Enclave rifle's scope zoomed in automatically on Marty's back. Two doorways in the rear wall of the garage spat Infected into the room like meat oozing out of a grinder. Marty unloaded the SPAS into the crowd, cheering. Every so often, he'd yell "Headshot" or "Fatality." Each time a belch of orange came from the front of the shotgun, a detonation of blood and pulp flew.

Gene, apparently in a panic, ran face first into a tool cart and fell. Screaming, he rolled upright, seated, and offloaded his grenade launcher into the oncoming throng. As soon as the loud *foomp* sound went off, Marty flung his arm up, putting the trenchcoat over his face before an explosion showered him with gore. He backpedaled, gagging and puking on the run.

Kevin sighted on Marty's face, half tempted to put a bullet in his brain when no one would notice… but he had no blood or fleshy bits anywhere near his mouth or eyes. He switched aim and triggered twice, taking down a handful of Infected with each bullet as the slugs tore through three or four close-stacked bodies each.

An infected fell in from a hole on the roof, landing within feet of Gene. Another rifle fired twice, detonating a rotting woman's head. A patch of scalp trailing once-ginger hair sailed off like a frightened flying squirrel. Gene leapt to his feet, shrieking, and ran for the door while looking back over his shoulder.

"Gene, look out!" yelled Paul, firing a short burst into the two once-women pursuing him.

Gene tripped over the ridge of a maintenance pit under one of the jacks and fell out of sight. Orange light flashed on the walls of the sunken chamber as an M-16 went off on fully automatic. Tris joined in from the left with the AK, detonating about eight heads. Though she likely fired single shots, she triggered fast enough to sound like a machine gun. Kevin fired as fast as he could pull the trigger into the onrush. Between all the bullets flying, Infected bodies burst open and rained gore. Some fell by the wayside, trampled by the unrelenting press of an endless stream of disease-riddled people forcing their way in. The throng, despite the assault, spilled like a lava flow into the pit.

Gene's scream cut off with a gurgle as if he'd gone underwater.

Marty emptied the SPAS and seemed half tempted to jump in after him. He stood in place, screaming "Gene!" over and over.

"Come on!" yelled Tris. "He's gone!"

Paul somehow managed to contain himself, firing deliberate single shots into one Infected after the next.

"Time to go!" shouted Kevin. "This is fucked. Stop wasting ammo!"

Marty jogged out of the garage, looking dazed. He stuffed shells from his pocket into the SPAS and kept trying to force another one in after he'd filled it. Tris ran up behind him, yelling at him to get rid of his coat. While Paul and Tris fired into the crowd, he scooped shotgun shells out of his pockets and dropped them to the ground. Once he emptied his pockets, he peeled the coat off and flung it.

Tris looked him over. "I don't see any blood on you."

Marty stared at her. "Gene's gone... Gene's not supposed to die; he's one of the player characters."

She grabbed his arm and dragged him to the bus. Paul hustled over to the shotgun ammo and collected it in the thigh pockets of his fatigues. With the Infected occupied by the momentary distraction of a screaming body in a pit, Kevin ran for the bus, disconnected the charging cable, and sprinted to the driver's seat.

Tris shoved Marty up the stairs. Paul followed, headed right away for the rear ladder and climbing it high enough to allow him to aim over the edge. Kevin grabbed the wheel and exhaled. *Here goes.* He shifted into reverse and stepped on the pedal. The lights faltered, but the bus didn't go anywhere.

"Oh, shit." Tris jumped on to the forward ladder.

Kevin stomped the accelerator to the floor. The bus lurched backward, causing Tris to swing away from the rungs for a second, screaming. Marty fell into a seat, his forlorn stare going into space. Creaks and groans shuddered in the frame as Kevin maneuvered the bus into a turn. Tires chirped when he slammed it into drive and charged the yard gate. The bus laughed at the chain link fence, launching it against the brick wall to the left.

Paul's Mp5 went off a few more times and fell quiet. An empty magazine clattered to the floor inside the bus a few seconds before he reloaded.

Marty roared. "I'm gonna kill them all!"

"Save your ammo," yelled Kevin.

Small cars bounced like tiddlywinks off the front bumper, spinning into collisions with walls or bashing through storefronts. The sand-filled construction barriers burst open on impact. He veered left, brushing the tail end of a box truck. Paul's legs swung off the ladder, but he held on to the roof.

Not prepared for the boggy braking, Kevin came close to crashing into the face of a building on the first right turn. He took out a few more parked cars, tossing old fallout ash into the air. Cracks splintered the windshield. Something flew up and slammed into the left side with a hollow metallic *whump*, but stalled on the scrap metal.

Tris slid down the ladder. "Road's clear behind us."

Marty climbed to the roof, armpit deep in the hole, muttering 'sons of bitches' in an endless loop.

Kevin didn't bother trying to avoid the crude barricades of dead cars, relying on mass and a steady, albeit slow, pace to push them out of the way. Paul twitched, but held his fire.

"Couple behind us," yelled Marty. "Four blocks back, looking confused."

Oh, good. He's sane again. He counted side streets and cornered left where Rod's map indicated. The next right put him on Fullerton about a half mile from the building. With the street relatively clear, he accelerated for a little while until the building came into view. He brought the bus to a halt, half turned into the little parking lot.

"Move the Challenger." He gave Tris a light nudge.

She blinked. "Really? You want me—"

"No time. Go."

Tris darted out the door, ran around the bus, and hurried to the car. The mere sight of it made him long for a vehicle with agility and acceleration. She hopped in, and within a few seconds, rolled it backward out of the way. Kevin eased the bus forward, parking it as close to under the ladder as the first floor columns would allow.

He slapped it in park and climbed the ladder after Marty, onto the roof. Patricia's head poked out the fifth-floor window.

Kevin waved. "Change of plans. This train is heading out *now*."

"They're coming," yelled Marty.

Patricia nodded, and disappeared into the building, shouting orders.

The two men and the Asian woman who had first met him shimmied down the flexible ladder to the bus. Marty and Paul helped guide them to safety. Six more people, three women, two men, and Cody, clambered down soon after. Kevin hovered at the side of the flexible ladder, spinning in a paranoid's dance, and aiming the Enclave rifle at every shift in shadow. Cody seemed intent to stay on the roof with a handgun out, but Paul stuffed him down into the hatch.

A child's wailing at the top caused a delay. Star shrieked and threw a tantrum when they brought her to the window. "I don't wanna!" echoed in the canyon of skyscrapers.

"Duct tape," yelled Marty.

Danielle backed off, letting others go while she tried to quiet the girl. Nine more men came down. The last, in his seventies, lost his grip on the ladder when his shoe slipped. He fell three stories, landing flat on his back on the bus roof. He made no attempt to move, face twisted in a grimace of pain. Paul and one of the fifth-floor sentries carried him to a hatch and lowered in him inside. An elderly woman made it down intact, followed by Dennis, Patricia, and two more women in their early twenties, one of whom screamed at the top of her lungs.

Everyone turned to look where she pointed. A handful of Infected, all in shredded business suits, crept around the corner of the building by the front of the bus. Marty, Patricia, and three of the fifth-floor sentries opened fire. Star, wailing and sniveling, crept out onto the ladder at Danielle's prodding. Kevin moved under, rifle over his back, arms out. The girl clamped on to the swaying ladder, refusing to climb. Gunfire roared everywhere. The younger women hurried down the hatch into the bus. Cody tried to climb up, but Paul roared at him to stay down.

A stream of obscenities flew from Marty's mouth before and after each discharge of the SPAS.

Danielle shouted, "Star, honey, you have to go now!"

The child stared up at her mother and started to climb down. Her trembling shook the flexible ladder, making the tail end whip against the bus.

"Come on, Star. You're okay. Don't look down. One foot after the other," yelled Dennis.

When Star reached about halfway, Danielle backed out the window and got on the ladder. An unusually loud moan drew Kevin's attention to the shambling throng as a rotting man pulled a handful of gore from his chest and hurled it. A wet *splat* came from the right. Kevin ducked and spun that way. One of the fifth-floor sentries had a patch of Infected skin on his face, blood everywhere. Dennis pushed him to the far edge of the roof.

"I'm sorry, Tarik…"

The man spat to the right and gagged. He smacked his lips, making a face as though he tasted something foul. When realization dawned, he sent a defeated look down and handed his rifle to Dennis.

"Ain't right. They throwing pieces now." Tarik closed his eyes and nodded. "Don't wanna be one of them fuckers. Do it."

Dennis shot Tarik in the chest, and he fell backward off the bus. People inside screamed.

"Watch for that shit," yelled Dennis. "Virus-bearing projectiles."

Metallic clattering announced a hand grenade skipping across the parking lot from the direction of the Challenger. Tris had tossed it to the side of the building, out of sight. When it exploded, a spray of crimson and pieces rained. Fortunately, the building shielded the survivors from particles.

A surge of Infected swarmed around the building from the other side, overwhelming the continuous barrage of fire.

Marty yelled, "I'm out!" and waved his shotgun around.

Dennis tossed him Tarik's M-16.

Star's high-pitched scream seemed to freeze time. At the level of the second story, she hung by one hand. An Infected had made it past the defensive fire and gotten a hand on the tail end of the ladder. The rotting woman yanked and jerked on it, staring at the little girl dangling overhead like a dog after a bit of filet. Kevin reacted fastest, shooting the crazed Infected in the face.

The ladder sprang upward when the dead woman's weight no longer burdened it. Star's grip failed, and she fell. Kevin's grab passed an instant too slow. The child bounced off the corner of the bus roof and hit the parking lot. Two infected surged toward her.

"Star!" Danielle shouted and let go of the ladder.

She fell three stories onto the back of a lumbering Asian man with no skin left on his face. Her impact knocked the Infected flat, his fingers inches from Star's toes. The child shrieked and backpedaled, heading for the recessed wall of the first floor—away from the bus.

Kevin stared at the girl, and at the nine or ten Infected desperately trying to rush her. Without thinking, he jumped to the ground and charged to her. He skidded to a halt at her side, one-handing the rifle and firing at the oncoming group as fast as he could pull the trigger.

"Mommy!" screamed Star.

Kevin glanced to his right. Three infected advanced, seconds from swarming over Danielle. Dennis flung himself off the bus, flying sideways into a tackle that took all three of them down. Star let off a scream that felt as if it ruptured Kevin's left eardrum. The stream of Infected coming around the building by the front end of the bus trailed off to one man. A fast-walking figure with dark skin, wearing pink shorts and a tank top, loped into view. He had a thin and lanky build, but stood close to seven feet tall. Most of a puffy afro dangled against the side of his head on a strand of skin, exposing skull. He moaned, head tilted to an unnatural angle, and headed right for Kevin.

Star shrieked and lapsed into hysterics at the sight of him.

"Oh, God!" Danielle took a step as if to run *to* the Infected man, but backed against the side of the bus. "Carl!"

Kevin started at a flash of white that zoomed by. Star vanished with a brief squeak of a scream. Kevin, on the verge of total panic, spun toward the motion. Tris carried the terrified girl at a superhuman sprint to the bus door. A burst of automatic fire came from high and right. Carl's chest splattered open. Reason returned to the man's brown eyes. For an instant, he stared at Kevin and then convulsed as if to vomit.

A symbiote serpent burst up from Carl's mouth. The writhing, jet-black creature seemed to zero in on Kevin, staring for a half second before it launched from the dead man's throat. Kevin twisted to the side, swinging his rifle. His first (and hopefully only) attempt at playing eel baseball resulted in a line drive that splattered the creature into the jagged metal bars on the side of the bus, where it draped like a limp hose, twisting and squirming. Silver ooze leaked from numerous slices in the fleshy sheath the nanites constructed. Three corpses rolled away from Dennis, killed by Paul and Marty from the roof. The Asian woman and Patricia stood at the rear end of the bus, firing at an onrushing crowd a block away.

Kevin *almost* shit his pants at the sight of the street packed wall to wall with thousands upon thousands of infected. On autopilot, he sprinted to Dennis and Danielle. "Go! Get in!"

Danielle ran toward the bus door, rushing toward the wails of her daughter inside. Dennis didn't move.

"Dennis... get on the fucking bus!" Kevin pushed him.

"No." He turned to face Kevin. A bite hole in his cheek exposed several teeth, and blood streamed down his arm from two more wounds.

"Shit."

Dennis didn't seem the least bit frightened or sad. He glanced to the left at Danielle, safe inside the bus, and smiled before looking at Kevin's rifle. "Do it. I'm dead already."

The second and a half Kevin stared into the man's eyes felt like forever. *I can't.* He pulled the Glock-17 out from under his left arm and offered it. "Seventeen in the mag, one in the pipe."

Dennis took the gun. "Get them outta here. Tell Tris her father was a good man. He wasn't wrong... and I'm sorry." He walked past the bus, headed for the oncoming crowd.

People atop the bus with weapons stared at their leader's injuries. Funeral quiet, broken only by the fast approaching moans and shuffling noises of Infected, fell over everyone.

"Sorry?" yelled Kevin.

Dennis stopped. "For helping them make this God-awful virus. I thought the resistance could stop it..."

Kevin couldn't move. Half paralyzed by his terror of Infected, half by his inability to process what the man said. Dennis shot the closest infected in the face. A fat man fell, causing a minor domino effect to spread over the front of the swarm.

"I'm here. Come get me you rotting bastards. Come to Daddy!" Dennis shot another one and headed north toward the nearby ash-covered park, still yelling and taunting.

"Two," muttered Kevin.

"Nowhere for me to go!" yelled Dennis. He fired again. Another Infected moaned and slumped dead.

The last of the survivors hurried down the ladder as Dennis hustled away, attracting the attention of the crowd. With each shot, Kevin muttered a number. Soon Marty joined in.

"That's it you stupid bastards. Come and get me!" *Bang. Bang.*

"Thirteen, fourteen," said Kevin and Marty at the same time.

Dennis, leading the flood of Infected, vanished amid dead trees.

Bang.

"Fifteen," muttered Kevin.

Even people inside the bus had caught on, and repeated it.

Bang. A distant gurgling moan echoed off nearby buildings.

"Sixteen," whispered everyone.

Silence hung thick for almost a full minute.

Bang.

Kevin lowered his head. *Seventeen.*

Bang.

No one spoke the word. Everyone knew where the last bullet went.

ABSOLUTON

K evin came close to shitting his pants a second time when Tris grabbed his arm from behind. The lingering moment of silence gave way to fear and worry. None of the people on the roof wanted to fire at the confused crowd of Infected three blocks away. They shuffled about, waving their heads as if trying to smell people on the wind. Dennis had led them far enough away to momentarily lose track of the survivors. He glanced at the window, at the muted screams of a child. Inside, Danielle kept her hand over Star's mouth and tried to rock her. Fog on the windows reduced most of the people to blurs of color.

"Car or Bus?" asked Kevin.

"What?" Tris blinked.

"You wanna drive the car or the bus?" Kevin grabbed her arms. "I don't wanna let go of you."

She sniffled.

"I got the bus," said Paul. "I can drive this pig. Cover us."

Paul hustled to the forward ladder and hurried to the driver's seat. Kevin hesitated for a second before grabbing Tris by the arm and hauling her toward the Challenger. Their footsteps echoed loud enough to draw notice. A few Infected outside the parking lot let off loud moans and proceeded to walk repeatedly into the chest-high stone wall. They bumped and jostled, staring at him with their arms raised, as if they couldn't figure out why forward motion wasn't happening.

"Good thing they're stupid sometimes." Kevin threw the Enclave rifle in the back seat and jumped in.

The bus backed out onto the road, stopped, and pulled away.

As soon as Tris got in, the Challenger's tires smoked. Kevin let off the accelerator enough to let them catch and squealed out onto the road.

"Oops. Damn, that thing's a pig. Gotta floor it to notice anything."

Infected came racing out of side streets and from between cars, flinging themselves at the bus. Muzzle flare lit up the windows, as bits of glass and gore sprayed from both sides. Kevin swerved right, firing the M60s into a large pack a few seconds before the bus smashed them like biological bowling pins.

Eight or nine clung to the side, holding on to and impaled by the spiked metal slats. Kevin dodged out of the way of an upside down car sticking into the street, swerved back into the right lane, and accelerated. Marty climbed up and roof-surfed the bus, shaving two Infected from the side with the SPAS.

Kevin accelerated, reaching over his head for the incendiary trigger cable. He caught up to the front end, yanked the cord, and slammed on the brakes. Bright orange filled the driver's side window for two seconds, until the bus passed, and he let go. A stripe of fire clung to the tangled mass of welded metal and diseased bodies; one by one, the Infected fell away and broke apart into burning chunks. Kevin swung behind the bus to avoid contaminating the undercarriage and tucked up on the rear bumper.

Marty held the SPAS over his head in both arms, pumping it up and down in some manner of triumphant salute. The influx of Infected ceased coming from in front of them and poured into the road behind them. Kevin flicked on the rearview monitor and pondered opening up with the trunk guns, but even at the bus's pathetic 54 mph, the horde had no shot in hell of catching up on foot.

"Is Marty a risk? He's acting odd."

"He's always been like that. He thinks he's living inside a video game." Tris exhaled. "I… think he's okay. I didn't see any blood on his face. His coat took the splash. For a heavy guy, he's got good reflexes."

He broke out in a sweat, remembering how the infection had spread last time. One person too curious… too careless. Kevin stared into space for a few seconds, reliving the worst parts of his childhood in short flashes. Tris's hand on his arm snapped him back to the present.

"Hey… I can't believe you ran *at* infected."

Kevin swallowed a mouthful of saliva that had collected under his tongue. "Yeah… That kid screaming…"

She squeezed his hand. "You owned your fear. You saved her."

He forced a smile despite trembling, trying not to see the faces of the two teens who realized they were doomed, or hear their mother's screaming as they walked away to kill themselves. "Dennis said something I'm not sure if I should tell you."

"Doctor Andrews?" Her expression fell somber. "It's not fair."

He pulled left into the oncoming lane and sped up until they were even with the driver's seat. Paul looked frustrated. Tris rolled her window down and waved.

Once Paul opened the sliding glass, Kevin yelled. "Gonna take point. Follow me."

Paul gave a thumbs up.

"Yeah… Doctor Andrews." He pulled in front of the bus with about a three car-length cushion between the two vehicles. "Keep an eye out to the rear, 'kay?"

Tris leaned to her right and watched the door mirror. "Sure. So what about him?"

"Before he walked off… he wanted me to tell you he was sorry. He helped them make the Virus."

"Yeah. I know. He had a lot of guilt."

Kevin exhaled. "Kind of ironic he's killed by his own crea—" He snapped his head to the right, staring at her. "Wait a minute… he was Enclave. Didn't he have the vaccine?"

"Yes."

"So he wasn't sick." He shifted his attention back to the flashes of painted white lines on the road. "He wanted to die…" He growled. "Shit, I should've stopped him."

"If you helped inflict *that* on people who managed to survive a nuclear war… would *you* be able to live with it? I guess he trusted us to get them out of here. The Resistance failed. He kept himself going to help those people, and now they're safe. Maybe he wanted absolution." She pulled the mag out of her AK to count bullets. "I wonder if it was him."

"If what was him?" Kevin eyed the oncoming forest with suspicion, half-expecting to see an Enclave aircraft overhead.

"All those religious passages written on the stairwell wall." She inserted the magazine again. "Sorry I used so much ammo."

"Don't worry about it." Kevin eyed the horizon, and scraps of junk and shrubs on either side of the paving. "Those people aren't safe yet." Ten minutes or so of silence later, he glanced at her. "Sorry. I know he had answers to questions you didn't even ask yet."

"Yeah, well." Tris looked ready to cry for a second, but emotion faded to determination. "Maybe I'll be happier not asking them." She took the magazine out of her AK again and popped more bullets into it. "At least we got them out of Chicago."

"Gene… Poor clumsy bastard." Kevin rolled his head around to stretch his neck.

Tris bowed her head.

TWO HOURS LATER, OVERGROWN GRASSY FIELDS BLURRED PAST ON EITHER side of the road. He squeezed the wheel, making his gloves creak. The bus kept up. Nothing in the rearview screen hinted at any problems. Tris fidgeted.

"What?" asked Kevin.

"Gotta pee, but don't stop. I can wait." She sat high in the seat with her back to the door, looking around in a three-sixty. "It's too damn quiet out here. I don't like it."

"We're pretty far east. Isn't much out here for anyone to steal. If there *is* anyone living here, it's an isolated family or two living off the land. We can stop if you want."

She looked over with a hint of fear in her eyes. "Didn't go so well for me last time."

"Stay close to the car then." He pulled over.

The bus came to a stop behind him. When Kevin got out, Paul shrugged from behind the wheel. Kevin pointed at his crotch and off the side of the road. Paul nodded, and turned away, presumably announcing the piss break to the rest of the survivors. Tris brought her AK and only moved a few feet off the road. Kevin kept her in view out of the corner of his eye, enough to remain alert for threats.

Several people made hasty trips outside to relieve themselves. A few men let fly from the bus roof. Marty and Patricia pried charred bodies off the window slats. Eventually, those who needed to had made use of the grass, and the convoy resumed.

A touch over five hours after leaving Chicago, Kevin pulled into the same parking space he'd used twice before at Whazzat's roadhouse. He hopped out and waved his arms around, directing Paul to back up to a space, so the charging cable would reach the plug in the rear. When the bus stopped and the door opened, Kevin leaned in. Cody, asleep, sat in his father's lap, clinging like a boy half his age.

"It's almost two in the morning. Go 'head and shut it down for now. If it takes a shit, not a big deal. There's no Infected for miles around here."

Paul let go of the large steering wheel and cradled his son. A moment later, he sniffled. "Thank you."

Kevin looked down at his boots. "Credit ain't mine. All I did was fix a stupid battery." He backed out of the bus. "I'm goin' inside for food and a bed."

The Challenger locked and emitted a *chirp*. Kevin smiled. Tris walked up to his side, sans-AK, but she had the katana on her back. Patricia plodded up to the barrier between the driver and the rest of the bus, a grim look on her face.

"Artie didn't make it."

Paul shifted out from under Cody, leaving the sleeping boy in the driver's chair. After a few seconds' hesitation, he pushed the shutdown button and the bus went dark. Patricia walked back inside, followed by Paul.

Kevin headed for the roadhouse, pausing by the front door to watch them carry the remains of the seventy-ish man who fell off the ladder out into the field. Everyone filed out in a line and followed in a procession.

Tris pulled her hair off her face, squinting into the breeze. "Should we go?"

"Nah. It's their moment." He pushed the door open and went in.

KEVIN RAISED AN ARM OVER HIS FACE IN A FUTILE ATTEMPT TO BLOCK OUT the dreaded daystar. Tris gave him a light shove and climbed out of the bed they'd shared. Nothing had happened but sleep. Three in the morning plus the rebound crash from too much adrenaline had put him out within seconds of head-to-pillow contact.

He moaned. "What time is it?"

"Almost noon." She rustled around for a few minutes. When she leaned over him again, she had the plain white tank top on. "Come on. We gotta get going."

"I can see your tits right through that." He grinned.

"It's not covered in blood." She wadded up the leather shirt and tucked it under her arm. "I'm going to check out the bus before they try and turn it on."

"'Kay."

He left his arm balanced across his eyes for a minute that turned into ten. *Crap. I'm going to sit here all day if I don't move now.* Kevin dragged himself upright, dressed, and stumbled to the food court. The survivors more or less filled the place. He dropped a pair of coins on the counter, walking away a short time later with two skewers of dust-hopper meat. People offered smiles, nods, and raised hands as he walked among the tables, taking his food outside.

"Hey," yelled Whazzat. "Mek sure ya bring back 'dem skewers."

"Right," said Kevin.

"Whazzat?"

Kevin laughed on the way to the bus. All four wheel motors' hatch covers were propped open like awnings on thin metal rods. Tris crouched under the flap of the right side rear, a few inches from a tattered strip of burned flesh dangling from a jagged slat. He found another direction to look in while taking a bite of his food.

"How is it?"

She leaned up and let her knees touch the ground. "Well, one good thing about the Infected is they don't shoot at us. The motors are fine. Big question is if the system will handle the shock of powering up. The voltage regulator is the problem. We had this thing charging all night. I was so tired I didn't think about it... might've failed to stop charging when it was full."

"I hate fire." Kevin chuckled.

"Stupid mistake, but no smoke is a good sign." She shut the semicircular hatch over the wheel hub and kicked it to make sure it closed all the way. "If it didn't overcharge, it might start."

He stood in place eating while she ran around to close the other three wheels before climbing half in to the battery compartment. Survivors made their way outside and gathered in a crowd about ten paces from the bus door. One or two went off to water the grass. Danielle looked like she'd been up all night crying, but had put on a strong face for her daughter. The six-year-old seemed to have forgotten about the mad dash through streets packed with rotting people and flashed a warm smile at Kevin.

He turned sideways to slip past the others coming out and handed

Whazzat back the empty skewers. The old man nodded and traded him a large black coffee.

"On th' house. Thanks fer bringin' in so much biz." Whazzat let out a wheezing chuckle that reeked of whiskey, chewing tobacco, and half-digested dust-hopper.

Kevin cringed, but smiled. "Thanks."

Outside, Paul paced around the bus door. Cody hovered nearby, arms folded, looking lost and despondent.

Kevin cleared his throat to avoid startling the man as he approached. "You can calm down. Zoe's fine. The settlement she's in is safe."

Paul exhaled. "I never should've let her go alone."

"Sounds like your people were dying off at a pretty scary rate." Kevin exhaled. "You wanted to protect her."

Tris came around the front end. "I don't see any obvious problems with the bus."

Paul mumbled. "I... dunno if it was the right thing to do. Might never have seen her again."

Kevin glanced left, at one of the doors covering a luggage compartment along the ground. It wasn't quite closed. "How sneaky are Infected?" He pulled the .45 and crept over, took a breath, and flung the hatch up with his boot. A dim rectangular space held only dust and one suitcase. "Damn. Must've rattled open on the road." Thoughts of Zoe made him tense up. What if some other kid hid in it and no one found him. He stooped to reach in, unsettled by the eerie feeling of being watched. As if some kid's ghost sat next to the case he'd died in. He held his breath, reaching for the handle.

"What's up?" asked Tris.

"Gah!" Kevin jumped and hit his head on the hatch. "Dammit."

"Sorry." She jumped back.

He lifted the lid, finding it full of little books and boxes. With a sigh of relief, he let the lid down and stood.

"Whoa, you okay?" Tris blinked.

Kevin rubbed the bridge of his nose. "Yeah. Just... imagining things. You believe in ghosts?"

Tris shrugged one shoulder. "Never thought about it."

He holstered the pistol and slammed the hatch.

"Okay, everyone wait there while I hit the button," said Paul. "If this thing blows up..."

"No way, Paul." A Hispanic man in his later forties approached, shaking his head. "You got a kid to get back to. I'll do it."

"Harold…" Paul held his hands up.

"No arguments." The older man brushed past him and climbed into the bus.

Seconds later, the interior lights flickered on. The familiar *buzz* alarm to warn the driver that a charging cable remained connected went off. Before long, the survivors boarded the bus, Kevin crawled behind the wheel of his car, and they drove off.

IMPASSE

Kevin swung north, skirting Boulder as much as he could while following a small dirt road south through sparse trees to where Route 119 cut west. Within a half hour, the welcome sight of a pair of dump truck beds greeted him. The same pewter-haired older man waved from the left side of the gate, gesturing at someone out of sight on the ground.

The trucks started, and a few seconds later, the beds closed to the frames with the grating screech of steel sliding over pavement. He drove into Nederland, past the pitiful little 'circle,' and parked near the orange building on the corner, which apparently served as the city hall. The bus squealed to a stop close behind and let off a hiss as the parking brake kicked in.

Word had apparently preceded their arrival. Zoe came sprinting down the road from the direction of the red house, followed some distance behind by Ann. Paul tripped and fell down the bus steps in his haste to get out, managing to get up to his knees before the little blonde missile collided with him, screaming "Daddy!"

Both father and daughter burst into tears.

Cody ran outside and jumped into the hug.

Tris, grinning from ear to ear, leaned up and kissed Kevin. Survivors disembarked, gathering in the open lot on the other side of the street between two rusting excavators. A few minutes later, Bill cleared his throat.

Kevin looked up from the kiss. "Found a couple more people wanting a ride."

Bill chuckled.

An ear-piercing child's scream followed a fleshy *thump*.

Guns rattled from all around as Kevin whirled. A male figure apparently made out of the same bricks as the building across the parking lot from the orange one held Zoe off the ground, boxy pistol to the side of her head. Paul lay on his front, twitching, not quite unconscious. Tiny blue sparks danced over his back from a spray of small metal Xs. The sight of them tightened the muscles on the back of Kevin's neck from remembered agony.

The man holding Zoe shimmered; brick texture gave way to black Enclave armor. Four more figures stepped away from nearby walls, neatly surrounding Bill, the four Nederland militia with him, and all of the survivors.

"Change of plan," said the man holding Zoe. He ignored her kicking and squirming. "We would rather Tris accompany us alive, back home where she belongs. If I see one of you Neanderthals move wrong, everyone dies, starting with this wretched little grub."

Kevin glared.

Tris held her hands up as tears ran down her cheeks. "Okay. I'll go. Don't hurt any of these people."

"Tris… they don't want to kidnap you, they want to *kill* you."

She closed her eyes. "I'm sorry. I can't risk these people for—"

Boom.

Two lines of blood exploded from the man's helmet; a smaller geyser spurted from the left temple toward the bus, a larger torrent flew from the back of the head in the opposite direction. Zoe slipped from his dead arms, landing on all fours.

Kevin didn't bother going for his .45. He sprinted forward as gunfire erupted everywhere. In a not too smooth roll, he landed on top of Zoe and slapped his hand down on the Enclave pistol that had, seconds before, been against the side of her head. Survivors as well as the Nederland militia scrambled for cover while trading shots with the armored figures.

Zoe struggled to get away from him and crawl to her father. Before her dress tore off in his hand, Kevin traded a fistful of denim for clamping a hand around her ankle while firing at a man in black armor perched behind one of the derelict backhoes. The high-tech pistol felt and sounded like any other gun he'd used, though the trigger clicked like an electric button. Still, bullets failed to penetrate the suit, appearing as silvery-grey dots on the deep black.

"Lemme go!" shouted Zoe.

"No!" Kevin dragged her back and pinned her under his hip. "He's electrified. It'll hurt you."

Tris's Beretta burped like an automatic weapon somewhere behind and to his left. Screams of pain mixed with curses and commands to 'get down' or 'cover me' in various voices. Heavy *booms* thundered over the street, a sound as though someone had rigged a cannon for automatic. Blood squirted from the head of the man Kevin's borrowed pistol failed to hurt as the body spiraled to the ground in a heap. Cracked like an eggshell, the helmet split open revealing a stunned expression.

Kevin rolled over, dragging Zoe into his lap and scooting to put his back to the front end of the bus. The child fought as hard as her little limbs could fight, but he held her down. Tris wrestled with a larger male figure in black armor. He overpowered her, forcing her onto her back. Kevin shot him in the helmet and shoulder, but the Enclave soldier ignored the pistol as if it spat wads of soaked paper instead of bullets. He gathered Tris's wrists in one hand, and drew his sidearm.

Boom.

A geyser of red sprayed out of his chest, leaving a tunnel through him the size of a man's thumb. Tris flung the body to the side and crawled under the rear end of the Challenger. Gunfire trailed off, a few stray pops lingered over several seconds until it got quiet.

A woman moaned in pain. Multiple male voices growled.

"They're down," yelled a woman.

Bill shouted, "Nobody move. There's one more."

Kevin stared at the gaping hole in the back of the man who'd pounced Tris.

Answering shouts followed: "I don't see anyone." "Nothing here." "Got shit."

He set the pistol down on the road, cradled the still-struggling Zoe in both arms, and peered around the corner of the bus. One of the luggage compartments was open. *Son of a bitch.*

"Shots came from that way," said an unfamiliar woman.

"Zara?" yelled Kevin.

"What?" Bill popped up from behind a dead car parked on the side of the orange building.

Tris, flat on her belly under the Challenger, widened her eyes. She looked apologetic and guilty.

A woman's voice came from the roof of the bus. "Yes."

"What now?" asked Kevin.

"You can tell Tris we're even."

Kevin looked up at a shimmery blur against the sky in the approximate shape of a helmet stuck over the edge above him. "So…"

Zara raised one hand. "I've got two rounds left and I'm not planning to waste them on anyone here."

Bill stood. "Who the hell are you talking to?"

"It's clear." Kevin got to his feet, cradling Zoe. "This one's friendly."

Gasps sounded among the survivors and militia as Zara's armored suit turned black, causing her to materialize out of thin air. She climbed down from the bus roof, holding her five-foot-long sniper rifle in as non-threatening a posture as one could conceivably hold such a weapon. Her helmet disassembled itself and collapsed into the pod behind her neck.

"It's spent." Zara nodded at Paul. "They won't shock her now."

Kevin released Zoe, who ran over and jumped on her father, sobbing. Militia emerged from cover and set to the task of tending to the wounded. At a quick glance, Kevin counted nine wounded and two, maybe three, friendlies dead. Marty clutched a bloody left shin. Patricia clamped a hand over her left bicep; blood oozed through her fingers.

Bill yelled and waved his arms, directing people about. A woman with Native American features and green camouflage pointed a Colt M4 at Zara from a cautious distance.

Tris crawled out from under the car and approached Kevin and Zara. "I thought you wanted to go back to comfort."

Zara looked down. "You were right. They didn't want to come get me. I sat around that stinking hovel for days, but not one person showed up until you came back with that… monstrosity. I had no idea the Enclave was planning an ambush."

Kevin chuckled. "I figured that when you shot them."

The militiawoman lowered her colt. "Sergeant Vasquez? What about this one?"

Bill looked at Zara, then Kevin. "What's her story?"

Kevin explained as others carted the wounded away. Paul woke up around the time Kevin got to the point where they'd left her tied at the roadhouse. Zoe's sobbing became gleeful cheering when her father 'returned from the dead.'

Zara frowned. "These people don't look half as bad as I thought they would."

"What did you expect?" asked Bill.

"Face paint, dirt, minimal clothing, spears, cannibalism…" Zara shrugged. "You know, total primitive."

Bill smirked. "We try."

Crackling emanated from the helmet of the man who'd pinned Tris. Kevin tilted his head.

"… status report. What the hell is going on out there? Why is there so much red on the status monitor?"

Tris took a knee by the corpse and squeezed something at his neck. The front of the helmet split into dozens of metal slivers, opening like insectoid legs to expose a pale face with blood draining from the mouth and nose. Bright silvery electronics around glowing domes on either side of the head flickered with light and projected a holographic screen a few inches into the air, bearing a man's face over a field of blue.

Nathan's annoyance melted to cool hostility. "Tris."

"Asshole." She glared.

"Hey, that's me." Kevin pointed a thumb at his chest.

"Well, you are certainly proving to be an unusually stubborn thorn." Nathan clucked his tongue.

"Why am I so important to you? You know the data's useless. I'm no threat."

"But you had The Cure in your head all along." Nathan flashed a saccharin smile. A band of shift slid down the digital image from right to left. He chuckled.

"Okay, you're a complete hardon, but I have to at least say that was clever." Kevin pointed at the screen. "You're still a piece of shit for doing that to her."

Nathan ignored him. "Oh, well. I suppose I'll have to keep trying."

"Why?" Tris yelled. "I'm not coming back. What are you afraid of? I've got nothing you need."

Kevin put an arm around her. "The kind of dick that would put *music* in your implant probably can't sleep at night leaving a piece of his plan out of place."

An imperious frown spread over Nathan's lips. "For a cretin, your powers of observation are remarkably sharp. Hmm, I wonder if I can offer you something to put my mind at ease. Ten thousand coins perhaps?"

"Not happening." Kevin glared.

Tris fumed for a few seconds. "So this is just some petty revenge thing? I didn't even *do* anything to you. The Resistance is already gone."

"It's amusing me." He smiled.

Her eyes narrowed. "This is an official frequency, isn't it. You know the Council of Four has software listeners that react to people saying certain things like oh, '*The Council of Four.*'"

Nathan turned pale. He swiped at the right of the screen, though nothing changed.

"Oh, now you're worried." Tris leaned closer to the screen. "Can't kill the channel? That means they're listening. Do you think the *Council of Four* would approve that you've gotten nine or ten Enclave citizens killed on a pointless vanity quest to kill me when doing so provides zero value? I'm sure they're not going to be happy."

Static laced the screen in thin, drifting lines. A sixty-ish woman with pewter hair in a tight bun and a pronounced expression of displeasure appeared. Black epaulets bore silver bars atop the grey shoulders of a military-looking jacket.

"Director Gerhardt." Tris stiffened. "Forgive me if I don't bow... but I'm pretty sure my citizenship has been terminated. That's okay. I don't want it back."

Despite being holographic, the woman's steel-grey eyes seemed to drill holes in reality. "Nathan..." One eyebrow rose a quarter inch. "You will leave this little one to suffer in the Wildlands without further squandering of resources. Or the next precious life lost over her will be yours."

The floating panel faded to black.

Tris put a hand over mouth. She looked like a little girl who'd just gotten her annoying older brother in trouble and wanted so much to laugh at him.

"I wasn't expecting that." Kevin pulled her close. "Maybe you can stop worrying now?"

She laid her head on his chest. "Maybe. There's still bandits, giant scorpions, slavers, Glimmertown, Infected, disease, starvation, radiation—"

He kissed her.

"Giant scorpions?" asked an unfamiliar male voice. "Where?"

"They're always in the historical documentaries," said Zara.

Kevin chuckled, but Tris didn't stop kissing him.

"Get a room," yelled Bill.

Tris leaned back and stared into his eyes. "That's a great idea."

A SLIGHT MISCALCULATION

K evin drained the jar of homemade beer and set it on the table. Ann lugged a whole roast dust-hopper over in a baking tray and set it in the middle of the table. Tris sat close at his left, with Bill at the far end of the table on one side. Paul, Zoe, and Cody crammed together on the facing side, and an open seat on the right waited for Ann.

Three days had passed since their arrival, and the Chicago survivors all decided to settle in Nederland. Few had anywhere else to be, and none of them had a way out other than walking. Talk of Infected as close as Boulder—and a lack of high-rise buildings here—didn't go over well, though a population nearing four hundred plus ample weapons and a lot of empty ground helped.

One thing Infected seemed to detest was wide-open space.

Kevin shivered. *They love to leap out from dark places.*

Bill carved the dust-hopper, and soon everyone had a plate piled high with meat and vegetables. After a few minutes of face-stuffing, Kevin smiled at Zoe. She seemed like an entirely different person from the creepy little waif that gave him nightmares. He kept back from the conversation going around the table. Paul discussed his request to join the militia with Bill, which seemed appealing to both sides.

As Bill cleared empty plates from the table, Tris got up to help, ignoring protests about being a guest.

Paul reached over the table and dropped a heavy sock with a knot in it in front of Kevin. It jingled with coins. "Well, a deal's a deal. I made a slight error in my math. That's about seventeen hundred coin, not quite the two thousand I'm supposed to have. It's all I got left. I want you to take it." He stood. "Oh... Gimme a second."

Tris leaned over, forehead to Kevin's shoulder. "Well, there's your Roadhouse."

Kevin picked the sock up, twirling it around a finger before letting it drop. Cody stared at him with a face that said 'please don't kill my dad.' Zoe bared all her teeth in a huge grin, and tilted her head.

Paul returned with a doll and sat. To Zoe's horror, he turned its dress inside out and stuck a finger into the hollow head. After extricating a bit of folded paper, he handed the doll to Zoe, who glared at him as she fixed the little dress back to rights. Paul slid the paper over the blue and white checkered tablecloth.

Ann set a pitcher of home brewed beer down.

"A while back, I found a cache of prewar swag in Kansas. This place had a bigass warehouse full of everything you can think of. Last time I was there, the building looked untouched. That's a map to the place. I got no interest in running around anymore. Course, you'll need something bigger than that car of yours to collect stuff in... like a bus."

"And a little help..." Kevin pushed the sock back to Paul. "Keep it. You got a family, you'll need it more than me."

"Not really a whole lot of use for coins here," said Bill. "I suppose that might change if we start dealin' with the outside world... but for now..."

Kevin smiled. "I ain't in no hurry. That's the funny thing about a long journey. Sometimes where you think you're going isn't where you really want to go." He put an arm around Tris and pulled her close. "A 'house ain't the most important thing."

She stared at him with a mixture of shock, adoration, and tears in her eyes.

"You sure?" asked Paul.

Kevin twisted the folded map in his fingers, turning it over, letting the light play off the yellowing notebook page. He kept his right arm firmly around Tris, flicked the map to the table and picked up his beer. "Yeah. What's one more run?"

A GOOD RUN OF BAD LUCK

K evin leaned against the front left fender of the Challenger, snapping 7.62x51 ammo into metal clips, adding to the belt for the M60. The salvage run Paul suggested seemed like a reasonably safe prospect, though he still didn't like the idea of bringing the kids along. As soon as Paul arrived, he'd start an argument that he expected would meander through the ultimatum of 'I'm not leaving her again' and wind up with him frustrated and dealing with the worry of protecting an armed little girl. Bandits would—most of the time—ignore children, but if she had a gun... He shivered. Maybe he could find a compromise at insisting she keep her head down and not make herself a target. He chuckled to himself.

Could always pack her in a suitcase.

He sighed, snapping another round in place. The scuffing of boots along the gravel road became louder to his right.

"Morning," said Bill.

Kevin looked up.

Bill and Brett walked up the driveway carrying brick-shaped cardboard boxes that seemed heavy.

"Morning." Kevin offered a nod of greeting.

"I didn't want to say anything till the town elders stopped quibbling. We wanted to do something for you to thank you for leavin' all that enclave hardware here. You made Ned a safer place."

Kevin held back the cringe that came from being guilted into doing something he didn't want to do. "Yeah, well…"

"This here's 3000 coins. $25 in pennies and $50 in nickels. Consider it a fair trade for the guns and ammo… not to mention a little bit of pay for taking out that raider group."

Tris bolted out from a hiding spot at the corner of the house, grinning. She hit Kevin from behind with a wraparound hug and bounced up and down.

"You knew?" He leaned to the left to fire a playful accusatory look over his right shoulder.

"I asked her not to let you leave till I could get back." Bill winked. "Like I said, we don't have much use for coins. They're more for wanderers, and something tells me you're not quite ready to settle down here."

Kevin gazed down at his boots, shaking his head and chuckling. "Not rightly yet, no. As nice as it is in Ned…"

"You've been wanting something so long it's like part of you." Bill handed him the box of pennies. "If you ever change your mind, there's a place for you here."

After a strong handshake, Kevin nodded once. "'Preciate that. If things don't work out, maybe we'll be back."

Paul, Zoe, and Cody appeared at the far end of the looping road to the left. Except for the AR-15 in her hands, the little blonde looked like the picture of happy innocence.

Kevin pinched the bridge of his nose. "Help me out here. I need to talk him into letting his kids stay here where it's safe."

"You know no matter how much you try to tell him it isn't necessary, Paul's determined to 'pay you back' for getting him out of Chicago. He's also not about to spend another minute separated from his family." Bill scratched his head. "That old warehouse he found doesn't seem like it's in too bad a spot. Suppose Ned could spare some militia for extra security if you're willing to negotiate on some of the spoils. Be safer for everyone."

"Yeah." He tapped his fingers on the penny box. "Feels kinda strange to be holding my dream in my hands. No sense takin' a dumb chance now. Deal."

———————————————

THREE WEEKS LATER, THE CHALLENGER CRUNCHED OVER THE SAND-SWEPT parking lot of an abandoned rest stop off Route 80 about twenty minutes west of what used to be Rawlins, Wyoming. Kevin's heart raced no less than seven times on the way in when other vehicles passed. None turned out to be hostile, and encountering more traffic in one day than he'd seen in a month gave him hope the spot might work out. He regarded the battered building; the remains of a huge filling station sat to the left of the main structure. From the looks of it, the pre-war owner had been slow to adapt to the e-conversion, and many of the spaces still had dead gasoline pumps. He cringed at the thought of the mess lurking in underground tanks, but it's not like getting the fuel system up and running was a worry.

The building looked more promising. Nowhere near as large as the one Whazzat stumbled on, it still had plenty of space to convert into rentable rooms as well as an old fast food restaurant, which, even if it couldn't be salvaged, would offer a place to install a new kitchen. The unexpected influx of coin from Bill would bankroll any additional equipment he needed. From a structural standpoint, it had no major issues. The wide-open field behind it with park benches and picturesque puffs of green scrub brush lent a nice touch. The scene looked like it belonged as a painting on the wall in a steakhouse. A battered shack stood a quarter mile to the right by the start of the approach ramp, next to the derelict hulk of an old dump truck. Whatever was in there could wait; nothing had disturbed it for decades... another few months wouldn't hurt.

Paul's warehouse idea turned out well, all things considered. They'd only run into one pack of bandits. Zoe had listened to her dad and stayed down while adults traded bullets between moving vehicles. Kevin had no idea who 'Amazon' had been or why she had a giant warehouse full of so many different items. Everything from books to underpants to cat litter. There had been food as well, but not even God could've saved it after fifty plus years. Bill, who'd wound up coming along, appropriated a bunch of camping supplies for Ned as well as some clothes and other tools. Despite what the militia kept, the bus remained packed to the brim with stuff—inside as well as on the roof. Zoe had hit a stuffed-animal gold mine while Cody had barely said a word to anyone after making off with several large boxes full of books.

The bus rolled up and parked sideways across the fading paint of several car-sized spots.

"Doesn't look like much yet, but what do you think?"

Tris reached over and slid her arm around his shoulders. "I think it looks like weeks of ass-breaking work." She grinned.

"Yeah. That it does, but no one will be shooting at us." He patted his armored jacket. "I'm gonna need a glass-walled case."

"I still can't believe Amarillo. So big... and... all those people." She bit her lip. "I'm glad the Enclave doesn't know about it."

"They have to. And they're probably terrified of pissing them off like everyone else is." He chuckled.

"So... five thousand coins gone like that huh?" She shook her head. "Your whole life's work."

"It's an investment." He smiled. "They should be here in a few days with the solar panels, sign, and charging hardware."

"You sure they're coming?"

"Yep." He gestured over his shoulder at the trunk. "Another five grand waiting. Plus that whole 'code' thing. Wayne's gotta be crying in his beer right about now. That ol' bastard kept waitin' for me to get myself killed so he could keep my bankroll."

She smiled. "Really?"

"Well... he probably wasn't *hoping* for it, but I doubt he'd have been too upset if it happened."

"Would you let me die to get ten thousand coins?" She peered up at him.

He smirked. "Why do women always ask crap like that? Of course not."

She leaned into him. "You mean that?"

Kevin stared into the glass front doors of his soon-to-be roadhouse. "Yeah... I never really thought about anything else but not getting dead and getting my ass off the road. Now... If someone told me I could have my roadhouse or be with you, I wouldn't even hesitate." He kissed her.

She let her tongue linger in his mouth for a moment before pulling back with a smile. "So you do like me more than your car?"

"Hey now. Let's not get too crazy." He chuckled.

Tris smirked and jabbed him in the side, smiling. "Ass."

Paul walked over in no great hurry, stretching hours of driving out of his legs. Zoe squealed and laughed nearby, running in circles holding a big stuffed green dragon with purple wings over her head.

Kevin got out, as did Tris.

"Looks like a fixer-upper," said Paul.

"That it is." Kevin stretched.

Paul stuffed his hands in his pockets. "Could probably stick around a week or two till you get it off the ground. Don't think Bill would mind."

He clapped Paul on the shoulder. "Alright. Best work fast though. Ann's going to kill you if you don't bring Zoe back soon."

Paul chuckled.

Tris grabbed Kevin's hand. "Ready to go inside?"

Kevin squinted at the weakening afternoon sun. *Well, Dad, guess I made it.* He offered a moment of silence for the father he barely knew before heading for the door. "Been ready for this for years… never thought I'd live to see it."

She tugged him to a halt as his hand touched the door. When he looked over to ask why, she leaned up and kissed him on the lips. Zoe zoomed along in the background, pretending her plush dragon flew around. Kevin smiled, much happier to see her without a gun. Tris watched her go by with such a starry-eyed expression, he wondered if the life of a courier would be *less* scary than what waited for him.

"Aww, Hell." He scooped her up into his arms and carried her past the doors. "We're home."

fin

ACKNOWLEDGMENTS

Thank you for reading One More Run!

I'd like to thank Wilbert Stanton, (author of The Artful and Gears of Fate) for his suggestion to expand this story. One More Run started life as a short story, and Wilbert's reaction to it (and subsequent enthusiastic suggestions to expand that world) resulted in this series.

Also, thanks to Mark W. Woodring for editing (even if he did hate the pun).

Thank you also to Alexandria Thompson for the cover art!

ABOUT THE AUTHOR

Originally from South Amboy NJ, Matthew has been creating science fiction and fantasy worlds for most of his reasoning life. Since 1996, he has developed the "Divergent Fates" world, in which *Division Zero, Virtual Immortality, The Awakened Series, The Harmony Paradox, and the Daughter of Mars series* take place. Along with being an editor at Curiosity Quills press, he has worked in IT and technical support.

Matthew is an avid gamer, a recovered WoW addict, Gamemaster for two custom RPG systems, and a fan of anime, British humour, and intellectual science fiction that questions the nature of reality, life, and what happens after it.

He is also fond of cats.

Visit me online at:
    Facebook: https://www.facebook.com/MatthewSCoxAuthor
    Amazon: https://www.amazon.com/author/mscox
    Pinterest: https://www.pinterest.com/matthewcox10420/
    Goodreads: https://www.goodreads.com/author/show/7712730.Matthew_S_Cox
    Email: mcox2112@gmail.com

OTHER BOOKS BY MATTHEW S. COX

Divergent Fates Universe Novels

Division Zero series

- Division Zero
- Lex De Mortuis
- Thrall
- Guardian
- Harbinger

The Awakened series

- Prophet of the Badlands
- Archon's Queen
- Grey Ronin
- Daughter of Ash
- Zero Rogue
- Angel Descended

Daughter of Mars series

- The Hand of Raziel
- Araphel
- Ghost Black

Virtual Immortality series

- Virtual Immortality
- The Harmony Paradox

Prophet of the Badlands Series

- Prophet's Journey

Divergent Fates Anthology

(Fiction Novels - Adult)

The Roadhouse Chronicles Series

- One More Run
- The Redeemed
- Dead Man's Number

Faded Skies series

- Heir Ascendant
- Ascendant Unrest
- Ascendant Revolution

Temporal Armistice Series

- Nascent Shadow
- The Shadow Collector
- The Gate to Oblivion
- The Queen of Discord

Vampire Innocent series

- A Nighttime of Forever
- A Beginner's Guide to Fangs
- The Artist of Ruin
- The Last Family Road Trip
- The Phantom Oracle
- How Not to Summon Demons
- Ordinary Problems of a College Vampire
- A Vampire's Guide to Surviving Holidays
- An Introduction to Paranormal Diplomacy

Standalones

- Wayfarer: AV494
- Axillon99
- Chiaroscuro: The Mouse and the Candle

- The Spirits of Six Minstrel Run
- Sophie's Light
- The Far Side of Promise anthology
- Operation: Chimera (with Tony Healey)
- The Dysfunctional Conspiracy (with Christopher Veltmann)
- Of Myth and Shadow
- The Girl Who Found the Sun

Winter Solstice series (with J.R. Rain)

- Convergence
- Containment
- Catalyst

Alexis Silver series (with J.R. Rain)

- Silver Light
- Deep Silver
- Silver Quarrel

Samantha Moon Origins series (with J.R. Rain)

- New Moon Rising
- Moon Mourning

Vampire For Hire series (with J.R. Rain)

- Moon Master
- Dead Moon
- Lost Moon

Maddy Wimsey series (with J.R. Rain)

- The Devil's Eye
- The Drifting Gloom
- Dark Mercy

Samantha Moon Case Files series (with J.R. Rain)

- Blood Moon

Immortal Operative series (with J.R. Rain)

- Broken Ice

Four Elements series (with J.R. Rain)

- The Elementalist
- The Black Rose
- The Wakefield Curse

Young Adult Novels

The Eldritch Heart Series

- The Eldritch Heart
- The Cursed Crown

Evergreen Series

- Evergreen
- The World That Remains
- The Lucky Ones
- Nuclear Summer

Standalones

- Caller 107
- The Summer the World Ended
- Nine Candles of Deepest Black
- The Forest Beyond the Earth
- Out of Sight

Middle Grade Novels

The Adventures of Ubergirl series

- My Dad is a Mad Scientist
- Aliens Ate My Homework
- The End of all Halloweens

Tales of Widowswood series

- Emma and the Banderwigh
- Emma and the Silk Thieves
- Emma and the Silverbell Faeries
- Emma and the Elixir of Madness
- Emma and the Weeping Spirit

Standalones

- Citadel: The Concordant Sequence
- The Cursed Codex
- The Menagerie of Jenkins Bailey